I0675185

The Shadow of the Berg

Zach Otto

Copyright © 2025 Zach Otto

All rights reserved.

ISBN-13: 979-8-9942623-0-6

To my partner,

my pocket of sunshine.

For always making

my life just a little brighter.

I love you, Kait.

CONTENTS

PROLOGUE

A young boy, dressed in what barely passed for rags on some children, ran down a familiar narrow city street. He urged his body forward, away from the night guardsmen he knew must be close behind. Tiny splashes accompanied the patter of leather on stone, echoing off the tall buildings on either side. A damp, sickly odor hung in the air while dimly lit streetlamps lining the walkway painted his surroundings with a dull orange glow, like the fading heartbeat of a dying city.

He had been running for what felt like forever. His legs burned with fatigue and his chest constricted, cold air forcing its way into his lungs, breath after breath. He knew with every fiber of his being that he couldn't stop now. If the night guardsmen caught him out after curfew again, they would throw him in the dungeon faster than he could count to ten.

He slid around a corner. The glare from a light glinting off a window blinded him long enough that he didn't see the hulking mass standing there until it was too late.

A wild stinging sensation painfully flooded his arm as he looked up from the ground. A large, portly man wearing a butcher's apron and grimy, canvas trousers stood over the child with a cleaver in one hand and an oil lantern in the other. He had been dumping the remains of a pig he had slaughtered into the street when the boy ran into him.

The butcher looked down at the child in puzzlement before lacing the cleaver into his belt and stretching his arm downward.

As the boy clumsily climbed to his feet, the butcher's face shone in the light of the lantern with a concerned expression. "You best be getting home, lad," the large man urged. "It's well past curfew, and your parents must be worried sick about you. Little boys got no business being out this late what with that killer on the loose and the High Councilman's personal guard out for blood. Dangerous streets these days."

The boy patted some of the dirt off his legs, though he found that the water and pig's blood from his fall made cleaning difficult. "Thank you, sir. I was on my way home when some of the older boys stole the bread that I was taking home to my parents. You wouldn't happen to have anything you could spare? I know my family would be very grateful."

"Of course, I do. End of the day there's always something left. Shame to throw it away, but people can't buy pork shoulders and cow livers when they can't even pay their bloody taxes. Wish I could give it away more if I'm truthful," the butcher disappeared momentarily and returned with a morsel of meat wrapped in dirty brown paper. "Here you go, lad. Now hurry on home."

The little boy bowed slightly after taking the morsel. "Thank you, sir. I'll be sure to give my parents your regards."

A warm smile spread across the butcher's face. "It's no trouble at all, lad. Now get going before the guards catch you out." The man returned to his storefront without delay, closing the door behind him.

The boy begrudgingly tucked the parcel beneath his arm and continued onward. He disliked showing adults respect, but he wasn't foolish enough to think that he could afford not to. The adults were, after all, the reason life in Corina was so harsh.

Rage bubbled in his chest as he walked down the empty streets. It wasn't fair that the High Council lived so lavishly while he was doomed to live in filth. His anger subsided quickly, however, when he saw a family sitting in their home enjoying the company of a small, ragged cat with matted orange fur.

He crept to the window of the house and looked at his reflection. His gnarled, long, dark hair fell in front of weary blue eyes. The wool clothing he had gathered long ago hung from his sickly limbs awkwardly, making him look even smaller than he was.

The boy watched the family laugh and share bread in the candlelight. A blonde-haired man and a woman with large red curls and pale skin smiled as they held one another, watching their children play with the cat. Amid everything awful in the world and despite the sorry state of the city, they were happy.

He turned away after far too long, trying to ignore the tears welling in his eyes.

He wiped his face with dirty hands before walking down the familiar alleys of the city until he finally arrived home. In a small nook, hidden away from watchful eyes, a straw bed lay on the ground next to a pile of wet kindling and ash. He sat on the bed and uncovered a box hidden beneath the mattress. It contained a broken wooden horse that he had taken from the garbage sitting behind a house, a small stuffed bear that was missing an arm, and a bit of coin that could be used in absolute emergencies.

He knew the kindling was too wet to start a fire and cook the meat the butcher had given him, but at least the night's sky did not betray more rain. He would have a generous breakfast the next day.

At the height of the midday sun, the young boy walked to the city center. The weekly marketplace flooded the streets that day, and he knew he would have the opportunity to pocket portions of food that people either did not want or could not afford. The city center, located next to the largest guard post and an equally large chapel to the Great Carpenter, was crowded with a mess of hungry city dwellers that towered over him. He was hidden by his size, practically vanishing in the busy hive of preoccupied people.

Slowly, he made his way through the crowd, swiping an empty linen sack that a trader had discarded and draping it lazily over his shoulder. He finally arrived at a cart selling fresh produce. The smell was faint in the bustle of the crowd, but he could make out a mix of sweet peppers, beets, and potatoes on the cart in front of him. He walked to the back of the cart to the pile of vegetables that had been deemed rotten by the wagon's customers. After sorting out the items that were still good enough to eat, he filled his sack and left the marketplace to make his way back to his home.

As he left the market, content with the full sack of vegetables slung over his bony shoulder, he caught the scent of freshly baked sweet cakes in a nearby storefront. He could not resist the temptation, the sweet aroma dancing on his tongue and in his nostrils. He entered the bakery, stunned at the wall-to-wall selection stacked on countless shelves. The store looked as if it would burst! Cakes, pastries, donuts, sweet rolls, and freshly baked dessert breads of all shapes and sizes flooded his senses with a flurry of colors and smells that made his stomach turn hungrily.

His mouth watered as he gazed upon various frosted donuts and coffee cakes. It had been so long since he had enjoyed something as decadent as that. He looked around for a moment. Despite the rush of people outside and the wealth of delicious pastries inside, there were few customers in the bakery. The baker was preoccupied making small talk with a lavishly dressed noble, so the boy reached under the glass of one of the display cases and grabbed an especially delicious-looking chocolate frosted pastry.

He carefully placed it in his bag making sure not to disturb its careful decoration.

He left the bakery quietly and walked almost two full city blocks before he ate his pastry. The sweet, delicate flavor of the cake and the dense, rich chocolate frosting filled his mouth with an exciting sensation that he could seldom enjoy. He finished eating and licked his fingers, sloppily savoring every last crumb, only to have his attention caught by the baker emerging from his shop.

The man jogged to catch up to him, calling the guards over to grab the boy and bring him back.

He was familiar with what was about to happen next. He threw the sack of vegetables over his shoulder and ran as quickly as his short legs would carry him. He twisted through the elaborate, narrow alleys of the city making sure to keep the guards off balance, trying to compensate for the weight of the sack as he went.

Once the yells of the guards vanished, he slowed his pace and relaxed. The heavy sack of vegetables dragged slightly against the ground, but he found it hard to care very much about such things at that moment. He lazily observed his surroundings, trying to piece together exactly how to reach his little nook with his bed. It was hard to tell exactly where he was in the maze of massively tall buildings, but he did see a school in the distance that looked familiar.

He walked around the corner of a street, grabbing the nearby lamp post casually and swinging his sack of vegetables over his shoulder.

An alarming crack rang through his ears as he fell to the ground, pain coursing through his pounding head. His vision blurred, and a pained groan escaped his lips. He felt another hard crack at the base of his skull and the world around him faded to black.

***

The boy woke to the sound of a metal tray clashing on a stone floor. He looked around and saw dark stone walls reaching high above him. The sound of a droplet of water occasionally echoed throughout the chamber as his eyes adjusted to reveal a row of vertical bars forbidding his exit.

He knew immediately he was in the underground prison beneath the Corina High Councilman's palace. Slowly rising to his feet and stumbling forward, he picked up the tray and begrudgingly sat. The cold tray held a lump of stale bread with some gray mush that the boy assumed was made from chicken and cream along with a small amount of blandly prepared green beans. Most people thought the food made in the prison was horrid, but he accepted it for what it was and always ate it without complaint.

The harsh sound of a cane clanking on the bars in front of him echoed through the halls of the dungeon.

A man in rich purple robes embroidered with golden thread along the sleeves and a small raven stitched on the man's chest stood on the other side of the bars. His fine black shoe tapped the ground, mimicking the sound of his cane. His dark, oily hair glimmered in the dull torchlight, offsetting his slightly rotund features.

He looked down at the boy. "Do you know who I am?"

"No," the boy stated defiantly. "Should I? You don't seem like much to me."

The man laughed insidiously. "Easy to have a quick tongue behind bars, *child*. I am Faerhen Belson, the High Councilman of Edenhall, visiting Corina on behalf of Gregor Moline. You do know Lord Moline, don't you? He is the High Councilman of Corina, and owner of the cell you seem to be occupying at the moment." He paused for a moment, running his thick fingers through his greasy hair.

After the boy said nothing, he continued. "I arrived in the city just two days ago and have found that the people here are...ungrateful for the services that the Council provides. Now imagine what a surprise it was to me when my favorite baker in all of Corina informed me that I wouldn't be able to enjoy his wares?" Faerhen lifted his hands and shrugged mockingly. "The pastry you stole from that man was made especially for me. He merely had it on display to show the masses what beautiful work he could produce."

"Well, it tasted real good. You made a good choice with that guy. Real great work, though I'm not sure it was the best idea to hang that sort of thing over the heads of starving little children," the boy retorted as disrespectfully as he could.

Faerhen only smiled wickedly, crooked teeth glistening in the torchlight. "When you stole from that baker, you stole from me, *boy*. I assure you that I am not a kind man. I am not a merciful man. Do you know what the punishment is for stealing from a High Councilman of Rakksberg?"

"Let me guess," the boy started with a smile, his pride and arrogance growing with each passing comment. "Thirty lashings? Maybe the hot coals or an ice bath?"

The councilman now billowed in laughter, causing his plump belly to chortle as his shoulders rose and fell. "After I have the baker's hand removed as a reminder of what happens when a shop keeper slacks off, I will see to it that another *rat* such as yourself is removed from the city. Surely, it's the only reasonable thing a man in my position could do. How else will the people see what comes for those who take what doesn't belong to them?" His smile twisted into a sneer. "I'll see you at the gallows in three days. Have a nice life, boy. I do hope the pastry was worth it."

Faerhen left the boy to sit alone in his cell, dumbfounded by the consequences of his actions. He had been arrested for theft before, but the burning hot coals were by far the worst punishment he had ever received. He clenched his fists in anger. *I guess the rules are a bit different when the right person is calling the shots,* he thought.

That night, he felt nothing but a cold emptiness as if he had been expecting this day for quite some time.

He opened his eyes the next morning to the feeling of a sharp, cold blade pressed against his throat. Careful not to make any sudden movements, his eyes adjusted to make out a hooded figure crouched over him. Gleaming teeth shined though a dim shadow that betrayed only glints of reflected light in the figure's eyes. The man's strong grip on the child would have left him paralyzed if his fear had not done so already.

The man noticed the child's eyes processing what was happening and began to speak. His voice was deep, cold, and hard yet smooth and clear. "You may not speak. You may not move or attempt to relieve yourself of my grasp. I have been watching you for a few days now and I find myself taken by your tenacity. I believe you possess a certain set of qualities that will provide useful to us as you grow. There is a group of people, a fiercely loyal and extensively skilled group of people, who will welcome you as a family, but you must leave your life here behind and come with me now."

After being given permission to speak, the boy responded, "I don't have much of a life here and they just told me that in a few days I won't have a life at all. But your knife there isn't real comforting. Why should I trust you? What will happen if I don't go with you?"

The man's crooked mouth widened into a grin, his teeth seemingly glowing in the dim light of the cell. "You have no reason to believe me or to trust me beyond the simple fact that you have a blade pressed to your throat. I can teach you many things, and one day you may find yourself in a position similar to my own. As for what were to happen to you if you reject my offer? Nothing. Though I must warn you that I have spilled much younger blood than yours and if you find the urge to speak of our meeting, I will have no problem easing the executioner's work schedule."

"I guess I don't have much of a choice. I stay for the hanging, or I leave with you." The boy rose to his feet after the dagger was removed from his neck. He carefully watched the cloaked man sheathe the black-bladed dagger. "How exactly do you plan to get me out of here? We aren't really alone."

"You don't have to worry about that, Chase," the man answered, beckoning the child forward. "Guards who value their lives or the lives of their loved ones have a certain respect for our family."

Chase smiled and stretched his arms outward. He brushed dirt and grime from his ragged clothes and stifled a laugh. "I could get used to that."

CHAPTER 1
ANOTHER DAY

Chase heard the distinct clack of horses' hooves on a cobblestone road. He opened his eyes and turned his gaze downward to see a nervous, scrawny wagon driver accompanied by two of the cheapest bodyguards that money could buy. The man to the driver's left wore several mismatched plates from various sets of armor and carried a small cudgel across his lap while the larger man to the driver's right held a short sword across rusted chain leggings.

The gaunt driver whipped his horses to go faster, hurrying to arrive at Edenhall in the waking hours of the next day. Chase shifted his position and rose to his haunches, readying himself for the coming moments. He took a deep breath, estimating the pace of the wagon below.

One. Two. Three.

At just the right moment, Chase stepped from his

branch and unsheathed his dagger in a fluid movement. Landing behind his targets, he spun on the spot, sweeping his leg out to deliver a sharp blow to the side of the plate-wearing mercenary's head. The other armed man moved to respond, raising his rusted sword high above his head—readying for a downward blow.

Chase saw the strike before it landed and with a swift thrust, he felt the blade of his dagger slide into the man's throat. The thin knife hit its mark, and with a violent gurgling sound, the mercenary slumped onto the wagon, choking while he fell. Far too late, Chase noticed his grip on his dagger was too loose. The weight of the dying man jerked the blade from his hand scattering it somewhere unseen.

Shit. That was sloppy.

Chase grappled the panicking wagon driver and threw him out of his seat into the rear of the cart. Resisting the urge to flourish out of habit, Chase drew his bastard sword, tucked his shoulder, and spun. Before the victim could raise further alarm, Chase came down with a slash of his blade and removed the farmer's head in one smooth stroke.

That's better, but I'm not clear yet. Stay Focused.

Chase whirled around to see the plate-clad thug stumbling to his feet, slowly regaining his bearings. The mercenary saw his two dead companions before turning his gaze on Chase. Seeing black leather paired with the assassin's signature black-bladed bastard sword, all the remaining color left the man's face. Chase stood calmly with his sword drawn at his side.

Without warning, the cart hit a cracked stone protruding from the worn surface of the road, knocking the mercenary off balance. Chase seized the opportunity and lunged forward, dragging the tip of his blade upward. In a single graceful motion, Chase hooked the man's leg and flipped the mercenary on his back.

Chase spun his weapon in an exaggerated and unnecessary flourish before thrusting the tip downward. He felt the blade break through the man's rusted plate armor and slide deep into his chest, and soon after the body at his feet went limp and lifeless.

He took a deep breath and wiped the blood from his blade. His stomach turned unpleasantly and bile rose in his throat at the grim reality of his job, but a small part of him—buried deep somewhere in the back of his mind—reveled. The brief thrill of a successful contract flooded him, his heart pounding in his ears like a drum. Sweat beaded on his furrowed brow, and for a moment he felt an unexpected sense of elation. However, that elation was quickly drowned out by the all too familiar acrid twisting of disgust in his gut.

He fought the urge to empty his stomach off the side of the slowing wagon. Chase took no joy in ending another's life, especially townsfolk simply struggling to survive just as he had all those years ago. If life had been different, he may have found himself in that wagon, slowly making his way to the promise of some coin and a hot meal. He always wished it could be different, but he dismissed those wishes as futile and focused on the task at hand.

Chase sighed. *That was messy. I'm out of practice. Maybe next time I can act like more than an initiate. And Cole would have my head for that dumb flourish at the end.*

Without their driver urging them forward, the horses pulling the wagon halted. Chase retrieved his dagger before searching the dead bodies. Nausea washed over him despite his best efforts to ignore the pit in his stomach. *I've got no choice. I don't have to like it, but I've got a job to do.* It was his life now, and he was good at it, all things considered. Even still, he could never ignore that part of him that triumphed following the last moments of his contract. Sometimes he felt like that just made everything worse.

Shaking away his nerves, Chase continued his grim work. His dossier claimed the group should have enough coin between them to repay the debt they owed to High Councilman Faerhen's associate. However, to no surprise, the three men did not.

For a moment Chase second guessed himself. *Damn, is this the right wagon?* After only a moment's hesitation, he shook his head. All three targets perfectly matched the physical descriptions given to him in the contract.

These are the marks. They must be. I need to leave before some farmer's daughter sees me and I have a fourth body to dispose of. Chase gathered what little coin the three men had stashed in a hidden compartment of the cart and leapt to the ground. If the horses were well trained, which he suspected they were by the look of them, they would continue until they arrived at

Edenhall's gates. He smacked the nearest horse on the haunches, and it whinnied obediently before trotting away.

Chase returned to Lightfoot and hoisted himself into his saddle. The job was never done until he received payment. He cut the lead secured to a nearby oak tree and spurred the horse forward. Lightfoot was a strong-willed mare and would gallop as long as Chase demanded it, but he knew better than to push the horse too hard. He was grateful to have such a dependable mount, though. He had heard that his best friend, Richard, was once forced to walk beside his horse for three days after a contract because the thing wouldn't let him go anywhere near its saddle.

No longer feeling the pressure of meeting a deadline, Chase took in the drab landscape and listened carefully as he rode. The aggravated caw of a nearby crow or the buzzing of jays flying overhead was a familiar sound in Rakksberg. On some rare occasions, one might hear the chatter of a squirrel sitting in some bramble, or the distant cackle of a coyote finding shelter from the harsh winds flowing in from the sea. Dull shades of green and gray from dead or dying trees blurred against the overcast sky above. Ever the picture of bleakness, the Berg never failed to underwhelm.

The ride gave Chase a chance to ease his mind and breathe in the damp, cool air of the nearby sea. It was a small but necessary relief, finally finishing his contract after tracking and studying his targets for the past few days—not to mention after the deed itself was complete.

As Chase approached the wooden gate that marked the border of Edenhall, he pulled his black hood over his eyes to conceal his face from watchful eyes. He knocked sharply on the wicket. The old wooden gate was sturdy, though it left something to be desired compared to the surrounding stone wall that had stood for hundreds of years according to the stories.

A peek hole slid open to reveal an old guard wearing an even older iron helm. His leathery skin held bushy, gray brows that drooped over tired, brown eyes. The guard barked in a crude tone, his voice rasping, "Who goes?"

"I am a shadow," Chase spoke softly under his hood, ensuring only the guard could hear. The nicknames the assassins in the Burrow created for one another served a dual purpose. As an assassin gained notoriety, their name spread and created a sort of legend surrounding the member until almost every guard in any major city, and those of many smaller villages, knew the name at once.

It usually felt odd to say the name aloud, especially about himself, but Chase accepted its purpose. He was a shadow, and to some that meant he may very well be some strange monster that emerged from dark corners to steal away their loved ones.

The guard's eyes widened in horror, memory serving to fuel the assassin's reputation. The peek hole slid shut, and Chase heard yelling as the guard beckoned for someone to open the gate. Chase walked through the city walls without any mention of an entry tax and continued onward. As he strode down the crowded streets and passed familiar buildings, he felt the troubled gazes of passersby following him.

Carrying weaponry within the city walls was forbidden and punishable with lashings at the gallows, although Chase's signature black-dyed leathers gave him amnesty that was born from fear of his guild. The black woolen cloak may have hidden his weapons enough to prevent townsfolk from panicking, but people knew what he was. To those that saw him, there was no way of knowing why the assassin had come to their city, and no guarantee Chase wasn't there for someone they knew or loved.

After leaving Lightfoot at the stable near the city gate, Chase made his way through crowded streets, making a certain detour he always took when in Edenhall. Most of the stone buildings were worn and weathered, seemingly as old as the walls that surrounded them. Their thatched roofs were marred by holes that had been sloppily patched, and the muddy streets were in shambles after decades of neglect.

So, Chase found a path sheltered from the damp, salty air carried by harsh winds.

He stepped through a tunnel running beneath a particularly crowded road, wind howling so fiercely it threatened to pull the stone from its mortar. He shifted his cloak and momentarily lowered his hood. Being seen and identified here was a risk, but the cowl made it harder to see in the dim firelight of the tunnel.

Chase quietly sidestepped a haggard, sleeping beggar that smelled strongly of vomit and brandy before navigating the maze of tunnels that ran beneath the roads of Edenhall. A pang of sympathy flashed across his mind when he saw the unconscious man. *Was he alone? Did he have a family, or has he been left to suffer in solitude? Is he down here to tempt the fates, the dangers of such a place be damned?* Chase silently dismissed his concerns, thankful that none of those dangers would be foolish enough to attack a Black Blade.

Emerging from the tunnels sometime later, hood raised over his eyes once more, Chase was only two city blocks from the Councilman's palace. It stood as a large, castle-like building, stone towers stretching into the gray skies above with a massive courtyard. The surrounding stone wall was secured by an iron gate, adorned in ornate golden figurines inlaid with various precious gemstones. Chase was stopped by a palace guard standing watch at the gate with a finely crafted steel poleaxe meant to intimidate as much as it was to kill.

The palace guards wore gilded breast plates with the symbol of High Councilman Faerhen's family crest emblazoned on inlaid copper. A raven with a maple branch in its beak shined in the sunlight.

One of the guards looked at Chase with cold, cobalt eyes through his silver helm, trimmed in gold with a braid of brown horsehair hanging from its peak. He pushed his poleaxe against the young stranger's chest and spat. "State your business."

"The High Councilman has summoned me as his formal guest." Chase kept his gaze low without lifting his face to the man. "I was supposed to arrive at sunrise tomorrow, but my carriage ran ahead of schedule. If you would be so kind as to grant me entrance, I'm sure your lord would be pleasantly surprised at our good fortune. Besides, I'd hate to see what Lord Belson would do if he were told that his guest had been kept waiting."

"He's in the middle of an important dinner with fellow members of the High Council, boy." The guard's lowborn accent was well hidden, but it was still there. He pressed the poleaxe further into Chase's chest and smacked his lips as if contemplating a bitter taste. "Your business with him will just have to wait."

Chase pushed the poleaxe aside nonchalantly with a single gauntleted hand. He turned his head toward the guard and laced his voice with cold steel. "Members of the Black Blades are not accustomed to waiting." The guard shuttered slightly at the mention of the assassins, but he kept his composure better than most would. "But if this meeting is so important, I suppose I can spend my evening visiting the home of a certain low born palace guard. After all, I'm sure a respectable member of the guard like yourself had no problem finding a partner." The man's eyes widened behind his silver helm. "Ah, yes. I am sure that in your prime, you surely found yourself a respectable woman. Maybe one with a nice dowry? Or perhaps an innocent farm girl from the countryside?

"No matter. I'm sure either way, a strapping

young man of your stature managed to sprout a few babes with a woman of any sort." The guard was trembling, unable to hide his fear any longer. "A son? A daughter? Perhaps both or maybe a whole flock. The blackened steel of my blade doesn't care one way or the other. I can't say for certain what could happen during my stay within the city walls. That is, unless that certain palace guard were to open a certain palace gate at this very moment to ensure the Shadow's stay in the city is as brief as it can be."

He studied the quivering man for a moment, bile threatening to rise in his own throat even as he kept his eyes cold and indifferent. Threatening innocent bystanders may have been effective, but Chase hated doing it. *Death threats for a guard just trying to provide for his family? At the very least, he doesn't need to know that I'd never act on it if I could help it.*

The guard was petrified for much longer than was expected before he finally dropped his weapon. All color had vanished from his complexion. "Whatever you do," the man rasped. "Let my family live. Please. Our boy has only just passed his third name day. Please, don't harm him."

Chase stood—silent and motionless—while the palace guard scrambled to open the gate, ignoring the protests of another guard on duty. Silence often made people more uncomfortable than any words could. They always tended to fill in the gaps on their own, their frightened minds assuming all sorts of unmentionable things that Chase would likely never even consider. Instead, he simply stayed silent and continued into the palace courtyard.

The yard overflowed with hedges and trees trimmed to represent various aspects of Faerhen Belson that he demanded to showcase to his servants and underlings—a wolf for cunning, a bear for strength, and even an owl for wisdom. At the back of the courtyard in the center of an elaborate fountain, a topiary shaped like a giant raven stood overlooking a massive maple tree. Lining the path to the palace entrance were grey and blue flowers accented by more pruned greenery.

Chase strode through the courtyard and stopped before the raven.

He thought for a moment what the councilman would have to say about his precious family symbol if it had been slashed or burned. *It would certainly look much better than it does now.* As much as he disdained Faerhen for the death sentence he had once received, Chase knew that the repeated lessens from his Dark-Father were right. The High Councilmen in Rakksberg were far from desirable or honorable, but they filled the assassins' coin purses all the same.

He shook his head and focused. There were two more guards outside the palace door, but now that Chase was within the gated walls, he could continue without being bothered.

Upon entering the main hall, he almost admired Faerhen's blatant overindulgence. Lush red carpet and purple silk drapes glowed and shimmered against the stone walls that were covered with paintings of what he could only assume were Belson's family. Each silver-trimmed table was arranged with expensive cutlery and golden trinkets of all sorts, but the truly dazzling feature in the hall was the immense golden chandelier that bathed the chamber in a warm, orange light.

Chase climbed a wide staircase and walked through the halls of the palace in search of High Councilman Faerhen. The rich décor of the main hall was mimicked throughout the palace, the raven clutching a maple branch etched into nearly every piece of metal on display. Chase vaguely knew his way around the palace from collecting payments in the past, but if he wasn't careful, he would get lost in the maze of red, purple, gold, and silver.

After a few minutes of wandering the palace halls, Chase saw several chambermaids and cooks running down a walkway to his left, urgently carting a collection of desserts. He assumed they were rushing to serve the council members, so he followed quietly. When he finally arrived at the double door that led into the dining room, Chase waited for a break in the bustling servants leaving and entering the room. He held his ear to the door and heard three mumbling voices. When he entered, their conversation stopped.

Sitting near the center of the chamber was High Councilman Faerhen with his two guests. To Faerhen's left was the rounder High Councilman Randall Fink, wearing the sage and brown garb of the Lowlands. On the other side was the petite and frail figure of High Councilwoman Jivera Thorne, adorned in the yellow and crimson of the neighboring territory, Haverson. The two guests shared slight touches of grey through their hair, shadows betraying wrinkles in the creases of their faces. Faerhen, on the other hand, sported a full head of silver hair, though his complexion failed to reflect his old age.

He looks so different than he did all those years ago, and yet, so similar.

Chase reached under his cloak, causing the two guests to flinch. He smiled slightly and withdrew three purses from his belt, tied together with a short length of twine. He strode forward and casually tossed the pouches on the table in front of Faerhen.

Chase couldn't help the urge to taunt the man he despised so much in front of his guests. "I hope that the next time your associate decides to gamble, he decides to do so with more refutable sorts. Not sure you've noticed, but some people out there have the nerve to dodge a debt collector. *Some* people out there are dangerous."

Chase made sure to emphasize his last point by moving his arm slightly, lifting his cloak just enough to briefly flash the pummel of his sword to the councilman.

"Mind your tongue, boy," Faerhen spoke shrilly. "And your blade." The councilman wiped his mouth with a bit of grimy red cloth. "You may wear those hideous black garments, but in my halls, you will treat me with the respect I command. I could have your head for threatening me in my own palace like that. A disrespectful rat such as yourself wouldn't be missed, either." Faerhen took the pouches in his hand and felt their weight. He sneered and tossed them back to the assassin. "That should cover whatever payment you desire. Now leave us before I have my guards throw you on the executioner's block at once."

Rage bubbled in Chase's chest, but he kept his nerves steady. In an exaggerated show of courtesy, he smiled and bowed to the councilmen. "With all due respect, Faerhen," he turned his back to the man, his tone as sharp as steel. "It didn't work last time you tried, and it wouldn't work this time either."

CHAPTER 2
BAD NEWS

Chase walked purposefully out of the palace as quickly as he could. He opened each of the coin pouches and counted his payment. It was a meager sum, no more than fifty silver lairens altogether, but it was all he could expect from such a routine assignment. He counted his blessings and decided the opportunity to frighten a few of the High Councilmen was payment enough.

Soon, Chase was standing just beyond the palace gate, looking down on the slums of Edenhall—a collection of tattered and half-destroyed buildings that stretched as far as he could see. The sun began to set over the horizon, casting an unsettling shadow on the city. The wind lingered just as it always had, even if it had relented to little more than a gentle breeze. A few angry crows cawed in the distance, no doubt fighting over a tavern's scraps from the day.

Chase quietly swore to himself. There wasn't

enough daylight to make it back to the Burrow before nightfall.

He walked openly through the streets of Edenhall now that the crowds of people working throughout the city had dispersed for the night. Only a fool would dare to accost him in the tunnels beneath the city, but it was equally foolish to linger down there longer than was necessary.

Under normal circumstances, Chase kept to the alleys and shadows, winding through the worn stone buildings that seemed on the verge of toppling over one another while remaining out of sight. But when those lesser traveled routes weren't an option, he walked as smoothly and casually as he could. There was no need to raise suspicion by acting out of the ordinary, especially after his contract was complete.

Of course, that didn't mean he would carelessly make himself known to every prying eye in the city either. He avoided the first inn he saw. It was too close to the nearest guard post. Eventually, he stumbled upon a quiet place not far from the city walls that would do nicely.

The Wounded Mare was a modest inn at best. It rose two stories with a third for the owners, workers, and their families. The dull, gray stone was as worn as any in the streets of Edenhall, the harsh weather unkind to places that couldn't afford repairs. A faint wooden sign was nailed over the doorframe depicting a horse lying on its side next to a fire pit. Dim light shined through clouded and dirty glass windows, and little sound found its way to the street outside.

Chase entered through the old, iron-bound door

and looked around the dimly lit common room. Hardly any of the furnishings matched one another and little to no decorations hung on the walls, save for an old riding crop displayed over the fireplace. A small party of city dwellers sat in the corner somberly drinking from flagons of ale, while a few outsiders— wishing to be out of the bitter winds for the night— occupied the bar.

A bard dressed in dirty linen pants with a roughly sewn cotton shirt lingered in the corner strumming on an old lute and singing "Take Me Home." It was a sad melody about a man and woman trying to find their way home after becoming stranded in the Lowlands. The tune always made Chase stop to listen for a while, though he was never sure why it did.

The dull hum filled the tavern, accompanied by the occasional tap of flagons as the patrons raised and lowered their drinks. Chase approached the bar and placed his hand on the counter where an old, portly man in a greasy cotton shirt with more hair on his chin than on his head stood.

The bartender was cleaning a dusty mug with a dirty rag held in fingers as thick as sausages. He saw Chase approach and set the mug down. "Can I help you, lad?" The old man's voice sounded as if his throat was full of gravel.

"Just a room for the night," Chase replied in a smooth tone under the cowl of his woolen hood. "And if you have a kitchen, I'd appreciate some food. I'm not picky and I have good coin for both."

"Aye," the old man answered, rubbing the gray stubble on his chin. "We got a kitchen. Not much to offer, I'm afraid. You'll have to settle for some stew we've had over the fire for a few days. Haven't seen much else on this side of town."

Chase nodded. "That will do."

He sat on a nearby stool while the old man left through a door behind the counter. A few moments passed before the inn keeper returned with a wooden bowl filled with hot gray liquid. Chase stirred the stew in a moment of hesitation—a small amount of stringy brown meat along with some potatoes and barley that all smelled bitter. It wasn't much, but he appreciated the warm food and ate without complaint, thanking the inn keeper for the ale between bites.

After finishing his food and drink in silence, he handed the innkeeper a few silver lairens for the accommodations. The old man grunted, inspecting the coins carefully before handing Chase a room key. He rose from the bar to retire for the night, but instead he was greeted by a patron that had clearly enjoyed a few too many flagons of ale.

A tall and lanky man with sandy blonde hair and a nose that seemed to have been broken too many times, swayed slightly as he spoke. "Hey, you! What are you playing at? What kind of man eats with a hood?" He turned to face his friends sitting at a nearby table. "Man's wearing a hood indoors." The drunkard turned back to Chase and hiccupped. "Dishonest is what it is. Who are you?"

Acting on instinct, Chase's hand shifted under his cloak very slightly toward his cleaving dagger. *Cole would cuff my wrists for allowing someone to speak to a Black Blade with so much disrespect, but he's just some drunkard.*

Poor bastard is probably more afraid than suspicious. I can't say I blame him.

Before anyone could do anything they would later regret, the old innkeeper barked at the drunken patron. "He's a paying customer is what his is, Dale. You mind your mouth, or you'll be sleeping outside." He turned to Chase before continuing in his rasping tone. "Sorry, lad. Not too often we get guests beyond what you see here. Even the outsiders have familiar faces after a while. Never mind Dale and his like. Bunch of drunk idiots if I ever saw one."

Chase's hand relaxed and he smiled at the old man. "No need. I'm used to suspicion in my line of work." He shifted uncomfortably despite his best efforts to remain poised. "Thank you for your kindness. I don't think I'll need anything else for the evening. You'll find I'm a quiet tenant." Chase continued to his room, leaving the drunken patrons and the sounds of the somber bard behind him.

He woke early the following morning to the faint sound of glasses and mugs being set on the tables in the common room of The Wounded Mare. He dressed, fastened his weapons, and left his room after dawning his black cloak. Raising his hood over his head, Chase approached the bar where the round-faced inn keeper stood wiping the wooden surface with a wet washcloth.

Without wasting any time, he slurped another bowl of mysterious stew from the night before and drank a mug of sheep's milk that was uncomfortably warm. He politely excused himself from the inn, leaving behind a meager sum of coin to cover the meal. Chase smiled to himself when he saw the drunken patron named Dale sitting on the ground with his back against the tavern's wall—dead to the world.

He remained unnoticed while he quickly made his way to Edenhall's gate to retrieve Lightfoot. Thankfully, people out at this hour were mostly concerned with tending to their storefronts or getting to their work before their foreman had an excuse to flog them.

After giving Lightfoot a carrot from one of its saddlebags, the horse was happy to carry Chase home. Soon after he left the city, he passed the cart from the day before, slowly making its way back to its rightful owner.

The dead bodies still lay where they had fallen. Chase's stomach turned. The cart would cause a stir when it finally arrived at Edenhall, but he and the rest of the assassins counted on such things to fuel their reputation. Even still, he couldn't help the pit of guilt that ached in his chest when he thought of the people he had killed.

It's just a job. I don't have to like it.

Chase rode for most of the morning to the melody of Lightfoot's clacking hooves on stone, broken only occasionally by a crow in the distance. Dalin, the farmer under the protection of the Blades in exchange for the use of his livestock, was tending his farm when Chase returned Lightfoot to her stable.

He walked back to the familiar cliff face and found the path leading down to the Burrow. The cliff wasn't terribly tall, and he knew the water below was safe even if it did make his knees go weak when he peered over the edge. On warm summer days as children, many of the assassins spent their spare time cliff diving from that very spot, but he never had.

Chase made his way to the waterfall concealing the Burrow and proceeded through the hidden entrance.

Eyes still adjusting to the dim light of the cavern, he felt a blunt thud on his chest as he walked into a short feminine shape.

"Dammit, Chase," a harsh woman's voice chastised him as the figure stepped away from the clumsy young man. "Watch where you're going! For a *shadow*, you sure know how to get in the way."

Chase rubbed his eyes, and the figure came into focus. Standing a few paces away from him was Ditri, a hot-headed blonde woman that joined the family shortly after Chase had. Chase smiled, but Ditri's emerald eyes glared daggers at him. "Relax, Di." Chase didn't know what to say, so he resorted to the first thing that came to his mind. "You don't have to tackle me to get my attention."

Ditri's eyes narrowed to slits, her hands clenched into fists and planted firmly on her hips. "I think the Carpenter hammered your head a few too many times." She snorted and bumped into Chase's shoulder as she continued down the hall to her own quarters. Chase smiled to himself, turning toward the commons.

Soon, Chase joined the rest of his family in the

common area of their strange dwelling. It smelled damp, just like the rest of the cave had, and it was just as dark, as well. In fact, it was wholly unremarkable, all things considered. It was simply the only chamber in the Burrow that happened to be larger than any of their quarters, so they took it upon themselves to contribute some simple furniture and decorations to create a modest social area. At first, their Dark-Father was reluctant, but after seeing what they had done, he decided to let them keep their common room.

Chase saw Richard laughing and enjoying a hearty lunch beside Veronika. Richard's immense stature, thick features, and broad shoulders with cascading blonde hair was almost comically contrasted by Veronika's petite frame and raven locks. Chase had a history with the sharp-eyed woman across from his friend, but he would rather avoid talking about it if he could. *My neck still aches sometimes from where she held her throwing knife.*

Before joining the eating pair, Chase saw Ricket's wiry red hair across the chamber bobbing up and down as he talked with the shaggy, brown-haired Jerod; a former farmhand and convicted murderer that joined the family just a few months prior. Ricket was the youngest member of the family by a few years and was certainly the smallest.

A dim figure sat in the corner of the room that Chase assumed was the reclusive Barric, who never socialized more than he had to. Chase was certain the large burn scar that covered most of the man's face had something to do with that.

Chase sat across from Richard and grabbed a

piece of bacon from his friend's plate. He eagerly bit off a piece. "You two seem to be enjoying yourselves well enough." Without saying a word, Veronika huffed and briskly rose from the table before leaving the commons. Chase laughed and looked at Richard. "You know, I've been back for hardly half an hour, and she is the second woman in this family to have done that to me today."

"You have such a way with women," Richard smiled as he scooped a spoonful of salted potatoes into his mouth.

"You're one to talk. Tell me, are you the mighty bear or the cowardly cub when we find ourselves enjoying a drink in mixed company?"

Richard laughed sarcastically. "Better a bashful cub than a silent shadow." He quickly changed the subject. "Weren't you the one telling me the other day about High Councilman Tallin's new wheat tax in Darkwater?"

Chase wasn't surprised to hear about another tax increase, but Darkwater in the northeastern corner of Rakksberg was having a hard enough time keeping their people fed with their harbors being in such disrepair for so long. "No, I didn't, but that's a shame. It's not like those people are fat and merry by any means."

Richard swallowed a particularly large portion of eggs and wiped his mouth with the back of his hand. "Ah, must have been Ricket, or maybe Sal. I just hope one of us finally gets a contract for that bastard. All the other High Councilmen, too."

"You know we don't get contracts for the Councilmen, Richard." Chase tore into a piece of ham with his teeth. "They are usually the ones contracting us. They're the only ones that can afford us."

"Aye," Richard sighed. "It's just frustrating, is all. Every tax they pass is a whole other lot of people that go hungry and starve." A bleak disappointment washed across his features as he returned his attention to his food.

He's right. I wish there was something any of us could do about it, but it's more likely the whole damned council will be deposed than they actually do *anything for the good of the people.* Chase awkwardly tried, and failed, to hide his own disappointment. "Not much we can do about it while the Council hold all the cards." Chase paused for a moment before changing the subject. "By the way, where *is* Sal? He doesn't usually pass on a meal like this."

Richard shook his head, his long, tangled hair bouncing from side to side. "Contract in Dirnhell. He left early this morning with Korvall. Speaking of contracts, how did yours go?"

"If I'm being honest, it was rather boring. I'm not entirely sure why a High Councilman would go out of his way to hire an assassin to hit some poor villagers when some hired thugs would have gotten the job done for less. The Carpenter knows the Blood Moons and Sun Fangs are always looking for work."

"Maybe he wanted it done quietly." Ricket's small voice chimed in as the wiry young man joined their table. It was slightly reminiscent of a creaking wagon wheel, though he managed to put the sound of authority behind it when he needed to. "The Blood Moons do seem to always cause a scene, and the Sun Fangs would have burned the entire forest to the ground."

"Please, Ricket," Ditri rolled her eyes as she sat down as well. Chase noticed she was no longer wearing her black leather armor, instead opting for a loose-fitting shirt and linen pants. She must have come back from her own contract at nearly the same time Chase had.

He was unsurprised that the two fellow assassins had joined their table. Voices carried in the tiny common area.

Ditri had little patience for melodrama. She flipped her hair with a hand as if to emphasize her point as she continued. "I am sure they'd know well enough how to collect a gambling debt. Chase has a point. It doesn't make sense that a veteran assassin was hired for something like this, much less the bloody golden child. Richard told me about your contract, Chase, and I don't think it adds up either. We aren't exactly cheap, and I can't see how Cole would ever agree to take on something so trivial. What if you were captured? What if your horse slipped and fell on you? Hell, the Sun Fangs could have even stumbled upon you and taken you for ransom."

Richard frowned as he ran a hand over his cheek in thought. "Business has been slow, I suppose. But even still... Dammit, Chase, you need to go to Cole and figure this out. Too many things don't feel right."

Chase nodded. "Aye. You're right. None of this

makes sense, but I trust our Dark-Father. Cole had to have a reason for sending me. I better get this over with."

He excused himself from the commons and proceeded to his Dark-Father's study. He knocked on the door, and after hearing a muffled voice beckoning him in, he entered the room.

It was a modest chamber, although it was packed with everything the leader of the Black Blades would ever need. Lined from wall to wall with bookcases, a meager fireplace cast a shadow on the older man while he sat at his desk, thoughtfully smoking his pipe. The desk was covered with stacks of papers, folders filled with all sorts of parchments, ink wells and quills, and even a half full mug of a sweet-smelling liquid completely foreign to Chase.

Chase stepped into the room and closed the door behind him, waiting for Cole to speak. The guild leader did not stir for a long moment, and Chase felt an enormous pressure in the air—as if Cole was searching for the right words. Suddenly, the creases on the old man's features seemed deeper and darker than normal, his hair grayer and his eyes more worn.

Chase's stomach twisted in knots as he stood in silence.

It was unusual for Cole to act so aloof. In a deep and somber tone, Cole finally spoke, "Chase, come in further. It isn't proper to have you standing like an initiate ready to be scorned. You're welcome to sit if you'd like." The man gestured to a chair opposite his own before taking a long drag from his intricately carved tobacco pipe.

Reluctantly, Chase accepted the offer and sat next to his Dark-Father in the luxuriously cushioned chair meant for guests—the only lavish thing in the room aside from the gilded portraits of previous Dark-Fathers. He looked down at his master's desk dreading what things Cole may be contemplating. The scent of burning logs in the fire did little to ease his nerves.

"Dark-Father, I wished to speak with you about my previous contract. Something doesn't feel right. I don't mean to be disrespectful, but—"

The old man smiled, smoke gently falling from his lips and nostrils. He raised a hand in assurance. "Please, Chase. We can dispense with the formalities. You know my name well enough. It's an unnecessary burden on us both. Now, what do you mean? Tell me. Did the contract go well? I was sure you wouldn't find any trouble with the assignment."

Chase looked at Cole, trying to read the old man. It always seemed the Dark-Father knew more than he let on, but none of the Blades would ever know the truth of the matter. *I wish there was an easier way to go about this.* Chase answered before the pause grew too long. "That's just it, Cole. The contract was easy—probably too easy. I'd expect it to be given to an initiate, or possibly one of the less experienced neophytes. I don't understand why you awarded the contract to me." *Carpenter's Hammer, I am going to be scrubbing the dishes for weeks.*

"There was once a time," Cole retorted with a distinct aggression Chase had not expected, "when you would have thanked me for the easy coin and been on with your day. Tell me, what are you really trying to ask me, Chase?"

Chase's cheeks flushed in embarrassment. *I'll be lucky to scrub the dishes.* Even still, it was too late. He had gone this far, and he needed to press on. "The job was beneath me, Cole, and you know it as well as I do." Chase felt the heat rise in his cheeks as his voice grew louder. "I'm a veteran in the Blades while this glorified debt collection could have been handled by a thug. So, I ask again, *why* was I awarded this contract?"

Cole's demeanor grew harsh before dissolving away. Chase saw his Dark-Father's shoulders relax while the old man prepared to speak. "Aye. I suppose you must know the truth one way or another and it would be best if you heard it from me." He took a deep breath before setting his pipe on the desk in front of him. "I gave you the contract so I could think longer about something I received.

"Five days ago, a letter stamped in wax without a seal was given to Dalin. He had opened the letter without realizing what it contained, although once he knew he asked one of your fellow neophytes to deliver the message straight to me." Cole smiled faintly, more to himself than to his guest. "Luckily, Richard was wise enough not to read the opened letter. I gave you the contract that you feel was so beneath you to get you out of the Burrow."

Chase was taken aback by the reasoning. "Cole, what was in that letter?"

"It was a message," Cole said as he half-heartedly raised his pipe to his lips once more. "Or a summoning, if you will. The letter wasn't signed, nor did it reveal the identity of its author. Even its origin is in question, as far as I can work out. Whomever wrote this invitation claims to be in the heart of the Widower's Woods, which is highly unlikely." The old Dark-Father shook his head in disbelief. "No, I don't believe the author is telling the truth. I believe this is a trap to draw our family out of hiding."

"Where do you need me, Dark-Father?" Chase felt his heart race. "What must I do?"

"I don't know how to put this." Cole took a deep breath and paused as he looked into his pupil's piercing blue eyes. Chase trembled inwardly when he saw the indecision on his mentor's face, his throat tightening and his mouth going dry. Cole shifted uneasily in his seat and drew a puff from his pipe before straightening. He met the eyes of his pupil with a steely resolve fit for a judge. "You are to be exiled."

"What?" Chase's voice stuck in his throat momentarily before he had finally processed what had been said. He had not been able to control himself and stood over his mentor's desk with his fists clenched on the table. "What do you mean, exiled? You *cannot* be serious. No member of the Blades has ever been exiled. You don't leave this family unless it's by the blade. How can you say such a thing?"

Cole did not rise, but his voice grew loud and authoritative. "I say such a thing because it will be so. Am I to ignore the mysterious summons that arrived at my doorstep asking for one of my assassins, *by name*, to report to the heart of Widower's Woods?

You have been compromised, Chase, and you have put the family in danger." Cole's voice leveled, and he regained his cool demeanor. "Whoever summoned you knows where the Burrow is. What exactly am I to do? Custom dictates I have you killed. Am I to execute you in front of your family as Faerhen would have? No. You are to be exiled at once. I've made up my mind, and I will not hear otherwise."

Chase stood back, his mind racing. "Can I see this *letter* for myself to see what this is all about?"

"No." Cole's voice was as cold as ice, all empathy gone in that moment. "You may not. I have told you all you need to know about that, and you are not to ask again."

Chase was desperate for something—anything— he could do to change his Dark-Father's mind. But alas, nothing came to him.

This can't be happening. Not again.

He thought back to his life as a homeless orphan, longing for a family to care for him and keep him safe. He thought back to the children he saw playing with their cat, their parents watching with nothing short of adoration despite the sad state of the world outside their home. And he thought back to all the years he spent in the Burrow, laughing and training with his friends between contracts.

But now, he was losing the only family he had ever had.

I'll be alone… again.

Tears welled at the corners of his eyes, but Chase swallowed the lump in his throat and took a slow, shaking breath. With no other choice, he submitted— head down and voice lowered. "What should I do?"

Cole rose and placed a hand on Chase's shoulder. "Leave. Go far away from this place and never come back. I promise nothing will happen to you. You are my son. Even if I must exile you, I will not put you in danger unless I absolutely must. Trust that I am trying to do what is best for you *and* for the family."

Chase nodded, unsure of what to do. He wanted to embrace his mentor—perhaps for the last time— but he couldn't shake the urge to smack some sense into the old man. He wanted to curl up and stay in this room forever just as much as he wanted to scream before running away as fast as he could. Turmoil and conflict swirled in his every thought.

This can't be the only way. It can't be.

Please.

It can't.

Defeated and resigned to his fate, Chase turned toward the door before forcing words out. "May the darkness embrace your mind, father."

Though shaken by the gesture, Cole returned the sentiment. "And may the shadows guide your blade, my son, and may the night shelter you from her enemies."

CHAPTER 3
NO MORE RESTFUL NIGHTS

Struggling to keep his composure, Chase left his Dark-Father's quarters.

It can't be. This can't be happening.

He stumbled a few more steps.

The Burrow is everything. This can't be happening.

Pausing for a moment, he placed a hand on the damp stone wall. He took a deep, slow breath to steady his nerves. *I need to get ahold of myself. Getting upset isn't going to change Cole's mind. Besides, the others shouldn't see me like this. They all think I'm some stone-faced, cool-headed killer that always wears a smile. It's probably best they keep thinking that until I'm gone.*

With shaking, uneasy breaths, Chase returned to the commons on wobbly legs. *At least I'm not going to be executed. That's a start.* To his surprise, Richard was the only assassin left in the hall. Chase thought he should be disappointed, but instead he was relieved.

Maybe I can run off somewhere.

"Bloody hell," the boisterous, blonde-haired man swore after Chase had finished recounting the details of his meeting with Cole. "Exile? That seems a bit much. So, a letter showed up with your name on it. Seems harsh to turn you away for good over the scratching's of some goat-brained madman from Carpenter knows where. I seriously doubt anyone is living in those woods."

I could work on a farm, or in a smithy.

"Cole thinks it's an attack on the family and that I am putting all of the Blades at risk if I stay here." Chase sighed, rubbing his hands against his temples while feebly trying to think clearly for even a moment. The Burrow had been his home far longer than it had not, and the life of an assassin was now the only one he knew. "He thinks that if whoever wrote that letter could find us, then others can as well. The worst part is that I can't confidently say that he's wrong. Can you imagine if the Death Bringers came knocking at our door?"

Who am I kidding? I don't know the first thing about smithing.

"It'd be a blood bath. Even we can't stop an army." Richard took a deep breath before looking his friend in the eye. He threw his burly arms around Chase, catching him by surprise. Upon releasing his grip, he pounded his fist on the table in frustration. He paused briefly, looking for something to say. "What are you planning to do now? Where will you go?"

That's the question, isn't it? Countless possibilities

51

had been rushing through his mind, but there was only one path forward that would grant him any closure in this horrible twist of fate—one path that was the clear option above all others.

After some hesitation he spoke with a harsher, more frustrated tone than he had intended. "I'm going to the Widower's Woods. It's the only thing I know about this damned letter. And if I can't get answers, I'll at least get to gut the man responsible for my exile. That is, if there even *is* a man in the center of those Carpenter-forsaken woods."

"Well," Richard's tone grew in excitement much to Chase's surprise. "Then I'm going with you. If we can get to the bottom of this, Cole will have to see reason and accept you back into our ranks. He's a reasonable man, even if he is a bloody bastard sometimes."

"Richard, if you come with me, you'll be labeled a deserter." Chase's heart sank and an uncomfortable lump formed in his throat. As much as he wanted his friend to come with him, he knew that would only put a target on Richard's head. "I am exiled as soon as I leave the Burrow, and you will be branded a traitor as soon as you do the same. No. I won't allow you to leave a good future and a safe home."

"Dammit, Chase. You were always as stubborn as an ass, weren't you? I don't think you understand. I am going with you, treason be damned, and that's final. This place may be my home, and these people may be my family in name, but *you* are my family. Don't argue." Richard smiled wryly, patting his friend on the shoulder a bit harder than he should have.

"You know it won't work."

Chase sighed in relief. He agreed to the wishes of his old friend after a great deal of consternation. He knew Richard wouldn't take no for an answer and he wasn't foolish enough to turn the man away.

They each returned to their quarters and gathered their belongings. Chase dawned his black, studded leathers and fastened his collection of blades while scooping up his traveling pack with as many provisions as he could take from the Burrow's food stores and supply cabinets. *I'm not exiled* yet. *They can't stop me from making sure I don't die on the road.*

After ensuring he had not forgotten any essentials, Chase returned to the commons where Richard was standing, eagerly awaiting their departure. The thick-limbed man was armed with his double-hefted great axe, meant as much to intimidate as it was to cleave, and a hatchet with an oddly curved handle.

Not wishing to dwell on their fate, they hastily left the Burrow before any of the others returned and asked unwanted questions. As Chase walked up the cliffside path toward Dalin's stable, his heart grew heavy.

The late summer sun began to fall toward the horizon as they began their ride northward. Chase rode atop Lightfoot, as he always did, while Richard rode a stallion named Thunder. It was one of the few horses at Dalin's farm that could hold Richard's heavy frame for any length of time.

They briefly debated whether it was wise to take

their usual horses from the stable master. The odds of returning to the Burrow were slim, and horse theft was not commonplace for the Black Blades. Eventually, they begrudgingly accepted that gambling on unfamiliar horses would be the poorer decision. After all, they weren't Black Blades any longer.

After riding for as long as they could before nightfall to get far away from Dalin's farm, Chase and Richard situated a small camp for the night. Sleeping on the road was no strange occurrence for either of them, but neither were thrilled at the prospect of a night on the cold, hard ground.

Chase put together a make-shift cot using his cloak to pad his bedroll and his travelling pack as a pillow. It was just enough to make the days between inns slightly more tolerable. After trying to enjoy an evening of conversation to forget the day's tragic events, they ate a few helpings of dried ham and mushrooms before dousing their small fire. They were eager to get an early start the following morning.

***

Chase startled awake to the smell of smoke, forcing his eyes open to see a fiery, burning city. The sounds of screaming women and children rang in his ears as he clambered to his feet, trying to orient himself in the glow of intense firelight. The cries and screams raged on, growing louder and louder until his ears rang and his temples ached. He stumbled into a nearby shale-roofed house, grasping his ears in pain.

The screams were muffled within the decrepit walls of the ruined house. Chase heard a man barking orders just outside a door on the far wall of the room.

Reluctantly, he walked through the exit. Outside, a row of women with their children in tow lined a nearby stone wall. They were crying and pleading with strange men who wore black plate armor over chain shirts, their helms each shaped like a wolf's head, teeth bared around emotionless faces.

They wore a sigil unfamiliar to Chase—a man surrounded by black teeth, sewn on a field of red.

A slim man with a face hidden in shadow barked orders over the screams of the city, wearing red-dyed leathers with touches of gray. He turned to his subordinates and dropped his raised arm to his side.

The snaps of several bowstrings rang through the smoky air. In a painfully quick moment, the captives were struck with arrows, crumpling lifelessly to the ground. The silence that followed was more disturbing than their screaming moments before.

Not knowing what was happening, where he was, or why he could not find it in himself to step in and stop the massacre, Chase did the only thing he could and watched in horror. He shifted his gaze and stared at the wicked commander. The Man in Red cackled with a crazed expression, rousing himself into a maniacal stupor.

The commander's eyes glowed in the orange firelight with wicked pleasure. He dismissed his archers with a distracted wave of his gauntleted hand. As the red glow in the air flickered with the dancing flames around them, Chase realized that the blood-crazed man who had ordered the execution was none other than the twisted image of himself.

***

Chase awoke with a scream, covered in sweat and struggling against his bedding in desperate confusion. His ears were still ringing, and the sulfurous smell of smoke still flooded his senses.

"Chase!" He heard the voice from afar, his eyes slowly adjusting to the blue-gray light of the early morning. Richard knelt over him with both his hands grasping his shivering friend's shoulders. The familiar voice became clearer as Richard shook him. "What the bloody hell happened, Chase? Are you okay? Carpenter's Hammer, say something you sod!"

Chase was disoriented, but his senses were returning slowly. The soft sounds of jays and crows cawing filled the crisp morning air. Chase panted. "Just... a nightmare, Richard. Nothing to worry yourself over."

"My ass, it was just a nightmare." Richard spat, still holding onto Chase's arm as he sat up. "You scream like that—sweating and panting like you've been running all night—and you say it's *just* a nightmare? You were shaking like nothing I've ever seen! Carpenter's bloody Hammer."

Chase's head fell forward, and he sighed. *What the bloody hell was that? Was that really me?* Chase knew assassins weren't kind people, but executing women and children while they begged for mercy? That was leagues beyond anything he felt he could do. He shook any doubts from his mind.

Just a dream. It had to be.

He raised his head and desperately tried to sound

positive even if he didn't feel particularly optimistic. "Don't worry yourself, Richard. I'm sure I was feverish or ill. It's probably the stress from everything that's happened. Now, I think that if I were any hungrier, my stomach would growl loud enough to scare away the birds. What's for breakfast?"

CHAPTER 4
INTO THE WOODS

The two assassins shared a skillet of fried pork sausage and potatoes before gathering their belongings and continuing northward. Chase was quiet through the morning, deep in thought, allowing Lightfoot's gentle rocking side to side to put him at ease.

Cole had taken Chase from a life of poverty and suffering, days away from a public execution. The assassins had been told every day of their training that they ensured the greater good for of all the people of Rakksberg. They were a necessary evil that kept people in line through their reputation as well as their actions.

Sooner or later, each initiate accepted that killing was a tool. Chase had even grown to enjoy his life at times even if his line of work brought him no joy. He looked especially fondly at the time spent with his brothers and sisters in the Burrow. There were good memories buried between the grim realities of the profession that was forced upon them.

He never thought any members of the Blades were capable of a mass execution like the one he had witnessed.

A night of tossing and turning without respite left Chase sore and tired. As Lightfoot continued down the trail behind Thunder, Chase's muscles burned, and his joints ached. His eyelids were heavy, and he fought an insatiable urge to yawn. And when he succumbed to the urge, it only made things worse.

As they traveled down the empty road, Chase repeatedly rubbed his eyes to keep from closing them. He couldn't shake his exhaustion no matter how hard he tried. It felt unlike anything he had experienced before. It felt unnatural.

Early in the afternoon, Richard looked back to Chase from atop Thunder to break the silence of the morning. "Belford is half a day's ride to the east. We could ride there and get you a decent bed to sleep in for the night. We don't need to rush into the damned Widower's Woods. I'm sure if there is someone there looking for you, they won't be going anywhere."

"No." Chase shook his head to clear his thoughts, waving a hand at his companion dismissively. "I don't want to cost us a full day's ride because of a little nightmare. We're almost to the woods, anyway. Before we know it, we'll be there."

Richard grunted and shifted uncomfortably in his saddle. "I don't see what the bloody rush is. And I don't think that was just some nightmare. You didn't see the way you thrashed about this morning. What do you expect we'll find, anyway? Local legends say that no one's ever ventured into the woods and come back to tell the tale."

"That's hogwash and you know it," Chase replied with a weak chuckle. His tense ribs panged uncomfortably at the sudden jerking of his laugh. "Sure, there are poor, old sods who go missing in the woods, but the gargoyles, forest spiders, and mind fungus might have something to do with that."

"That's what I'm saying. What the hell kind of person lives in a place like that?" Richard snorted angrily and threw his hands up in exacerbation before turning forward again. "I guess we'll find out soon enough."

Chase smiled to himself. Richard always lightened his mood without trying. The brutish man's thick wit and blunt logic added a refreshing perspective on things, especially compared to the constant mystery some of the Black Blades seemed to live by. Chase fondly remembered a time when he and Richard had worked on a contract together. After hours of plotting the most efficient way to infiltrate a money laundering Baron's homestead, Richard suggested they merely knock on the door. Chase had laughed for days after that job. *The great thing was that the fool's plan actually worked.*

The nearby pines, oaks, and bramble thickened as the travelers drew closer to the forest until the road was tangled with weeds reaching through cracks in the cobblestone and brush spilling over the sides of the path. Chase saw a clump of crows and jays in the distance mobbing a gargoyle as the odd creature flew away. The horribly ugly things flew more awkwardly than they walked.

Eventually the sun hid behind a veil of needles and leaves overhead, and the travelers were bathed in shadows. Wind gently combed through the trees around them, twigs crackling and leaves shifting behind the occasional cackle of a wild dog. The trees grew livelier in the wake of bad weather, but as they continued into the thicket, the world around them grew silent.

Grey clouds darkened behind the cracks in the canopy above and the air thickened while Chase and Richard approached a wooden sign nailed to a large oak that had grown into the pathway. Chase climbed down from Lightfoot and approached the sign, brushing away vines and moss. It read, *Widower's Woods: Turn Back*.

The trees along the road ahead grew a full arm span in diameter and the pine needles extended longer than the width of his palm. Bramble and wild berry bushes along the edges of the path were covered in wild, dagger-like thorns reaching toward the decrepit cobblestone road as if to dissuade travelers from continuing further. Dim, gray light cast a ghostly hue through the canopy, sapping the life from the world around them. And while the road continued to the center of the woods, the path grew narrower and more overgrown with each step.

Chase glanced at Richard, who craned his neck to see what lay ahead. "Do you think the horses can make do on the path?" Chase asked. "It doesn't seem too narrow, but I can't tell if the path will curve or twist. I don't know if the rumors about this place can be trusted, but it might be best to assume the worst."

Richard frowned slightly. "Aye. I don't think it's a good idea. Thunder and Lightfoot are good horses, and the path we rode here seemed straight enough. Do you think they'll make it back on their own?"

Chase patted Lightfoot gently and whispered a comforting remark in the mare's ear before looking back at Richard. "I suppose they'll have to. This wouldn't be the first time some of Dalin's horses were left to find their own way home. They always seem to make it back one way or another."

They patted their horses' flanks, urging them to ride south. Chase stared down the path heading deeper into the woods as dread crept up his spine. His muscles still ached weakly, and his joints occasionally creaked as a reminder of the night before. His mind was foggy from a strange and unnatural presence—though, he was unsure if it was just him or if the rumored mind fungus within the woods was already affecting him. *At least Richard seems fine.*

As they continued onward, the enormous trees became covered in thick, twisting branches blocking most of the light from the sky above. More brambles crawled across the ground around them with each step, covered in those sharp thorns that looked like claws that yearned to grab passersby and drag them into the darkness beyond the path. The musty air hung uncomfortably around them, weighing them down in a blanket of sickly smelling sap and mud.

Chase heard a nearby branch crack and flinched. His attention snapped to a clump of leaves rustling in the distance. He noticed Richard had heard the same sound and began searching for its source among the darkened woods. There was a faint rustling in the canopy, but the path remained still and quiet. Branches snapped again, and Chase silently unsheathed his bastard sword.

The black blade reflected the dim, gray light from above while Chase waited for the disturbance to reveal itself. After a few still moments, a dark shape leapt from the bushes and blocked the path, staring at the two strange outsiders. When the creature refrained from attacking, Chase lowered his weapon slightly.

The gargoyle stood waist-high, using its bony appendages to support its gaunt, twisted figure as though it struggled to stay upright in a tangle of mangy, mottled fur and battered, leathery wings. At the end of each of its limbs was a bent paw with three long claws. A slender neck protruded from its emaciated body to support a slightly-too-large head that forced the gargoyle to slouch awkwardly. It boasted a large lower jaw with coarse, yellow fangs poking up into the air. Above its small, reptilian nostrils were two empty black eyes that held a blank expression, observing the intruders to its forest with little more than indifference.

Chase's sigh rang through the silence like the bellowing of a war horn.

The gargoyle hissed and leapt at Chase, brandishing its claws and opening its mouth, revealing countless sharp, yellow fangs. Acting on instinct, Chase dropped a knee to the ground and lifted the tip of his sword at the oncoming attacker. The blade twisted in his grip while the creature slammed into him, allowing its momentum to carry his sword hand before he dropped his shoulder and pivoted. With a flick of his wrist, Chase threw the gargoyle into a nearby tree.

The mass of fur and fangs fell to the ground in a bloody heap, twitching and writhing as it coughed and squeaked before passing in silence. Chase wiped the blood from his blade and sheathed it while Richard approached the body for inspection. The gruff man used the handle of his axe to roll the corpse onto its back. Its empty, lifeless eyes remained open, gazing up at the trees, thick, black blood oozing from its chest.

Chase soon joined his friend by the gargoyle. The smell of wet fur and blood wasn't overwhelming, but it wasn't pleasant either. "I don't think that's a very large one," Chase spoke in a quiet, level tone, analyzing the body to ensure any lingering danger was long gone. "I've heard stories from the farmers to the west, and I think we saw one on the way into the woods that was much larger. This one's wings don't look fully grown and it seemed to be hiding in the bramble. I'd guess it was a juvenile."

Richard huffed and spat on the ground through a sneer. "Let's hope we don't see any of the big ones. They're ugly enough as it is. I don't think we could handle the larger ones in these tight quarters."

Chase yawned and looked at the leafy canopy

above. *Carpenter's Hammer, I'm tired. I don't think I could make it much further if I wanted to.* The cracks of dim sky shining through the trees had grown darker. *It'll be night soon. Good thing, too. I could use some rest.* He looked back to his friend. "I think we should stop and camp for the night. If one of the larger ones comes around, I'd like to be ready for it. Hopefully, a fire will keep them away through the night."

"Aye. I'll work on that fire while you get rid of the body." Richard smiled wryly. "It was your kill, after all."

After unpacking their bedrolls, they gathered some modest cookware to heat an additional helping of their dried sausages over the fire. The partners began discussing what they had heard about the rise in gargoyle populations in the woods when Chase felt his eyes close involuntarily. Richard offered to stay awake for a while in case something else came by, and in Chase's current state he couldn't bring himself to argue otherwise.

He lay on his cot and drifted to sleep quicker than he anticipated.

***

Once again, Chase stood in a city bathed in fire.

His limbs swayed as he stumbled between rows of burning houses. It was no city he could recognize, though the mix of stone and wood buildings roofed in a mess of shale and thatch reminded him of Darkwater. The smell of the sea was absent, replaced by the stench of rotten eggs and brimstone. Chase struggled to stay on his feet and proceeded down an empty cobblestone street until he heard the muffled screams of a woman in a nearby house with a thatched roofed.

Chase tripped and fell into the door, the wood giving way to leave him lying on the floor of the house. The room was empty save for ruined and scattered furniture. A table lay broken beside a mess of toppled chairs and a cracked stone fireplace. Whatever decorations had been there once were either taken, torn, or burned. The smell of charred wood and blood hung thick in the air.

Chase's chest tightened.

The screams grew louder, though they were still muffled behind something. As Chase climbed to his feet and stumbled through the house, he heard an occasional sharp crack or dull thud accompanied by the harsh voice of a man yelling. After fumbling around on legs that felt like water, Chase finally reached out to a nearby door handle and pulled.

Chase froze in the doorway when he saw a man standing over a panicking woman. The man laughed between frenzied screams and desperate cries, the woman desperately fighting to get away from her assailant. Between feeble whimpers, the man hit her so hard it made Chase's own jaw tighten in pain. He clenched his teeth and watched in horror as the man swung a small club at the woman over and over, relishing in the pain he caused her with sick satisfaction.

Chase tried to look away, or intervene, or do *anything* but stand there watching. Every muscle in his weary body was frozen in place, as if some unseen force held him still. He was stuck watching the man beat the woman senselessly, and all Chase could do was stand in shock and horror with tears streaming down his face—helpless to do anything at all.

After the man grew bored of the hellish display, he tossed the woman to the side like she was nothing more than a nuisance. She fell to the ground with a loud crack, her head slamming into the nearby end table. The bruised and broken woman curled on the floor, weeping. The man walked to the bloody table and procured a scrap of cloth. Laughing to himself for only a moment, he wiped a light smear of blood from his cheek before turning his attention to the cowering body at his feet. "Next time I expect you to put up a little more of a fight, or I'll burn you from the inside out."

The voice was as cold as steel, laced with an oddly familiar, unmistakable venom. The man had Chase's dark hair and lean frame. He had the same scars in the same places. And when he finally turned to face the door, he stopped to look at the frozen observer. Chase gasped as the fiery red light illuminated the mirror image of himself.

***

Chase sprang upright, screaming in the dead of night. Richard's expression darkened with concern while Chase frantically looked around and slowly remembered where he was. Shaking from the lingering mess of emotions, he rubbed his eyes as much in frustration as confusion. Richard gently placed his large hand on Chase's shoulder before helping him rearrange the bedding that had twisted askew during the nightmare.

After steadying his breath and calming his shaking hands, Chase could finally speak to his friend without stumbling over his words. "I-I don't know w-what's happening to me, Richard." Chase licked his lips uneasily, a bead of sweat falling from his brow. He may have stopped his hands from shaking, but he still felt the rest of his body shiver underneath his clothes. "This feels un-unnatural. Like someone, or something, is *doing* this to me, but the bloody Carpenter kn-knows who would do this—or how. My dreams don't feel like my own."

Chase continued to recount the dream, skipping over the unnecessary details. *He doesn't need to know everything. I don't want to remember everything.*

Even so, Richard's eyes widened in horror. "Carpenter's bloody Hammer, I can't believe this. This must have something to do with that damned message. Chase, are you sure we aren't just walking into a trap? If somebody's controlling your dreams, they might be controlling your actions, too. For all we know there's something in these woods meant to kill us, and the person that sent that message to the Burrow is miles away in some tavern enjoying a drink and a good laugh at our expense."

"I don't know either, Richard." Chase paused despite himself. He always had an answer—always knew what was ahead—and if he didn't, he always had a quip or a joke to lighten the mood. Rarely did Chase find himself in situations where he was completely at the mercy of someone or something else. He finally responded, trying not to sound defeated. "It doesn't feel like someone else is in control. I feel free enough to make my own decisions.

"Besides, magic, mind control, ancient hexes, and curses are just children's stories. Even if we could think of a person with enough reason to do this to us, there is still the matter of how. *How* would they be controlling me? Still…" Chase rubbed his eyes again. His vision was blurred and somewhat unfocused. "I feel drunk. No. I feel hungover, like I drank a whole cask of ale to myself. Not to mention my body aches like I was run down by Thunder. Things aren't adding up."

He stretched his arms above his head as he looked out into the darkness of the night. The small fire bathed the area in a warm glow, but it shrouded the woods beyond in an ominous darkness. Occasionally, the rustling of a bush, snap of a twig, or crackling of a burning ember broke the silence that hung over the travelers like an unseen weight. It was as if something were just beyond the comforting light of the campfire, waiting for the right time to strike.

Chase couldn't force himself to sleep again that night.

CHAPTER 5
TOO MANY LEGS

The night slowly faded into morning, the forest glowing with an eerie, gray light. Compared to the near pitch black of night, the odd light that found its way through the dense canopy above was a welcomed sight. The weary companions slowly gathered their things, making sure not to leave behind any signs of their presence. Step by heavy step, they ventured deeper into the unknown.

Two days with only a few hours of sleep took its toll on Chase. His entire body felt sluggish and heavy, like he was pulling a wagon with no wheels. Chase slowly arched his back and rolled his shoulders, his joints popping and cracking uncomfortably. He rubbed his eyes and saw Richard watching him intently. Chase smiled and stifled a yawn. "Shouldn't you be watching where you're going?"

Richard sighed and forced a weak smile. His hand involuntarily rose to the back of his head when he spoke. "I was trying to, but your cracking old joints are distracting. You sound like an old cart on a broken road." His smile faded, replaced with concern. "Are you going to be okay, mate?"

"I'll be fine." Chase returned his focus to the overgrown path, taking care not to catch his sleeve on a bramble thorn that stuck out awkwardly. *I don't know what's happening to me, Richard, but you don't need to worry about that.*

Chase continued to force his way down the path. Minutes rolled into hours, and hours felt like days on that overgrown trail in the heart of the Widower's Woods. Occasionally, they stopped and ate a bit of dried meat, berries, and bread to give their groaning stomachs something to digest, but they wasted little time. The disturbingly silent forest was growing thicker and wilder with each passing minute, and it became harder and harder to follow their path forward.

The air had grown thick with mist when Chase stopped at the side of the path. A white, sticky substance ran between the branches of a nearby thorn bush. He inspected the silk carefully, rubbing it between his fingertips and watching it cling to his gauntleted fingers before clumping. Chase turned his gaze to Richard. "We must be heading into forest spider territory. Looks like webs to me."

Richard shook his head. "First gargoyles and now bloody forest spiders. I was hoping these damned things really were just a story meant to scare folk away from the woods."

"Stories often hold a least a piece or two of

truth." Chase wiped his gauntlet on his thigh and slowly stood. "Let's just hope the spiders aren't as large as the shepherds say they are when they have a few too many pints in them."

Soon, the stringy white silk covered the bushes and bramble around the road until they were nearly surrounded by it. The path twisted and turned, silk stretching across the trail, making it more difficult to avoid. After a painfully slow and careful trek, Chase and Richard found themselves outside the rocky opening to a cave lined with thick webs. The trees and undergrowth around the opening had grown far too thick to proceed around it. And unfortunately, neither of them saw an alternate route.

Chase's stomach turned uncomfortably. The thought that this may be a dead end rather than a tunnel forward sent shivers up his spine. *I hate caves. They're dark, damp, and whatever is living there knows where you're going before you do. That's why the Blades made the Burrow in the first place.* Chase looked to his friend and silently nodded. Richard nodded in reply and slowly readied his axe.

Silently, Richard took a step forward, tightening his grip on his battle axe. Chase followed in kind, carefully stepping exactly where Richard had. They slowly entered the cave, the ground beneath them shifting from broken cobblestone to dirt and jagged stone. The silk on the walls prevented any moisture from falling from the ceiling, leaving a disturbingly calm silence to hang in the air.

After an hour of carefully walking through the twisting cavern, they stopped in an open chamber that split into three smaller tunnels. The first tunnel to the left was the smallest, blocked by a jagged rocky outcropping that made it nearly impassable. The middle cavern was wide enough for a single man but seemed to twist before rising towards the cavern ceiling. The final tunnel on the right appeared large enough for three men to walk abreast, with flat ground and a high ceiling.

Chase gestured to the tunnel furthest to the right. He didn't know where it would lead, but they had little choice. The damp air was beginning to weigh down on them, and if they didn't find a way out of the cave soon, they would have to turn around and head back the way they came. Richard slowly nodded and crept toward the passage. After only one step, he froze in place.

Slowly and steadily, Chase turned his head and—to his dismay—saw the source of the silken webs plastered along every inch of the cave. The creature stared at the two intruders, its eight, hair-covered legs twitching restlessly. A bead of sweat formed on Chase's brow, his breath catching in his throat.

Standing before them was a massive forest spider. The creature was larger than a hound—two shining, black fangs protruding a few inches below a row of gleaming, black eyes that studied the two men with piqued interest.

The spider didn't move. Chase's muscles burned in protest as he tried to stand perfectly still. After a tense moment of silence, a drop of sweat from Chase's brow fell to the ground. The faint sound of water hitting a flat stone rang throughout the empty cave like church bells at dawn.

With alarming speed, the wicked spider lurched at Chase. But before the creature's massive front legs could land a lethal strike, Chase maneuvered his blade to deflect the attack. Not wasting a second, Richard quickly swung his axe, lopping two of the spider's legs clean off its body. The beast fell to the ground, its pained squeal echoing through the cavern.

Chase flinched at the spider's ear-splitting cry. *What the hell was that?*

The distraction, however short, was enough for the monstrous beast to strike again. With six legs intact, the spider recovered and swung at Chase again. The creature's leg hit his thigh with a dull thud, and Chase's legs buckled under him bringing him to the ground. Richard swung at the thing's thorax, nearly cleaving its hairy body in two. The spider squealed again, black blood spurting from the wound. It turned, exposing its rear to Chase.

This time, Chase didn't hesitate. Lunging forward, he drove his sword into the monster's carapace with little resistance, allowing Richard to swing his axe one more time. With a final screech, the spider collapsed on the ground and writhed in pain. Eventually, the squirming stopped, and the cave was silent once more.

Chase wiped the blood from his blade and looked at his friend. They laughed together before Richard blurted out. "That went better than I thought it would."

Richard regretted the words as soon as they left

his lips. The chamber quickly filled with its brethren, the eight-legged monstrosities crawling out of the shadows and surrounding Chase and Richard. Each beast stood poised to attack, their empty, gleaming eyes staring down the two intruders. The spiders were cold and emotionless, interested only in feeding on those that entered their home.

Chase tightened his grip on his bastard sword while Richard lifted his massive axe to face their foes. *You had to say something, didn't you?*

Without warning, the monsters charged them. Chase and Richard leapt apart to divide the attention of the horde's immense numbers. Chase swung his sword at one spider's legs, causing it to crash to the ground with an unpleasant screech. With a swift, downward thrust of his sword, he felt its strange exoskeleton crack and splinter. Before he had time to think, Chase withdrew the blade and swung again, slicing a spider's fangs and forcing it to recoil.

He tried the same maneuver on another spider, only for his sword to taste nothing but the stale cave air. The spider lunged at him with its front legs raised, but Chase quickly parried the attack before twisting his arm and driving his blade through the beast's abdomen.

Chase allowed his instincts to take over. He slashed and stabbed and parried and dodged countless times without a thought—as if he were dancing to a number he'd heard countless times before.

Suddenly, in the heat of the battle, Chase's focus was ripped away by a muffled grunt. He paused for only a moment to see Richard struggling with two of the massive spiders. Panic rising in his chest, Chase reached under his cloak. In a single motion, he drew his cleaving dagger and hurled the blade at one of the spiders attacking Richard. The beast shrieked as the long blade dug into its small abdomen before it fell to the ground in a twitching mess.

The other spider attacking Richard swung wildly at his burly legs. To Chase's horror, his friend fell to the ground, dropping his axe a few paces away. Chase ran to him but was blocked by yet another giant spider. After spinning and slicing his way through the monster, he watched helplessly as the spider on top of Richard arched its back and bared its fangs.

No! Richard! No!

Chase screamed wordlessly as the monster struck the soft belly of the fallen man. Richard let out an ear shattering scream of pain before falling silent.

He stepped toward Richard, but a nearby shriek forced him to turn. Chase had just enough time to raise his blade before the leaping beast slammed into him, knocking him to the ground. With every ounce of strength he had left, he pushed back against the spider to keep the monster away from his chest. But with the flat of his sword pressed against his face, he could do little more than struggle while the spider lunged and jerked unnaturally. Finally, Chase kicked its sensitive underbelly and rolled to his side, narrowly dodging the lunging fangs of another.

After springing to his feet, Chase slashed violently at his attackers until the rest of the spiders in the cavern had either died or retreated into the darkness. Minutes had passed in the chaos of the battle, but

Chase was finally left alone to catch his breath.

He looked to where Richard had fallen. To Chase's surprise, he saw that the spiders were retreating into the rightmost tunnel, pulling Richard's limp body behind them. Panic surged through his mind. As fast as he could, Chase sheathed his sword and gathered his dagger in stride, charging forward with his limbs screaming in silent agony. He banished any thoughts of rest from his mind.

Richard needs my help, dammit.

He could already be dead.

No! He's not dead. You're going to get him out of this hell hole.

After a few minutes of desperate pursuit, Chase's single-minded focus was broken by the strange appearance of an old, oil-soaked torch mounted on the tunnel wall. Before he had time to ponder on the oddness of such a human convenience that no spider would need, the tunnel grew brighter, lit by several more of the strange torches.

Chase shivered, a sudden, cold breeze flowing over his sweaty skin. The impossibly fresh air originated further down the cavern, and he grew more apprehensive as he ran.

When the tunnel grew larger and straighter, Chase slowed his pace. Suddenly, the tunnel gave way to a massive, open chamber. A walkway lit by several torches led to the center. Hesitantly, Chase ensured he was hidden in the shadow of a large outcropping of rocks as he approached.

He scanned the chamber and saw a crudely carved

stone altar basked in fiery red light. The altar was made of dark stone, adorned with images of human skeletons holding up a sacrificial plinth. The spiders had placed Richard's body in front of the altar before retreating to the darkness once again. Chase tried to make out just how many spiders were in the vast room, but his eyes struggled to see more than vague shapes beyond the torchlight.

Behind the altar, Chase noticed a misshapen stone throne surrounded by piles of bones. He strained his eyes, searching for someone or something that would sit on such a throne, but he saw nothing. After returning his thoughts to Richard, a shrill womanly voice rang throughout the chamber. "Come out and face your Queen, intruder. I wish to see the *monster* that has slain so many of my children." The words seemed to slide in a crass slur as the high pitch sounds echoed off the chamber walls.

Exhaling, Chase stepped out from behind his rock and into the heart of the cavern, stopping just short of his friend at the center of the chamber. He forced himself to smile at the shadows and reply to the womanly voice with a confidence he didn't have. "Here is your *monster*—the Bane of Spiders. It seems many of your children have met their end today and more might, as well. Release my friend and grant us safe passage from this place before you regret bringing him here."

The creature laughed and emerged from the darkness. Her womanly shape from the waist up was disturbingly elegant, save for the dark bristles covering every inch of her bare skin. Long, bony arms with jagged, clawed fingers twirled gracefully, drawing attention to her hungry smile and wicked fangs.

Chase's stomach dropped. As she inched into the torchlight, her hips seamlessly joined to the mottled body of a giant forest spider. She crept toward her uninvited guest, seemingly gliding as her eight legs shuffled silently across the cave floor. She stopped ten paces away and pointed at Richard's motionless body. Four pitch-black eyes glistened in the dim light as they focused on Chase. "You came for *him*?"

"Aye," Chase's words failed him in her horrifying presence. The blood drained from his face as she closed the gap to him without making a sound. Fangs shining and a sickly-sweet scent wafting over Chase from somewhere unseen, the creature lifted a bony hand and stroked his cheek. Her yellow-brown claws grazed his stubble, her mouth twisting into a terrifying smile.

She laughed with a surprisingly smooth melody that grated with her harsh tone. "You caught me at a gracious time. It's not often I'm treated to *human*." She stretched out her bony arm, looking at the back of her hand to admire her wicked claws. "Men are just so... *sweet*. Animals do well enough for my children, but I try not to settle for such vile things. Your *friend* will be plenty to satisfy my hunger. But then, of course, there is the matter of replenishing my children's numbers. And you are so very *appealing*."

Chase shivered as her words crept into his mind. *Bloody hell.* The Spider Queen eyed him as though she were starving.

He smirked and managed to keep his voice level as he resorted to the only thing he could think to say—a joke. "I'm sorry, but you're not really my type. I tend to fancy those with two legs rather than eight."

"Funny, too. I like that." Black eyes fixated on Chase even more hungrily, a glistening drop of saliva hanging from one of her putrid yellow fangs. "It's always nice to play with my meal before laying my eggs."

She finally crept back to the grotesque throne behind her and settled upon it. Her arachnid body rustled against the cold stone, her spindly legs folding beneath her. The creature posed with one arm forward, as if presenting herself as a prize.

Chase looked down at Richard and then back to the ravenous Spider Queen. His voice was cold and sharp. "I don't intend to be anyone or anything's meal today—nor will I be a glorified egg sac, for that matter. Unless you like the idea of being skewered, I suggest you and your children let me take my friend and leave."

The Spider Queen smiled and held her hand out to her side. Silence hung in the air for a moment before an oddly plump spider emerged from the shadows, presenting its queen with a crude, curved blade like an offering.

She gently accepted the gift, bristles twitching unnervingly as she inspected Chase from head to toe. "If you can best me in single combat, you are welcome to do what you please. I cannot promise, however, that my children will simply allow you to leave. I would imagine so. They are feral, not stupid—although they may become enraged at the sight of their dearest mother being vanquished. Who knows, really? I find it hard to understand them at times. Care to find out for yourself?"

Countless dark shapes shifted in the shadows. The ground was level and hard-packed despite the state of the rest of the caverns. The sickly stench was gone, and a cool breeze flowed through the chamber, calming Chase's nerves.

He turned his attention to the challenger, studying the creature's anatomy while trying to think of a weakness he could exploit. After a long, contemplative moment, he drew his sword and passed it from one hand to the other. He muttered wryly—more to himself than anyone else—although his voice carried in the silent chamber. "I do enjoy a challenge."

The monster lifted her blade with a surprising grace, like a ballroom dancer. Slowly, the sword pointed at Chase while she twisted her arm this way and that. The Queen's lips pursed into a terrifying smile, and she swayed to the motion of the blade as if she was trying to lull Chase into a trance.

The Spider Queen dashed in a sudden fluid movement and slashed. Chase jumped back and retaliated as quickly as he could. She parried with astonishing speed and finesse, gliding eerily with hardly a sound. Chase focused on blocking each of the Queen's strikes until he found a rhythm to the swings.

His exhausted body seemed heavy and slow, but he thankfully mustered enough strength to meet his opponent. After a painfully long time matching the Queen blow for blow, Chase leapt backward and stood his ground, allowing the fierce song of clashing metal to fade. Breathing heavily, he felt sweat drip from his brow.

Dammit, I'm in no condition for this. I need to end it quickly.

If he were fully rested, Chase could've ended the fight without much of a struggle. Instead, he was forced to fight defensively in hopes that the Queen would tire. It didn't take long to see that she would not give in so easily. Chase knew he had to do something different, or he wouldn't last much longer.

An idea came to him. He steadied his breath and calmed his nerves.

As quickly as he could, Chase slashed and thrusted furiously from many different angles, trying to find even the tiniest opening. The Spider Queen had not anticipated the sudden burst of energy but had little trouble deflecting the attacks. Strike after strike, she strode from side to side, gliding across the cavern floor.

Chase stopped momentarily and backed away. Throughout the fight, it had become clear that the Queen was using her long limbs to keep him away from her. *I've got one chance to pull this off.* Standing at the ready, Chase waited for her to make the next move.

The Queen smiled. "You are very skilled, human. I can already tell that you'll taste sweet." Though she tried to mask it, her voice shook as she fought to hold back gasps for air.

This was not time to get ahead of himself. Chase

focused on the fight. Sweat beaded on his forehead, and he felt his legs scream in silent protest. *One chance.*

The Spider Queen crept toward him with ghastly steadiness and swung her sword one last time. Rather than sidestepping the attack, Chase stepped forward with his sword held high. Their blades clashed, the sound of steel-on-steel echoing through the chamber like the clash of a symbol. Without a moment's hesitation, Chase grabbed hold of her bony arm. He pulled the monster in and stomped his foot down on one of her outstretched arachnoid legs.

The leg snapped with a disturbing crunch and the Queen howled in pain, her wretched body buckling slightly as her footing gave way. Chase released her arm and spun as close to her as he could. In one fluid motion, Chase drew the small dagger from his belt and drove it into the Queen's thorax. Using the handle to hoist himself onto the beast, he straddled her spider-like body to face her exposed, bristly back.

She twisted wildly, panic rising and arms flailing. Chase grabbed the Queen's bare neck and squeezed. She dropped her sword, desperately grasping at his gloved hand with jagged claws. For a moment, they struggled against one another until Chase finally thrust his sword with another unsettling crunch, skewering her through her humanoid chest.

With a piercing shriek and a rasping, shuttering gasp for air, the Queen fell to the cavern floor and went still.

Chase withdrew his blade and stumbled to the ground. He gathered his dagger and ran as fast as he could to his friend's motionless body. The spider's fangs had penetrated deep into Richard's stomach, but the wounds looked superficial. There was still a chance his friend was alive.

Looking up, Chase expected the remaining spiders to pounce. To his relief they were cowering and backing away into the shadows beyond the torchlight after witnessing the demise of their queen. He sighed and sheathed his sword. Carefully, he picked Richard up under the arms and hoisted his massive body over his shoulders. Chase swore to himself, wishing Richard was as small as the other assassins from the Burrow.

Slowly, he made his way through the tunnels, following the cool current of damp air while avoiding the way they came. Eventually, the winding tunnel filled with a blue glow as he approached the exit. Chase dragged Richard out of the cave and down the overgrown path of the forest until they were far enough away to avoid any more of the wretched spiders.

Battered and exhausted, Chase gently lowered Richard to the soft earth at his feet. He sighed heavily, leaning on a tree with aching joints and burning muscles. His eyes were heavy, and his throat was dry. Looking at his unconscious friend, he wished he knew some way to clean or treat the wound in Richard's stomach that had dried over with sticky, thick blood.

Without warning, the air grew thick, and a putrid smell filled Chase's nostrils. He looked around in the dim light, trying to find the source of the stench. Suddenly, a sharp pain surged through his entire body unlike any pain he had ever felt before. He fell to the ground, his body jerking wildly. His hands clenched and twisted, his muscles tensing all at once.

Something unseen grabbed the back of his neck and lifted him to his feet. Pain raced through his mind in an unrelenting wave, making it impossible to think. His legs moved on their own while his upper body continued to convulse, as if someone was working him like a puppet on strings. Slowly, his body walked toward a large bush covered in massive thorns.

The shaking grew more violent with each jerking movement. Chase's hand was forced to reach out and break a giant thorn from a nearby branch. With a dagger-length thorn in his possession, he turned and walked back to his friend. Fear flooding his every thought, Chase tried to resist, but any efforts just caused more blinding, white-hot pain.

Forced to kneel beside his friend, Chase lifted the thorn over Richard's body. He tried to close his eyes, afraid to watch what was about to happen. After his hands twisted and jerked unpleasantly, he watched himself break the piece of plant in two. A strange liquid oozed from the thorn and into the bloody wound on Richard's midsection.

Richard flinched, but little else happened. Once all the liquid had been drained from the thorn, Chase's body went limp, and he collapsed on the ground.

CHAPTER 6
BABBLING PROPHECY

Chase opened his eyes. He was lying on a cold, damp city street bathed in red light. The screams of women and children assaulted his ears, his head splitting in pain from the onslaught of horrible cries.

Slowly prying his body from the ground, Chase rose to his feet. To his surprise, he felt surprisingly rejuvenated. The aches and pains from days on the road and his fight with the Spider Queen were gone. He cracked his back and stretched his arms while the smell of smoke and charred wood thickened the air. After brushing the dirt from his legs, Chase looked around the vacant street for any sign of what he had to do or what he needed to see before he would be allowed to wake from his nightmare.

He walked until he discovered a large house at the end of an alleyway. All the windows were cracked and broken, and nearly all the wood paneling was falling from the walls. Even the heavy door of the dilapidated building was broken, hanging from a single cracked hinge. *I suppose this is as good a place as any. I can't really see anything else in this Carpenter-damned street.*

The screams from the outside world muffled with each step through the halls of the home. Pictures were torn off the walls and tables turned on end. Chairs lay scattered around the various rooms and mounds of melted candle wax had hardened where they formed. The air was stale and empty, void of any scent or breeze. The stark silence of the ruined building felt more unsettling than the cries from outside.

After what seemed like ages of wandering the apparently endless, ruined home, Chase heard the desperate screams of a young man. He followed the source of the sound as quickly as he could.

Right. Left. Right again.

Chase ran through an impossibly large maze of halls, faster with each step until he was out of breath. A sharp pain shot through his head as the sound grew louder and louder. At first, Chase couldn't distinguish words amid the screaming, but when he approached a large wooden door left slightly ajar, he heard what the man was yelling about.

"Why don't you just kill me already?" the screaming voice pleaded in desperation, shaking between gasps and sobs. "I've told you want you want! You can just kill me! Why don't you just do it, already?"

Chase waited for another voice to reply. Rather

than an answer to the man's questions, a wicked laugh echoed from the room, followed by another deafening scream. Chase swung the door open to see a bloody and beaten man splayed out, tied to a wooden board. The man was covered with cuts, bruises, and visibly broken bones, but he wanted to empty his stomach on the floor at the sight of a gaping wound across the man's gut.

Struggling to keep his composure, Chase held a gloved hand to his mouth. The air suddenly stank of blood and hot iron. The torturer pulled a red-hot dagger from the prisoner's flesh before turning to Chase. The Man in Red, the mirror image of the young assassin dressed in blood red leathers with splashes of gray, stood before him—covered in blood. His crooked, crazed smile was enough to make Chase's skin crawl.

Chase closed his eyes and felt the world around him disappear.

***

Chase woke slowly, his brow damp with cold sweat. As his vision cleared, he realized he was no longer on the path near the Spider Queen's cave. He was still on the ground, but in a small clearing surrounded by massive trees. Unlike the rest of the Widower's Woods, there were no messy clumps of thorn bushes and untamed bramble. This clearing seemed intentionally maintained.

Exhausted, Chase clambered to his feet. *Bloody hell, my head feels like I've just been trampled.* His muscles burned horribly, and his joints cracked uncomfortably. His ears rang unpleasantly at the familiar calls of jays and nuthatches, accompanied by the occasional chittering of a squirrel.

Richard was gone.

Immediately, a series of horrifying images rushed through Chase's mind, but he forced himself to clear his thoughts. *I need to focus. Panicking won't save my friend.*

In the quiet ambience of the forest, Chase faintly heard water trickling on rocks nearby. Step by step, he made his way toward the sound, passing a huge oak tree where the grove grew large enough to fit a sizeable pond.

The surface of the water was black glass, glistening in the moonlight that shone in the cloudless night sky. Ripples and waves erupted on the surface every so often, revealing a sense of life that had been absent from the woods until then. The smell of fresh water and moss filled Chase's nostrils while he gazed in wonderment at the plant life that seemed almost alien to him. All sorts of wildly colored mushrooms and weeds littered the shore. In the shade of a willow tree at the edge of the pond, Chase saw a patch of shimmering flowers resting upon jagged, branching stems.

Am I still in the woods? I can't be. There's no place in all the Berg like this. Chase's gaze wandered about the clearing until he spotted an old shanty. Its wooden planks appeared rotten and damp, while its thatched roof was falling in some places. Outside the home was a small fire pit accompanied by a tanning rack and an empty rotisserie spit. Chase proceeded cautiously to the strange, old house, tightening his grip on his sword. As he approached, he heard sounds coming from within—two distinct voices mumbling inside.

With calculated, silent footsteps, Chase slowly made his way to the front door. As he drew closer, he noticed unsettling things about the home. Various herbs and plants unfamiliar to him were strung up to dry, along with several squirrel carcasses and a recently trapped beaver. A pile of chickens and gargoyles with their heads removed lay next to a stone basin filled with the black water from the pond. Next to the fire, the apparatus that Chase thought was a tanning rack held an entire deer carcass. The sight of the animal, strung up to allow its entrails to spill out and dry, made Chase's stomach turn uncomfortably.

He finally reached the door and stood silently, listening to the conversation in the house for some indication that he could enter. The first man seemed to have a rasping, gravelly voice, while the second man's voice was familiar.

Richard. He sounds well enough, but I don't trust it. None of this makes any sense.

Chase swallowed the lump in his throat and further tightened his grip on his sword. The door creaked loudly, and the two men abruptly stopped their conversation.

Chase resisted the urge to jump as he entered the house at the sight of several petrified body parts in jars. The cluttered room was filled from floor to ceiling with all sorts of metal and stone charms hanging from short lengths of hide, as well as various animal parts fermenting in strangely colored and putrid smelling fluids. The shelves lining the walls were so cluttered with strange collections that further items—such as dried animal parts, vegetables, and roots—hung from the ceiling.

Still grasping his sheathed blade, Chase walked through the decrepit door frame into the next room.

As soon as Chase crossed the threshold, his body froze in place. A hunchbacked old man approached him, limping and leaning on a withered branch fashioned into a cane. The man had dark, wrinkled skin, and wore clanking jewelry made from various animal bones and horns joined by strips of hide. His stringy gray hair protruded haphazardly around a balding crown while his wobbling legs shook uncontrollably with each step toward Chase.

The man coughed and stammered to himself. His aged green eyes, set deeply in his creased face, darted wildly from side to side. "You there, boy. I know you. You are a shadow. No. Not just a shadow. The Shadow. The Shadow of Death." The man let out a manic crackling laugh to expose his jagged yellow teeth. His voice trembled and squeaked with every word.

Chase's stomach dropped—he couldn't move nor could he defend himself. His heart began to pound in his ears, and he felt his hands become clammy inside his gauntlets.

The old man continued, "Shadows follow light. No. They don't follow it. They are created by it. No. Not quite. Cast by those in the light. Ah, yes. A shadow is cast down by those who find themselves in the light. What light brings this Shadow? Death is cast down by steel. Is this Shadow cast down by steel? No, no, no. Not steel. Words. Yes. This Shadow of Death is cast by words. Words on paper. My words."

Chase's mind clicked at the utterance of the last phrase. He was looking at the author of the letter that led to his banishment. His teeth clenched in frustration. *All this way to find some bloody madman babbling in a rotted shack on a pond in the middle of some Carpenter-forsaken woods. If I had known this was what I was going to find, I wouldn't have come here.*

The old man took a few steps, clanking his cane clumsily on the ground. He smiled again while he raised a pouch up to Chase's eyes. "This is powder. Powder made from flowers. Flowers grow on the water. Flowers get ground to powder. Powder gets in the mind." A wrinkled finger with a jagged, untrimmed nail tapped the old man's temple. "The mind freezes. It freezes the body, too. No worries." The strange old man shook violently as he smiled wider and held his arms out. "Body will thaw. This Shadow should be grateful. Flowers mix with other flowers to make other powders. Other powders helped the Friend of Shadow."

So, whoever this is, he claims to have helped us. Chase silently resented the comment. *I know I couldn't have done anything better, but I don't see how* this *helps anything.*

He noticed a slight prickling at the ends of his hands and feet while the old man shook his head fiercely. "The Shadow wonders. Wonders why he is here. Wonders who I am. These things are no big trouble. All will be said. All will be known. I see inside the Shadow's mind. I see many things." The man pointed to the ceiling of the rotten cabin. "The Great

Carpenter speaks to me. Tells me the Shadow must be cast west. Come, come. All will be told."

The stinging sensation crept up Chase's limbs to his torso. He was confused, but he had come this far and wasn't about to leave without hearing what the man had to say.

The hermit tossed his pouch onto a nearby table. "I sent for the Shadow for many reasons. Many reasons will all be explained. The Shadow can be cast by death, but light bends around the shadow now. The Shadow will rise to light. All will be explained. Come now. Powder has worn off and Friend of Shadow waits. Yes, yes. I know shadows can dance. Now, come."

Chase's regained feeling throughout his limbs, and his mind raced. The old hermit's babbling amounted to nothing more than confused segments. *At least Richard is okay. He must be.* It only took a few more moments for the stinging sensation to run through his entire body, and with it, the ability move returned. Chase relaxed his grip on his sword and cracked his neck. The old hermit cocked his head to the side before beckoning him to another small room.

With stiff legs, Chase followed the old man and saw Richard sitting in a wooden chair next to a small fire sipping a strange, hot tea out of a dusty iron mug. The hermit's jewelry and charms clattered loudly as he plopped himself down in a matching chair.

The room was relatively sparse compared to the rest of the household. A blanched deer skull hanging over the fireplace and a petrified rodent in a jar sitting on a small table were the only decorations in sight.

Chase staggered next to his friend and sat in an unoccupied stool while he watched the eccentric host. Richard nudged his arm and motioned to an additional cup of tea that had been set out for him. He reluctantly reached for the cup sitting next to the preserved rodent. *Violets and wildflowers… and is that field grass? No poison that I can smell…*

He sipped the drink, letting the warm liquid flow into his stomach. He then turned to Richard and spoke softly. "Who is this man?"

"I'm not sure," Richard whispered with a wry smile. "I think he mentioned his name at some point in the babble. Benjyn? Whoever he is, he sure is a riot. Just a minute ago I could have sworn he was waving around a chicken bone."

Chase smiled and shifted in his seat. He turned his gaze to the shaking old man who had taken the moment to mutter incoherently to himself under his breath. "You said you'd tell me why I'm here."

The hermit cocked his head at his guest, causing his jewelry to clack together loudly. He looked confused. "I did?" Recognition flashed across his eyes. "Ah, yes, of course I did. The Shadow must be cast and there must be light to cast it. Firstly. Well, no. Not firstly. It came after the whispers. That nasty spider woman needed to be dealt with. She ate my goat. I liked that goat. Did she eat it?" He stared into the distance, momentarily lost in thought before returning to his stammering. "I think she did. Could have been one of her spiderlings, though. Either way, I must thank the Shadow and Friend of Shadow. Benjyn's goat will rest now."

Richard snorted, clearly resisting the urge to laugh with great effort.

The hermit continued, ignoring anything his guests did. "Now, firstly, Benjyn hears whispers of the Great Carpenter. Many whispers. Many times. Once heard whispers of death. Now hear whispers of shadows in darkness. The Shadow of Death. The Shadow of Death must be cast west and turned to the light. Light consumes the shadow. Light consumes all. Shadow cast from steel and blood consumed by light. Talk to the light. Turned by the light. Beyond the rocks that cast a shadow on the Berg. Light consumes rock. No. Light leaves rock. Light comes from within rock. Light consumes shadow."

"What are you saying, Benjyn?" Chase interrupted, growing impatient. "Speak clearly for Carpenter's sake. I don't understand."

The hermit's head cocked the other way, looking at Chase with a dazed expression. "West. The Shadow must be cast west to be consumed by light." The old man's tone suggested he was stating something as plainly as the weather. "Why can't the Shadow hear this? Light consumes the Shadow, and the Shadow becomes the Light. Shining fury on silver wings from the west." By now, Chase was certain the man's frantic arm waving was going to yank him from his seat. "Light shines from silver wings onto the east from the west. West!"

"What do you mean, on wings?" Chase spun the cup of tea in his hands absentmindedly to ease his frustration. "Benjyn, you need to speak more plainly."

Benjyn suddenly grew very confused. He looked

at the two young men like he had never seen them before. Fear grew in the man's expression, replacing any confidence he held moments before. "Who are you? Why are you here? Do I know you?"

Richard placed his hand on Chase's knee and gave him a comforting smile. He turned to the hermit. "Benjyn, you saved us from the Spider Queen's cave. I am the Bear, Friend of Shadow. This is the Shadow."

What the bloody hell is going on? Richard just nodded. Recognition flashed on Benjyn's face again as he smiled and nodded vigorously. His bone jewelry clacked together loudly. "Ah, yes! The Shadow and the Friend of Shadow. Yes, yes, yes. The Shadow must be cast west."

"You mentioned that." Chase spoke carefully, struggling to keep his tone calm. *This man is trying my patience.* "Why must the Shadow go west? What must he find to the west?"

"Find? Ah, yes. Find is a word. A fine word. A fine calling. Just the word Benjyn needs. The shadow must be cast west to *find* the light."

Chase and Richard rolled their eyes and drooped their heads.

"Find the gate to the light. First through dark, then through light, then on silver wings. Bring light to the east. Bad men bend to silver wings. Bad women, also. Bend forward, not backward. Light consumes all. Shadow becomes light."

Richard seemed just as confused as Chase—however he was far more entertained than Chase was.

I am glad one of us is enjoying this. Chase returned his gaze to the hermit, ready to ask further questions, but was cut off by more rambling.

"You can't wait. Never wait. Go. *Now.* Shadows can dance. Light consumes Shadow. Go. Path goes west. Out of woods. Go beyond all things—beyond the rocks that stand in the west. *Go.*"

The old hermit motioned to his guests, wildly clacking his jewelry while his arms shook. They finished the dregs of tea left in their mugs while the old man shimmied them out of the room. Desperately trying not to crash into the myriad of shelves and dangling charms, they hurried out of the house only for the door to slam shut behind them.

Chase wheeled around to see Richard bracing himself—hands on knees—laughing.

"What an odd man," Chase remarked.

Richard caught his breath. "What a guy! I haven't had a good laugh in a while. I can't believe he got Cole's feathers in such a tussle. Benjyn couldn't hurt the family even if he tried."

"Maybe," Chase answered bitterly. *He still managed to get me exiled.*

"Well, do we go where he says? As far as I know, beyond the Iron Hills, the Blackridge Mountains are the only thing to the west."

Chase nodded. "Aye. And from what I read in the Burrow's library, the mountains are too treacherous to cross. I don't think anyone has ever done it before even if that crazed old man says we need to go 'beyond the rocks.' The legends all say there's nothing but an endless sea on the other side." Chase ran his hands through his hair in frustration. "Cole must have had more reason to exile me than this man's ramblings. Not to mention Cole never allowed me to read the letter for myself. Whatever Benjyn wrote was something that Cole didn't want me to know."

"We could return to the Burrow and talk to him. It's odd he didn't even let you see the note."

"I'm afraid that if we return, they'll just kill us on sight." Chase sighed, shaking his head. "No, I don't think that's an option as much as I want to go back."

Richard frowned. "I suppose we don't have a choice. We get to the Blackridge Mountains and then find a way to cross them. I'd rather chase down the ramblings of a madman than sit and do nothing."

Chase nodded in agreement. *He's right. We* don't *have a choice.* They had to follow the cryptic messages of this hermit and head west. If they didn't, they would be relegated to simple mercenary work for the rest of their days, never learning why Chase had been exiled. What this strange man had told them—however little that may be—was his only hope of ever returning to the Burrow, if that hope remained at all.

They followed the westward trail from Benjyn's cabin, but it was late. The pair were exhausted, and they didn't get far before fatigue set in, forcing them to stop to rest once again.

CHAPTER 7
AMBUSH

Chase and Richard trudged onward for the remainder of the week, determined to leave the woods as soon as they could. Each morning, Chase woke covered in sweat after yet another nightmare. And each day, his body protested more as the pain coursing through his body only grew worse.

Fog hung over his every thought as if his aching joints weren't enough. His legs stiffened and burned with each step, the uneven ground occasionally sending jolts of pain up his spine. It took great effort not to limp in front of his friend, but his legs felt clumsy. His arms were heavy, and his hands were weak. When his body felt cold, his face flushed as if bathed in steam. When his face cooled, his arms and legs turned to fire.

He could hardly think straight, but the road ahead was clear and—for the time being—that was enough.

The path leading away from Benjyn's hovel was long and difficult, but cracks of light eventually opened like narrow windows in the canopy above. Richard let out a heavy sigh of relief, but Chase simply smiled. After being shrouded by the leafy canopy above for days on end, they longed to feel the reassuring warmth of the sun on their skin. Despite himself, Chase chuckled when his friend joked about how Chase was convinced they wouldn't get out of the woods alive. Of course, Richard believed they would all along.

Eventually the trees shrank, and the surrounding thorn bushes and bramble thinned until they were all but gone. Half-dead oak trees, wiry birch groves, and decrepit pine forests still littered the dull, grey landscape, but they could finally feel the sun on their skin and breathe in the crisp, fresh air. To be clear of the Widower's Woods and all the dangers it held was a massive relief for both weary travelers.

Richard and Chase allowed the outdoors to brighten their moods and ease their efforts. They kept up their pace, eager to stay at an inn with an actual bed for once but still made frequent stops on their way. Soon, they approached the small farming settlement of Blanchard. As they approached, they kept their weapons hidden, hoping the townspeople wouldn't realize where the travelers had come from or why they wore such strange, black leathers.

Blanchard was a dreary town with little to see. Chase had previously passed through the town on the way to Haverson to contact High Councilwoman Jivera, but he never had a reason to stay any longer than was required.

Potatoes and dried grains regularly left the town loaded on horse-drawn wagons, though they received little in the form of compensation for them and the ramshackle state of the village showed. The muddy cobblestone roads were cracked and worn from years of use. Many of the houses were covered in patches of rotting wood or mite holes, and their thatched or shale roofing had seen better days. The inn at the center of the town, situated near a small chapel to the Great Carpenter, was in marginally better condition, but a large hole in the roof still allowed rain to fall into one of the guest rooms.

The Laughing Dog Inn, marked by a sign painted with a foxhound juggling brightly colored balls while wearing a court jester's bell-ridden cap, was empty— save for a few local patrons in a candlelit corner of the room. Plainly decorated with few ornamentations, a painting matching the sign hung over a meager fireplace. Simple oak furnishings were scattered throughout the room, but the inn seemed to expect more guests than it probably ever had.

A portly, brown haired woman with fair, green eyes that Chase assumed was the inn keeper's daughter quietly sang to the room. The song was about a wandering man who was welcomed into a stranger's company, but it turned out he was the stranger's cousin. Chase and Richard talked over flagons of sour wheat ale, along with bowls of soup made from a dried lamb shank and beets before retiring for the night.

By now, Richard knew Chase was dreading each night's sleep.

Yet again, Chase rose in a cold sweat the following morning, panting and flushed in the face. The inn keeper offered some wheatgrass and wildflower tea that he promised would keep any further bad dreams away. *It's a wonder the whole damn town didn't hear me last night. Carpenter's Bloody Hammer, I'll do anything to get these damned nightmares to stop.* Chase took the tea, as humiliating as it was, and refilled their food packs with items they bought from the inn's stockroom while Richard tracked down the local stable master to procure new horses.

After several days of slow, but steady progress, they tied their horses to a tree and stopped for some rest. Chase had become dizzy, almost falling from his horse when Richard demanded they stop.

Exhausted, Chase found a large rock near a fallen oak tree to sit on. He closed his eyes and rubbed his eyelids. He was beginning to see things from his nightmares when he kept his eyes closed for too long, but the relief from doing so was too much to resist. He opened his eyes and looked at Richard. "You're not going to make it."

Richard landed on the ground and chuckled while he caught his breath. "Just wait," he replied. "I'm going to get a nice plump apple for each of us."

Chase smiled. It had been an hour since Chase bet his friend that he couldn't grab an apple from one of the nearby trees without climbing it. Richard was still as positive as ever, convinced he could jump as high as the lowest fruit bearing branch. "Just let me know when you give up." Chase wryly laughed to himself, ignoring the pain it caused in his chest. "And do it soon or we'll be here all day. You never did know when to give up and admit defeat."

Suddenly, Chase heard a faint thump followed by a hissing sound as an arrow shot passed him. It narrowly missed Richard's arm while he reached for an apple, landing in the tree trunk with a sharp crack.

Chase spun from his seat, swearing to himself and drawing his blade, only to be overwhelmed by two men clad in bright red. His sword fell to the cobblestone road with a loud clang as Chase fell to his back. One of the men grabbed a dagger from his belt and raised it high into the air, ready to strike. Chase squirmed desperately, but his strained muscles burned in silent protest.

Dammit. I haven't made it this far to be gutted by some thug.

Before the attacker's hand could drive the dagger downward, Chase heard a loud, whooshing sound. Richard's axe swept over Chase and struck the assailant on the side of the head. With an unpleasant crunching sound, the attacker rolled limply to the ground, freeing Chase's arm.

The second attacker was so surprised by the blow that he froze in place—unable to react. Chase seized the opportunity and swung a gauntleted fist, connecting with the man's exposed jaw beneath his crude, steel skullcap.

The man lost his hold on Chase long enough for him to scramble to his feet. The small clearing that had been empty moments before was now filled with soldiers. The foes were adorned in a haphazard mix of chainmail, heavy studded leather, and tattered plate, but they all wore bright red tunics unfamiliar to Chase. For a moment, he could have sworn they were stitched with the haunting sigil of a man surrounded by black teeth.

He blinked, however, and the sigil was gone.

No. It can't be that. Not that. Not here.

He shook his head. Their chances looked grim, and Chase knew it. The Black Blades were some of the most skilled combatants in Rakksberg, but their success hinged on planning and preparation. If altercations came to blows, any Black Blade could best any hired thug, but they were hard pressed to last long when pitted against an army.

Chase grabbed the handle of the thick, curved dagger strapped to his lower back. He drew the blade with a reverse grip in preparation for a brawl. Any duelist knew better than to carry a weapon like that, but he intended to get as close to his attackers as he could. If these fighters were undisciplined, they would refrain from swinging at their fellow mercenaries.

Four soldiers, backed by several others, waited in nervous anticipation. An aged man with dirty chainmail and a freshly sharpened short sword fidgeted on the spot, his grey stubble dripping with sweat. Next to him, a lean young man stood ready with a bludgeon, and then a woman with a pair of daggers in studded leathers bouncing from side to side, her hair tied behind her head with a bit of ribbon. The last man watched anxiously from behind a sword and buckler, his dented plate pushing his scarlet tabard out in awkward places. He was shaking so badly that Chase could see it fifteen paces away.

The world began to slow. Each heartbeat felt like a lifetime. Chase took a deep breath and steadied himself for the task before him.

The old man lunged abruptly, slashing wildly with his sword. Chase sidestepped, deflecting the blow with ease before spinning closer and stabbing him through the neck. Without hesitation, he pushed forward, only to be met by the lean, younger man closing the distance to him. After blocking a hefty blow from the man's cudgel, Chase swung a clenched fist at his attacker's nose.

The red-clad soldier staggered back—yowling in pain—holding a hand to his face. Chase rushed him and grabbed hold of his loose-fitting tabard, quickly thrusting his dagger into the soldier's belly. Chase released him and dropped to a knee, narrowly avoiding the horizontal swing of a broadsword before he threw another slash that tore open his next opponent's leg. With a harsh cry, the mercenary fell to the ground, dropping his buckler with a loud clang.

Chase sprang to his feet, anticipating an attack from the dagger wielding woman. He spun to find Richard in the chaos of battle, but instead of his companion, he met eyes with a towering, bald, shirtless man.

Sweat shined from bulging muscles and a vein in the man's forehead pulsed with rage. The hulking man carried a large, two-handed hammer resembling a mallet more than a weapon. Its immense head gleamed in the sunlight with each step the man took toward his quarry. Chase recognized the man: Varrix

Strongbrow, leader of the Blood Moons mercenary guild.

Chase quickly flung a throwing knife at his foe. It whistled as it flew, hitting the large man's shoulder with a dull thud.

Strongbrow barely flinched. He simply laughed haughtily, lifting his hammer with both hands before running at Chase.

Chase held his ground.

Not yet.

Strongbrow closed in, sweat glistening off his rippling muscles.

Almost there.

Varrix roared and swung his hammer in a single mighty blow.

Now!

Chase dove out of the way. Strongbrow's hammer slammed into the ground, leaving behind a sizeable crater with a loud thud.

Hoping to overcome the man with speed, Chase flung himself at his attacker, but he was too slow. The brute threw his elbow back, slamming into Chase's cheek bone. He staggered, ears ringing and vision blurring as he tried to regain his composure.

His senses returned just in time to see Strongbrow's hammer swinging at his head. Without a second to spare, Chase raised his dagger to meet to blow.

The impact was enough to rip the blade from

Chase's hand and knock him back several paces. Slow on his feet and exhausted from fighting, Chase faltered for a moment too long. His entire world dissolved into a crushing pain in his chest as he fell to the ground.

Chase screamed, struggling through broken ribs from the strongman's hammer blow. His mind was flooded with white-hot pain. Nothing mattered anymore. There was only the jagged misery that crescendoed with each ragged breath.

After far too long, his vision returned. Strongbrow stood over him with a wicked grin painted across his wide features, his hammer held high. Quickly fading, the world blurred into a foggy haze. Just as he saw another silhouette come into view, everything faded to black.

***

Chase opened his eyes and found himself in the nightmare realm that had become so familiar to him. The air stank of ash and burning wood, and the light glowed a deep red. The cityscape around him burned, stone buildings collapsing and thatched rooves ablaze as the sound of frightened men, women, and children filled his mind.

He was in a small cul-de-sac lined with several houses made from a mix of grey stone and darkened wood. A few blocks over, a burst of screams unnaturally deafened all other sounds. A plume of black smoke rose above the line of houses beyond the cul-de-sac.

I guess that's where I need to go. No sense in waiting.

Chase's first steps were hesitant, more from habit than anything else, but he soon quickened his pace. The burning stench hanging in the air made it difficult to breathe, but Chase had learned by now there was no sense in prolonging the inevitable. If he waited, he would never leave. If he walked the other way, something would undoubtedly turn him around or he would absentmindedly find himself walking in the right direction again. If he closed his eyes and waited for the horrors of the place to pass, something would force them open. There was no way to avoid whatever he was supposed to see.

He saw a group of soldiers pushing a frail looking woman into a house, all wearing the sigil of a man surrounded by black teeth on a field of red. He stopped and watched, although he wasn't sure why he did. Something in this place compelled him to wait, so he waited.

The screaming woman was overpowered and thrown into the broken-down home. Soldiers repeated the process for two more women and a handful of children before closing the door and barring it shut. The Man in Red conducted them—like he was leading some sick symphony—and his men were his orchestra.

Chase's heart sank when the man swung an arm in an exaggerated show of excitement, instructing two soldiers to continue before they lit the house ablaze.

His gut wrenched and tears streamed down his cheeks while the house erupted in flames. Soon, the only thing anyone could hear were the screams of the poor innocents burning alive inside. That, and the shrill, cold laughter of the Man in Red.

Chase was forced to stay in the dream and watch his alter ego systematically burn five more houses. Each time, a group of soldiers forcefully escorted prisoners into the house before razing it to the ground.

After the sixth house was set ablaze, Chase was drained of any emotion he had left. Screams and cries flooded his mind while a sickening stench forced its way into his nose and mouth. All he wanted was to leave this waking nightmare and return to his broken body.

Just wake up. There were no more prisoners to burn, yet he was still trapped in this place. *Why can't I wake up? Please. Just let me wake up.* For the first time since the ritual burning started, Chase noticed his nightmare counterpart was no longer laughing.

Chase turned to see the Man in Red glaring back at him, smiling. A cold shiver ran down his spine as a putrid, unexplainably horrible sensation seeped from the man's very presence. Chase was about to turn away when the Man in Red opened his mouth, and the familiar voice said, "Are you having fun yet?"

CHAPTER 8
STRANGE COMPANY

Chase gasped, his chest tightening violently and sending a dull, throbbing pain through his entire body. Covered in cold sweat, he realized he was in an unfamiliar room, lying on a soft bed atop white linen sheets. The scent of pine trees and wildflowers pleasantly filled the air. Chase realized a little too slowly that he wore soft cotton pants with a large linen bandage wrapped around his torso.

He stood from the bed and stretched his arms toward the ceiling. Amazingly, he didn't feel any of the sharp pains throughout his body that he had come to expect. In fact, he felt better than he had before the attack. His chest where he'd been struck by the hammer was understandably tender, and taking a deep breath sent a jolt of pain through his torso, but his joints no longer ached, and his eyes no longer burned. His muscles were still fatigued, but his limbs no longer felt heavy and unwieldy.

The room was simple but comforting. A small, pinewood dresser painted the color of lilacs sat under a mirror, and in the corner of the room was a matching table accompanied by a simple oaken chair. A plate with rye bread and a hunk of cheese were set on the table, along with a steaming cup of liquid that perfumed the air with a pleasant aroma. He walked over to the dresser and looked in the mirror.

Chase winced when he saw a large, purple bruise on his cheek where Strongbrow had elbowed him. Bile rose in his throat at the thought of the soldiers he had killed during the altercation. *It was them or me. Anyone would have done the same.* He took a deep, shaky breath and closed his eyes, but the fiery images from the night before felt burned into his eyelids. His eyes ached when he looked back into the mirror and sighed.

After carefully inspecting the wound on his cheek, Chase noticed the acrid feeling in his throat had been quickly replaced by an intense hunger. He had no idea how long it had been since he last ate, so he sat at the nearby table and tore into the food set out for him. The thought of poisoning crossed his mind, but he immediately dismissed the suspicions as paranoid nonsense. *If whoever brought me here wanted to kill me, they wouldn't have bandaged me up and given me a bed. Carpenter's Hammer, I'm starving.*

The bread and cheese were gone too soon. Chase drank the tea in a single large gulp and stood. The pine flavor of the hot liquid was pleasant, and the wildflowers in the brew helped ease his breathing, although Chase didn't understand why. As he was about to leave the room, a little girl walked through the door.

The girl looked like she had dressed for a tea party. Her dark hair was arranged in pigtails tied by pink bows, and she wore a simple cotton dress. Her rosy cheeks shined, and her wide eyes twinkled at the sight of Chase standing out of bed. Her silver-buckled black shoes clicked loudly against the floor while she bounced on the balls of her feet and clapped.

"You ate the food I set out for you!" she squeaked excitedly, bouncing as she spoke. "I'm so glad to see that you woke up. You tossed and turned an awful lot in your sleep. I was so worried you would fall to your fever, but now you're awake! How are you feeling?"

Chase couldn't help but smile. Her small voice, rapidly changing expressions, and wild enthusiasm was amusing and oddly comforting. He looked around in confusion before returning his attention to her. "I feel good, actually. Tell me, little girl, what's your name? Where am I?"

She smiled from ear to ear. "My name is Madelyn. Madelyn Taph." She pointed at herself squarely in the chest with her thumb. "And you are at my house! Your friend, Richard, brought you here after you were attacked, and I healed you all up."

Chase's grin faded more with each word she spoke. It was as if she had just told him the sky was green. *I thought things couldn't get any stranger after the damned Spider Queen.* "Wait. *You* healed me? *You* took care of me, dressed my wounds, and prepared this food? Don't you mean your parents? Where are they, anyway?"

Madelyn laughed and clapped her hand against her knee in an exaggerated motion. Seeing that Chase didn't share her sense of humor, she snorted. "Chase, my parents have been dead for nearly twenty years."

Twenty years? That can't be right. Chase's jaw dropped. "But how? You don't look older than seven years old. Are you sure you know how long that is?"

"Six years old, actually!" She spoke with such defiance and conviction that Chase didn't know how to react. He just stood, dumbfounded.

"This is all fine and well, Madelyn, but–"

"Please, call me Maddie. Madelyn was my nana."

"Ah, yes. *Maddie*, this is all fine and well, but it's time you take me to your parents."

She chuckled once again. "For such a scary assassin, you really are quite silly, Chase. I could take you to my parents, but it wouldn't be much to see. Just a couple of stones in the ground with some words on them. It'd be quite sad, actually." She paused for the briefest of moments, looking at nothing before returning her attention to Chase. "Why don't I just take you to see your friend, and I'll explain some things to you that I already did to him? Or else you could just pretend my parents are still alive, but that would be ridiculous."

Without delay, she left the room. Chase blinked twice, frozen in place—then shook his head and rubbed his eyes.

This is a dream. It must *be a dream. No one has died and there isn't quite enough fire, but it must be a dream. I guess I should still follow her. What's the worst that could happen?*

Chase put on a clean cotton shirt that had been laid out for him before following through the door.

The rest of the house was small, but warm and bright. The furniture was made of stained, dyed, or painted wood, cushioned with large red and green pillows. An assortment of rugs with numerous colorful patterns were scattered across the floor while countless elaborately framed paintings covered the walls. Chase finally stopped when he saw his friend sitting in a small room with a relieved smile painted across his features.

Madelyn sat next to Richard on a well-cushioned chair at a slightly-too-small table before drinking some tea that flooded the air with a sweet and spicy aroma. She chuckled at something Richard said as she sat down, smiling warmly.

Richard sipped on his tea and watched his friend stumble into the room in confusion. He laughed and gave a wry wink. "I think you need to stop waking up in places you don't recognize."

Chase smiled dryly. "No kidding. I'll try not to make a habit of it." He joined his friend at the table where a cup sat ready for him. Gingerly, he picked up the mug and sipped the tea. The hot liquid warmed his chest while the taste of cinnamon and sugar tickled his tongue. Setting the cup down, he took a deep breath and turned his gaze to Madelyn. He waved a hand to gesture to the room. "Okay. I think I'm ready to hear whatever ridiculous story justifies all of *this.*"

She giggled while carefully placing her own mug on the table. "Oh, you certainly get so frumpy." She cleared her throat and sat up slightly straighter. "It all started when I was a little girl. Now that I think of it, I'm still pretty little." She giggled softly. "About twenty years ago, my family worked on a nearby farm and lived in this house. It was a little different then. There were curtains and the rugs were arranged differently. My momma always had a garden with green beans in it."

Madelyn paused for a few moments while Chase waited for the rest of the explanation. He glanced over at Richard, who nodded before she spoke again. "One day, my family was visited by a mysterious stranger. She was an odd woman with a funny hat. Anyway, she tricked my momma and poppa into drinking a smelly potion that just so happened to teleport them to a magic prison or some such nonsense. The woman then confronted me and told me that the only way to bring back my parents was to drink this sort of blue, glowing stuff."

She took a sip of her tea and shrugged. "Obviously, I did it—but all I did was help the mean old lady kill my momma and poppa. She said the potion shoved their souls in some sort of medallion. Anyway, she said some scary magic did something to my soul, and I've been stuck at six years old ever since."

Chase rubbed his eyes in frustration. The whole thing sounded like a tale out of a children's book. Evil witches and magic potions were outrageous. Every sane person in the Berg knew that was all hogwash. He took another sip of tea to collect his thoughts, dismissing the nonsense she spouted. "So, how did you care to my wounds?"

"Isn't that obvious?" Madelyn giggled, absent-mindedly swinging her feet from the chair that was slightly too tall for her to reach the floor. "I've been studying alchemy! Well, that and a touch of herbalism and botany on the side. Except those are just hobbies. My momma always said that you should find ways to spend your time wisely or you'll turn into a fool!"

Chase's head began to ache as Madelyn sipped her tea, lifting her delicately painted cup with both hands. He knew none of this could be true, but he decided to accept her story for the time being and remain grateful he survived the ambush. Chase turned to Richard. "The people who attacked us were the Blood Moons, weren't they? I saw the color of their tunics, and I swear that was Strongbrow that hit me with that hammer."

Richard swallowed his tea before shaking his head. "No. Strongbrow left the Blood Moons after they made some pact with the Iron Wardens. It was the Scarlet Furies."

"Who the hell would send the Furies after us?"

There were eleven mercenary guilds throughout the Berg, all with their own hierarchies and allegiances. The Scarlet Furies were one of the more viscous and power-hungry groups. There was a certain degree of lawlessness in Rakksberg since the High Council allowed the guilds to work freely and openly in place of a unified army. That allowed the Black Blades to remain within their cave, but it also allowed groups like the Scarlet Furies to flourish and grow out of control.

The leader of the Scarlet Furies, a man named Korin, had made a deal with Cole allowing both parties to exist without conflict. If they had been the ones to attack Chase and Richard, it would indicate the treaty had been broken.

"I don't know," Richard rubbed his neck thoughtfully, a worried expression clear on his face. "But something bad has happened. The treaty was supposed to be in place for as long as both Korin and Cole were in power. I suspect our run-in with Strongbrow may have been more than a coincidence."

Chase drank the last of his tea. "If Strongbrow is in control of the Scarlet Furies, they'll be dissolved by the end of winter. I think Korin may have just convinced the man to be his right-hand man, or something along those lines."

"Carpenter's Hammer." Richard rubbed his jaw in disbelief. "I don't like the bloody implications of that. Either Korin just breached the treaty, or Cole is dead."

Chase set his mug on the table and leaned back in his cushioned seat. "Or Cole was more serious about our exile than we had expected, and we're no longer protected by the terms of the treaty. In any case, whatever happened is out of our control. We need to stay vigilant. If the Scarlet Furies have it out for us, others may as well."

Madelyn suddenly clapped her hands excitedly. "Oh, boy! You two are so much fun!" She shifted slightly in her seat. "What are you going to do now? I hope you are off to go kill those nasty scarlet fellows. They sound like the worst!"

Chase looked at Richard and nodded before answering her. "We need to get to the Blackridge Mountains. We aren't exactly sure where, but we know there is something we're meant to find there. Thank you for all your help, but we need to be going now."

Madelyn clapped twice. "Not so fast, you two!" Her tone was suddenly sharp. "You need to rest. Your wounds are barely healed, and my salves only help if you stay still. You need at least three more nights of bedrest before I'll let you leave! Then you can go wherever those horses of yours will take you."

Chase and Richard glanced at each other, astounded at the shift in her demeanor. Richard reluctantly raised a questioning finger at her. "So, that's it? No catch? No crazy witch scheme to trap us here, forcing us to kill you? We stay here for a few days while we recover, and then we just *leave*… just like that?"

Madelyn laughed for longer than the questions warranted. "Of course I'm not going to kill you. You assassins are the funniest people I've met in long time. I've had enough evil plots and even if I haven't, I'm sure Gertrude will be back again sometime. No, when life grows as quiet as it has, I just enjoy the company of a few lost travelers.

"Chase, I'm sure I can show you how to make some creams that will help with your aching muscles. Don't look at me like that! Richard told me all about it. Now, would either of you like some more tea or maybe some cookies? I can make shortbread cookies with this *really* tasty jelly in them. Oh, or I could make some sweet cakes that will knock your boots off!"

Chase was about to counter her offer, but the twinge in his ribs and the hopeful look from his friend practically begged him to stay. After enjoying another cup of tea and the wonderful cookies Madelyn baked for them, they walked around the cottage to get some air. The landscape was open and vast, the foothills of the Blackridge Mountains in sight to the west. A pleasant pine scent hung in the air, accompanied by the chatter of several nuthatches and the annoyed buzzing of jays in the distance.

Chase sighed, wincing at the sharp pain radiating from his side. Richard grew concerned before asking, "How are you feeling?"

"Remarkably well, actually." Chase rolled his shoulders and arched his back. "Whatever Maddie did has dulled most of the pain already. Even my recent injuries feel better than they should."

"It's the nightshade," Madelyn spoke defiantly as she made her presence known to her guests while they walked. "With a dash of hemlock. The smell is mostly from the pine sap and goat's milk I use to create a paste of the right consistency—along with some flour, of course"

Richard turned to their undersized host. "Bloody hell, Maddie, aren't those poisons?"

She suddenly frowned before she scuttled over and briskly kicked him in the shin. "Language, mister!" Madelyn yelled. "I don't care if you are big,

119

scary assassins. If you aren't careful, I'll wash your mouth out with soap just like my momma used to."

Richard hopped on one leg and hissed in pain while Chase suppressed a laugh.

"Now, to answer your question—yes." Madelyn firmly placed her fists on her hips. "Nightshade and hemlock are poisons when you dry them, grind them to a powder, and dissolve them in a bit of sugar water before ingesting them. However, if you pluck the flower and work it to a pulp before applying it to the skin, it can mask aches and pains."

Chase was astonished for what felt like the hundredth time that morning. He turned to his friend who just shrugged sourly. Chase returned his gaze to Madelyn. "Was the story you told us earlier true? About some old witch and a magic curse?"

Madelyn smiled and rolled her eyes in amusement. "Of course it was. I suppose magic is really the wrong word for it. Gertrude never did anything to my parents at first. When I met her, she told me they were gone and the only way to bring them back was to drink some strange liquid. It turned out to be a large dose of toothed wrackweed she gathered from near the sea. It made me sleep for a long time. Long enough that momma and poppa thought I was dead when they found me."

Madelyn suddenly grew somber, her tone softening as her cheerful demeanor faded away. "Gertrude lied and told momma the only way to save me was to have her and poppa drink something else. They did, without realizing it was essence of foxglove. When I woke up... they were gone. Gertrude told me the potion I had drank had granted me eternal life. So, here I am."

By the time she finished her story, she sat on the ground with tears welling in her eyes. Chase wasn't sure what to say, but thankfully, Richard broke the brief silence. "We're sorry, Maddie. That's a cruel way to kill someone."

She sniffed abruptly before springing to her feet and patting her dress. "Oh, well. That happened a long time ago and there is no sense in dwelling on things. Gertrude is a cruel woman, but my poppa always said to make the most of things when something bad happens. So, now I spend most of my time learning about stuff to help sick people get better." She made it a point to smile at her guests. "Now, who wants more tea?"

The next few days in Madelyn's cottage were entertaining. She constantly hovered over Chase's wounds, inspecting them closely and constantly reapplying different creams and salves. She even had him drink a few concoctions in case he had internal damage they couldn't see. The potions always tasted horrible, but Madelyn was quick to supply a delicious assortment of teas and treats after each dose.

Chase got immense joy from the periodic smacks and kicks Madelyn threw at Richard for his foul language. Each time she furrowed her brow, threatening to wash his mouth out with soap—then giggled at the spectacle of Richard's over-the-top reactions. Chase swore that by the third day, he caught Richard smiling while he swore and made exaggerated displays of protest that provoked their host even more.

After four days of enjoying baked treats and lovely company, Chase and Richard departed from the cottage—but not before their host saw to their every need. Madelyn reminded Chase to continue to rub his muscles with her various remedies, and she gave them a few recipes to recreate the medicines using goods he could buy at any marketplace. Before they left, she ensured their packs were full of the essentials, including a small satchel of cookies she knew Richard loved.

They thanked the strange little girl for everything she had done before riding away. Chase looked back to see her bouncing up and down as she waved goodbye.

It was the last friendly company they would keep for quite some time.

CHAPTER 9
ENTRANCE

With Madelyn's cabin far behind them, Chase and Richard casually rode west. The pale, browning grass betrayed the start of an early fall stretching out to the dim, gray horizon. Oak and birch trees slowly faded away while spindly pines lined the path and dotted the landscape. As they approached the mountains through the rolling Iron Hills, the animals shifted with the landscape as well. Squirrels and the scant pack of coyotes made way for occasional horned goats and deer, while crows were replaced with ravens.

Chase's nightmares continued to haunt him each night. Thanks to Madelyn and her myriad of ointments, tonics, and lotions, he could dull his aches and pains—but it was little comfort in the face of life draining sleep deprivation. Chase often caught himself staring at the path below or at a distant tree only to realize too late that the path had turned or the tree had gone.

Some of the nightmares repeated themselves and others did not. It didn't matter much in the end. The Man in Red always forced Chase to see it through to the end one way or another, and Chase was always left to collect himself in a worried mess after he finally awoke.

After a few days of easy riding and a few nights without sleep, they arrived at the jagged cliff faces at the base of the Blackridge Mountains. Huge pillars of twisted stone looked like they were ripped from the ground by the hands of giants, reaching toward the clouds where snow replaced life. The mountains stretched as far as the eye could see, and they both knew nothing except the Great Seas lay beyond the range in either direction.

In fact, for all they knew, they were standing at the end of the world.

A few hours prior, the pair had tried to see something—anything—that would give them a clue of where to go next. A single tower in the walled city of Iron Hold jutted over the horizon to the north, its peaked roof as small as an insect. As they traced the mountains south, Richard saw an irregular rock formation that somehow seemed unnatural. A large crease in the mountainside slanted downward, but there was a gap, as if part of the mountain had folded over itself.

Chase and Richard agreed that it was as good a sign as any. If they were lucky, the gap may mark the entrance to a cavern or tunnel that would eventually lead through the mountains. Approaching the strange rock formation, Chase's stomach knotted.

"Chase," Richard beckoned, taking a careful step forward. "Bloody hell, Chase. I think we've done it."

Chase approached the odd stone and found the hidden tunnel entrance tucked behind a jagged outcropping. *Go beyond all things—beyond the rocks that stand in the west.* "I agree. Going over the mountains seems about as possible as sprouting wings and flying. Going through is likely the better bet. Now we just need to hope this leads somewhere nice." He sighed and rubbed his eyes with a gauntleted hand. "Great Carpenter, I hope it leads somewhere nice."

"I wouldn't trust our luck."

"Maddie was pleasant, and I'm sure you enjoyed Benjyn's garbled nonsense enough for us both. Besides, the last few days have almost been boring. Maybe our luck is finally looking up." Chase smiled back at his friend, but it was clearly a hollow gesture.

Richard visibly resisted the urge to spit. "Yes, well, I also almost died. You almost died. A spider thing almost ate us, and an entire damn band of bloody mercenaries is out to kill us—along with Carpenter knows what else."

Chase failed to stifle a laugh. "When you put it that way, what's the worst that could happen? Our luck may not be the best, but it can't get much worse, I suppose." *Carpenter's Hammer, I hope this leads somewhere nice.*

The rocks were rough, and the passage ahead was too dark to discern if danger loomed ahead. Chase and Richard once again abandoned their horses, hoping they would find their way to a helpful stable master somewhere nearby. The pair entered through the crease in the mountain to find a narrow tunnel running deep into the mountain. Its steely gray walls of jagged stone were slightly damp and cool to the touch.

Twenty paces in, the air had already grown thick, the walls closing in around them like a cage that may never let them go. Moisture dripped from countless stalactites, feeding the lichen and mushrooms that sprouted in patches along the floor. The stench of wet moss filled the air, and the sound of trickling water echoed in the emptiness of the cave.

Eventually, the cave grew so dark that they were forced to light torches. Immediately, the damp stone walls were bathed in a warm, orange glow. Cold washed over Chase like icy rain with each step they took deeper into the tunnel. The overwhelming feeling that someone—or something—was watching them made his skin crawl.

The walls continued to squeeze around them until they were sure they had gone all this way only to find a dead end.

After walking for what felt like hours, the tunnel widened, becoming more uniform and artificial. The jagged stone smoothed and the curved surfaces flattened until the tunnel resembled something otherworldly, carved into a perfect, square hallway as straight as an arrow. A faint torchlight peered through the darkness in the distance.

Chase shivered. *Beyond the rocks that stand in the west.* After sharing a knowing glance with his friend, they silently readied their weapons and crept onward.

As they walked closer to the light at the end of the tunnel, Chase's stomach turned. His mouth became dry, and his mind raced. He could feel his partner's tension growing from beside him, as well. Eventually, they could see a pair of torches hanging on either side of the cavern. Between the lights, a large object sat in the middle of the path ahead.

Their progress was slow, but they soon stood a stone's throw away from an angular, stone seat. The light from the torches shimmered, revealing the skeletal remains of someone covered in cobwebs and tattered robes sitting upon the throne.

A putrid taste filled the back of Chase's mouth as he inspected the body. Besides its dusty bones, there was just enough muscle and tendon remaining to keep the corpse intact. Ragged shreds of what was once rich, padded cotton were draped over parts of the skeleton and a pair of dirty leather boots, chewed through by rats, covered its bony feet. Sitting upon its sinewy skull was a tarnished, jeweled crown.

Chase's leather gauntlet creaked in the silence of the tomb, his grip tightening on his sword. He startled when the corpse's skull slowly rose to face the intruders. A portion of decayed muscle snapped, leaving its jaw to hang unsettlingly from one side. The blood in Chase's face drained while Richard shifted nervously—both men desperately trying to keep their composure.

The skeleton gazed at them in silence with deep, empty eye sockets.

Slowly, the skeleton's arm feebly lifted from its place on the throne. The sound of bone scraping against bone echoed throughout the empty tomb until the skeleton's hand came to a rest with its finger pointed at Chase. A faint voice sounded from the skeleton's still mouth as if it was a whisper on the wind. "Who comes to disturb me?"

Chase swallowed roughly. "...A Bear and its Shadow." *If Benjyn had any sense in him at all, those names might mean something. Dammit, I don't think this is going to lead to somewhere nice.*

The skeleton remained motionless, gazing into the darkness. "I have been expecting you. My keeper is quite...particular about those who enter our halls." The ghastly words passed through Chase, his heart growing as cold as ice in his chest.

With the grinding sound of bone scraping against bone, the skeleton's arm slowly returned to the throne, but it continued to gaze into the dark abyss behind Chase and Richard. The whispers continued. "Many have passed through these halls by your blades. Be warned, young reapers. Your time may come sooner than you expect."

Chase jolted back to his senses. The skeleton's head slowly dropped until its skull hung lifelessly by its spine, and a gust of wind swept through the passage.

In the moments of calm that followed, Chase tried his best to concentrate, and Richard did the same. Desperately, they searched the dark surroundings. A creeping cold consumed Chase from head to toe, his strained eyes struggling to see past the torchlight. An unnatural sense of dread fell over the travelers unlike anything they had felt before.

The sound of metal chains grinding together echoed through the empty hall, followed by the scraping of chains against stone. Chase and Richard stood nervously listening to the ominous noises echoing off the passage walls. As the sounds grew louder, the unseen intruder slowly and deliberately crept toward them, and their bodies stiffened in fear—fear that only grew stronger with each passing breath.

After a painstaking stretch of ear-grating clacking and scraping, the trudging menace stepped into the light. A man loomed over them, much taller than Richard, with long pale arms and ragged cloth pants covering gangly legs. The greasy black hair falling against his shoulders contrasted starkly with his unnaturally pale complexion.

Chase shuttered, realizing the awful sounds ringing through the tomb came from an assortment of iron shackles protruding from the man in a frightening manner. The massive links were woven into his body like a series of growths, two rusted chains sprouting from his arms before falling to the stone floor.

Somehow worse than the grotesque pair of chains were the gaping black holes where the man's eyes ought to be.

For a moment, the three men stood in near silence, narrated by the faint dripping of water splashing on the cold stone floor. Chase stepped back, watching the newest addition to the chamber carefully. The ominous figure shook its arm, snapping a length of the chain like a whip. Chase glanced over to Richard and nodded.

"Now!" Chase yelled.

Richard leapt to the side as the deafening clang of chain striking the stone floor boomed. The intruder prepared his next strike while Chase closed in on his foe, tightening his grip on his sword. He barely ducked under a large chain swinging at his head before it smashed against the stone wall with another deafening bang.

Richard stumbled forward clumsily. In a flash, the chained man effortlessly threw an arm upward. A heavy chain connected with a loud thud, lifting Richard off his feet before he crumpled to the floor.

Chase jumped to his feet and lunged his blade forward, only to connect with an odd mix of chain links and the brittle flesh of the man's shoulder.

The chained man suddenly snapped his head to Chase, the black pits where his eyes should have been looking directly into his. A frigid cold coursed through Chase's body, starting at his feet and crawling up his spine like ice water flowing through his bones. Dread consumed him, darkness closing in around him. The horrifying man ruthlessly twisted his arms, wrapping Chase's blade in rusted chains.

Without warning, the sword was ripped from Chase's hand and launched behind the stone throne. It clattered against the wall, knocking one of the torches off its mount. Without hesitation, the man grabbed Chase and threw him aside like a child's doll.

He slammed against the wall and collapsed to the ground with a muffled grunt.

The chained man stepped toward Chase and rattled the links connected to his dangling arm. Chase groaned absentmindedly, pushing himself up on his elbows as he returned his opponent's gaze. The silent man approached, unconsciously rattling the chains protruding from his body as he moved.

Against his better judgement, Chase spared a glance at his fallen friend.

Richard slowly rose to his feet. Carefully, he stepped toward the center of the room where the skeleton sat on its throne. Without making a sound, he withdrew a small stone from his belt and unbuckled his hatchet. He stopped next to the throne and gingerly placed something that Chase couldn't see in the skeleton's lap.

The chained man lifted one of his whips in the air, ready to strike. Before he could act, however, a sharp whistle sounded from across the chamber. The man stopped and looked over his shoulder only to see Richard strike the rock in his hand against his hatchet. A flame erupted from the throne, bathing the stone chamber in an intense yellow-orange light.

A piercing screech burst from the strange man as he frantically covered the gaping holes where his eyes should have been. Chase scrambled to his feet, narrowly avoiding a chain that rushed past his head. Instinctively, he leapt to his sword behind the burning throne. As soon as his hand met its handle, he felt a vigorous tug on his cloak from behind. Chase whirled on the spot, ready to strike only to see Richard pulling him toward a makeshift doorway.

I could have sworn that door wasn't there a moment ago.

Without hesitation, they fled from their attacker. Barreling through the doorway, they frantically threw the stone slab shut behind them. They both fumbled in the dark until they found a hinged locking bar mounted to the door. With a great effort through the burning pain in his limbs, Chase threw his body weight behind him and pulled the lock into place.

As they caught their breath, their eyes slowly adjusted to the darkness. The small chamber resembled a hallway rather than a cave or stone tunnel. There were no branches, no torches, and no apparent exit beyond a wooden door at the opposite end of the hall.

"Chase, are you alright, mate?" Richard asked as he sucked in the damp, cold air. "You took quite the fall."

Chase smiled, his breath slowly returning to him. "It was more of a toss than a fall, but I think I'll live. I'm just a bit shaken. How'd you figure the fire would work?"

Richard brushed his legs, inspecting himself for any injuries. "I didn't, but the way those eyes looked, I figured it was worth a shot. If it didn't scare him, I was about to tear that damn skeleton's head off and throw it at him."

Chase felt a sharp pang in his ribcage as he let out a laugh. "Honest, as always. I know I don't fancy round two with our new friend. You don't suppose that door down there leads to something that won't try to kill us at first glance?"

"Not bloody likely. Benjyn better have been right about all this. If this doesn't lead through the damned mountains, I'll go back to the damned Widower's Woods myself and set the damned fool straight."

After stumbling in the dark for a while, they found a torch to provide them with some much-needed light. They investigated the stone hallway, only to find grooves carved in the stone door frame written in a language neither of them recognized. The dark brown wood of the door on the opposite side of the short hallway looked aged, and the old ironwork that held the planks together was tarnished heavily with rust.

Richard snorted. "After you, mate. Not sure I want to be the first to see what's on the other side of this one. With our luck it'll be a ghost, or a troll, or some other bloody nonsense. This whole bloody trip's getting to be a bit too strange if you ask me."

Chase reached out and rested his gauntleted hand on the wooden door's cold, iron handle. He lifted the latch and pushed the door open, revealing another short passage that matched the style of the door. A red carpet and torches lined the hall, leading to a stairwell on the opposite end of the passage.

Quietly, Chase walked past the threshold with Richard close behind. But before Richard could follow, the wooden barrier slammed shut.

Chase spun around and yanked on the latch in desperation, but the door wouldn't budge. He beat his fists against the old wood panels, shouting for his friend, but the only response through the heavy door was silence.

CHAPTER 10
THE PRICE OF A PROMISE

After realizing the door was not going to open despite his best efforts, Chase faced the mysterious passageway. The thought of leaving his friend at the door infuriated him, but waiting for something to suddenly happen was pointless. If he was lucky, he may find a key to unlock the door or a pry bar to force it open. *The Carpenter knows I'm not that lucky.*

The passageway was peculiar, seemingly plucked from somewhere far away. Faded portraits of several strange people hung from the walls in the gaps between lit torches. Most of the canvas or hide artworks were torn, covered in dirt and grime that tarnished the once regal images. Rotting carpet lined the ground in the areas that had not been kicked away, and numerous tables were covered in a thick layer of dust. Several place settings had been toppled over, as if someone had fled from this place long ago.

Chase walked slowly down the hall, uncertainty thrumming through his limbs. The faded carpet shifted under his feet with each step he took. Weary, he reached the stairwell and reluctantly descended the spiral stairs. Eventually, the torchlight ceased.

As the light dimmed, the passage grew colder.

Another old wooden door stood at the bottom of the winding, stone stairs—almost identical to the one he had seen earlier in the passage. However, this door was covered from floor to ceiling in a thin layer of frost.

Unease flooded Chase's mind.

Richard's still stuck back there, but I can't find anything around this damned place to help him.

His stomach turned.

If there's another one of those things *with chains, I'm dead and Richard is lost. If I stay here, he'll be lost anyway.*

His throat tightened and his mouth became dry.

I guess there's nothing left but to go through *the mountain and hope I find some way to get Richard out of here.*

Slowly and cautiously, Chase reached for the handle. But before he could open the door, he quickly withdrew his hand. The chilled iron burned—even through his leather gauntlet. He paused as he stared at the door, gathering his wits before reaching for the handle once more. Ignoring the icy burn against his fingers, he opened the door slowly.

A mix of shock from the stinging cold air and awe at the vast, empty wasteland stole Chase's breath away. He stepped forward, overcome with a chill that seeped into his bones. The bitter air stung his exposed skin, and his eyes watered uncomfortably. His joints screamed in pain, the harsh air assaulting his worn body. His leathers became stiff and unyielding, crunching at even the slightest movement.

After closing the wooden door behind him, Chase stood in the middle of a white void staring out at a blank horizon. The floor was a bed of dry, hard packed salt, stretching as far as he could see. The gray sky above showed no signs of sun or clouds—nothing but endless emptiness above the stark landscape.

As the harsh sting of cold air flooded his chest and the smell of salt filled his nostrils, Chase's muscles tightened and quivered. He extracted a length of wool from his pack and wrapped his face and ears with shaking fingers before raising his hood.

A line of steel braziers led to something far away in the distance and was Chase's only guiding path in the salt flats. The flame that filled each pedestal was pitch black, emitting a harsh cold that—to Chase's disbelief—could be felt even through the already frozen air of the void around him. When he approached one of the braziers, Chase's joints screamed in silent protest and his hands clenched involuntarily.

In a matter of moments, the cold consumed his every thought.

A metallic clatter rang by a nearby brazier, like it had been struck. A small orb of black smoke collected over the flaming pedestal, slowly growing. The smoke twirled and spun before morphing into a man's silhouette. The figure swirled and smoked—its shadowy body born from the black flames that lead further into the void.

Two piercing white orbs opened where the man's eyes should have been. A moment of silence passed before Chase heard a whisper from right beside his ear, speaking slowly. "Come."

Let's follow the smoke monster. Sure. It's not like I'm going anywhere else.

Chase followed the mysterious figure down the path. He quickly lost feeling in his toes, and then his feet, his worn leather boots failing to fend off the brutal cold. He routinely slapped his thighs with gauntleted hands just to keep some feeling in his fingers. The wool wrapped around his face had frozen from the moisture of his breath, and his ears stung uncomfortably. If he didn't leave this place soon, he feared he may not leave at all.

For what felt like hours they walked in silence until the braziers that lined the path ended.

Without warning, Chase's shadowy guide faded away, abandoning him in the barren waste. Alone once again, he scanned the frozen emptiness around him, hoping to find any clues as to where he was—or why he was there. Before long, a collection of voices reached his ears, varying in pitch—as though several men and women spoke as one. "Hello, Chase."

Chase searched the void around him, desperately trying to locate the source of the voices. There—only a few paces away—he saw another smoking figure. However, this one was different. It stood taller and more confidently, its extremities bulkier than the first. The smoke rose from its black body, twirling in a chaotic dance. Under its strange, white orbs that took the place of eyes, a tiny crack of white spread across its jawline like a twisted, crooked smile. The crack widened and the voices continued. "I am so glad to see my Shadow."

"Who are y-you?" Chase choked against the cold, even behind his makeshift mask.

"I have many names," the voices replied. "But you may call me Lucius."

The voices bothered Chase to his core. The eerie chorus seemed to vibrate as the jagged white crack upon Lucius' face split and moved. Chase tried to relax his tense muscles to no avail. "Okay, Lucius. W-Where am I?" He couldn't keep his voice from shaking, his jaw chattering against his will. *Bloody hell, it's hard to think straight. I've never been this cold.*

"You're home, Chase. This is where you belong. It's where you were always meant to be."

Chase's stomach turned, but he kept his composure. "How do I leave?"

The voices laughed causing a pit to form in Chase's stomach, his skin crawling at the horrific sound. "Oh, Chase. You're not leaving." The shadowy figure raised its arms, smoke twirling upward. "I want you to stay so we can talk for a while. I rarely get a decent conversation all the way down here."

"What do you want to talk about, Lucius?" Chase resisted the urge to slap his thighs again. He was losing the feeling in his fingers quickly. Struggling to think straight and losing his patience, Chase quipped, "I can't imagine the weather here is all that exciting."

The crack on the shadowy figure's face widened. "You."

"What about me?" The crushing cold was now seeping into every part of Chase's body, but that wasn't all. His stomach felt hollow, and an unseen weight pressed on his chest. It was hard to breathe.

"I want you to think back, Chase," Lucius replied, the jagged white rip nearly splitting the figure's face in two. "Think back to all the things you have done. You have quite the history, and I'd like to see what things may come in your future."

"What are you playing at, Lucius?" His toes were burning, his heart was pounding, and breath was becoming labored. It was as if a rope was squeezing him tighter with each passing word the shade spoke. *I need to get out of here.*

"Let's look back. What have you accomplished with your short life so far? It seems you have been quite busy, especially to someone like me."

Chase paused to think, but his mind was shrouded by a strange presence. While his heartbeat quickened and his throat tightened, his thoughts grew slow and lethargic.

Lucius smiled. "A member of a cult of murderers in a land ruled by mercenaries. You've filled your time rather well, if I do say so myself. I've seen the fruits of your labor, and I must admit I'm impressed. Do you keep a tally or a log? I lost count some time ago."

"What I do to survive is my own business." Heat rose in Chase's chest, but it was immediately consumed by the oppressive cold. "And who are you to judge me? You sit in this barren waste to what? Sit and think?" *Carpenter's Bloody Hammer, I'm cold.*

Lucius laughed. Chase trembled at the sound.

"You haven't a clue where we are, do you?" Lucius paused for a moment. "I'd like you to think about all those who have fallen to your blade. Do you have an idea of where they go when they die? Do you understand what happens when you so thoughtlessly take the lives of others? I can't imagine you do."

One by one, shadowy forms appeared behind his host, all smoking in stark contrast to their empty white eyes. The blood drained from Chase's face and retreated from his hands as his stomach twisted, begging to be emptied. Sorrow and hopelessness left his insides aching, and no matter how hard he tried, he couldn't force the feelings away.

Chase looked at the two glowing lights and the bright crack on Lucius' face. He tried to keep his voice level, but his words came out in a shaking mess instead. "S-s-peak plainly, L-l-lucius. What m-m-matter of cruelty is this? W-why am I here?"

Lucius' harsh, white mouth gaped. The shade's garish laugh rang through the cold air. "Hold on to that feeling, Shadow. I want you to embrace it. Your soul is pocked. It's a wretched, shriveled thing tainted by your misdeeds. And you have *so many* misdeeds to your name. Stay here, in my realm, and I'll give you everything you've ever wanted."

Chase's mind raced through the haze that hung over him.

He's right.

No, he can't be right.

Great Carpenter, he's not right. I know he's not.

The raging heat of his desires and the sheer cold of Lucius' words battled within him. Chase had always tried to do the right thing by his family in the Burrow, even if that did mean killing in the name of the Black Blades. He took no joy in killing. He never had, and he never *wanted* the life that Cole gave him all those years ago—thrust upon him with the hangman's noose as his only other option.

Chase had killed his fair share for the guild, but it was always just a job. The High Council made sure that every person in the Berg struggled to survive, getting by however they could. That is all his position as an assassin ever was, and Chase was sure of that. He may have been a killer, but it was for the right reasons, wasn't it?

But then again, he couldn't ignore the rush he felt after a successful contract. A part of him, no matter how small, relished that moment when the life left his target. He enjoyed what his black leathers allowed him to do. That small part of him coveted the power he had as a Black Blade. He could go anywhere—*do* anything in the cities of the Berg while those who should stop him stood back in fear that he may turn on them next. Was that who he *really* was? Was that the *real* him and the rest just a façade?

Indecision clear on his features and conflict

ringing through his voice, Chase feigned a smile and responded with a poor attempt at humor to deflect his host's words. "Th-This is all fine and well, Lucius, but I-I can't imagine you pay well, and this place is awfully c-cold for my taste."

Lucius glared, his white, orb-like eyes narrowing to slits. "You cannot deny your true nature with a bad joke. You're a murderer." The smoking figure's expression relaxed, and his jagged smile returned. "You wear it like a badge of honor. Now, if you were to stay, it would be just that.

"You would be honored among my shades. You already hide in the shadows, so why not become one? No person in the mortal realm would dare to cross you. Never again would you face the hangman's wrath or struggle to put food on your table. All those years honing your skills as a killer would be put to good use, and never again would *anyone* cast you aside like you are nothing more than a liability. You would be my most valued follower... forever."

The haze closed in around Chase's mind, and the heat in his chest waned against the cold that threatened to crush him.

Am I nothing more than a killer? It's the only path I've known for so long. I didn't ask to be a Blade, but does that even matter anymore?

He tried maintaining the charade. "You assume I'd b-be so willing."

"Ah, but I know you are. That small part of your mind that you would never share with anyone—the part you fight against even at this very moment? *That* is the killer in you. That part yearns for the thrill of the hunt, stalking your target like a wolf stalks a deer. All I am asking is for you to embrace the darkness within you and succumb to what you know to be true—that you are nothing more than an assassin, and you *like* it that way."

Inwardly, Chase reeled. He wanted nothing more than to leave this place and pretend that none of this ever happened. He wanted to wake up from his nightmare and be back with his friend, camped just off some road in the Berg with the warmth of a fire there to help him shake this oppressive cold. But that was just it. He wasn't dreaming. This wasn't a nightmare, and Lucius wasn't some figment of his imagination like the Man in Red was.

He's right. I'm a killer. That's what I really *am and that's all I'll ever be.*

Seeing the pain painted across Chase's features, Lucius' smile grew even more. The chorus of voices nearly roared in triumph. "You even dragged your friend along with you. I wonder how long it will take for your blade to find its way to him."

A slight jerk of warmth returned to Chase's chest within the cold abyss that swallowed him whole.

I would never. Not Richard. I know I wouldn't.

However, that conviction was quickly replaced with denial. "It was n-never that way. I kill because I m-must, not because I want to."

"Of course. Of course it wasn't. You're just misunderstood, trying to do what's right for that wretched family in that Carpenter damned cave."

Lucius' wry tone flattened, becoming more serious. "Face it, Chase. You're already halfway there. Your stomach may turn, but you know what I say is true. You try to bury your nature beneath humor and good intentions. I ask that you simply... stop. Stop hiding from yourself. Stop denying your true nature. Stop running and stand proudly beside me forever."

"That's... not true. I'm n-not what you say I am." Chase no longer believed his own words.

Lucius is right. I'm a murderer.

"I implore you to think rationally." Lucius paused for a moment in contemplation. "If you would prefer not to think of your past, think of your future. What I offer is more than you may realize. You'd be a true shadow, striking fear in all those who would oppose you. And here, in my court alongside the lost and damned you see before you, you would always have a place. You would never be alone again."

The promise of power tickled that dark part of him that Chase wished was not there. It swelled with pride when he remembered the feeling he had whenever he completed a contract, and it roared with desire at the thought of the power Lucius promised. But it was more than just that small and terrifying part of him.

The rest of him, hurt by his exile and the abandonment of his family, settled with a wave of relief.

Chase had been cast aside as an orphan in an unforgiving world. He had been left as a child to fend for himself or die trying, and when he managed to survive despite the state of the Berg, the High Council had sentenced him to death. And then, years later, he had been cast aside by the only family he had ever known. His Dark-Father had thrown him out at the first sign that he had overstayed his welcome.

And now, he would never be cast aside again.

This must have been what Benjyn had sent him to do—and why Cole never let him see the letter that led to his banishment. Everything had led to this very moment, standing before a smoking demon that promised him power, but more importantly a place to belong—to embrace who he really was and to be celebrated for doing so.

What little heat that remained in Chase finally died out, surrendering once and for all.

I belong here. Richard will understand. It's for his own good as much as it is for mine.

"Okay," Chase whispered in a soft, accepting voice. "I'll do it. I'll stay. What do you need me to do?"

The jagged smile widened even more. "All I require is that shriveled lump lying deep inside you. A soul is a small price, really."

"Very well."

Lucius sneered. "Good. Now come to me. Come stand by your new master."

Dread was replaced by defeated obedience as his weary legs carried him toward the smoking shade. He prepared to forfeit himself in exchange for the gift Lucius offered. He would become a *real* shadow once and for all.

The white crack split the smoking figure's face in two. "This will only last a moment. Then you will sit among my shades in a seat of honor."

Lucius reached forward with a black hand, raising it to Chase's chest. Smoke danced off the shade's arm while Chase waited dejectedly. Acceptance flooded him, and he closed his eyes. The smoking hand continued forward until its longest finger passed through Chase's leather jerkin.

The chill returned, colder than ever before. It rushed through him like a freezing storm.

Gasping, his knees buckled, and he nearly collapsed from the pain. Lucius didn't stop, reaching into Chase's chest until he firmly gripped the young man's heart.

As the hand tightened around Chase's heart, images of his life flashed through his mind. He saw Cole teaching him the finer points of wielding a blade. He saw Ricket and Ditri laughing with Richard at a dinner table in the Burrow. He saw Richard standing in a stone passage, banging on a locked wooden door, screaming for his friend to answer his calls. Chase opened his eyes to gaze deep into Lucius' glowing white orbs, madness streaked across the shade's expression.

What am I doing?

This is not *what I came for, I know it's not.*

I won't submit to this.

With a newfound vigor, Chase tried to pull away,

but with Lucius' hand around his heart, he couldn't move. He panicked at the sudden realization that he was stuck. Unable to jerk out of the shade's grip, he did the only thing he could think of. He thrust his own gauntleted hand forward into the depths of the specter's chest before finding a cold pulsing mass. Chase grabbed hold of the mass within Lucius' chest, taking the shade by surprise, and pulled as hard as he could.

The smoking figure shrieked in pain, withdrawing its hand from Chase's chest and releasing his heart. Gasping for air and falling to his knees, the shade screamed in horror. Lucius heaved and convulsed, vomiting black sludge from the stark white crack that split his face in two. Shortly after the gagging and choking stopped, Lucius collapsed and slowly faded away.

The pulsing, smoking, black heart Chase had pulled from Lucius beat faster in his hand and began to glow. In a sudden burst of sound and black mist, the heart caved in on itself—condensing into a pure black stone. He stood in silence, staring at the otherworldly marble.

The crowd of shades disappeared, replaced by a wooden door held together by rusted iron struts.

Chase pocketed the marble, his senses slowly returning to him. The sheer cold of the void returned, and his body began to ache. His eyes watered and his skin stung. The pit in his stomach slowly faded, and his heart relented in his chest. As the last traces of the shade's terrible presence fled, he took a deep yet ragged breath.

Desperate to leave this place, and with no other option before him, Chase grabbed the iron latch before him and pulled the door open.

CHAPTER 11
A CHOICE

Chase stood on a rough bridge staring at a massive stone castle. The sudden warmth of the damp air prickled and burned his skin while the sweet smell of maple trees replaced the dry, salty scent that dominated his senses just moments before. A small, orange songbird was nestled on the branch of a nearby tree filling the air with its trilling song in harsh contrast to the overwhelming silence of the void.

Chase's hands shook even after the last traces Lucius's presence faded, and his knees wobbled uncomfortably despite his best efforts. His eyes strained in the dim light, but the world slowly came into focus, and the dull ache behind his eyes faded.

The castle stood alone atop a dark, grass-covered hill with two looming, peak-roofed towers at its corners. Its high walls stood as hulking gray slabs without any sigil or family symbol—its windows too small to reveal what waited for Chase inside.

No way to go but forward...

Chase silently cursed Benjyn's babbled nonsense as he made his way toward the castle. The feeling of sturdy cobblestone beneath his feet was a welcomed change, but something about this place felt wrong. A buzz of tension lingered in the air, and Chase couldn't shake the feeling he was being watched.

He slowly opened the tall wooden gate barring entrance to the keep. The castle felt oddly familiar to Chase, although the details were somehow off. An uncanny veneer lingered atop everything in sight that made his gut uneasy.

Lush purple and green banners hung from the walls, however the sigils stitched upon them changed whenever Chase looked away from them. One moment there was a deer leaping over a crescent moon, and the next a badger brandishing its claws. Matching carpets covered the stone floor, but the material changed with each passing breath. Platters of gold and silver cutlery sat atop finely woven tablecloths the rippled in a breeze that wasn't there. No single detail in the vast chamber felt like it belonged.

A velvet path led to a small table in the center of the room that was adorned with a large silver sculpture of a fish that shimmered and shifted as though it were alive. Chase's gaze settled on an old man in rich purple robes sitting on a padded wooden throne that shifted in its impressive filagree just as much as its surroundings—one moment its carvings depicted crashing waves and the next a brilliant sunrise over rolling hills.

Uncertainty laced Chase's every thought.

What is this place? Is Lucius truly gone?

He waited for a sign—any sign—that it was okay to proceed further into the keep.

I can't be in the Berg, can I?

His heart raced.

No. I don't believe I am, but if I'm no longer in the Berg… where am I?

A servant dressed in simple sack cloth and white linen bowed before the guest and gestured toward the man on the shifting throne. The ominous host had short, chestnut hair touched with splashes of gray at the temples that matched his neatly trimmed beard. His creased, pale skin and blue eyes were greatly contrasted by his dark robes, and his bony fingers lay adorned with various rings inlaid with sizable gemstones.

He looked up from his plate of roasted chicken seasoned with aromatic herbs and steamed peas. His piercing gaze fixed on his guest, and Chase felt the color drain from his features. His mouth became dry, and the sudden need to leave this strange place flooded his every thought.

After an uncomfortably long silence, the old man spoke in a harsh tone, making Chase wince. "Do you have the stone?"

It took a moment for Chase to realize what the

man meant. He reached into his belt pouch and procured the black marble. "This?" His voice caught awkwardly in his quickly tightening throat before he could say more.

"Yes. Toss it here." The man's voice was cold enough to freeze a flame. "Don't just stand there with it, boy. And I suggest you close your mouth. You look like a fish out of water."

Chase snapped his jaw shut and threw the marble across the table. The robed man caught the stone with ease and absentmindedly placed it in a leather pouch hanging from the arm of his ornate throne. The marble landed in the bag with a muffled, grinding clack, betraying the presence of other similar stones.

"What is it?" Chase's tongue felt thick and clumsy, but he choked the words out all the same. "And what was that place? Where am I, now?"

"Silence, boy." An uncomfortable silence followed. For a moment, Chase thought his questions would simply go unanswered, but his host finally responded between sips of wine. "That *place* was a part of you. The thing you saw was something that needed to be cleansed. That's all you need to know."

"Okay, then… where am I now?"

"Somewhere far away from the Berg."

Chase waited for the man to elaborate. When it was clear his host wouldn't, he continued. "And who, exactly, are you?"

"You cannot see for yourself?" The man scowled, as though he had eaten something rotten. "That's a shame. After all you've been through, I hoped you'd have enough wit to piece things together."

A lump formed in Chase's throat, but he took a deep breath to collect himself as he sat across from his host. "You'll have to excuse me. It's been a long day." Lost for words, Chase flashed a weak smile with a half-hearted joke. "I don't suppose there's a guidebook or manual somewhere I can read as long as you're not interested in telling me more?"

"Watch your tongue, boy. I can see to it that you never leave my kingdom and never see your friend again. Years of scrubbing pots would clean that insolent tone from your mouth well enough."

"My apologies," Chase bowed his head, averting his eyes for as long as he knew most of the High Councilmen would require of their own servants. *I need to be more careful if I want to leave here in one piece.*

"Better." The man tore a piece of chicken from the bone and chewed noisily before swallowing. "Who I am is of no concern to you. I have occupied my domain for longer than you can imagine, and the depths of your world run deeper than anything you've thought possible. Just know that I have been watching you for quite some time, and I believe you are uniquely suited to fulfill my needs." His tone sharpened enough to cut steel. "Pray that I was not mistaken."

Chase wanted nothing more than to spring to his feet and leave the castle as fast as his legs could carry him, but he merely sat in stunned silence. After far too long, he responded. "You must be the one I can thank for my exile."

"I may have been correct in my choice, after all." The man's expression softened slightly before hardening again. "It seems you can string a few thoughts together on occasion."

Heart pounding in his chest, Chase lifted a nearby goblet of water to his lips. The cool liquid was refreshing at first, but to his horror it soon left his mouth ashen, a rotten taste coating the back of his throat. He tried to keep his voice level—desperate to keep his composure—but it came out in a hoarse croak. "So, am I to believe you are some kind of god if you managed to bring me all the way here?"

The older man drank from his own silver goblet. "I don't care what you believe. Your people hold far too much value in beliefs. I'm sitting in front of you. What you choose to do with what's presented before you is your own business."

Chase sighed and spoke before he could stop himself. "Then what do I call you? Do you have a name?" His heart skipped a beat, but it seemed his host either did not notice his candor or simply did not care.

"Will." The old man looked largely disinterested in his guest, inspecting a particularly large chunk of chicken. "You may call me Will. It was a name given to me long ago."

Awkward silence hung in the air once more. Soon, Will shifted his gaze to his guest, disinterest replaced by the overwhelming sense that the man was measuring Chase where he sat.

Chase averted his own eyes, looking down at a

food covered platter that had been set out for him. With an intricately engraved silver fork, he moved a steaming piece of broccoli to his lips. Bile rose in his throat, but he chewed the morsel carefully and swallowed so as not to offend Will any further.

"Okay... so why am I here?" Chase nearly choked on the words as the bitter taste of burnt coal lingered uncomfortably.

Will nodded slightly, seemingly satisfied by something Chase did or said. He contemplated another morsel of chicken for long enough to make his guest shift in his seat uncomfortably before taking another bite. Will chewed loudly while he spoke. "I will try to keep things brief. I suspect you might go mad if everything was revealed to you at once." He swallowed and drank deeply from his goblet before continuing.

"Long ago—about one hundred and fifty years— a man from your homeland thought himself above the natural order of the world and crossed me. I can see to many things from my realm, but even I have my limits." Will shook his head. "I often lament how tenacious your kind can be. It has its uses on some occasions, but I find humans meddle too often in affairs that do not concern them. It causes far more trouble than you are worth.

"The man found a way to circumvent my authority and steal something very powerful and very important to me. He returned to your land to become a tyrant for a short time until his confidence grew to hubris and his kingdom rebelled. I can't say that I'm surprised."

Chase frowned. "What exactly am I supposed to do about something that happened generations before I was born?"

"Don't interrupt me, boy." Will's voice rose before falling again to its normal apathetic tone. "You will be told what I want you to know when I want you to know it.

"That man who crossed me all those generations ago wasn't killed that day. The naïve fools who overthrew him banished him to his eventual death in solitude. They thought it was a fairer punishment than a public execution. They claimed some false superiority in the gesture, but it was weakness. Your *High Council* underestimated the man's power and for that, it will be their inevitable downfall."

Chase waited a moment, ensuring Will had finished his story before responding. "That's all quite the tale, but what do you want me to do about it?"

"What I want you to *do* is what you are told."

"But the man is clearly gone, and the High Council rules over the land with a dagger at its throat." Chase felt heat rise in his cheeks, losing his patience against his better judgement. "I can't do anything to right some wrong done to you more than a century ago."

"You are quickly making me resent my choice in bringing you here." Will's eyes narrowed and the heat in his voice returned. "What you can *do* is sit and listen without snapping like little more than a rabid dog."

Chase flushed, and the hair on his neck stood on

end. Will's eyes were cold and distant, but the heat in his voice was enough to muffle his guest. Chase folded his hands in his lap, fearing they would shake too much if he didn't.

Will's tone grew eerie, quiet, and cold. "You would think a contract killer would be better at listening to direction.

"When you and your little friend leave my domain, continue westward. You will find yourselves in an unfamiliar land but try not to be overwhelmed. Find your way to the far west and you will be presented with a gift." Will suddenly smiled, but there was no warmth in the expression. On the contrary, the man looked more dangerous than ever. "I can be gracious for those with the wisdom to respect their place and do as they are told."

I'm getting so sick of prophecies, half-truths, and misguided quests. "I don't suppose you plan to tell me what this gift will be?"

Chase regretted the words as soon as he said them.

Will set his cutlery down and glared at his guest. His eyes darkened and the flickering light of the chandelier above their heads dimmed. An immense pressure filled the air, and Chase suddenly felt a weight bearing down on him. His ears popped and his joints screamed in pain.

"You're lucky I don't rip your soul from you where you sit you insignificant, ungrateful *human*." Will soon returned his attention to the portion of steamed peas that he had left untouched, and the pressure subsided. The heat in his voice vanished, but rage still bubbled behind his harsh features. "Fortunately for you, I see value in your skills and there is a certain admiration in your diligence. There are few other humans I would entrust to see your fate carried out to its end."

"It doesn't sound like I have much of a choice in the matter." Chase tried to keep his voice as cool as possible, although he couldn't help but feel the heat rise in his cheeks as he spoke. "Just like every step I've taken since I left the Burrow, I imagine I'll find that there's no way to go but forward, and I'll do your bidding whether I want to or not."

"There is always a choice, Chase."

As Will spoke, two doors faded into view on the nearest wall. The door on the left was plain and wooden, bound by rusted iron, just like the doors Chase had seen throughout the mountains. The door on the right, however, was made from rich, deep mahogany bound in silver intricately engraved with a myriad of animals that Chase had never seen before.

"The door on the left leads to the passage where you left your companion. You will then leave the mountains and return to your home with nothing to show for it. You'll return to your life in the Berg, hunted by those who would see you dead, ruled by those who would leave you to starve, and ignored by the family that cast you aside.

"The door on the right leads to the same passage where you will find your friend, but you will not return to your home. You will proceed to a world wholly unfamiliar to you until you see your journey through to its end. It is then and only then that you will learn *exactly* what my generosity has to offer." Will's mouth turned into a crooked smile, but there was still no warmth behind his cold, hard eyes.

Chase thought for a moment before speaking. "What would stop me from taking the door to the right and then ignoring this quest of yours? With no guarantee of what may come or even a clue about what you want from me I can hardly say you've made a tempting proposition."

"Nothing is stopping you. Not in the slightest." Will picked up a tomato before inspecting it carefully and casting it aside. "However, if I've chosen correctly, I'm confident you will see this through to the end. It may be today, or tomorrow, or even years from now, but eventually you will see what waits for you beyond the sea."

Indecision rippled through Chase's mind. A part of him wanted to return to the Berg, put all this behind him, join some band of mercenaries, and forget that anything in the last three weeks had ever happened. Richard could find some woman to treat him well and give him beautiful children, and Chase could continue to do what he did best. To return to the Berg would be to return to routine, and routine carried with it a sense of comfort in knowing what the future might have in store.

However, something about the ornate door pulled at him. Chase's heart bled for all those struggling to survive under the High Council's abusive reign. Every day brought with it a new tax or law that would see that countless citizens starve just to line the council's pockets further. Whether it was a poor drunkard drowning his sorrows day after day in the slums of Edenhall, or a pair of young men making ends meet taking on a job to protect a cart driver only to find their end to an assassin's blade—the people of the Berg were always suffering at the hands of oppressive rulers that valued coin over morals.

But now, Chase might be able to do something about it. He had no way of knowing what Will's offer would entail. But after years of accepting the harsh reality of life in Rakksberg for what it was, he could feel a faint sense of hope somewhere deep inside him. If Will really was as powerful as he seemed, what sort of gift awaited him? Could he return to the Berg one day and use that gift to *help* the people he had seen suffering for so long?

Of course, the third option was also appealing. Chase and Richard could leave the Berg behind, shed their mantle of assassin, and live out their days in peace. He had been an assassin—a hired killer—for so long. Constantly distancing himself from the bleakness of his profession had made him forget that there may be a different way to live altogether. *Peace. That's not something I ever thought I would find.*

However, if they chose a life of peace, there was no guarantee that his nightmares would end.

The nightmares. The thought crept into Chase's mind as he continued to stare at the choice that lay before him. He turned to face Will, but before he could speak, the old man interjected as if he was reading his guest's mind. "Chase, I know what you fear. If you choose to walk away from this right here and now, the nightmares that plague your every night *might* come to an end. However, I can assure you that if seek out my gift beyond the mountains, the nightmares *will* end in time."

Chase's heart sank. He could turn his back on everything and hope that these nightmares would cease as quickly as they started. After all, they had only started when he had decided to seek out Benjyn in the Widower's Woods. However, there was no guarantee the two things were related at all, and if he fled back to the Berg only for the nightmares to continue, there was no way of knowing for certain that he would be able to return to this place to accept Will's offer later.

I guess I don't have much of a choice after all. One more misguided quest.

Chase sighed, resisting the urge to rub his tired eyes. His throat was tight and the acrid taste of bile in his mouth was stronger than ever, but he resigned himself to accept the hand he was dealt. "I suppose I won't be back again."

"If I chose correctly, then no." The cold smile remained until Will's expression darkened. "If I chose incorrectly, I suspect I will see you again very soon."

On wobbling knees and with shaking hands that he fought to hide as much as he could, Chase rose from his seat and proceeded to the rich mahogany door. His stomach felt ready to empty itself right where he stood, but he simply swallowed roughly and reached for the door.

Chase paused for a moment.

Am I doing the right thing? What would Richard want me to do?

Sweat beaded on his brow, and his heart raced.

Would he want to go back to the Berg?

Just then he remembered the encouragement his oldest and best friend had always given him. He remembered Richard's tenacity and all the times he urged Chase onward, even before their journey started. Richard was always the first one to jump headlong into a problem, consequences be damned.

No. I don't think he would. One more misguided quest for us both.

As Chase walked through the doorway, Will and the throne room behind him vanished. A moment later, he was standing in the passage within the Blackridge Mountains once again.

Chase closed the door behind him with a dull click. It remained silent for a few moments before a hand on the other side began pounding against it. He heard the muffled sound of Richard's voice just beyond the wooden barrier.

Richard barreled through the door, almost knocking his friend over. "Ack! What the bloody hell was that for, you damned bastard? After what we just saw, you think it's bloody well and good to lock the damn door behind you?"

Chase stepped back from his panting friend and wiped his brow with his sleeve. "I'm sorry, Richard. I don't know what happened. I walked through the door ahead of you and the next thing I knew we were separated. I had no intention of being gone for so long."

Richard brushed dirt off his jerkin before looking back at his friend in bewilderment. "What are you on about? Is this some kind of joke or something?"

"What?"

"Some joke it was, anyway." Richard spat on the ground, rubbing a sore spot on his chest gingerly. "Slam the door in my face and let me pound for a good long minute. Keep me locked in a dark passage with nothing but a wall between me and a murderous chained whatever the hell that thing was. Really funny, Chase."

Has it only been a minute? Chase rubbed his sore and tired eyes, his head beginning to ache at his temples. He couldn't say for certain what he had seen in the last few hours, but Chase knew he could confide in his friend when they had time to talk.

They spent hours walking through a vast winding maze of stone corridors. The odd décor continued to flood the passageways—ruined and rotting tables with tarnished gold and silver houseware spilled haphazardly with a healthy coating of dust and cobwebs. Faded and torn paintings littered the walls while ripped and soiled carpets bunched in more places than not.

Chase and Richard finally arrived in a room just big enough for an immense double door that rose to a point near the chamber's ceiling.

"We've been in this bloody mountain for hours and all we find is another damned door," Richard spat on the ground before raising his hands to his neck in frustration.

I shouldn't tell him about what happened. Not now. Dammit, I don't even know if what happened was real. "We should stop for the time being. Carpenter knows what time it is, but I'm exhausted. This room is as good of a place as any to set our bedrolls down and get some rest. Whatever is behind those doors can wait until tomorrow."

CHAPTER 12
OUT OF THE DARK, INTO THE LIGHT

Chase gasped. His heart raced as he struggled to catch his breath. The darkness of the chamber closed in around him threatening to swallow him whole. Sweat drenched his underclothes, and the cold ground pressed against him as though the earth itself wanted nothing more than to push him away—to be rid of him from within the Blackridge Mountains

Several long moments passed before his vision cleared and his breathing slowed. Chase had lived through the scene with the helpless young woman in the ruined house once again. It wasn't the first time the nightmare had repeated itself, either. And if that wasn't bad enough, it was getting harder to recover from the wicked dreams, the lines between the real world and the nightmare realm steadily blurring with each passing day.

His muscles eager to remind him of just how sore they had become, Chase reached for a cream Madelyn had given him. Silently, he worked the rich smelling paste into his limbs, back, and neck. The pain slowly faded, and Chase's thoughts wandered back to his nightmare.

No. I can't think about it. I won't. It's not me. It can't be me. I don't care what he looks like.

It's not me.

By the time he had finished with Madelyn's cream, Richard stirred. After filling their growling stomachs with dried bread, cheese, and a splash of wine from their nearly empty wineskins, they gathered their belongings.

With a labored push from their combined efforts, Chase and Richard heaved the massive, heavy doors open. A grating shriek from rusted hinges greeted them before a rush of cool, damp air flooded the chamber. Just a few steps away a narrow, dark cave waited for them not unlike the cavern they had entered the day before.

The sound of dripping water echoed through the passage and strange plants grew all around them. An odd brown moss clung to the walls, deadening the sound that would normally echo through the stone chamber leading to an eerie quiet that felt oddly peaceful. Toadstools and wildly colored hanging plants littered the cavern and filled the air with a strangely pleasant musk. Chase couldn't stop the smile that crept across his features as he breathed in the soothing aroma.

By the time they reached the mouth of the cave, Richard was almost running in excitement. "I hate bloody caves!" he shouted to no one in particular. "I hope I never step foot in another one as long as I live!"

Filled with a vigor that had been absent since they breached the cavern into the mountains, Chase quickened his pace to keep up with his friend. Without warning, he slammed into Richard's back with a dull thud.

The landscape that lay before them was stunning. It looked unlike any place in the Berg the two travelers had ever even heard of. The grass was a rich, bright green that nearly sparkled in the light of the rising sun and filled the air with a fresh, sweet scent. Large, rolling hills stretched out as far as the eye could see, adorned with lush trees kissed by touches of orange, red, and gold. Bushes bearing sweet fruit and berries hugged the trees like eager children, giving shelter to foxes, rabbits, deer, and other stranger animals.

The crisp air was filled with the mixing sounds of countless colorful songbirds and leaves rustling in the gentle breeze. It filled their lungs with a distinctly clean feeling, their eyes watering in the morning light as they gazed up at a sky painted in a beautiful array of purples and blues.

Chase and Richard turned to each other and laughed. They couldn't help it. They were so covered in dirt and grime that they could hardly see their faces. Richard looked back at the hillside and pointed at a nearby pond. "The water there looks clean enough. Feeling up for a bath?"

"I think you may need it more than I do by the smell of you." Chase grinned even wider, but Richard simply snorted before the pair made their way to the cool, clean water.

The sounds of birds and squirrels and leaves swirled around them while they walked. Small fish and aquatic plants filled the pond and while Chase could recognize a perch swimming through some nearby weeds, the rest of the critters scattered around them were wholly unfamiliar to him. A few ducks with brilliant, green heads rustled their feathers before flying from the pond, leaving a web of tiny ripples while a strange deer covered in spots huffed and fled into the trees behind it.

Chase bent down and raised the cool water to his mouth in cupped hands. The crisp feeling in the back of his throat was startling at first, but once he started, he couldn't stop gulping down the water without restraint. Richard chuckled before dunking his entire head into the water, flinging it back and spraying the air with water. With a hearty laugh, the grizzly man rubbed his grimy face with his hands before plunging his head into the water again.

With a splash of water on his face, Chase scrub away the dirt and grime. In the dim light of the torches, it had been hard to see just how dirty they had gotten by wandering through the cave. Chase looked up, happy that his face felt clean again and smiled at Richard.

Richard ceased his splashing. His expression grew

distant and nervous, as though he were looking at a complete stranger. Shoving his damp hair out of his face, Richard spoke in disbelief. "What the hell is on your face, mate?"

Chase looked down in confusion to see his reflection in the rippling water. A strange black mark surrounded his left eye. Two unfinished rings circled his eye from the center of his brow line to his nostril, intersected by four lines reaching outward. The two longer, middle lines were crossed by smaller dashes resembling crosses. The black design was crude, like it was carved into his flesh with a knife.

He touched a hand to the markings in disbelief before gathering another handful of water to wipe away any stray dirt and sighing. "I guess I have a tattoo now."

"You guess? You don't seem as surprised as you should be. I know if had some bloody tattoo I didn't ask for I'd be carving it out of my skin by now. Why are you so damn calm about it? How did you get that thing, anyway? I was with you the whole time, and I never saw a needle and ink. You pick up a new hobby without telling me? I swear, if I find you put some mark on me while I was asleep, I'll knock the snot out of you."

Chase sighed. *Now is as good a time as any.* He proceeded to tell Richard everything that had happened to him in the cave. He explained that what had been a minute to Richard had been several hours to him. He described his meetings with Lucius and Will and what each had told him.

When Chase got to the part of his tale regarding

the doors and his ultimate choice that decided the pair's fate, he paused. Richard looked at him expectantly, and his stomach knotted. *Did I make the right choice? What if I tell Richard about it and he's upset? I know I would be if someone made that choice for me without being able to decide for myself. I know Richard well—better than anyone else—but is that enough?*

Carpenter's Hammer, what if he gets so mad he leaves?

The thought hung in his mind for far too long.

What if he leaves?

"Mate." Richard waved his hand in front of Chase's eyes in an exaggerated show to get his attention. "What happened next? Will told you about the gift and then what?"

His throat tightened for a moment, but he spoke without delay. "Sorry. I must be more tired than I realized. Will told me about his gift beyond the sea, and a door appeared next to him. He explained where it would take me, so I walked through it and found myself on the opposite side of that wall from you."

"Bloody hell. So, a couple minutes of banging away at a door was hours of whatever that was for you?" Chase nodded, and Richard snorted grumpily in return. "Given everything else we've seen I suppose it's not completely crazy. It *is* crazy, though. I don't suppose this has anything to do with what that hermit had to say, would it?"

"If everything Will said is true, then yes." Chase shrugged. "Benjyn's incoherent gibberish was exactly the thing that Will was relying on to get us to follow his trail into the Blackridge mountains.

"And then there's the issue of whatever *gift* Will has in store for us. I must admit I don't recall much of Benjyn's message, but I remember some bits about light and shadow as we headed west. That could refer to us, or it could have just been a clue about Lucius and Will." Chase rubbed his eyes in frustration. "Do you remember anything else Benjyn said? Anything about after we head west that Will might have overlooked him telling us?"

Richard frowned in thought, trying not to stare at Chase's tattoo. "Something about wings," he muttered. "Dammit, I can't remember a blasted thing that man said. I must've been looking at the man more than really listening to him."

On silver wings. "Right, I guess there's nothing else to it. Will was convinced we would eventually see this to its end even if we decided not to. I don't think there's a reason to delay it longer than we need to."

"Before we go anywhere, we need to figure out just where the hell we are. You mentioned it wouldn't be the Berg. So, where in the bloody world are we? Last I heard there wasn't anything beyond the Blackridge Mountains but another sea."

Chase looked beyond the pond thoughtfully. "I think I saw a road when we left that cave." He scooped another handful of water into his mouth. "With any amount of luck, and the Carpenter knows we deserve it by now, that road will lead to a town or village. Maybe once we're there, we can find an inn, figure out precisely where we are, and go from there. Hopefully, whoever lives here is friendly."

He could feel the dull throbbing in his temples

return. Following these vague directions and half promises was growing more frustrating by the day, but deep down he knew there was no other choice now that they were in this strange, new land.

There is always a choice.

Will's statement rang through Chase's mind.

There is always a choice, and I made mine. I just wish I didn't have to make Richard's as well. Dammit, I wish I could tell him, but I just can't. He can't leave me—not after everything that's happened.

A pit deepened in his stomach that Chase desperately tried to ignore.

"Aye." Richard nodded in agreement after contemplating their options. "And maybe we can get a decent meal while we're at it. I am getting tired of dried meats, old cheese, and stale bread. The wine is gone, too. You know, this whole vacation of ours is turning out to be a royal pain in the ass."

Chase chuckled before drinking deeply from the pond one last time, but the weight of his decision still hung over him.

I'll tell him soon. I just need to make sure we are okay here, and then I'll tell him.

They filled their empty skins with the water, with minimal grumbling about wine from Richard, before walking back up the nearby hill to get a better look.

Many of the animals had retreated into the wilderness as morning faded to afternoon leaving them in a serene scene punctuated by the gentle breeze that still rustled the nearby trees. Much of their view was obscured by the lush hills, but Richard made out a faint stream of black smoke rising from the crest of one of the smaller hills.

As they walked toward the plume of smoke, the landscape bustled with life around them. Sparrows and goldfinches as well as vivid orange and black birds that neither of them recognized filled the air with a pleasant mix of trilling songs. Wildflowers completely unfamiliar to the outsiders dotted the roadside, the air sweet with their scent. Splashes or pink, purple, white, and blue flooded the bushes and roadsides in the days before the bitter autumn cold would eventually strip the flowers away. The trees themselves even shifted from needle-ridden evergreens and white trunked birches to immense trees, bigger than they had imagined possible.

Well into the day, it became apparent that what had appeared to be a single pillar of black smoke was several smoke streams rising from the treetops ahead. Stopping only briefly to finish the last of their dried meat and bread, Chase and Richard continued through the day until the bird songs vanished and the orange-red glow of the sunset bathed landscape.

Only after ferns and underbrush filled nearly every inch of their surroundings did the forest part to reveal a small settlement in a sunken basin. The town glowed warmly in the dim light, and the pair could hear the dull buzz of people from far away.

An unsettling thought crept into Chase's mind. *This all seems too good to be true, but Will never mentioned if this strange place would welcome strangers such as us.* "Richard." The man paused mid step. "It's probably better to approach with caution. We can't be certain we'll be welcome at this hour."

Richard thought for a moment before answering. "Aye. Could be a curfew that we don't know about. Or they might decide they just don't like the look of us." His eyes lingered on Chase's tattoo for a little too long before he cracked a wry smile. "I'm not worried about me, but you're a mighty ugly bloke. Don't want you scaring off the children."

Chase rolled his eyes but wrapped his heavy black cloak around himself all the same. They approached the first house casually, trying to look as inconspicuous as two men dressed in midnight black could. It was a small, yet elegant house—the white painted planks trimmed with ornately carved dark-stained wood. Hunks of gray stone complimented the home's foundation, along with a speckling of windows, various wind chimes, and garden charms. The décor was eclectic, fit for a farmer or an herbalist, although they must be a very wealthy one to afford such a place.

Without warning, an old woman called out to the wanderers from near the doorway. "Well, 'ello there strangers!"

They nearly leapt from their boots in alarm. The woman's gray hair was tied in a bun that bobbed as she swayed in her oak rocking chair. She wore a modest cotton dress dyed light blue with a white half-apron and buckled leather shoes. Waving emphatically, she gave them a toothy grin that stretched her wrinkled skin. "I 'aven't seen you lot 'round 'ere before. What brings ya' both to these parts?"

Chase was lost for words at the woman's unfamiliar accent and cheerful demeanor. His heart raced for a moment while he desperately tried to think of something—anything—to say but thankfully, Richard quickly chimed in. "Just passing through, miss."

Taking a slow breath, Chase tried to calm down. *It's just an old woman. Carpenter's Hammer, I can manage to threaten a palace guard well enough, but I can't even say hello?*

"Oh!" the woman shouted enthusiastically. "We get lots of travelers 'ere! Why don't ya' take a trot on over to the tavern! Spit Pig's the name, run by a fellow goes by Val. It's just across the way not two blocks in on the right. I 'eard they're havin' a mighty fine shindig tonight, but I 'member when the mayor's daughter was wed. Now *that* the 'ole town was out 'till dawn! I never did catch you folks' names. What's yer names, then?"

"We are a shadow and a bear." The words came out faster and more muffled than Chase had intended. Even if his words had returned to him, he couldn't shake the unease that laced his every thought. *She seems nice enough... but still. What if it's just a ruse? What if there is someone waiting around the corner until we walk by the house? What if—*

"What?" The old woman threw her arms in the air in disbelief. "No, yer not! Yer two men! I don't see no bears round 'ere and yer certainly not just a shadow! You tryin' to pull somethin' or what?"

Richard hurriedly waved his arms to smooth

things over. "No, no, no, miss. Nothing of the sort. Forgive my friend. We've been on the road for a long time. Not sure who you can trust, you know?"

The woman bent her lips into a discontented frown. "I suppose. But I'm not goin' to hurt ya'. Go on now. What are yer names?"

"Right," Chase finally answered. *What is wrong with me? Did Will do something to me while I was in that cave?* "My name is Chase, and this is my companion, Richard."

"That wasn't so 'ard, was it? The name's Patty. Patty Branod. You two go on now and 'ave some fun b'fore yer old like me!" The old woman stood from her rocker and returned to her home through the white painted door.

"Thank you, Patty," Richard shouted as the door slid shut with a quiet clack. "It was nice to meet you."

The tension finally fled from Chase's shoulders and his heartbeat slowed. The acrid twisting in his stomach that he only just noticed faded away. Chase wet his dry lips and sighed.

Richard turned his attention to his friend and frowned. "What was that about? Have you gone daft?"

"I must just be tired, Richard. I'll be fine."

Richard eyed him with an expression that clearly showed he didn't believe his friend, but he thankfully let the topic die as they continued onward. *Just tired. That's all.*

Chase was in awe over the craftsmanship that

went into the buildings they passed as they followed Patty's directions into the town. They each followed the same pattern of white planks, dark carved wood, and stone. But as the buildings grew bigger, the designs became even more ornate—as if everyone in this town was a wealthy landowner or some kind of artisan to carve the wood and place the stone themselves.

They eventually arrived at a large building with a swinging sign depicting a pig standing on its hind legs, turning the crank of a spit roast. Loud chatter and cheerful music seeped outside the inn, and several drunken patrons staggered onto the street, ready to retire for the night. The bustling of the inn seemed to burst forth as the heavy door swung open, only to become muffled again when the latch clicked shut behind a pair of odd-looking women in strange clothing.

The entire building was packed wall to wall with people dancing and laughing and singing. The rich scents of honey, ale, and a strange herb-roasted meat Chase couldn't recognize filled the air.

The vast mix of all sorts of strange looking people was overwhelming at first. There were people wearing odd, layered silks with dark skin and hair as black as night, while others wore animal hides and furs over their heavily tattooed skin. One woman with scarlet hair as straight as freshly pressed curtains—dressed in billowing, white cotton that would look at home in a ballroom—danced with a man wearing nothing more than simple work pants and a dirty wool shirt.

Even in the mix of every sort of person

imaginable, it was impossible for Chase to feel more out of place at that moment.

After making their way clumsily through the massive crowd of people, trying desperately to find a place to sit and rest, Chase heard someone yell from a nearby table. "You two, newcomers! Over here!"

It was hard to hear over the ambient roar of the pub, but Chase turned to the source of the call. An odd-looking pair sat at a table in the corner of the inn, away from the madness. Richard saw them as well, and without warning, grabbed Chase's arm and dragged him to the strangers. "Evening there, mates," Richard nearly shouted to be heard over the bustling tavern. "What can we do you for?"

The man at the table laughed in a cool, almost sinister tone. He was one of the people in the tavern with terribly pale skin. Upon closer inspection, the man had a long face with a pronounced chin and pointed ears. He had deep, dark red eyes, which strangely complimented his long, carefully combed hair of the same color. He wore a lavish, white cotton shirt under a black leather coat lined with rich red velvet, and a strange, short, cylindrical hat with a long, flat brim hung on the man's knee.

The pale man continued to speak in the same cool tone. "What you can do for us is drink and talk. There's nothing quite like good company and good drink is there, Remi?"

Remi—the woman that had yelled to get their attention—nodded her head. "Right you are, Klaus." Remi was a short woman with a rich, black braid draped on her shoulder and dark skin that glistened in the light of the tavern. She wore leathers like Chase's own, however, hers were dyed yellow, wrapped in brilliant blue and purple silk. Her short, thick fingers grasped the handle of a flagon that she raised to her lips to take a long drink.

Chase looked at Richard who, to his surprise, was flagging down a tavern worker and ordering beer for each of them.

Chase smiled, leaning back in his chair while Remi finished her gulp and wiped her mouth with a small, white handcloth. Remi smiled warmly as she addressed her new drinking companions. "You two don't seem from around these parts, but as you can clearly see by our current arrangement of company, not many people here are." Her voice was thick in an accent that made it sound like the words were tumbling from her mouth, but she was well-spoken, nonetheless. "Where do two young lads like you call home?"

Chase reluctantly paused and contemplated revealing the name of their home country to these strangers. *I'm not even sure they would know what the Berg is.* Richard cut in before Chase could answer, speaking as casually as if he was stating that the sky was blue. "We just crossed the Blackridge Mountains."

His heart in his throat, Chase intently watched the two strangers attempt to discern Richard's answer. Finally, Remi responded after another swig of sweet honey ale. "I am unfamiliar. Do you mean the Ardent Rise? The mountains to the east have not been crossed by foot in a very long time, or so the local legends say."

The Blackridge Mountains were clearly known by another name here. To quell any suspicion, Chase realized they needed to be more careful when using the names they knew the world by. Unlike Chase, however, Richard seemed caught up in the energy of the tavern and carelessly blurted out, "We are from Haverson; a province of Rakksberg. Apparently, the world is a bit bigger than we thought it was. Eh, Chase?"

Chase's heart dropped and his chest tightened. *Carpenter's Hammer, Richard, could you at least wait until we know they aren't dangerous?* The strangers suddenly put their drinks down on the table and stared at their new guests. Remi wiped her shining brow with her handcloth and began to twist the end of her braid. "Interesting. Very interesting."

"And why exactly is that *interesting*?" Chase remarked. His heart raced. It suddenly became harder to catch his breath, an unseen band squeezing his chest.

"You see," Klaus answered, trying very clearly to make himself understood plainly while maintaining his cool and smooth tone of voice, like water sliding over rocks. "Your home country—Rakksberg you call it—must have been isolated from the rest of the world for a very long time if that is really where you call home. Most folks swear that nothing but The Dread Wastes and Dead Seas lie on the eastern side of the Ardent Rise. Local legends and a few of the more controversial texts suggest that the last person to cross those mountains did so over a century ago, and he wasn't exactly a pleasant man."

Remi laughed. "That's an understatement to be certain. The man supposedly traversed the Ardent Rise only to raid three towns after meeting that abomination of his—Terror—and then flew off to return to The Dread Wastes." A sudden light shined in the woman's dark eyes as realization struck her. "Is your entire land not in ruin by now? If there are many people in The Dread Wastes, I am quite surprised to learn that more have not tried to cross the mountains by now, although I suppose Terror had that effect on people—if the legends are true."

"What the bloody hell are you two on about?" Richard griped, now gulping ale seemingly by the flagon.

"You don't know, do you?" Remi asked in a sincere tone. Chase knew that, in his friend's rapidly increasing drunken state, Richard had completely forgotten what Chase had told him about his conversation with Will. Chase felt the band around his chest tightened slightly. He gripped his flagon with both hands, worried they would start to shake.

Too many people. Would need to run. Out the window? No. Out the back door. There must be a back door. We'll need to—

"Well, let me buy you two some food." Remi spoke carefully, her gaze lingering on Chase longer than he would have liked. A dazzling smile splashed across Remi's features as she returned to a more jovial tone. "We will speak on the subject. Oh, do not object. You look famished and I have more than enough coin for two weary travelers. I would suggest the rosemary-ginger pork chops with a side of the garlic potatoes. The Spit Pig's special is always especially delectable. Val does know how to serve a crowd, after all."

CHAPTER 13
UNEXPECTED CHARITY

Remi waved over a waitress who took their order quickly. She soon brought back two helpings of food along with two new flagons of ale. The aroma was intoxicating. A rich herbal smell that reminded Chase of pine trees flooded his nostrils, accompanied by the scents of ginger and garlic. The two smells were odd, but strikingly pleasant. Richard ripped into the pork chop without hesitation and Chase quickly followed, unable to hold himself back. He was convinced at that moment it was the best food he had ever eaten in his life.

Remi smiled warmly and continued the lesson as soon as she saw a chance to begin. "A long time ago, at least a century and a half ago according to most accounts, a man travelled here from across the Ardent Rise claiming to be from a beyond the mountains. The people of Galland were clearly interested in such a strange figure, so the man told them all about his home—even helping them to draft maps and write records of its history. However, I must admit that practically all those records have been lost in the generations since—if they ever even existed in the first place.

"According to the legends, the man demanded passage to the fabled Dragonstone in return. Only a single farmhand had ever heard of the place, and reluctantly, he led the man there as best as he could." Remi took a long drink from her flagon. "There are tales that say the farmhand slowly went mad simply being in the man's presence, although that seems highly unlikely to me—if I may be so bold to say. In either case, the man finally arrived at his destination where he met Terror.

"The man paid the farmhand back for this favor by plunging a dagger into his heart." Remi shook her head sadly for a moment. "While flying across the country to return to The Dread Wastes, the man used Terror to raid three separate towns, turning them into little more than ash. Tarentoll and Ghael were eventually rebuilt, but they say that the lost town of Berringer was reduced to dust that scattered in a strong eastern wind. If we assume the legends are true—even though I assure you I do not make such assumptions lightly—then that was the last anyone in Galland had heard of him or his home."

Chase gulped a particularly large amount of ale before breaking the pause in conversation. "You said this was a hundred and fifty years ago?"

"Yes," answered Klaus in his cool, smooth voice. "If the tales are true, it was about that long ago. Why do you ask?"

Chase set his drink down on the table. His voice caught uncomfortably in his throat. *What can I tell them? Dammit, they could be probing us for information, or worse.*

He reluctantly swallowed his apprehension. "Around that time a group of politicians rose to power in Rakksberg when the people in our land revolted against a tyrant. They exiled the last king of the Berg after he had committed some sort of crime, and we've been ruled by the High Council ever since." Chase suppressed a sigh. "It's hard to say since the Council doesn't allow folks to learn about our history, but I think the man that was banished from our home is the same man from your legends."

"Ah, yes," Remi twisted the end of her braid in thought. "That would be a logical conclusion, of course. An astute observation, indeed."

The table sat in silence for a moment of reflection before Richard blurted out, "Wait a second! How the hell do you two know all this? It was a hundred and fifty years ago. Surely you weren't alive back then, were you?"

The two strangers laughed before Klaus answered, "We know because we were taught the legends as children. Think of them like bedtime stories. Remi even researched the matter on her own, though I've always called her a fool for doing so. Come to think of it, I don't think I'll be able to make that claim after our conversation tonight, as long as you're telling the truth. I can tell by your accents that you're not Gallanders... Anyway, you don't take a dragon, raise three villages to the ground, and escape mention in history lessons."

The comment came and went just like any other casual statement until Chase and Richard realized what Klaus had said. They nearly jumped up from their seats. "Dragon?! What do you mean, dragon?!"

Klaus and Remi laughed even more heartily, nearly spilling their drinks this time. "Yes, lad, a dragon," Remi confirmed. "What did you think Terror was? A great big ogre of a thing, too, from the stories they tell."

"I certainly didn't think Terror was a dragon," Richard was so exasperated he looked ready to shake the table as he spoke. "Usually, terror just bloody well means the same thing as fear."

"And *what* would be so terrible to be able to lay waste to the countryside without contest, young one?" Klaus asked with a grin that exposed what Chase could have sworn was a fang at each corner of his mouth.

"Oh, I don't know. You all speak strange here, anyway! None of what you say makes a lick of sense." Richard snarled more than Chase had expected him to. "All legends and myths and stories. And now, to make matters worse, you speak in riddles." Frustration seeped from the man's posture as he sulked in his seat. For all the knowledge Cole taught his disciples in the Burrow, they knew very little about things the Dark-Father viewed as *impractical*.

As the two strangers continued to laugh and poke fun at Richard, Chase interrupted the conversation.

"So, have you ever seen a dragon? I remember reading a fairy tale when I was a child in Corina, but it was just a story."

"Oh, they are more than stories, lad. Or at least they seem to be depending on what book you find," Remi replied, still shaking off the last bits of laughter from her voice. "But no, I nor my companion has ever seen a dragon in the flesh. There are still many that believe the legends are false and that dragons do not exist at all, but I gather there's more to it." She waved to a nearby waiter with a smile to order another round of drinks. "According to the texts, Terror was the last of the dragons to leave Dragonstone, and even before him, it had been countless generations since any recordings of dragons were collected.

"I had once read a particularly rare account that described a tale nearly lost to time. The legend of the dragons dates back to before people recorded their history, when they relied on stories to carry their words through the generations. At the dawn of time, the dragons fell into chaos that ravaged the land. That was until a great green dragon brokered peace between them.

"As penance for their misdeeds, the dragon exiled his entire race to the confines of Dragonstone, only allowing those chosen to be bound to a rider to ever leave. Even then, they had to wait until their marked rider sailed to their island to be free again. They were forbidden from leaving their home on their own accord."

"Damn. Would have really liked to see one of

those," Richard replied sourly. "How did someone get marked to be a dragon rider?"

Chase had a sinking suspicion he knew the answer to that particular question.

"Why don't you ask your friend there, young one," Klaus smirked as he gestured in Chase's direction. "He has a mark right there around his eye."

"What?" Richard blurted out while he swiveled to look at his friend. His eyes were glassy, and his tone was oddly blunt, even by his standards.

Just how much has he had to drink? When Chase simply shrugged, Richard scoffed and returned his attention to the strangers at the table. "No, no, no. That's not right. No bloody way that's what that is. You must be having a good laugh with all this *mark* rubbish."

Klaus casually drank from his flagon of honey ale before responding. "Yes. If I'm not mistaken, from what Remi's found on scraps of parchment hidden away from the world, markings like the one your friend has around his eye are just the kind of markings used to designate a dragon rider. 'A cryptic symbol emblazoned on the flesh with pitch black ink, darker than any ink any man can mix or refine.' It's reasonable to think that however you got that tattoo, you were somehow bound to a dragon."

"Bullshit," Richard slurred rather adamantly. "Dragons can't be real. I don't care what you say about them. They just aren't. They are big, scary monsters meant to scare little children into behaving and that's that."

Klaus smiled with an odd twinkle in his eye. "Ah, a sentiment shared by many. Even those who were alive during Terror's sacking of the countryside believed they were just stories. In fact, outside of Galland, hardly anyone believed the rumors were true. Dragons are regarded by most as nothing more than a myth, and you'd be reasonable to assume the same. Although, based on what my friend has learned, and our meeting two strange young men from beyond the Ardent Rise here tonight, I'd wager they are slightly more than a story for children."

Chase gripped his flagon more tightly for fear his hands might be shaking. *Can I trust these strangers are telling the truth? Why would they lie to us? What would they have to gain? If it is true what does that mean for me?* Will had promised him a gift, but there was no way it could be something such as this. Strange people in a strange land, prophecies, quests, and now dragons?

It seemed more likely Chase would wake from a dream to find himself back in the Burrow than for these two strangers to be telling him the truth. But, then again, why would they lie to him? *Two strangers walk into a bar, so you decide to lie to them with some tall tale about dragons? If it weren't for Will, I'd say that might be the case... but what if it's true? A damned dragon. For me.* The thought sent shivers down his spine. Chase realized his knuckles had gone pale, and he hadn't spoken for quite some time.

On silver wings.

"Can you bring us to Dragonstone?"

"What?" Richard perked up with half-open eyes. "Are we going on an adventure again?"

Remi laughed. "That is quite a tall request, lad. How do you suppose you'll be able to pay us for our trouble? I hope you don't mind me saying, you don't seem to have much gold between the two of you."

The pit in Chase's stomach deepened. *Maybe it's all one big joke, after all.*

Richard drunkenly raised his flagon. "We will pay you in good company and rich stories." He hiccupped softly, trying to keep his expression even to no avail.

Klaus chuckled while he dabbed his forehead with a small square of finely embroidered cloth. "I doubt the stories would be all that rich, but the company would surely be very *good.*"

Chase pushed the whirling maelstrom from his mind as best he could. "Why would you tell us all these stories?" He tried to keep his voice level. "You both clearly believe the tales you've shared with us. Why tell us all this if you didn't plan to help us in the end? If friendly tavern talk was all you wanted, you could've asked anyone else to join your table.

"It seems to me you recognized this symbol on my face. It's not like I can hide the damned thing. And from the moment we sat down, you've been trying to impress us with tales and myths and legends. That's why you beckoned us to your table. You wanted to see if we knew exactly what it meant and since we didn't, you gladly gave us a free lesson to help us find our way. I would even gamble that you counted on our ignorance so that the two charitable tavern goers could gracefully offer their services as guides to this *Dragonstone*. It seems to me you wanted a chance to land in those stories you've been so intent on sharing."

Chase's heart was pounding in his ears, and he could feel his voice begin to shake. He desperately hoped he had hidden his nerves well enough to go unnoticed.

Klaus laughed coldly between gulps of ale. "You certainly are cleverer than your friend. Maybe the stories *will* be rich."

"Oh, be nice to them, Klaus," Remi said, smacking her friend gently on his coat sleeve with the back of her hand. She turned to Chase. "It seems you are right about some things at the very least. I recognized the tattoo as a possible dragon mark, and Klaus suggested we speak to you to learn what each of you knew about it. I must admit, it was not our intention to guide you all the way to the capital and beyond."

Klaus nodded in agreement but let his friend continue.

"But after speaking with you, it is plain to see that you are quite clever," Remi continued. "And you enjoy good company with a tall flagon of ale. I almost want to take straight to Haven ourselves. Something about your presence is *interesting*. Yes, very interesting indeed. I apologize for the apparent deceit. It was not my intention, of course. It's not every day one has a dragon rider fall into their lap. Though, you were wrong about one detail, lad."

"And what's that?"

"It was never my intention to impress you with my stories." Remi smiled brilliantly as she flagged down someone to order more drinks. "I must admit I simply enjoy them, myself."

Chase wasn't comfortable throwing in with people he had only just met, but he and Richard were desperate. For now, he buried his instincts and accepted the strangers for what they appeared to be. *This isn't the Berg, anymore. Not everyone wants to kill us, right? Patty seemed a nice enough woman...* After all, Remi and Klaus were a welcomed change to the normal caliber of person that would bother conversing with a couple of assassins.

Chase and Richard bought a room at a quieter inn nearby, hoping to avoid the wild festivities of the night. Over the inn's entrance hung a sign depicting a blacksmith pounding a handful of dice with his hammer. The Smithy's Contempt was smaller than The Spit Pig and considerably emptier, although a small crowd of thirsty patrons still filled most seats in the common area.

A woman with a lute stood in a corner, strumming away and singing a merry tune about a man who was tricked into marrying a goat. Pleasantly drunk from all the sweet ale, they sat and listened to the woman sing for a while before retreating to their modest room for the night.

***

After waking from another wretched nightmare, the pair bought large mugs of coffee from the inn's kitchen and—to their surprise—were given a complimentary fried egg with two sausage lengths each. The egg was peppered lightly, while the sausage was filled with a mix of strange herbs and spices.

Realizing their packs were empty and their wineskins were dry, the pair gathered their things and made their way to the local market without delay.

Aside from food, wine, and water, Chase needed to replace a few of his lost throwing knives. He approached a modest smith near the market—a home half-open to the world revealing a small forge along with numerous racks of tools on display. The portly blacksmith working the bellows wore a clean apron over a dirty leather vest, and when Chase showed him one of his knives, he looked at the hardware thoughtfully.

"Won't be cheap," he growled. "These got good balance. Must've been made by a real talented bloke. Not sure how he got the steel to be so black, though." The smith scratched the stubble on his plump chin absentmindedly while he looked Chase up a down with an undeniable skepticism. "You got money to pay for 'em?"

The coin purse fastened to Chase's belt was unfortunately full of High Council branded silver coins. He didn't know what the local currency looked like, but good silver should still do the trick regardless of the markings chiseled on the coins. Chase tossed the pouch to the blacksmith.

The blacksmith opened the purse with thick, hairy fingers and drew out a coin. "What the 'ell is this?" His cheeks flushed in confusion. "No coin I ever seen before. You tryin' to play me the fool? I'll not be played a fool when standing in me own damn forge."

"It's silver," Chase replied firmly. "What else do you care?"

The blacksmith nodded. "True, but this won't cover 'alf my cost. Hell, I can't imagine a smith worth 'is salt that could do four of those knives for less than triple what you're payin'. I can do 'alf of what you want for this much, and I'm takin' a loss. Don't know where you're from, boy, but 'round these parts we use gold, not silver."

"Half? You can only manage *two*?" Chase replied in disbelief. *That's enough to buy a whole damn sword in the Berg. The only people using gold are the High Council.* "That's all I have. Take the money and make the full order or I'll take my business elsewhere." It was a weak bluff, and he knew it. If the blacksmith was telling the truth, it wouldn't matter where Chase took his business. The answer would always be the same.

"Alright, I'll do it." The blacksmith sighed and shook his bald head. "Come back in a few 'ours and they'll be done. I'll need to keep a good one as a template, though." He begrudgingly set to work, waving a thick hand in the air dismissively.

Somberly, Chase and Richard ventured further into the market to see what food they could manage with Richard's remaining silver.

The market wasn't particularly large, filled with townspeople selling food from their gardens and family farms instead of proper merchants. However, the variety of food displayed on the tables scattered in the town center still amazed them—peppers, tomatoes, toadstools of at least three different colors, green beans, grains, dried meat... There was even a fresh food stand serving bowls of chicken and vegetable soup crammed in the tight village clearing.

The air was buzzing with the chatter of people bartering and bargaining, all with smiles painted across their faces.

Unfortunately, their silver proved more troublesome in the rest of the market than it had with the blacksmith. All thirty-seven High Council branded silver lairens in Richard's pouch were only enough to buy two loaves of bread, a pack of salted ham, and three potatoes. The food was enough for them both—*if* they could earn more coin later—but it would not last more than a few days. In the Berg, that amount of money would have easily bought them three or four times as much food as that.

After procuring Chase's knives from the smith, they headed to the spot near the northern exit of the village that Remi and Klaus had agreed upon the night before. Chase half expected their guides to be gone. Perhaps it was his lingering distrust for strangers, or perhaps he was just paranoid that their meeting the foreigners was too good to be true.

He was pleasantly surprised to see the pair waiting for them from atop two horses with saddlebags bursting with supplies. However, he was even more surprised to see two additional horses waiting for Richard and him. *Bloody hell, they must have just purchased those for us.*

"Thanks, mates," Richard called out, realizing the same thing Chase had. "We'll be good for it once we get some real bloody coin in our pockets. You wouldn't believe the looks we got from that gardener with the potatoes. Would've thought we were asking for them for free."

Remi bowed her head behind a thick neck wrap of purple silk that complimented her yellow-dyed leathers. "No worries, lad. I am not too proud to admit that I have more coin than I care to deal with, and we assumed you and your friend here may not be able to scrounge much."

"And it would appear our assumptions were correct." Klaus's voice was as cool as ever, his eyes glistening from beneath his strange, brimmed hat.

Chase nodded at Klaus before returning his attention to Remi. "Where exactly are we heading?" *First, I decided Richard's fate without his say, and now these strangers could very well lead us on without ours. I don't like this—but Carpenter's Hammer—I don't know what else we can do.*

"Redwood is in the southeast corner of Galland." Remi rearranged her silk wrapping, her black hair shimmering in the daylight. "You may study my atlas while we ride, if you like. I must admit I'm pleasantly surprised that you speak the common tongue, or else our conversation last night would have been much more difficult." She chortled to herself. "I have a particularly intriguing edition of *Panchert's World Maps* that I'm sure you would find most enlightening."

Klaus smiled as he dabbed his handkerchief to his forehead. "My dear friend, perhaps talk of books can wait a moment. At least until the young ones know where we're taking them."

Remi jumped in her saddle as if startled. "Ah, yes. Of course. I know a fisherman with a small vessel that can take you to the island, with a little persuasion, of course. He owes me for taking care of a small problem of his involving a particularly nasty bout with a karrencot. The last I'd heard, his home port was in Nareem. Although, he often docks in Haven to sell his goods. Of course, you must understand, even the most adept of fisherman could not deny the illustrious draw of the capital's trading port. They would be leaving gold on the table, so-to-speak."

"Wait one moment. What in the world is a karrencot?" Richard tried to keep his tone level, but his confusion overcame him. He always had a certain blunt curiosity that Chase admired.

Klaus smiled slyly. "It's a large wild cat that wanders down from Azalea from time to time. They aren't usually much to write about, but they can get aggressive if they're hungry enough."

Richard scoffed, "That doesn't sound so bad. A big cat?"

"Yes, indeed, lad." Remi emphatically waved a hand while her horse pitched her side to side. "Don't let my companion's casual demeanor fool you. I assure you Klaus has a nasty habit of glossing over the drama of such things. And I can tell you for certain my encounter with the karrencot in Nareem was quite *dramatic* if I do say so myself."

"It's an oversized house pet. I don't see what the big deal is."

"The *big deal* is that they have claws like daggers and teeth as long as fingers, young one." Klaus chuckled, sending a cold shiver down Chase's spine.

Richard barked with laughter. "If you think that is bad, Chase and I just had a run in with forest spiders.

Let me tell you about *dramatic*."

Chase smiled and let the conversation fade into the background as they passed trees with trunks as wide as horses that held all sorts of chattering critters. His smile faded when he saw a peculiar looking man standing in the shade of one of those massive trees.

He seemed to be the same age, weight, and height as Chase, but this man was dressed in sturdy leathers stained a deep, blood red with splashes of gray. Chase kicked his mare forward and kept his eyes on the man as the slow and constant step of his horse rocked him up and down.

The mysterious man finally returned his gaze. To Chase's surprise—in the middle of broad daylight—there stood the mirror image of himself. Or rather, the man standing before him was the slightly altered apparition that lived within Chase's nightmares.

It was the Man in Red.

CHAPTER 14
AN UNFAMILIAR INSTINCT

Chase rubbed his eyes before looking back at the base of the massive tree. The Man in Red disappeared without a trace—as if he'd never been there to begin with. Chase shook his head in disbelief.

It was nothing. Just a trick of the light. My imagination is playing tricks on me.

Dammit, I need some actual sleep. And soon.

Returning his attention to his traveling companions, Chase smiled and tried to mask his concern.

Klaus' smooth voice trilled with a pleasant laugh. "Not at all, young one. Vampires are nothing more than stories meant to keep children from talking to strangers. I can assure you that your neck is safe. I wouldn't dare take a bite." Klaus eyed Richard with a wicked smile and an almost hungry look in his eyes.

"Unless, of course, you wanted me to."

Richard's face grew as red as a tomato. He stammered slightly before grumbling something to himself that the others couldn't hear.

Chase stifled a laugh and tried to break the awkward tension that followed. "What's all this about vampires?"

"Oh, nothing, lad." Remi shook her head with a tired smile that suggested she was no stranger to her companion's coy demeanor. "Klaus is just having fun with your friend."

Klaus' smile revealed the slightly enlarged incisors that Chase had noticed the night before. "You see, young one, my people have a special relationship with blood. It's often seen as quite unpleasant by those unfamiliar with the Drakthul, but it poses a much greater threat to my kin than anyone else. There have always been stories of things like vampires told in Talvenna to warn about the dangers of partaking too heavily in our crafts. They are awful, terrible things capable of convincing you to surrender your life to them. Blood-sucking, mind controlling, manipulative, and dangerous creatures that steal children from their homes by simply asking their parents to give them away."

Klaus paused for a moment, distracted by something unspoken. "The realities of the Drakthul's Curse of Blood are often less romantic, but nonetheless, we tell stories to teach our young ones the dangers of our ways. It seems such stories have made their way from the northern Sun Isle to your own homeland—even if the details have been lost in translation. It's quite remarkable."

Chase turned in his saddle to Richard, leveling an amused smirk at him.

"Just wanted to bloody well know why he looks like a damned vampire," Richard grumbled, more to himself than to the group. "Pale skin and red eyes. Looks like a damned monster, if you ask me. Going to have to sleep with one eye open. Won't be biting my bloody neck anytime soon, that's for sure if I have anything to bloody say about it."

Remi rolled her eyes with a smile spreading across her face. She addressed her old friend jovially. "You don't have to tease the lad." She turned her attention to Richard while he brooded in his embarrassment. "If you don't mind me saying, lad, there is nothing for you to worry about. And I can say that as quite a matter of fact. Klaus may like to tease, but I will have you know his bark is quite a bit worse than his bite, or so the saying goes." Remi suddenly lowered her voice considerably, but it was still loud enough for Chase to hear. "Unless of course you would like him to. I can assure you, I don't mean to judge in the slightest. People of all walks enjoy the company of whomever they—"

"That's quite bloody enough, mate!" Richard roared, his face growing redder by the second. "All I bloody asked was why he has bloody fangs if he's not a bloody vampire!"

"Either way," Klaus said coolly with a wry smile. "Offer's on the table."

The group laughed while Richard huffed and

puffed for a little while longer. Thankfully, Remi changed the subject, allowing them to ride in relative peace. Even still, Chase could see Richard riding a few paces further away from their pale-skinned guide than he had before. He rolled his eyes but was glad to have a distraction from the Man in Red—even if it was at his friend's expense.

As they continued at a comfortable pace, Chase was soon lost in the awe of the giant, hulking trees that surrounded them. They made everything else look so small in comparison. Songbirds in all sorts of browns, reds, and yellows chirped in concert with the sound of rustling leaves in the gentle breeze. Foxes, strange white weasels, and muskrats were less common, but to Chase, they seemed to run wild. The smell of sap and field grass eased his shoulders while he breathed in the clean, crisp air.

A voice drew him back to his traveling companions and out of his preoccupied observations. Snapping back to the conversation, he stumbled over his words for a moment. "W-what was that?"

Remi smiled while her chestnut stallion, clad in considerably more packs and satchels than the other three horses, jostled her side to side. "Ah, yes, lad. You must tell us what it is like in your homeland. 'The Berg' as you call it—though, I certainly sympathize when a name such as *Rakksberg* seems so crude, even in the common tongue. Admittedly, it must sound much more appealing than our own term for the land beyond the Ardent Rise. More to my point, however, you must *describe* it to me. You see, I've only ever heard stories of what lies in the Dread Wastes, and I am now certain that these accounts are wildly inaccurate."

"Gray," Richard said bluntly.

"Well, then," Klaus suppressed a chuckle. "Our accounts of the Wastes may not be entirely inaccurate."

Chase sighed—more to himself than to the comment—before elaborating. "He's not wrong. The foliage on this side of the Blackridge Mountains, or Ardent Rise, is enough to make our home seem gray. Most wildlife is long dead, or at least it seems to be dying. The water is murky, the winds are harsh, and the sky seems to only ever be cloudy or storming. Some people say that the land is dead and that the people should have died a long time ago with it, but the more resilient folk keep their heads down as best as they can, even if the High Council never makes it easy."

Richard snarled bitterly. "The people aren't much better off than the animals. I don't think there is a single damned city in the Berg that doesn't have a food shortage most of the year outside the week of harvest. In some of the worst places, they don't even bother to bury the bloody dead once they starve. Faster and easier to burn them."

"That's... a shame," Klaus remarked solemnly. "It's truly unfortunate that your people live through such pain. There was once a time Talvenna shared a similar fate. Though—thankfully—that was long before I was born."

Richard spit in disgust and snorted. "Ack, the people don't care. They don't even care enough to police a gang of assassins that make their coin entirely from killing." The comment seemed harsh, but Chase's expression showed that he agreed with the sentiment. "Hell, there isn't even an organized army. The High Council just lets the mercenary guilds run rampant and pays them for their work accordingly." He turned to Chase. "What are there, now? Eleven? Twelve?"

"If the Blood Moons folded to the Scarlet Furies like I suspect they did, there are ten." Chase attempted to hide his shudder. *Sometimes, I think that's ten too many.*

"I see." Remi twisted the end of her braid, nearly lost in thought. "And what of the wildlife? Is it true that trolls roam the greater plains of the Dread Wastes?" She stumbled slightly over her words. "I-I mean to say the Berg, of course. Old habits fade with difficulty, as they say. I've always been quite interested in troll anatomy. It seems to change with each passing mile. They truly are a fascinating species. We have great dune trolls that wander the deserts of Soule, although they are seldom seen by those who live to tell their tale."

She was clearly trying to divert the topic away from politics.

Chase chuckled loudly. "No, no. There isn't anything quite as spectacular as trolls or dragons outside of children's stories in Rakksberg. Great Carpenter, it seems like all we have sometimes is an abundance of rats and crows. I suppose there are a good number of animals you probably see here in Galland." He paused for a moment. "Now that I think about it, we've encountered things even I thought were impossible since we were banished from the Burrow—spiders as big as bears, gargoyles..."

Klaus allowed for a small amount of surprise to show through his dark eyes. "Intriguing. You say you have gargoyles? I know a creature in Talvenna by the same name. By chance, are yours about as large as a horse, scaly and grey with the wings and face of a bat?"

"Smaller," Richard grunted. "Not so well put together, I'd say. Wings look like an accident, and the head always seems too large for the body. They have claws and teeth like daggers, though."

"Very interesting." Remi was on the edge of her saddle, as if the outlanders were telling her a tale of some great heroism. "I would very much like to sketch the likeness of such a beast when we find it appropriate to rest for the evening. And to even be called the same name as something across the world in another tongue? Very interesting, indeed. I can think of a few reasons why that may be, but I do not think I should be so hasty in sharing those ideas without proper research, as I'm sure you understand. You must tell us more as we ride. It will make for the most exciting conversation."

Chase, however, did not find the conversation as exciting as Remi. Although, he did find enjoyment in learning of his guides' homelands.

Soule—the native land of the Magi, where Remi was from—was a desert nation settled upon the coast. Remi spoke of many creatures Chase was not entirely sure he believed existed. Spirits of sand and wind wrapped in silks and ragged cloth called djinn supposedly roamed the desert in packs, waiting for unsuspecting travelers to stumble upon their home before enslaving them. Meanwhile, mighty beasts with the body of a lion and the tail of a giant scorpion known as manticores flew across the sky with terrible, bat-like wings searching for their prey.

However strange Soule seemed to a young man from the Berg, Talvenna was even stranger. Feral crosses between humans and wolves stalked the wilderness at night, and pale husks of former Drakthul citizens known as ghouls wandered the landscape, consumed by their need for blood. Their own breed of gargoyles hid in witchwood thickets along with a strange, reptilian beast called a basilisk. And if those wicked beasts weren't enough, Klaus shared stories of the trees themselves claiming the lives of unsuspecting farmers from time to time.

Eventually, the sun fell over the horizon through the cracks in the slowly thinning forest and the group decided to make camp before it was too dark. Still chatting about the various strange creatures from their homelands, Chase unpacked his belongings while silently thanking the Great Carpenter they could proceed on horseback.

"Of course, they are beautiful," Remi said while she patted her forehead with a bright piece of silk to dry the sweat from it. "But you must be careful. It's true that the fields of amaranth, and the occasional violets or tulips, make for a lovely bouquet for a lover and are completely harmless. Though, I do suppose a broken heart may not be as harmless as the flower."

She lost herself for a moment before returning to her original topic. "But yes, the largest of the flowers, mostly on the southern shores of Galland and very rarely seen elsewhere, are fierce. Certainly, aggressive enough to snap at any unwanted visitor or unsuspecting hand wishing to pluck the bud from its stem."

"Carpenter's Hammer!" Richard exclaimed. "A flower that would kill someone for picking it? If you would have told me that before this little trip of ours had started, I'd have some choice words in mind for you."

Remi chuckled, uncorking a bottle of strong mead she had imported from across the sea. The deep, herbal tones balanced the sweetness of the honey and the bitterness of the hops as the cool liquid washed across Chase's dry pallet. He wasn't accustomed to traveling so leisurely. People in Rakksberg enjoyed their time as much as they could, but compared to the folk here, they lived in a near constant state of dread.

I suppose the 'Dread Wastes' isn't far off from the truth, after all. I wish people back home could see this. Chase stared down into his wooden travel cup of tasty mead. *It's still a bit strange that our new friends don't seem the least bit worried about bandits, thieves, or any of those wild creatures they've been on about.* At their guides' insistence, they had even set their tents and campfire in the middle of the road, unbothered by what may be lurking in the dark.

Suddenly, almost as soon as his suspicions had left his mind, Chase heard a loud bang in the distance and saw a faint glow pulsing off the nearby trees. He searched for the source of the noise while Klaus and Remi stumbled to their feet. Without hesitation, Chase grabbed a torch from Remi's possessions, lit it with the campfire, and bolted toward the commotion.

Richard yelled something in protest, but it was too late. Chase was already a full twenty strides from the fire and gaining speed.

Chase arrived at the source of commotion, his three companions racing behind him. A crashed wagon burned brightly in the night, billowing flames licking the lower branches of the trees above like eager snake tongues. Heat slammed against his face so violently, he was forced to shield himself with an upstretched arm. Carts didn't drive themselves, but whoever had been driving the wagon was nowhere in sight.

Where in the world could they be? Wait a moment...

Chase had no reason to feel so panicked.

I'm no hero. They've probably been tossed aside, or worse they're already dead. I need to get ahold of myself before I do something foolish.

After a few brief moments of silence—broken only by the crackle of fire and the occasional pop of alcohol igniting—he heard the feint cries of a woman.

"Help!" she gasped from within the thick smoke. "Help me!"

An urge Chase had never felt before overcame him. He cast his torch aside and leapt toward the cart, ignoring the worried shouts from his companions. In a few long strides, he flung himself under the broken axel of the cart, sliding beside the scared woman. She

209

was crying, tears strewn down a dirty, soot-covered face. Chase pressed his hands on the beam above him and shifted slightly. The wood burned his hands through his gloves and the heat from the fire seared his face—but he didn't care.

She'll be okay. I just need to act quickly.

He strained in a great effort, pushing the cart in hopes that the woman would have time to crawl out from underneath the rapidly burning scrap pile. To his dismay, the woman made no attempt to escape. She was either too injured to move, or too content to lay down and die in the blaze surrounding them. Chase inhaled deeply, and as ash and soot-filled his lungs—his throat searing in pain—he let out a mighty roar.

With every ounce of his strength, Chase gave a final push against the burning cart above him. The cart lifted from the ground with a massive groan, flying through the air several horse-lengths away before the burning wood collapsed in a mess of sparks and tinder.

When Chase and the woman were safely away from the flames, she looked up at him with a mix of admiration and horror painted across her features. Chase's face still burned to the touch and his hands felt like they were about to burst, but he smiled slightly to ease the woman's fears.

"What the bloody hell was that?!"

Richard's outburst snapped Chase's attention to his friend.

"I honestly have no idea." Chase coughed, his

throat sore and full of lingering smoke. He looked back at the burning cart—now thirty paces away. Brushing the ash off his leather jerkin with a shrug, Chase returned his gaze to his friend. "It was like I was trying a new dance for the first time, but I already knew all the steps." He looked down at the woman, still quivering slightly. "Are you okay, miss? What's your name?"

"Sasha." The woman coughed and spat. "Sasha Reinhart. I'm okay, I think. My leg hurts, and my arm was badly burned."

Remi kneeled beside her and gently inspected her arm. "I think I have just the thing for that, lass. Come right this way, if you can bear to stand, and I will see to it that burn leaves little more than bad memories. And I do believe I should put a kettle on for some tea. Would you like that?"

The woman nodded and slowly rose to her feet. She used Richard as a brace while they made their way to the group's campfire, although she seemed to be moving steadily by then.

"Damn it, Chase. I'm not up for this again," Richard said in an exasperated tone, keeping a careful eye on Sasha to ensure she wouldn't fall. "The last time something like this happened, I was bit by one of those bloody spiders and a mad man forced you into helping me."

Chase laughed. "No, it's not like that," he assured his friend. "No one was in control this time." *That was me. I was in control the whole time.* "I simply didn't think about anything." *Why would I do that?* "I knew what I had to do. And if it didn't work and it had killed me, I didn't care."

He finally noticed something that gave him pause. That small part of him buried deep inside—that reveled in the moments following a successful contract—was notably silent, but something similar within him roared in triumph. Elation flooded Chase until he was nearly fit to burst and cry out. He had never felt this way before, but the thrill and joy and pride that he felt swelled.

Chase felt a smile creep across his face. He wanted nothing more than to howl out to the night, but he refrained. *Richard already thinks I've lost it. No need to make that worse.* He turned his gaze to Sasha, who coughed enough to make her stagger while she stumbled down the path.

"Besides," Richard began, sourly. "You're usually more of the killing type and not so much the saving type. And beyond that, how the hell did you throw a cart like it was some child's plaything—and what's wrong with your face?"

Chase looked back at Richard, who had raised his voice enough for Sasha to switch to using Remi as a makeshift crutch. "I don't *know*, Richard." He felt his smile widen. "And I'm not sure what happened to my face, but I bet it's still prettier than yours. So what? How badly did I get burned? It's so hot, it feels like it's still on fire."

Klaus reached into his pack and pulled out a piece of reflective glass. "Not exactly, young one. I think you should see this." He handed the glass to Chase.

Are they having a laugh?

Chase touched his face in disbelief. The tattooed markings around his eye were glowing like liquid fire. The outline of tattoo remained pitch black, while the rest of the mark was bright white—shimmering and swirling as if it were alive beneath his skin. It even emitted a dull light that flowed like smoke. Chase expected the mark to burn to the touch, but to his surprise, it felt no different than the rest of his skin. He looked at his companions and saw the grim expressions they all shared.

I guess that answers that. Not *having a laugh.*

"Interesting…" Remi clearly saw Chase's questioning expression as she stepped around a root sticking out in the path. "Very interesting. I have an idea what the implications of tonight may be, but I must sleep on the issue. Nothing like a good rest to clear your head, lad. Some rest may do us all some good, come to think of it. Sasha, why don't you let me see that arm."

The group returned to their camp in relative silence. Chase was dazed, absent-mindedly brushing his eye with his hand every so often. It slowly returned to normal and with it, the heat in his face subsided. Nothing remained of his moment of heroism—not a scratch or mark or burn to be seen.

They had insisted Sasha stay with them for the night before making her way to Redwood in the morning. Remi procured a small tent from her packs and set up another cot so that Sasha would have privacy. Still visibly shaken—and shooting suspicious glances at Chase's eye on occasion—the woman accepted their hospitality and retired to her tent shortly after they had constructed it.

Chase was eager to rest for the night, but he forced himself to sit by the fire with his companions. Richard was eating spiced pork jerky out of his pack with a blank expression, lost in thought as he stared at the fire. Klaus sat against a tree trunk with his arms folded, trading glances between the fire, Sasha's tent, and Chase. Remi sat cross-legged, stuffing her long wooden pipe with a cluster of tobacco mixed with some dried herbs Chase was unfamiliar with.

In a desperate effort to break the silence, Chase asked, "Why would a woman be traveling alone at this time of night? Are Gallanders not afraid of highwaymen and thieves?"

Klaus looked at the fire for a moment. "…Bandits are not uncommon in these lands, but they are sparse in the countryside. Trade routes are more frequent and prosperous inland, near Haven and the Harp. I imagine our young Sasha was returning from such places, eager to finish her route."

Muffled by a mouthful of jerky, Richard chewed noisily while he spoke. "Why the bloody hell—" He clumsily swallowed the morsel of meat he had bitten off. "Why the bloody hell would the cart go up like that? I've seen carts lose wheels and break axels but never flip in a blazing wreckage."

"I suspect she was carrying fire starters and brandy," Klaus shook his head. "Many traders overfill their carts to save time and money, although most know well enough to mix certain goods. Sasha is certainly not the first to make such a mistake, but if the barrels on her cart were filled with spirits, a fire accidentally igniting would be enough to cut her route short." His cool voice was somewhat chilling, even in the warmth of the fire.

Chase glanced at Remi who was muttering to herself through her tobacco smoke. He heard the occasional "interesting" among the mumbles while she absent-mindedly twisted the end of her braid.

"We can ask her for certain in the morning," Chase said with a sigh. "For now, I think I'll follow Remi's advice and get some sleep." *Not like it's going to help much.* He made his way to his own tent and lay on the rigid cot that held his bedroll.

Staring at the green fabric above him, he listened to faint muffled speech from outside. The small part of him no longer roared but rather basked in his accomplishment. It was like a fire had been lit inside him, and he couldn't explain why.

Does this have something to do with Will and Lucius? Then again, I've never done anything like that before. Even before this blasted quest began, I just put my head down and minded my own like everyone in the Berg.

An unfamiliar feeling lingered in the back of his mind nagging at him from far away.

I was in control. It was me—not like the time in the Widower's Woods.

His eyes grew heavy, the soothing sounds from outside his tent lulling him to sleep.

Never thought to be some hero.

Darkness closed in around him, and sleep took him once more.

CHAPTER 15
VISIONS OR PROPHECY?

Chase woke to find himself lying on his back in the middle of a town square. He rose slowly and brushed the dust from his clothes. His joints ached and his muscles burned in silent agony, but the pain faded quickly.

The more he had become accustomed to waking each night in this strange, nightmarish place, the more the sounds of screaming women and children faded into the background. The fiery red light that flooded the air almost seemed normal by now, and the odd pressure that hung in the air slid off his shoulders.

However, the putrid smell of burnt wood and rotten eggs flooded nose and coated his mouth until bile rose in his throat. No matter how accustomed he was to this place, he almost always felt the urge to empty his stomach while he walked through the nightmare realm.

Chase rubbed his eyes before seeing a single open door on the opposite side of the town square. He quickly made his way to the house. Delaying the inevitable would accomplish nothing. On more than one occasion, Chase had tried to simply wait until he woke up the next morning, but the result was always the same. He would always see what the Man in Red had in store for him, no matter what.

Upon entering the house, Chase was taken aback. He had expected to see a ruined interior not unlike every other building he'd entered in his relentless nightmares. Instead, Chase stood in a clearing with a burning cart thirty paces away.

The cart didn't unsettle him at first. After all, Chase had seen so many worse things in this world of nightmares. What bothered Chase was the dark outline of a dirty woman crouched on the ground, gasping and crying while desperately clutching her knees with her auburn hair hanging in front of her face.

Chase glanced to his left and saw a man sharing a startling resemblance to himself, dressed in dark red leathers, trimmed with splashes of gray.

The Man in Red smiled at him with a crazed look in his eyes that glimmered wickedly in the darkness of the night. "Go on," the man said with a laugh. "Go be a savior. Go be the hero. I promise I won't move before you have a chance to chat."

A rolling cold passed through his feet and legs, all the way to his head and fingertips. After taking a deep breath—fighting the urge to shiver at the sound of his own voice—Chase walked to the woman and knelt beside her. "It's okay," he assured her. "It'll all be okay. You're safe now."

The woman moaned between sobs. "It's not okay. It will *never* be okay."

Chase's stomach dropped, and his mouth became dry. "Nothing will hurt you now, Sasha. The fire is gone, and you are safe. You don't need to cry anymore."

He reached out to console the woman but quickly withdrew. Something wasn't right. It didn't *feel* right, but Chase couldn't explain why. There was buzzing in the air. Pain throbbed in his temples and his knees shook, threatening to give way and leave him curled on the ground next to the sobbing figure.

"Okay," the woman replied softly.

The buzzing grew louder. Chase's hands shook and sweat dripped from his brow.

Sasha's body began to blur and flicker. Chase rubbed his eyes—his heart racing faster and faster—but the image continued to twitch and contort. Soon, the flicker stopped. To Chase's horror, Sasha no longer knelt before him. Someone else had taken her place.

It was Richard.

Silence hung in the clearing save for the crackling embers of the nearby fire and the heaving sobs of Chase's oldest friend. His coarse blonde air clumped with mud and ash, hanging over his broad features. His shoulders rose and fell in shuddering motions, and his massive hands covered his face.

An unseen band tightened around Chase's chest. It was hard to breathe. His heart pounded in his ears like a drum. "R-Richard?"

The man simply cried.

Chase reached out a trembling hand.

Suddenly, Richard latched onto Chase's shoulders and jolted upright to reveal two gaping bloody holes where his eyes should be. Blood streamed down his cheeks and fell past the corners of his mouth to pool on the ground, staining his sack-cloth trousers. His jaw opened unnaturally, and he screamed.

"Look what you did to me!"

***

Chase let out a wild scream.

Daylight crept through the flaps of his tent.

Panting and sweating, he tried to reorient himself while his eyes adjusted to the light. He stumbled out of his tent, still dressed in the soot-covered leathers he had forgotten to take off before falling asleep. The smell of rotten eggs, fire, and blood lingered in his nose, and his temples throbbed with each step.

He opened his eyes, and he was back in the burning clearing. He blinked and saw Richard sitting by a fire. He blinked again, and the Man in Red stood beside him—laughing wickedly.

Richard's scream flooded his mind, and he fell to one knee gasping for air and choking on the smell of ash. Finally, the red hues of the nightmare realm faded away, replaced by a calm clearing in the dim blue light of an early morning in Galland.

Visibly struggling to regain his senses, Chase looked around to see Richard, Remi, and Klaus sitting at a newly lit campfire preparing a hot breakfast together. Panting, Chase ran his hand through his dirty, sweaty hair, breathing slowly trying to calm himself down.

In a deliberate effort, Chase closed his eyes and allowed the smell of spiced meat and fried potatoes to replace the pungent scent of rotten eggs. The echoing scream was replaced by crackling embers and sizzling meat. Soon, the cool, crisp morning air flooded his lungs and his heart finally relented to its normal pace.

With wobbly and uncertain legs, Chase rose to his feet and looked at his traveling companions, sweat dripping down his grimy features. The looks of concern painted across their expressions spoke louder than any words could.

"You haven't had one that bad for a while, mate." Richard's tone was laced with fear, worried for his oldest friend. "That may have been the worst yet."

"I-I-I'm fine, I think." Chase was still trying to calm himself, but he struggled to keep his breath steady. "This one was just… different. I-I don't know how to explain it, but it didn't make any sense. At least not the same way the others have."

Behind him, Chase heard Sasha's tent rustle. He nearly leapt out of his skin at the sound, but when he realized it was just their guest, he flashed a weak smile that looked absurd given the rest of his appearance. Without saying a word, she simply smiled politely and joined the others at the fire.

"Richard," Remi inquired. "You said *'in a while,'* as though these are common occurrences. If it is not too much for me to ask, I would quite like to hear more about these nightmares. I must admit, considering recent events, I find you and your friend most intriguing. When did they begin?"

"They started when we set off on this damned journey of ours," Richard answered while Chase gingerly sat next to the fire. "Every night, Chase goes to sleep. And every morning, he wakes up panting or screaming or shaking. It's never easy to see you like that, mate."

Chase looked at the ground. *I'm so sorry, Richard.*

"Some nights are worse than others. There are days I forget Chase even has the dreams, while other days... Well, it's just not what I ever want to see again—that's for damned sure."

"When the night terrors are bad, I sometimes tell Richard what happened, if he's up to hear it," Chase continued in response to Remi's clearly curious expression. He'd rather not share these dreams with his new companions, but if they were going to be together for the foreseeable future, there was no avoiding it. "He doesn't always want to listen, and I can't say that I always want to share. These dreams feel like more than just nightmares. They feel *real.* It feels like I'm there and recently it seems like... It seems like the dreams acknowledge me being there, as well. A man that appears every night has started to speak to me."

He paused for a long moment, struggling to find the words. He finally relented with a sigh. "I'm exhausted. The dreams always leave me more tired than I felt before I went to sleep. Our friend, Maddie, gave me some creams that keep me from collapsing in my saddle, but they don't help much with the rest."

"Interesting." Remi was twisting the end of her braid a tad more vigorously than moments before. "Very interesting. I seem to recall tales of men that are touched by madness after being exposed to certain items of peculiar origin. Although, it would not seem you and your friend have ever come across such an object. I must say this is most interesting, indeed."

Klaus shifted a handkerchief in his hand thoughtfully. "It may be visions of what has come to pass or what may be. Long ago in Talvenna, we thought those with the gift of foresight were wise. They often became clan leaders, but it's been so long since anyone was born with the gift that we only have stories now." A sorry expression flashed across his sharp features. "According to those tales, it was always found at birth. It never developed later."

Remi paused in thought before looking back to Chase. "Tell us, lad. What did you see last night? We would certainly know more about exactly what you are going through, which may allow us to help you—as long as you would be willing for us to offer our aid, of course. Although, I must admit, it may not help us at all, unfortunately."

Chase frowned at the fire, avoiding Remi's gaze. "Each night starts the same. I'm alone in some rotten and decrepit city. Everything is burning and the stench..." Chase's mouth became dry, and his hands grew clammy. "It's all rotten. Everything about the place is rotten. But I'm stuck there until I follow the dream to its end."

"You have agency in these dreams?" Klaus' eyebrows rose and his tone betrayed more surprise than Chase felt comfortable hearing.

"Yes. No matter how hard I try, I'm forced to keep going until I see what I'm meant to. I've tried waiting to let it pass, running away, closing my eyes and trying to ignore it all... Nothing ever works.

"Last night, I walked into a home only to find myself in the clearing with the burning cart from last night. That was strange enough. Until now, I've never left the city before I wake up. But when I saw the cart turned over something was off. It was just... *wrong*. One moment, Sasha was there, kneeling by the fire and the next..."

The words caught in Chase's throat. He locked eyes with Richard—his oldest and dearest friend— and his heart froze. The blood drained from his face. His stomach twisted uncomfortably.

He needs to know. I need to tell him. He'll understand. I'll just tell him what I saw.

Chase fought the urge to say nothing—to let the silence linger.

He needs to know what I saw. We still don't know what these dreams mean. It might be important.

His companions would eventually chime in. They would console him or ask him more questions. He didn't *need* to say the rest.

It's all because I made his choice for him. If anything happens to him...

Richard's eyes held a somber sorrow and pity that Chase had never seen before.

This is all my fault.

He couldn't bring himself to say more. He sat, silently fighting a battle within himself that none of the others could understand.

Eventually, Klaus broke the silence. "Have you had any other nightmares that were similar to events that occurred *after* you left your home?" Chase shook his head. "Then this most recent night seems to be the exception. And besides, you saved our fair lady as we can clearly see." The woman smiled slightly and awkwardly shrugged. Klaus returned his attention to Chase, smiling kindly. "Unless this vision is more abstract. In that case, it may be revealing a clue to a possible future of some kind—more symbolic than literal."

"Possible future? What do you mean?" Fear painted every inch of Chase's expression. He clenched his clammy hands into fists to stop them from shaking.

Klaus paused for a moment, but when he maintained his reassuring tone. "Yes. *Possible*, young one. There are many paths for all of us and each one is as set in stone as the next. Each one is also as fluid as the next." His tone grew more serious. "If these nightmares are not visions, then we are dealing with extraordinarily dark magic beyond any known sorcerer's abilities. No offense, dear Remi."

Remi shrugged as she pulled out her long tobacco pipe and stuffed the end with dry brown leaves. "Of course not, Klaus. I know exactly what you mean to say, and I must admit that I agree most wholeheartedly. If these were the product of some sort of magic, though I am unaware of what that might be, that would be truly astounding. Yes, given that the magic would have to be stronger than anything I have encountered in my travels, I highly doubt that this is the case. Much more likely, they are visions, unless of course they truly are nothing more than nightmares and the timing is sheer coincidence. We mustn't rule anything out. Very interesting, indeed." Remi puffed gently from her pipe and allowed the smoke to flow from her nostrils, deep in thought as she looked at the fire.

"Wait a bloody moment," Richard intervened, clearly upset by something he just heard. "Magic? First you tell us that dragons are real and now you two speak of magic like it's as bloody common as our bloody breakfast. Can you say that again, mate? I think I might have something stuck in my ear."

Chase rubbed his eyes to regain some semblance of composure. "Just the other day we accepted that dragons might be real, and you don't think magic could exist? Don't you think those things go hand-in-hand?"

Richard grumbled, looking down at his bowl of stew. "I don't know. I can't keep all these damned things straight. Before this all started, we were living day by day going from one contract to the next. Now, we run into monsters, dragons, and who knows what else?"

"We met Maddie," Chase added, trying as much to convince himself as to convince his friend. "She was clearly involved in something strange, even if she claimed it was ordinary herbalism and alchemy. How else can you explain a child stuck like that for so long?"

Klaus raised a finger at that. His voice was still cold and smooth, like water running over ice. "Yes, you mentioned her. You say she has been a child for a few decades or so? I think I'd very much like to meet her someday." He chuckled as if he had made a joke, but Chase failed to see the humor in it.

"At any rate," Richard interjected, "what exactly do you mean by magic, Remi? You should know by now that Chase and I don't bloody well know what you're talking about half the damn time. Is there any way that Chase is cursed? Or maybe both of us?"

"Wait—you two aren't from round these parts?" Sasha's voice was hoarse. "That's not too strange, given the likes you hold company with. It's just... You seem so much like Gallanders. You don't look Azalean. Wrong color eyes for it. Where are you from?"

Remi continued to twist her braid. "Young lass, these folk hail from beyond the Ardent Rise, of course." Chase couldn't help but grimace slightly as Sasha gawked in astonishment. "To answer your question, Richard, I don't believe so. Magic comes in many forms, taught in many ways. The Azaleans, for example, sing massive crystals from the earth to construct many great things. The Magi of Soule—my own kin—bend the energy in the air to carry out our will. And that, I may be so bold to say, is only the beginning. One could spend hours discussing magic in all its many forms from every corner of the world. It can all be quite impressive to say the least."

"The Drakthul of Talvenna channel power through blood," Klaus added. "It's quite jarring to any who haven't seen it before. It has earned many of us the reputation of blood drinkers or vampires. Although, I can assure you both, we are neither."

Richard's expression betrayed equal parts horror and excited intrigue. "So, what then? Are you some kind of warlock or something?"

"No, not necessarily," Klaus insisted coolly. "Although, we don't condemn such practices. You'd be surprised at the variety of rituals that are within a skilled Blood Mage's capability."

"It is quite the sight to see, indeed," Remi stated. She took a long drag from her pipe, slowly letting the burning leaves in the wooden basket sputter out before packing the instrument away. "I once met a fine young lad studying to become a warlock. It is quite a strange practice, depending on the school of magic the style is derived from. Though, it can be of some use if treated with respect. What was his name? Derrick? It may have been Devin, now that I think about it.

"But, yes. There are many types of magic, some of which Klaus and I know very little about, but none of them seem powerful enough to cause your perils." Remi shook her head emphatically. "No. Whatever plagues your mind is beyond us. It may be a dark future that awaits if you happen to follow the incorrect path. These visions may be a warning sent to you by the Sister of Compassion herself. They may even be a message from your god or gods to punish you for past crimes."

Will said he had nothing to do with the nightmares, but was he lying? No. It's got to be something—or someone—else. Chase took a deep, shaking breath before reaching for a bowl of breakfast stew. His nerves were slowly returning, but he still felt uneasy. This nightmare was the worst so far, and he feared they would only continue to get worse.

Thankfully, the warm stew lifted his spirits. A smile even crept across his face which made Remi's eyes shine with satisfaction. The rabbit meat, accompanied by thick cut carrots, potatoes, and celery, tasted better than anything Chase had eaten on the road before. Strange spices danced on his tongue and the aromatic herbs the Magi used cleared his head, wiping away some of the fear and anxiety from the previous night.

Chase wondered if he should tell his two new companions about his meetings with Will, Lucuis, or even the Man in Red. Something about Remi and Klaus eased his nerves. They seemed so genuine, and he wanted to believe they were being open and honest about their intentions, but a lingering apprehension tugged at him—warning him from sharing too much. *There's no guarantee they wouldn't claim I'm mad and leave me, anyway.*

They would just leave, anyway.

The thought echoed in Chase's mind, and for a moment he felt his heart race. He sipped more of his stew, smelling the food deeply to calm his sensitive nerves.

It's just the sleep. Carpenter's Hammer. When was the last time I slept through the night? I'm so tired.

Just need some sleep to clear my head...

Chase felt his head nod and his eyes close, but he jolted upright as Sasha broke the lingering silence. "Thank you." Contrary to her soft appearance, the woman was hardened by a life of honest work. "I don't know where you and your friend here call home, and I'm not sure I'm going to go believing anyone can live in the Dread Wastes. Magi have a reputation for telling tall tales." Remi smiled wryly and dipped her head in recognition. "Although, I do know you had no business helping me. So, thank you."

Sasha held out a hand expectantly. Chase rushed to return the gesture, nearly dropping his stew in the process. He felt heat rise in his cheeks while he shook the woman's hand, but she paid no mind to the fumble.

Richard slurped a spoonful of stew and laughed. "It was nothing, Miss Reinhart. We're happy to shelter a fellow traveler for a night."

"You didn't do nothing, you clouded pillock." Sasha shot him a sharp glare before looking back at Chase. "I'd be happy to go with you wherever your feet take you until I repay the favor, but I can't say I'd care to be gone so long from home. My father, Valric, owns a tavern in Redwood. One by the name of The Spit Pig, if you're familiar. Was on my way with a shipment for him, and it's best I get back and tell him what happened. The Smith knows he's going to set me to the pots for weeks after I burned his good cart, but it's what I get."

Sasha began to clamber to her feet, but Remi lifted a hand in protest. "Please, young lass. I insist you help yourself to some stew. I bought the rabbit from a hunter in Redwood named Geandrin and it really is exquisite—if you would excuse my boast."

The woman nodded. "Geandrin's a good hunter, if not as heavy headed as a drunken cow most days. Spoon me a bowl and I'll be on my feet. Just remember, you're all welcome at The Spit Pig any time you want. Mention me to the tender and I'll make sure you get a drink and a nice meal—on the house. Even this one." She waved her hand at Richard, which caused a wave of laughter among the group.

CHAPTER 16
A WORLD OF MAGIC

Chase slowly finished his breakfast, relieved at the lightened attitude around the fire. His aching joints felt like rusty hinges while he helped the others pack, but eventually the job was done all the same. They parted ways with Sasha to little pomp and circumstance, the young woman eager to return to her duties in Redwood.

I wonder if all Gallanders are as hardy as her. In the Berg it sometimes feels like folks are dragging along a weight, trudging from one thing to the next. There was so much spring in Sasha's step she was nearly bouncing.

After packing the horses and climbing in their saddles, the four men continued their casual ride onward. Hours went by filled with pleasant conversations before Remi looked over to Chase in the saddle of his beige mare. "How is your marking feeling, lad?"

Chase rubbed his face where—just the night before—it had glowed and burned white hot. A day later, it had returned to normal. "I'm fine. It's no different than the rest of me now; a bit sore, but no worse off for it. Thanks for asking, Remi."

"No trouble at all, lad," Remi smiled. Chase smiled back but didn't understand what she was up to. "I've noticed that a remarkable number of strange happenings and occurrences have surrounded you and your companion since the start of your journey. It is most interesting that two young men find themselves thrust into such strife."

"What are you playing at, Remi?" Richard interjected from a few strides ahead of them.

"Ah! Direct and to the point, lad! I must admit that I've been pondering your friend's dragonmark. I hope you both can understand. It is most fascinating, indeed!" Remi smiled as she continued. "I had a hunch previously, but the fine display by Chase last night confirmed my suspicions, or at the very least much of my curiosity. I believe Chase may have the capacity to manipulate toams."

"That's a bold claim, my friend," Klaus replied through a crooked smile.

Richard and Chase were both confused by the Magi's remarks, but Richard was the first one to inquire. "What the hell are you talking about? Is this more of that accursed magic talk?"

"Why, yes," Remi chuckled as she bounced up and down in her saddle. "It is! I believe Chase—through natural means or otherwise—may have gained the ability to manipulate the energy of the world around him, not unlike the Magi of Soule. I believe that is precisely the reason he was able to throw a cart weighing hundreds of pounds with as much effort as a child tossing a ball. I suspect the dragonmark serves as an indication that, with a fair amount of education and training, Chase could become a very powerful sorcerer. Of course, I may be wrong. Although, my suspicions are often correct in such matters."

Chase's mind swirled, growing hazy with each word the Magi said. He had only ever heard of magic and dragons in stories, but now—in the matter of a few days—Remi shared that not only was he somehow destined to become a dragon rider, but also that he may one day become some sort of wizard.

No matter how much Chase wanted to trust his new companions completely, a part of him still resisted. They were strangers, and in the Berg, strangers kept to themselves unless they wanted something from you. Even still, Remi and Klaus had shown them nothing but kindness. *All this just to possibly see a dragon...* "What's in it for you?" he finally asked.

Remi smiled but put her hand to her chest to feign offense. "I'm shocked you would accuse me of such tricks. Surely, my friend and I have been kind and informative—if not slightly imposing at times, for which I must apologize most dearly if you took offense. I must admit that I thought we must be past such distrust."

"We've only known you for a couple of days,"

Richard growled, sounding more resentful than he had intended to. "And in that time, you've told some pretty tall tales. Sasha said your people had a habit of that."

Klaus laughed. "And yet, the bear sleeps like a cub so far from his cave."

Richard grumbled a retort under his breath. But before anything came of it, Chase continued. "It's true. We get along well enough. But training a wizard or warlock or whatever you want to call it seems like it'll be a great deal of work. You know that I can't pay you for your services and I have nothing to my name beyond my weapons—even on my side of the mountains. And *those* will stay with me until I'm dead. So, what do you stand to gain by taking the time to train me in your ways of magic?"

A glint flashed in the stout woman's eye before Remi answered. "I was a teacher back in Soule. I truly enjoy the pursuit and passing of knowledge. Although, I must admit I find myself long winded at times as a result." Richard huffed while Klaus cracked a smile that said much the same. "I especially enjoy spreading the traditions of my people. Our ways seem strange to many on this side of the sea. The opportunity to spread my knowledge to someone from a world so far from my own is more than enough payment for me."

Chase struggled to see any deceit in the Magi's words. For so long he had been trained to never trust anyone outside the Burrow. Now, this seemingly kind-hearted stranger wanted to teach him something he had never even dreamed was possible. *Why should everyone be trying to get the better of me?*

His heart ached. Now that his eyes were open to life outside the Berg, he desperately wanted to believe the goodness he saw in these strangers was real. *If they really are this good at heart, what would that me for Richard and me...? Besides, becoming a wizard sounds like an enjoyable enough way to pass the time.*

"Ok. I'll do it."

Remi smiled from ear to ear with joy, but Richard scoffed and roared, "I can't believe you'd do this! You of all bloody people should know that no good can come from all this. Last time I checked, you didn't need magic to wedge that blade of yours between someone's ribs."

"True," Chase tried not to smile. "But what's the harm, really? It's not like we have much else to do in the evenings after we make camp. And if it *does* turn out that I can use magic like Remi claims I might, then I'll just have one more way to stick people in the ribs. I can't imagine Strongbrow would have gotten the better of me if I'd been able to throw a spell or two his way."

Richard groaned. "I suppose so but just know I want no bloody part of this. This whole damned trip is strange enough as it is without you waving your hands around conjuring Carpenter knows what. It's not natural."

"Noted."

As they continued their journey, songbirds of all sorts of shapes, sizes, and colors filled the trees around them. A pair of goldfinches fought over some thistle, reminding Chase of Richard and him, while the occasional squirrel or fox ran across the road from time to time. The gentle, cool breeze carried with it crisp air that almost seemed to wash away all his worries. Chase wasn't sure if it was his fantasies of conjuring lighting and fire and ice, or if it was simply the beautiful landscape that crept past him, but for the first time since leaving the Burrow, he felt hopeful.

That evening, after the camp had been constructed, the fire had been made, and the group had feasted on salted pork, hunks of aged yellow cheese, and a variety of root vegetables, Remi sat with Chase on the ground next to the campfire.

"In order for me to teach you the ways of the Magi, you first need to understand the foundations of our knowledge about the world around us," the sorceress said.

"Aye," Chase's mouth felt dry despite his full wineskin, and his stomach turned in nervous anticipation.

"You must know that this is only one type of magic. Magic itself is not as much a science as it is an art. While grounded in the realm of nature, magic varies widely from person to person. In fact, if Klaus were teaching you of these sorts of things, which I am certain he would find himself quite capable of doing so—if I know my friend as well as I think I do—the conversation would be quite different."

"Ha!" Klaus snorted with a twisted smile splashed across his face. "I'd be willing to teach you blood magic, but I'm sure you enjoy your blood in your body too much to partake." His tone grew more somber. "Besides, I'm not so sure you would be able to feel the flows to begin with."

Richard shuttered. "Why anyone in their right mind would lay a blade on their own flesh to conjure some sort of spell is beyond me."

"Some say the sensation is euphoric. If you ever find yourself in the company of a Drakthul for the night, don't be surprised if they approach the bed with a knife in their hand." Klaus laughed as he teased Richard. Chase always knew how to get under his friend's skin from time to time, but Klaus had a special talent for it.

"Drakthul are certainly a far cry from the worst company to enjoy a night with," Remi joked as she lit her pipe. "I once had the pleasure of meeting a woman that had escaped from the Orz'am, just south of Galland. She was vicious, yes. However, not in an altogether unpleasant manner, if I do say so myself. I believe her name was Anastasia. ...Although, it may have been Natasha."

Remi paused for a moment, lost in thought before returning her attention to her new pupil. "To return to the matter at hand. You must first understand how magic works to manipulate it; to walk before you can run, if you may. At the simplest level, the Magi are trained in manipulating the energy in the air around them. Everything you see is surrounded by countless tiny pieces, unseen by any human or beast. We Magi refer to these pieces as toams, and our school is focused on shaping their energy."

Richard snorted. "This sounds like some sort of

sick joke, Remi. Speckles that nobody can see? It's rubbish."

"Shut it, Richard," Chase snapped more than he wanted to. This all sounded strange, but everything Chase had heard in the past few weeks sounded strange. He couldn't take anything for granted anymore, and if Remi was telling the truth, then Chase wanted to listen very carefully. "Please, Remi. Continue."

The Magi shifted to a more comfortable position, rearranging the silk over her garments. She took a long drag from her pipe. "Right. To manipulate these toams, one must first learn how to sense them. At first, this is done through meditation. However, I've known some to feel them in other ways. It can be taught to those who cannot naturally feel them. Although, it is typically accepted that one must be sensitive to the toams to pursue training in their manipulations. Not everyone is fortunate enough to possess the necessary talents required to use our magic. In Soule, it is a common gift—while I would be so bold to guess that no person in The Dread Wastes has been able to do so for quite some time.

"Once a person has learned to feel the toams around them, they can bend the energy into something useful or deadly. Although, you must be aware that more powerful spells will take some time and practice to master. I've known many ill tidings to fall upon those who attempt to craft a spell beyond their own ability. It can consume the person completely, or it can leave them scarred or otherwise disfigured."

"I would imagine so," Chase replied politely. "And what sorts of things can a person do with these *toams*?"

Remi chuckled. "Nearly anything, if you have the ability and the knowledge. Of course, a healthy amount of imagination helps in some circumstances. Like this!" The mage held out her hand and spread her fingers out, her palm facing the sky. With the slightest twitch of her fingers, a globe of burning golden fire cracked into existence, floating above the woman's hand.

Richard leapt from his spot by the fire and shouted into the night. "Mother of all that's holy! Carpenter's Bloody Hammer, that's unnatural!"

"At least you believe it's real now," Klaus remarked through his sly, crooked smile. Richard huffed and returned to his seat at the fire while Remi closed her hand, causing the fire to vanish just as quickly as it had appeared.

Remi blew a ring of smoke from her mouth, seemingly lost in thought once again and suddenly more solemn than just moments before. "I must warn you, Chase. I cannot emphasize enough that every spell has its limit. While it may seem like you can theoretically do anything with our magic, every sorcerer knows that one must take the utmost care in showing restraint when bending the toams. They're wild and can often overcome the sorcerer with grave consequences. If you are unpracticed or otherwise unprepared, the toams may even swallow you whole. A training sorcerer must always grow their talents slowly and carefully."

Chase nodded silently, quietly contemplating the ramifications of the Magi's lesson.

Remi packed more dried leaves and herbs into her pipe. "While the magic from Soule may seem extraordinarily powerful, keep in mind its weaknesses and shortcomings. The Magi excel with a variety of practical problems, but we falter when it comes to the health and well-being of living creatures. The toams are simply ill fit for such matters.

"If the sorcerer cannot think it, they cannot do it, or so it is most simply stated. Living creatures are far too complex to make use of our skills. You can see that while I may be able to cauterize an open cut, there is a good chance I may cause drastic side effects if I were to attempt more than just that. Potions, alchemy, herbalism, and medicine are all more appropriate means of healing a wound, illness, or ailment. I have heard of some Elvari that practice healing by means of magic. However, I know little else of their druidism to speak on the matter further."

"And if you plan to bolster the harvest of a starving town somewhere along your travels," Klaus added. "Then you should leave it to someone else. Remi's style of magic may be flashy, but his thumb is far from green. Blood magic works well for that sort of thing in my experience."

Richard cringed at the thought of blood magic rituals, but Chase tried to stay focused. It was all a great deal to take in at once. *I feel like I'm a small child again learning the finer points of various blades and fighting styles.* He shifted slightly and tried to remain as attentive as he could with tired eyes and aching joints.

Remi wiped her brow with a small piece of teal colored silk and took a long puff from her pipe. "Klaus is right. I've also heard that Thornish rune shaping is particularly useful for imbuing magical properties into items. One could lose their entire life to the study and mastery of any one of these many crafts." Remi took a final puff from her pipe before setting it aside. "It's late. I don't want to overwhelm you with too much at once, if you don't mind me saying. This is quite a good start to your journey, but if you have further questions, ask. Even if you think they are foolish, ask. Better for you to feel embarrassed for a brief time than to feel what could be much worse if you don't fully understand the forces at play. For now, I think we all could use a good night's rest after such an exciting and thoughtful day."

With that, the group allowed themselves to relax for the remainder of the evening. Chase lay back in his cot and gazed at the brilliantly twinkling stars peeking through the branches of a nearby maple tree.

Similar to when he was a student in the Burrow, Chase silently reviewed Remi's lessons in his head a few times. But eventually, he simply listened to the sounds of the insects, owls, and other nocturnal animals while the wind shifted the trees back and forth. His muscles relaxed and the world around him slowly faded away to nothing.

CHAPTER 17
ON A BEETLE'S WINGS

Chase woke from another nightmare panting and damp with sweat. The malodorous stink of rotten eggs and charred wood hung in his nostrils, and he could feel the heat of fire licking his cheeks unpleasantly.

He opened his eyes, his vision blurring uncomfortably. When his eyes finally adjusted to the dim blue light of the morning, his heart nearly stopped in his chest—the Man in Red stood a mere ten paces away in the shade of a gnarled, aged oak tree.

Chase furiously blinked his eyes, rubbing the soreness away with shaking hands.

The Man in Red vanished only to reappear sitting at their smoldering fire, laughing maniacally at nothing. Chase's mind raced and his heart thudded in his ears like a horse's hooves in full gallop. The Man in Red flashed a wicked, wretched smile.

In an instant, Chase was back in burning town square surrounded by death and despair. An instant later, it was gone—and he was sitting, staring at the fire beside his friend.

He took a deep, steadying breath and looked up. The sky had grown dark and gray. The air felt thick and damp against his face and the wet smell of the coming rain replaced the awful stench from moments before. Chase glanced at Richard, glad that they had risen before their companions. He wiped the sweat from his brow and sighed.

Richard looked at his ragged friend. "Are you okay, mate?"

Chase stretched his arms slowly. The aching burn of tense muscles felt nice, even if it was a reminder of how little sleep he had gotten since they left the Burrow. He cracked his neck and replied with a weak smile. "Never been better."

His mind lingered on the question.

I should tell him. This is all my fault, and he never had a choice. What if something happens to him? Will said there is always a choice, but Richard didn't get one.

He gazed at his oldest friend across the fire and saw the pain that Richard failed to hide.

No. Not now. I can't tell him now. It's not the right time. Soon, though. I'll tell him soon—when he doesn't have so much to worry about.

Chase realized he had been silent for far too long. "How are you, Richard? Ever since this journey started, I've noticed our conversations have grown increasingly one-sided."

"Ha," Richard snorted as he stoked the red-hot coals in the makeshift fire pit. "You don't worry yourself about me. I'm not the one whose face is all painted up with a marked soul or some such nonsense."

"You don't believe them?" Chase asked. He couldn't deny he had doubts about Remi's various claims, but they had crossed the Blackridge Mountains—mountains that only one other man had ever crossed. Surely if that were possible, other things should be as well.

"I don't know what the bloody hell to believe anymore, Chase," Richard answered. He let out a long sigh and rubbed his temples in frustration. It was astonishing how much he had changed in such a short time. Chase could see deep, dark bags under his eyes and his blonde hair was matted and tangled.

Richard spit on the ground next to him. "Every day we see something or something happens to us that just doesn't make any sense. Maybe dragons are real, and maybe you can make your face glow. Maybe pigs can fly, and fairies exist. I don't know what the hell to think."

Chase nodded. He didn't know what else he could say. Richard was right. Before setting out from the Burrow, neither of the travelers would've ever believed in such tall tales as dragons and magic. Now, it seemed they were living in one. Chase's voice caught in his throat for a moment. "...And what do you think about Remi teaching me magic?"

"It's bloody unnatural, but I don't suppose I can say anything that will change your damned mind." His voice was cold and harsh, bitter resentment laced in every word. "I saw the look in your eyes, mate. You want it too badly." Richard shivered and poked the hot coals again even though it was clearly unnecessary.

Chase's stomach twisted uncomfortably. For a moment, he thought of reaching a hand to his friend's shoulder, but he folded his hands in his lap when he realized how silly the gesture would feel. "Think of all the good I can do," Chase finally answered.

He couldn't think of anything else to say. He couldn't blame Richard for the skepticism. He couldn't blame him for the animosity, either. Enough had happened to them both in the last few weeks to justify all the harsh feelings in the world.

"Good?" Richard nearly choked as he stumbled over a laugh. "You're an assassin, remember? And a damned ruthless one too, *Mr. Shadow.* Are you sure the beating from that bloke in the tombs didn't knock a few things lose?"

Chase didn't answer. He always knew what to say in these kinds of moments—always had the right quip or joke to lighten the mood. It made him come across as heartless in the past, but the reality was that he just found it easier to deal with the grim realities of his life that way. *I wish Richard could smile now… Carpenter knows nothing I say will make it better right now.*

I should tell him.

Chase knew the longer the waited the harder it

would be, but he couldn't bring himself to admit to his friend that *his* choice was the reason they were stuck here so far from home. It was the reason they were running off in pursuit of dragons and magic. And it was the reason they weren't going home any time soon.

What if he just… leaves?

Ice washed over Chase, and the color drained from his face. Richard must have realized something was wrong because he looked about to break the silence when Remi climbed out of her ornate, gold-trimmed tent.

When the time is better. Then I'll tell him.

Remi had just begun preparing the party's breakfast of dry biscuits covered in pork sausage and gravy when Klaus emerged from his own black canvas tent. In the dim light of the cloudy morning, Klaus looked even paler than normal in contrast to his dark hair, shimmering and swaying back and forth. He yawned and stretched before sitting down at the fire, eagerly awaiting the hot meal.

Chase swallowed the lump in his throat, glad to have the distraction of food to keep his mind off more troubling matters for the time being.

Once they had their fair share of breakfast, and their bellies were full and warm, Chase and Richard began to pack their belongings when Klaus interrupted. "You shouldn't bother, young ones. I suspect you'd rather not spend the next few days riding in the rain—or weeks for that matter. Although, seeing you two so waterlogged would be quite endearing."

"My companion is correct," Remi added as she sat back and took out her pipe. "Here in Galland, when it rains, it rains hard and continues for days. Sometimes weeks. It's worse south of The Harp, of course. I once stayed at an inn called The Dancing Mare in Glarrus when a particularly bad storm swept over the river from the north. Or was it The Jumping Mare?" Remi stared into the fire momentarily before she shivered slightly, snapping her attention back to the two foreigners. "Anyway, my tab was nearly seventy gold herons by the time the rain relented. I had hoped that we might arrive at Haven soon, but it would be far more foolish to try traveling amid a storm."

"How exactly do you suggest Chase and I stay dry then?" Richard snapped. "We don't have big, fancy tents like you. Klaus doesn't even have suitable shelter if the rain is as bad as you say it'll be."

Klaus' lips curled into a smile as he softly spoke. "So mistrusting, little bear cub."

Richard mumbled to himself, seemingly embarrassed at his own guarded response.

Remi lit the freshly packed tobacco in her pipe and took a few short puffs before responding to Richard's concern. "Don't worry. I can most certainly take care of that for us. In any event, it may be good for us to spend time together without the troubles of riding. Riding always seems the most favorable method of travelling until you have managed to rent a wagon. Much more comfortable in my experience. The horses should be fine as well. I'll make sure they stay dry and the two of you can feed them daily. Now, up. Yes, up. Get moving, you two."

Chase and Richard clambered to their feet and watched while Remi faced the campsite. Without explanation or warning, she raised her arm in the air, arching it over her head from one side to the other with her palm facing the fire. A moment later, the ringing sound of a single metallic drum beat erupted from midair, and a shimmer of light flashed across the camp. At the right angle, Chase could faintly see the outline of a transparent dome that covered the camp.

"Right. All set then." Remi clapped her hands and puffed at the pipe in the corner of her mouth.

Chase and Richard didn't know how to react, but Klaus nonchalantly reentered the campsite, walking through the dome as if nothing happened.

They followed reluctantly, but to Chase's surprise, nothing happened. Once they reached the smoldering fire and sat on the ground Chase turned to Remi. "What did you do? I thought I saw something, but it doesn't feel like anything changed. I can barely even see it anymore."

"A simple barrier," Remi smiled cheerfully. "They're quite easy to conjure and require very little effort. The toams in the air dance when various things flow through them. I simply altered them slightly to provide us with a barrier that will block any rain from falling on this spot. After we have a better fire pit, I'll do the same for the horses. We wouldn't want them to be waterlogged or to come down with an illness. I quite like this horse of mine, and it would pain me greatly to cause it unnecessary ill will."

"You sure it will work?" growled Richard skeptically.

"I'll tell you what, little cub," Klaus replied in his cool, even, and sarcastic tone. "You can be the first one to let us know if we spring a leak. I'm sure you'll be fine with a little rain."

Chase snorted louder than he wanted to, receiving a glare that could cut stone from the other Bergman. Ever since they had mistakenly shared their assassin aliases, Klaus couldn't help but tease Richard relentlessly with his moniker. *It's somewhat charming if you think about it, but Richard's pride does get in the way sometimes.* Chase glanced at Klaus only to see a certain, unmistakable glint in his eyes. *Then again, maybe* that's *the problem.*

At the behest of their guides, they gathered some of the larger rocks from around the camp to build a more permanent fire pit. Richard and Remi dug a shallow basin in the ground before carefully stacking the rocks in a ring around it. Meanwhile, Chase and Klaus gathered dry wood as fast as they could before the rain started. With weary arms silently screaming in protest, Chase shook his head at Remi. "Why don't you just use a spell or two and build the pit that way? Wouldn't it be faster and easier on us all?"

The weathered mage returned the look with a solemn expression. "Let this be your first lesson of the day. The day a sorcerer relies more on magic than their own hands is the day they lose everything. Magic is a wonderful and powerful thing, and Magi perform a particularly practical form of it, but it's important for each person to continue their lives using magic *sparingly*. Humanity, as taught by the wisest Magi in all of Soule, is the practice of human deeds. Tales from long ago speak of Magi elders that once devoted themselves completely to bending the toams.

"The sorcerers slowly lost themselves, and one by one the elders turned to stone where they sat in the Soulesian National Library. They were so consumed by power that the elders never tried to avoid their fate. They wrote that it was their rightful ascension, and that from the grave, they would continue to transcribe the knowledge they'd gain and provide guidance to all those who sought it. Sadly, once the last elder turned to stone, no books were written and those who wished for guidance were left wanting.

"Today, those statues still stand at the center of the library as a reminder to all those who practice magic. Toams provide us with power we use to shape the world, but they also can consume even the wisest of minds. The Magi are urged to use magic as a tool, not the entire tool belt. So, we work by hand when possible and use spells to grant us those things that we cannot easily obtain. It is a balance that was not stricken without a great deal of loss."

"I knew this magic business was not to be trusted," Richard insisted. "Chase, you're going to turn yourself into a rock."

"At least it'll be a pretty rock," Chase teased in reply, trying to mask his own concerns with a confident smile. "You'd better not try it though, mate. That'd be a mighty ugly stone. People around the world would gather and songs would be sung about the Boulder Beast of the Berg."

Klaus swiftly and calmly replied before Richard could get his own retort in. "This is no laughing matter, young ones. I've traveled to Soule and have seen those statues. The process of turning flesh to stone seems to be a painful one."

Chase and Richard immediately grew silent. The thought was sobering.

The gentle pitter-patter of rain began to fall on the trees around them. Chase was surprised to see that the barrier Remi had conjured was working exactly like the Magi said it would. Rain seemingly landed on a sheet of invisible glass before running down the side of the large, unseen dome that surrounded them.

Remi startled as she noticed the rain and broke the silence. "Ah, but those are tales of a history long ago. There has not been a case of any reasonable person losing themselves to the toams in a long time. And with the proper tutelage, there is nothing to concern yourself over. Some Magi insist those statues were carved by human hands to scare students into acting responsibly. However, I have read plenty of texts that presume otherwise. Now, I must ensure the horses stay nice and dry." Remi's voice lowered, and her expression grew somber. "Please, do not dwell on ghosts of the past. We have plenty of work to do."

Remi tended to the horses while the others tidied the campsite. Chase forced any thoughts of magical catastrophe from his mind, just as he had pushed any thoughts of death from his mind when training to become an assassin. If he wanted to learn the Magi's sorcery, he would need a clear head free from reservations.

After a brief respite, Remi filled a stone pot with rainwater from outside the camp's barrier and placed it directly in the hot coals of the fire. She withdrew a handful of chopped, dried tea leaves along with fragrant, unfamiliar spices. Cinnamon, cloves, nutmeg, and a particularly strange, peppery spice known to the Magi as daemon's tongue filled the air with a pleasantly rich aroma.

Remi returned her attention to Chase. "Are you ready for your first practical lesson? I understand if you are not, lad. And I can assure you—I would not judge you in the slightest if that were the case. We're about to embark on a journey few of your people could ever imagine, and once that journey begins, I'm afraid there will be no turning back. You cannot put the djinn back in the bottle, so to speak."

Richard nearly barked as he took his first bite from a lump of bread. "You sure you want to do this, Chase? I got a wretched feeling in my gut about this magic nonsense. Men of the Berg like us were never meant to wield the power of gods."

"Afraid he might get you wet, little cub?" Klaus smiled while Richard's cheeks flushed behind his newly growing beard.

Chase looked at his friend and his concern swelled.

He may have been taking the worse beating over their travels, but his friend didn't look much better. Richard's eyes had sunken with crow's feet formed at their corners. His cheeks were gaunter, and his brow was furrowed more than it was not. He rubbed his rough, dirty hands absentmindedly, scowling into the fire deep in thought.

Chase rubbed his own cheek and felt the coarse black stubble. "I'm sure, mate. I might be able to get by without it, but if my life's going to be filled with the troubles of dragons and magic, then I should be prepared. When I stop to think about it, considering everything that's happened to us, I see how different our journey might have been if I had magic on my side." He turned to his new mentor. "I'm ready whenever you are, Remi."

"Right," Remi eagerly rubbed her hands together. She poured the tea that had been brewing into four smaller mugs and gave one to each of the travelers, keeping one for herself. After blowing on the steaming drink and taking a small sip to ensure it had been brewed correctly, she continued. "In order to control the toams, it stands to reason you must first learn to feel the toams around you. Magi are normally told how to do this from a very young age, but it makes no difference for you. If I may be so bold, I strongly suspect that you will have no great issue once we begin. If I am indeed correct, we'll be able to move on to our next lesson in no time."

"So… where do I start?" Chase asked while Remi took a long sip from her tea. As he waited for an answer, he took a drink of his own. The warmth of the tea filled his chest pleasantly and the tastes of the spices danced on his tongue, the heat of the peppery daemon's tongue swelling in his throat.

"Sit calmly, with your mind open to all

possibilities," Remi finally responded. "And close your eyes. Try to focus on one thing, as small as you can imagine, and then think of something smaller. Continue to imagine things smaller and smaller, beyond what you believe is natural, and eventually you'll find the toams hanging in the world around you. Once you see the toams, try to reach out with your mind to touch them. Only once you can mentally hold onto the toams can you finally begin to move and bend them, but it will be quite some time before you are able to do something such as that."

"And take care not to bite off more toams than you can chew," Klaus added in his cool tone. "If you are lucky, you'll be stopped by your abilities before any real harm comes from it, but it's still nothing to be trifled with."

Chase nodded. He swallowed the lump that had formed in his throat. *Am I sweating? No. That must be the fire… or the tea.* He closed his eyes, but his mind continued to race. *It's definitely the tea. That's why I feel so damn warm.*

And itchy.

Why are my clothes itchy?

He took a long, deep breath counting backward from ten in his head. It was a simple trick the Black Blades taught their initiates to clear their minds to get ready for a kill. It only worked sometimes, but to Chase's relief it seemed to be enough. Soon, his racing heart slowed, and his mind became quiet.

At this point, I'll be relieved if nothing happens and happy if whatever does happen doesn't kill me.

Chase thought of a beetle that had been buzzing nearby and saw the creature in his mind, as clear as day. It had a vibrant, shining blue carapace with a large, twisted horn. He began to think of something smaller, fixating on the beetle's wing as it twitched and flapped. Each individual transparent fiber of the wing shined in the light of the fire.

Suddenly, it all started coming to him far too quickly. He could see the joint where the wing joined the body of the beetle. Then, he saw a speck of dust settled on the joint. He saw the ridges on the speck's surface, and then a single misshapen blob that seemed to consume other, smaller shapes as it wiggled through space.

His mind raced faster and faster—deeper and deeper—until he saw a single glowing orb of light, hanging in a vast empty space. Chase wanted desperately to stop and retreat from his vision, but he was no longer in control. The toam shimmered and swirled with brilliant, golden light—almost like it was alive—calling him to come closer.

In a moment of serene calm, Chase felt the urge to reach out and touch the orb.

Without warning, his mind dove into the toam. Pain screamed across his every thought. He tried to let go, but he couldn't find a way to release it. The longer he ventured inside the orb, the more intense the pain became until he screamed, the sound echoing as if from somewhere far away.

In that moment, there was nothing else.

There was only the searing, white-hot pain that

threatened to swallow him whole.

And Chase surrendered to it.

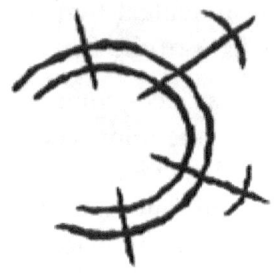

CHAPTER 18
STARTING WITH A BANG

Just as suddenly as it had all started, Chase was yanked from his vision. He panted heavily, sweat dripping from his brow and pain surging through his mind. Once his senses returned, Chase stared across the fire.

Remi sat with a thoughtful gaze while she twisted the end of her braid. Her expression held equal amounts of curiosity and excitement, a smile shining in the firelight.

"What the hell was that, Remi?" Chase asked between ragged breaths. "My entire body is on fire, and I saw some sort of glowing orb. And the orb drew me in or something, but something threw me out. Was that supposed to happen? Is that what other people see? Carpenter's Hammer, I can't stop shaking."

Remi took a long puff from her pipe. "Interesting.

I suspected you had great potential, but it seems as though I underestimated you. It takes most Magi many years of meditation before they can see a toam, let alone venture toward it. There have been cases to the contrary, of course. Some of the more gifted sorcerers in Soule begin to manipulate toams immediately. You don't seem there quite yet, but it appears that you're close. Very interesting."

"So, explain then, sorceress," Richard scolded. "Why is it that Chase was thrown out of his trance, or whatever that was? If he's so gifted, shouldn't he be casting spells now or something?"

"Does a child run on the first day they learn to walk?" Klaus remarked. Chase saw Richard flush again, but the comment was met with much less grumbling than those before.

"The toams are the smallest form of energy in the natural world, or so we suspect," Remi replied, unaffected by Richard's remarks. "And it is altogether unwise for someone to attempt entering one, as I suspect our friend just did. They are motes of energy. It would be as useless as trying to walk inside a boulder. I can assure you both—the simple fact that Chase managed to see and approach a toam is quite remarkable."

Remi took another drag from her pipe. "Chase. You must work on slowing your descent toward the toam—at least until you are more comfortable interacting with them. In time, you'll be able to call upon the toams without thought or effort. But, you still have quite a way until then, if you don't mind me saying.

"I assign you this as your next task. Continue to meditate on the toams, but do not reach out to them until you are ready. For now, practice working your way down to the toams slowly, and then coming back to this spot. When you feel yourself becoming more comfortable with this, you'll be able to do it easier and faster. Then, when you can call out to them in an instant and without excessive effort, we will begin bending the toams to suit your needs."

Chase nodded in reply, despite a sour look from his friend. *Trust me, Richard. If this works it will be best for us both.* Chase knew his guides would insist on staying right where they were until the last drops of water hit the ground and the sun shined in the sky. The thought of waiting with little more to do than sitting with his thoughts made him shiver. *If nothing else, it will be a nice distraction. Besides, the rain should end soon.*

The rain would not end soon.

Chase spent the next six days in near constant meditation. Remi had insisted that he do so and that the others would tend to the camp in his stead. Chase only stopped meditating to eat surprisingly diverse meals and to sleep—although, he was not particularly fond of the latter. He was still plagued by his nightmares, but practicing Remi's meditation helped keep him focused. On a few more occasions, Chase's mind slipped again resulting in a great amount of pain, but it had been three days since that had happened, and he could now see the glowing toams in a manner of seconds.

On the seventh day, after eating a breakfast of biscuits and spiced apple preserves with a pot of spiced tea, Remi stopped Chase from beginning his daily meditations. Rain still fell upon Remi's invisible boundary before sliding to the ground. The earth around the site was thick with mud while many of the nearby trees sagged or drooped to one side from the constant battering of wind. A thick, wet odor hung in the air just like it had for the last week.

Chase looked back at his mentor in eager anticipation. Learning and training brought back memories of when he was a student in the Black Blades. It filled him with a sense of vigor that had been vacant since they had been banished from the Burrow. Bittersweetly, it reminded him of the few things he missed from his home. When he thought back to those days, he couldn't help the pang of regret in his chest, but he tried to swallow his misgivings and focus on the task at hand.

"Now that you are comfortable with meditation," Remi instructed while the fire crackled in the pit next to her, "you must learn to feel the energy of the toams without it. If a Magi had to meditate each time they needed a flame, the flame would be useless—as good flint and steel would serve just as well. You know the feeling of the toams by now, Chase. Search for that feeling at your fingertip." Remi reached for her pot and filled it with rainwater, but instead of placing the kettle on the fire, she placed it on the ground in front of Chase.

"Gently nudging the toams is easier that bending them completely. Fire can be easy for some, but it is quite risky to conjure flames for your first few attempts. For each spell, carefully consider its cost. Remember, you must never reach beyond your own means to craft a spell beyond your abilities. It can be dangerous if not properly considered."

Chase nodded in acknowledgement. "...Is that all? Is there anything... else I need to be worried about?" *This is it. No going back now.*

"Only what Klaus and I have warned you about since you have started," Remi firmly nodded. "Now, since feeling the toams and bending them are so connected, I'm afraid it's nearly impossible to teach one without the other. This is one of the numerous drawbacks of our craft. When you sense the toams' energy at your fingertips, let it flow through you. *Feel* the toams as if they are a part of you, or they will never listen.

"Then, you must picture *precisely* what you want them to do. It is imperative that you know exactly what you want, down to the finest details. Otherwise, there will most certainly be unwanted consequences to your spell. A good mental image with strong intent is key to success. Without either, the effects could range from harmless to disastrous."

Klaus drank slowly from his morning tea. "It is quite common for young magicians across the world to oversimplify their spells. An apprentice blood mage may think they're enriching a field's soil to provide more fertile land, but in overlooking one aspect of their incantation, they can poison the entire crop."

"Precisely," Remi agreed, nodding her head excitedly. She took a puff from her pipe before returning her attention to Chase. "Once you have a clear image, perform a gesture to match your desire. If the toams are flowing through you and your intentions are clear in your mind to the finest details, then I'm certain it will come naturally. It doesn't matter what the motion is, and the gesture does not need to be unique nor consistent, but it *must* be present. This is what prevents a Magi from releasing their energy by mistake."

"If it weren't the case," Klaus remarked, "every time a Magi sorcerer thought about fire, the room around them would burst into flames. We wouldn't want you to singe the hairs off our little cub now, would we?"

Richard snorted, but Chase saw the slightest trace of a smile on his old friend's mouth. Chase returned his gaze to his mentor. "So, I feel it, think it, and then do it? Seems simple enough."

Remi laughed as she shook her head. "In so few words, yes. These are the three components to every Magi spell. Start slowly with this pot of water. Change it in some way that's unique so that we may observe when you have completed your task. I do not care what you chose to do, so long as it does not hurt any of us, of course." She chuckled, climbing to her feet and brushing the dirt from her yellow dyed leathers. "Come, now. You must begin. There's only so much time in a day."

Chase nodded in agreement and stared at the water in the kettle. He had to envision his spell first. Once he created a clear mental image, he reached out for the toams around the water with his mind. He felt himself slipping into meditation, like he had done so many times over the past week, but Chase resisted the urge and focused.

Nothing happened.

He concentrated as hard as he could, but he still couldn't feel a thing. The energy in the air was as invisible as it had always been, and for a moment Chase thought it would always be that way. *Maybe this was a waste of time after all. Maybe Remi was wrong about me...*

Chase took a steady, deep breath. *No. I can't give up so quickly.* With stubborn determination, Chase did the only thing he could. He sat, and he practiced.

Remi chimed in on occasion to give Chase advice, but progress was slow. Much to his frustration, Chase slipped back into meditation a few times, but when that happened, Remi gave him a small cup of spiced tea to warm his chest and revitalize his spirit. The hours slipped by, and soon the companions were gathered close by the fire to enjoy a meal of salted pork and potato stew.

The broth warmed Chase's belly—a welcomed reprieve on such a cold, damp day. Between spoonfuls of stew, Chase looked across the fire at his guides before clearing his throat. "You mentioned the Magi and Drakthul practice their own forms of magic. You also said something about Azalea, the Elvari... and the Thornish. Are there more?"

Remi smoothed her silk wrappings before answering thoughtfully through her thick accent. "Nearly all peoples in the world hold their own traditions dear to them. It's often said that when the tribes of old wandered the lands, they discovered magic in all its many forms. Passed on in stories and then eventually through the written word, magic became more refined and sophisticated over time.

"Some crafts, such as sorcery and crystal singing, are now honored by many while others…" Remi paused for a moment, struggling to find the right words before giving up on the thought altogether. She smiled and tried to shift the subject. "Many people go so far as to honor their families or their gods with their magic."

"And don't fool yourself, young one," Klaus added beneath his black, brimmed hat. "Not everyone has such a positive attitude toward magic like Remi and myself. In my own lands, many of the common folk condemn the ritualistic practice of blood magic. They prefer a more conservative approach to our craft. Crops, safeguards, and wellness—only the holiest of practices for our people."

"What sorts of rituals do you mean?" Richard inquired.

Richard was slowly coming around to the idea of magic in his own ways. He was asking questions, and the scowl he had been wearing for most of the last few days was softening. Chase smiled at his old friend. *Thanks, mate.*

Klaus smirked. His words slid from his lips like a cool stream. "Many of the young ones in Talvenna like to romanticize the bloodletting required for our magic. Many take it upon themselves to display these rituals in places that others consider far too public. It's a particular sticking point for most people during the harvest season."

Richard reflected on the words carefully before

responding. "I don't get it. What do you mean by ritual? What do they do?"

"Use your imagination, lad," Remi answered, tapping her nose with her finger with a glimmering smile that made Richard visibly recoil. "I'm told it can be quite the sight to behold, indeed." She turned to her friend. "I must admit, even I grow flush in the cheeks at some of the things one can see in Talvenna during the harvest season. It's all in good fun, I can assure you, and I would never dare to suggest that Klaus' people should not feel empowered to practice their magic in whatever ways they deem appropriate. Alas, it is not to my taste. I am perfectly content keeping my blood precisely where it should be."

Klaus smirked. "I always found it all quite amusing, although I tend to keep my private matters to myself." He shot a keen glance at Richard, the hungry gleam in his eye returning. Klaus gestured suggestively to his tent. "Of course, if you desire further demonstration…"

Richard's cheeks nearly glowed bright red above his scraggly beard as he fumbled on his words. "N-no thanks, mate. Think I got the idea."

Remi chuckled before returning her attention to Chase. "To answer your question, lad, there are too many types of magic to explain them all. Some are well known and praised throughout all the countries of the world, while others are secret.

"One can only assume, given the proliferation of such things, that the Valen have their own mystical artform—for example. But sadly, they shun outsiders and guard their ways fiercely." Remi thought for a moment and perked slightly, as if realizing something obvious. "In fact, I'm sure even your own people across the Ardent Rise have some forgotten art, lost over the many centuries of neglect and mystery."

Chase stared at the fire pit, allowing the last spoonfuls of stew to rest within his stomach. He waited until the warmth had settled in his belly and he collected his thoughts before he replied. "I highly doubt anything as unbelievable as this could come from the Berg..." Chase paused for a moment. "So, what *can* you tell us? You're aware Richard and I know very little beyond our lives in Rakksberg. For as long as either of us have lived, we thought the Great Sea was the only thing on this side of the Blackridge Mountains. Just knowing we aren't alone in the world is still a shock, but I'd still like to know more."

Remi set her empty bowl by her side and began preparing her tobacco pipe. She packed the dry, brown leaves and herbs into the wooden pipe. "To the north of Galland, in the country called Azalea, their magicians sing their songs into the land around them. I am unsure exactly how their magic works, and I've never personally met an Azalean willing to divulge their secrets, but the results are stunning. They sing crystals from the earth to create magnificent things. It's said that the flower folk of Azalea are among the most artistic and talented builders in the world."

"Legends say that the azaleas and wildflowers are what give the flower folk their strength," Klaus added. "I've even heard tales of crystal singers drawing in those who are listening, in a sort of trance that can be intoxicating to those who hear it."

Remi nodded in agreement before taking a long drag from her pipe—white smoke falling from her lips. "Not much is known of the Orz'am south of here, but there are the beast men of Black Rock, near my own homeland…" Remi's expression steadily changed from her normal, thoughtful, and peaceful stare to a scowl. "Their shamans conduct rituals to empower their tribes. They congregate in massive camps to construct bonfires with each passing full moon before doing all sorts of terrible, unspeakable things to each other. It's a barbaric and disgusting practice. Truly sickening."

Chase and Richard were equally taken aback by Remi's harsh response. They looked at one another, lost for words, trying to silently probe for an appropriate reply.

Klaus saw their discomfort and continued before the moment of silence drew on longer than it needed to. His voice was as smooth as glass, but he did not smile, and he did not laugh. "You must understand, young ones. My old friend speaks from her heart. For longer than either of us have been alive, the Magi of Soule have been at war with the Beasts of Black Rock. There has been much bloodshed, and they will be much more still."

Richard chimed in with his gruff tone. "If the Magi can conjure up bloody fireballs and Carpenter knows what else, how could anyone stand a chance in a fight?"

Anger flared in Remi's eyes until she seemed to realize her emotions were getting the better of her. She took a long, deep breath and sighed. "It is simple, lad. Their magic is known as nullification magic, or rather just *null*. Nobody knows for certain how they do it, but it seems to affect all kinds of magic. Their shamans can reach out and cut off your ties to your magic in an instant, leaving you to rely on your other skills in battle." Remi looked off in the distance pondering a memory from long ago. "It makes for a difficult conflict."

As Remi's words trailed off, Chase wondered what he might do with his magic. His mind wandered to all the people that had fallen victim to his blades. He was an assassin and a shadow, but was that really *him?* The tiny part of him buried somewhere deep in his mind that reveled in the thrill of a kill had always sickened him, and the triumph he felt when saving Sasha felt blinding in comparison.

So where does that leave me?

To his dismay, his thoughts then lingered on the Man in Red. Ever since his nightmares started, everything seemed to come back to the Man in Red—always. He was always there to remind him what darkness lay inside him.

Lost in thought, Chase couldn't help but reflect on the odd passageway within the Blackridge Mountains. It may not have been where his journey started, but it was certainly the day everything had changed so much. He remembered the conversations he had with Will and Lucius, burned into his memories like hot coals. He remembered the eyeless, chained man with his haunting stare and the skeleton on sitting on the throne, whispering words that flowed like a chilling breeze.

Chase snapped back to their conversation. "Is there magic that can bring the dead back to life?"

Remi and Klaus froze. It was like the question had knocked the wind from them. A moment of silence hung in the air before Remi answered. "There are those who practice that darkest form of magic, yes. Necromancy is condemned by nearly all magicians as evil and unnatural. Even the savage Beast-men spit at those who seek to raise the dead. We are not meant to linger in the world after our day has come."

Richard blurted out before he could stop himself. "Who practices it, then? If it's so damned awful, then—"

"The damnable Shishussan in the mountains of Shi, that's who!" Klaus shouted, his cool voice sharpening while his pale skin flushed. His usual calm and collected tone had left him, replaced by desperate hostility. "Many fear me simply because my people bleed themselves, but at least blood magic is used to provide *life*. We sacrifice our own life's blood to provide for those around us while those death crazed necromancers in the mountains continue to raise corpses from the soil behind their city walls!"

This time, Remi was the one to calm her companion. "Those people you're referring to have no love for the Shishussan necromancers, my friend." She looked at Chase and ended the conversation. "We must not speak of terrible things such as war and necromancy any longer. Shi is home to a dark and distrustful people. That is enough talk of magic for today. You must continue with your practice, Chase.

And the rest of us shall begin to clear the camp site. I predict the rain will halt in a few days. When it does, we should be on our way."

The tight pang of guilt coiled around Chase like a binding. His companions must know they had no intention of causing such a stir, but Chase's throat tightened all the same. He couldn't say he blamed their strange guides. He and Richard were no strangers to people assuming the worst about them, but the Blades *wanted* their ill reputation to carry on throughout the Berg. Remi and Klaus were clearly good meaning people. Chase had no idea magic could cause so much pain without a single spell being cast.

He licked his dry lips nervously before awkwardly returning his attention to the kettle of water on the ground in front of him. He practiced over and over without success. It was much harder to manipulate the toams than Chase had hoped it would be. An acrid frustration rose higher in his gut with each failed attempt to shape the toams into something else. A few times, he could feel the energy at his fingertips, but it quickly faded, and Chase was left staring at the still water sitting in the black kettle.

On the third day of practice, Chase sat with his kettle. *This is just a massive waste of time. Remi must have been wrong about whatever she saw in me.*

The pitter-patter of rain was getting lighter by the hour, and the air didn't feel quite as heavy as it did the day before. Chase closed his eyes and took a deep breath through his nose. The air felt clean. It washed away his uncertainties and filled him with stubborn resolve.

He formed a mental image of his spell and attempted once again to reach out and feel the energy of the toams around the water. At first, he was certain his efforts would end as they always had over the last few days. But suddenly—he felt something.

Chase struggled to stay calm and focused, but rather than losing the energy and failing like he had grown accustomed to, he felt the toams dragging him along the way. They danced on his skin, playfully inviting him to join them. It was almost like they were even more excited about the possibilities in front of them than he was.

He focused intently on the mental image of his spell. Heart beating in his ears, he clenched his shaking hand into a fist.

A massive bang rang through the trees.

Everyone jumped as the water in the kettle exploded with sound. Chase scrambled to his feet, checking himself for any holes that weren't there moments before. It was only after Richard tapped his shoulder that he looked down at a peculiar sight.

The water had erupted from the pot, rapidly freezing into a jagged and twisted shard, reaching to the sky above. Chase looked up at Remi with a broad smile. "I did it! Carpenter's Bloody Hammer, I actually *did* something. For a while there, I didn't think it was going to work, but it did!"

Remi put her tea on the ground next to her and smiled. "That certainly seems to be the case, lad. An interesting choice of spell, I must say. I know that I have little affinity for ice and cold, but even still, I would have chosen to boil the water by heating the toams in the air around the kettle. It is generally much easier to excite the toams than it is to calm them. Very interesting."

"You're just full of surprises, little shadow," Klaus remarked through his crooked smile.

"Will the spells he casts always be so...violent?" Richard asked. Concern and fear laced his every word despite his best efforts.

Remi chuckled with a warm smile. "No, no, no. Of course not. With practice and discipline, I am quite optimistic our new apprentice will keep his craft well under his control. After all, I've seen less talented sorcerers than Chase manage to do that much at the very least. There was a boy—I seem to recall his name was Maj or Taj—that would trip over his own boots if he didn't pay enough attention. And yet, he learned to create wonderful images seemingly out of thin air. The spells Chase crafts should be no more violent than mine in due time."

"Unless, of course," Klaus added coolly. "Our shadow wants them to be."

Chase dwelled on the thought. It was true—the idea of using this magic as a weapon constantly lingered in his mind. It was impossible not to consider the possibilities given the dangers they had faced recently. Chase half expected to feel something from that tiny part of him he tried so hard to ignore, but to his relief it was silent.

If it had been only a few months prior, Chase probably would have accepted this gift as just another weapon, helping him to do what needed to be done to survive. It would have been nothing more than an instrument to carry out contract after contract, just as he was—a tool.

But now? It was hard to explain.

I know who... I know what I was. Death will follow me whether I want it to or not. But still... Chase looked down at his hand, flexing his fingers, expecting something strange to happen. *Something is different now.* The part of him that roared after saving Sasha hummed in warm satisfaction.

I am different.

Chase finally returned Klaus' gaze and smiled. "I suppose they could be. We'll just have to wait and see."

CHAPTER 19
WHEN PREDATORS BECOME PREY

Chase eagerly returned to his kettle of twisted ice and continued practicing. Instead of melting the ice in the fire, he took it upon himself to melt it on his own with a spell. Following their tense conversation, apprehension whirled around Chase's mind, making it harder to feel the toams than he would have liked. To his disappointment, it took an entire evening of intense concentration to melt a small portion of the unnaturally cold ice.

After enjoying a hot meal of smothered chicken, carrots, and onions with a hint of daemon's tongue to warm their chests, Chase excused himself from the fire. He sighed and cracked his neck before lying in his cot, exhausted from the long days of training. Magi sorcery was proving to be emotionally and mentally exhausting, but it took an immense physical toll on him as well that he wasn't expecting in the slightest. *Just like the early days in the Burrow as a child, and in more ways than I thought it would.*

As he listened to the soft tapping of the rain falling on the tress around him, Chase allowed his mind to wander. He felt so far removed from his life in the Burrow. It hadn't been that long since they had been exiled, but it might as well have been an entire lifetime ago. All the pain and hardships—as well as the scant good memory here and there—washed away like faded ink in a dusty tome long forgotten.

He missed parts of that life. He'd be lying to himself if he said otherwise. Ricket and Ditri were his dearest friends behind Richard, and his time spent with Veronika left him smiling more than it had not. There were even a few good memories of Cole. The man was ruthlessly strict with all the assassins, but he had a soft spot for Chase and was the closest thing to a father that Chase had ever had.

Chase pushed all thoughts of the Blades and the Burrow from his mind. In his lethargic haze, his mind wandered to Benjyn and Madelyn. Benjyn was a peculiar man, but Madelyn was a delight, and Chase sincerely hoped he would see her again. She was an unexpected highlight to their travels. If they ever managed to get back to the Berg the thought of Madelyn, Richard, and Chase sharing another mug of tea with some of her delicious sweets made him smile to himself.

The tapping of raindrops on leaves slowly faded away as Chase drifted to sleep.

***

Chase opened his eyes to fire and ash and rot once again.

He was sitting on a bench in the middle of the same flaming courtyard as he had seen so many nights before. The smell of smoke and burnt flesh forced its way into his lungs, and it took much longer for his eyes to adjust to the dim, red light than he wanted. The sooner he could leave this place the better.

At least I'm sitting for once. He sighed, the heat making it hard to breathe. *Let's get this over with.*

The entire plaza was a chaotic mess of burning buildings and blocked roads, but there was a single alley nearby that was left untouched, leading Chase onward. Winding between flaming buildings, he stumbled forward. Chase knew he would eventually get to where he needed to be, so he let the road take him where it pleased. Left, then right, then left again until he stood in yet another town square.

A congregation of people were gathered, corralled by ominous guards wearing black and red plate armor, armed with various poleaxes and spears. Each wore the haunting sigil of a man surrounded by black teeth on a field of red. When Chase heard voices erupting from the center of the mob, he moved to get a better view.

"Please, no," a woman shouted. "We did nothing wrong, milord! We just wanted some more bread, is all. We're not thieves! Honest!"

"Silence!" an all too familiar voice commanded in reply.

The mob had gathered around a small group that

cowered together at its center: a man, woman, and their five children. Tears welled in Chase's eyes and a pang of sorrow surged through his chest. The family was dressed in little more than rags, their matted hair caked in mud. Each of the children—the eldest no older than six or seven years old—clung desperately to their parents with cheeks wet from tears.

Chase looked in horror at the expressions painted across their faces.

They're so scared...

Chase's stomach twisted when his gaze landed on the man who gave the command, standing in those wretched blood red leathers trimmed in splashes of gray. He was wrapped in a pitch-black cloak, embroidered with a sigil to match the armed guards.

The Man in Red continued in Chase's voice. "You had our fine baker sully his name by extending extra rations of bread and cheese to your pitiful family. Who are you to demand more food from your gentle king? Who are you to force my hand in disposing of my once beloved baker? You're all thieves and shall be punished as is appropriate for your crimes."

The cowering father raised his hands in a desperate plea for mercy, his voice shaking and cracking with every word. "Please, sir. We didn't steal nothing. We just asked, is all. Jorun gave us that bread of his own accord. Please, milord, our daughter is sick with the cold shakes. We just wanted more for 'er."

The Man in Red smiled. "Your daughter? You mean *her*?" The cruel man's voice cut the air like a knife. He gestured to the child clinging to her mother's dress with skin as pale as a ghost.

Chase's eyes widened in shock. His heart raced. She was *so* young. Her tiny arms looked like they would snap from a stiff breeze, and her knobby knees wobbled even while she crouched.

"Yes milord," answered the mother, tears streaming down her ash covered cheeks, soot dirtying her dress and hair. Her arm wrapped around her daughter instinctively, as if she were trying to shield the poor girl from the countless stares of the gathered crowd. "This is our daughter, Natasha. She's been sick for nearly a month, milord. We been told she's got the cold shakes. We just wanted the food for her, milord. Honest."

The Man in Red inspected the girl and smiled. He spoke softly. "So, this is the child you stole for? This is the child that killed Jorun Bartleby, our humble baker. Well, well, well... We know the penalty for taking another life in this city, don't we?"

Chase shuddered. His stomach turned over itself in the moment of silence that drew on for far too long. The Man in Red finally waved his hand in the air and a nearby guard let loose a crossbow bolt. A faint whistle and a dull thud echoed through the courtyard, bringing with it an unnatural silence as the bolt landed in the center of the child's chest. Natasha fell to the ground, and her family wept.

Tears fell down Chase's cheeks, his breath going shallow and ragged.

"Now," the Man in Red proclaimed with a newfound vigor that had not been in his voice moments before. "Do we have an understanding? Have you learned what happens to those who steal from their king, or do I need to make it clear to you?" The family sobbed inconsolably around their fallen child, but the father eventually nodded in agreement. The twisted king continued quietly, although not so quietly that the whole courtyard could not hear. "No. I think not."

Chase's breath caught in his chest. The Man in Red widened his stance and threw his hands in front of him, arms stretched out. A spark of light flickered before a cone of blinding white flames poured over the family. The Man in Red cackled while the family screamed.

The scream pierced Chase's soul. It echoed and reverberated in his thoughts, growing louder and louder until there was nothing else. The sound threatened to tear Chase's mind asunder while he was forced to watch the family burn to death, unable to pull his gaze away from the horror of it all. Finally, the gout of flames vanished, and the street fell silent.

The family's bodies lay in the street, charred and black, while the Man in Red stood amongst the crowd. The last thing Chase heard was his own voice, laughing with terrifying glee.

***

Chase woke, gasping for air. His heart pounded in his ears, and he struggled to catch his breath. For a moment, he was back in that hellish city street. The smell of burning bodies flooded his senses, causing him to choke and gag.

He rolled onto his side and forced his eyes open. There was nothing but fire and death surrounding him. He blinked and the cool blue light of the Gallander countryside welcomed him with a comforting glow. Another blink and the white flames from moments before flashed across his vision. He wretched and emptied his stomach on the ground next to his cot, pain surging in his temples.

Coughing and spitting, Chase rolled to his back. His heart skipped a beat. The Man in Red stood over his cot, but in a flash the man was gone, and Chase was alone once again.

Chase gasped, struggling to finally catch his breath. By the time he had calmed enough to think straight, he saw Klaus sitting by the fire. The Drakthul was watching Chase with a measuring expression, his sharp eyes observing with a critical keenness that nearly made Chase shiver.

"Quite the nightmare, young one." Klaus' tone held no warmth or compassion. On the contrary, he was cold and somewhat distant.

Chase could easily feel how guarded his guide was, and he didn't blame the man. They hadn't known each other for much longer than a week, after all. Chase tried to muster a smile. "They're not so bad when you get used to it."

"And *this* is not so bad?"

Chase rubbed his face with shaking hands. He was drenched in sweat. "This one was... bad." He looked away from the fire and out at the Gallander landscape. It was peaceful. Rolling hills covered in all sorts of trees, bathed in a cool blue light washed away the tension in Chase's shoulders. "This place is so beautiful." Klaus' eyebrow rose, but Chase continued. "I don't know if there is anywhere in all the Berg with a view quite like that."

Klaus' expression softened. "Yes. It's quite the sight to behold. From what you are Richard have shared, it would seem Talvenna and Rakksberg have quite a few things in common."

"Oh? How so?"

"Talvenna has... a charm that is lost on most." Klaus shifted in his seat. "It's quite barren with little of the comforts most enjoy. The witchwoods are cruel, home to all sorts of dangerous beasts. The countryside can feel quite dark and imposing at times, especially if you believe even half the stories of what lurks in the shadows. Not to mention our people have quite the dramatic taste when they build their cities.

"It's not all bad, though. Our farms could feed our country many times over and if you enjoy art, there are few places quite like Krovograd, our capital."

"Aye, lad." Remi rubbed her eyes as she joined the pair at the fire. "Klaus' kin have quite the way with poetry, I must admit. Make no mistake, they are quite talented in many of the arts of course, but their poetry is truly something to behold." Klaus nodded in agreement with a smug smile. Remi returned her gaze to Chase. "Now, lad. I hope you don't mind me saying so early in the day as I mean no offense, but I must remind you to practice your spell craft.

"The rain seems to have relented enough for us to depart and be on our way. I must apologize, but I get rather discontent staying in one place for so long. We will be able to pack our things and get back to the road ahead, but that does not mean it's time to neglect your studies! I may not have anything else to teach you for now, but you still have much to learn. Practice is key and—"

Chase nodded and smiled, but at a certain point Remi's rambling faded into the ambience. Birds sang, leaves rustled, and Remi talked.

He tried not to laugh, especially considering how much his head hurt, but Chase eventually clambered to his feet and helped his friends gather their belongings. With minimal grumbling from a lethargic Richard, they were soon on their way.

Practicing Magi sorcery proved the exact distraction Chase had wanted to keep from dwelling on his nightmares. He listened to the others while they were riding, but most of his time was spent focusing on slowly feeling the toams at his fingertips before letting them go. Time and time again he felt the unseen presence dance just beyond his reach, urging him to come closer before he relaxed and the presence faded away.

Even still, Chase enjoyed hearing more about their guides' homelands while they trudged onward.

According to Remi, the nobles in Soule lived in rich palaces, riding upon elegantly decorated beasts with tough, gray skin and large, ivory tusks known as elephants, while the poorer folk lived in meager clay and stone buildings. Horses were not uncommon in

Soule, but camels and other related animals were more ideal for traversing the country's massive desert. Chase especially enjoyed Remi's accounts of the djinn, the manticores, and the giant dune trolls.

Klaus also shared more about his home in Talvenna. Seeing Richard cause a fuss about the more gruesome parts of his home gave Klaus great joy as he focused on the more colorful aspects of his homeland. Awful, leechlike creatures known as woaditsk lived in the northern most region of the country—with gaping holes for mouths and insectoid limbs. Ghouls formed small colonies of bloodthirsty monsters, while half-wolf, half-crow corvid gryphons soared across the skies.

It was odd to Chase that manticores and gryphons could be so similar and yet so different. Remi and Klaus assured him that it was more common than he would have guessed. "According to most scholars, magic shaped the land and all its creatures, but only after the world's creation. It's commonly speculated that a single, prehistoric ancestor species was twisted by magic to take many forms, but I suspect the similarities are the result of similar magical forces exerted on various *different* ancestor species," Remi had explained. "Of course, I could be mistaken. The convergent and divergent shaping theories are often contested among experts. And after all, I am no expert."

Klaus added that this phenomenon was responsible for nearly every region of the world having some sort of winged, hybrid creature. Some cultures had even tamed them and used them as a form of transport. "Particularly, there is the staghorn gryphon, or hippogriff: part-stag, part-gray hawk. The Elvari supposedly use them to traverse their massive forests in Cendralli even if they *are* fairly secretive about it."

Two days passed with similar conversations while they continued their journey. When the group arrived at the river called the Amaranth—named after the flowers commonly found on its banks—they came to a halt.

The rain had ceased by then, revealing an intensely warm sun in the cloudless sky. Remi seemed right at home with the sun beating down on her, while Klaus resorted to wearing his thick, brimmed hat to cover his pale complexion as best as he could. Richard complained that his black-dyed leathers made the heat unbearable, but Chase enjoyed it compared to the dreariness they had endured for so long.

The view from the Amaranth's bank was picturesque. Water sparkled and shined in the sun, glowing brilliantly blue in contrast to the lush green grass and pink wildflowers that spotted the area. For a second, Chase gagged at the odor of charcoal and sulfur, but it was gone as quickly as it had come. Thankfully, the fragrance from the nearby flowers— coupled with grassy aromas and the smell of clean autumn air—were the only things left to fill his lungs and clear his mind.

Chase joined the others at the riverbank. He lifted a handful of the water to his lips and drank it. For a heartbeat, the taste of ash coated his mouth, but that too was gone in an instant, replaced by the cool, crisp taste of the liquid.

His heart slowed and the knot that had formed in his stomach loosened. *When did that happen? I must be more tired than I thought.* He rubbed his face with the water and looked at his companions. Richard and Remi were preoccupied with their own enjoyment, but Klaus paused abruptly.

Slowly rising from the riverbank, Klaus' keen gaze was fixed on a distant point to the east, away from the river. Carefully and deliberately, he placed his leather hat on his head, still fixated on some unseen threat. Chase searched for the source to no avail, and when he turned to look back at Klaus, he saw that the Drakthul had begun preparing a handheld crossbow.

"What do you see, Klaus?" Chase asked quietly, but as soon as the words left his mouth the odors of charcoal, smoke, and brimstone flooded his senses. He wretched at the pungent aroma before forcing himself to move beyond it. For a moment, he thought he was imagining things. He could have sworn that the world flashed to a sea of fire and smoke, but a moment later he was back on the riverbank with his companions. He wiped the sweat from his brow and drew his bastard sword.

While Chase had been struggling to discern what was happening, his friends prepared for the worst. Remi and Richard fled the water as quickly and silently as they could. Richard took his great axe from his horse's saddle while Remi uncovered a short spear from her own. Klaus now held his crossbow in one hand with a twisted dagger in the other. They each moved slowly and deliberately, preparing for whatever lay ahead.

Chase struggled to stay focused amid the weighty scent in the air. One moment, the group stood at the edge of a forest overlooking a vast field across the river. The next they were surrounded by broken and battered buildings, the cloudy sky glowing a fiery red orange. The demonic backdrop faded away as fast as it appeared, and Chase tried to let the sweet smell of maple sap and wild berries calm him. To his dismay, the stench of rotten eggs and smoke overpowered his senses. A bead of sweat fell from his brow, and Chase took a ragged breath.

His grip tightened on his black blade. Soon, he could hear the rustling of leaves in the nearby trees followed by a labored, heavy breathing. Harsh thuds rang out as the threat drew closer. Anticipation hung in the air, thick enough to cut with a knife as they waited for the intruder to appear. With heavy steps that rattled the earth, the monster emerged from the brush nearly forty paces from them.

Chase's heart sank. The monster stood on four massive legs, bulging muscles strained around thick limbs that ended in heavy hooves. It shook its disfigured ram's head knocking a nearby tree limb with a wretched curved horn. Harsh, strained breaths escaped from a grotesque fanged maw that dripped with spittle and sinew. Mottled and covered in patchy, grey fur that looked rotten in places, the beast moved like it was punishing the earth beneath its hooves. The immense creature finally stopped, stomping one of its hooves with a violent, rasping grunt.

The beast's massive legs tensed for just a moment before it charged. The ground shook with each step, threatening to toss the travelers from their feet. But before it could gain much ground, Remi leapt forward, taking great strides to close the distance between her and the beast. Chase was unsure whether to spring to the woman's aid or stand and watch as the Magi stood firmly with her spear poised beside her. After a quick flourish, Remi lunged with her chest and arms out. She bellowed a mighty roar.

An immense whirl of red flames emerged in front of Remi before twisting into the shape of a great elephant's head. Moments before their attacker could react, the fiery apparition shot toward its foe. Flames slammed into the foul beast, knocking it off kilter in a mess of burnt fur. The monster roared in frustration, its thick hooves struggling to find purchase on the tangled and knotted ground below.

Klaus let loose a crossbow bolt that landed with a dull thud in the beast's throat while Richard closed the gap to the monster and swung his great axe above his head. The creature twisted at the last moment with unnatural speed, knocking away the blow with a twisted horn to protect its vulnerable neck. Richard desperately parried and dodged the beast's thrashing attacks, but it was clear he was no match. He couldn't keep up his battle for much longer.

Remi flung orbs of fire at the beast's hooves while Klaus continued to flood the monster with a stream of bolts many times faster than the most skilled crossbowmen in the Berg could have managed.

The beast let out a mighty roar in anger that knocked Richard off balance before running through him. Richard tried to duck out of the way, but it was too late. A yelp of pain escaped his lips as the beast's horn connected with Richard's leg, throwing him to the ground.

Chase cursed while the beast rounded on the group.

Grunting and snorting, spit and blood spraying from the monster's snout, the creature battered the ground with its mighty hooves and directed its charge at the man pestering it with crossbow bolts. Without hesitation, Klaus ran his jagged blade across his forearm. Dark blood oozed from the wound and fell to the earth at his feet, but his attacker gained more speed with each bounding step forward.

Chanting a cold string of words in his native tongue, Klaus filled the air with a harsh incantation that made Chase's hair stand on end. Without warning, thick black tendrils of rock and soil burst from the earth in an explosion of sound. The charging monster stumbled for only a moment, but it was long enough for the lashes to reach out and grapple the beast's forelimbs, dragging it to the ground with a massive crash.

Chase bolted toward their foe, the sound of Klaus' incantation drifting through the air with each step he took. The beast writhed and struggled against the might of the earthen tendrils, but the wriggling masses held strong. A blast of hot air rushed past him as a bolt of fire struck the beast's flank. With a strained grunt, the monster twisted and turned, ripping at the arms that grasped him. It was only a matter of time before it was free of Klaus' spell.

With a few more steps and a massive leap, Chase thrust his bastard sword into the monster's exposed neck. The beast roared in anger, thrashing so violently it tossed him to the ground. He swore to himself at the sharp pain that shot through his ribs, but he pushed the pain from his mind. Scrambling to his feet, he held his sword at the ready. His stomach dropped and he cursed again. The force of the monster had snapped his blade in two, leaving him with little more than a battered cross guard.

With an ear-splitting roar, the beast tore itself from the earthen tendrils' grasp and clambered to its feet, spit and blood flying from its thick jaws. It stomped and thrashed wildly, filled with fury and frustration while it tried to dislodge the broken shard of metal from his throat. Its cries and rumbles rang out in deafening a storm of incessant rage. Remi tried her best to keep the monster at bay, cautiously thrusting her spear while avoiding its tantrum, but it was clear their foe was unbothered by the attempts.

Klaus returned to peppering the monster with crossbow bolts, Richard readied himself for another attack, and Chase sheathed what remained of his broken blade before drawing his cleaving dagger from the small of his back. The monster showed no signs of surrender, and the longer they fought, the more dangerous the battle became. Desperate for some way out of the fight, Chase tried to reach out to the toams.

However, as hard as he tried, nothing answered his call.

Suddenly, without warning, another monstrous screech flooded the landscape amidst the thrashing and grunting and pounding. Chase whirled around to find the source of the sound and froze when he saw the figure emerging from the nearby trees. Larger than any horse he had ever seen, a regal creature with the head, wings, and talons of a golden eagle fused with the body and hind legs of massive feline walked slowly toward the river.

Chase flinched when Remi patted his shoulder silently and gestured for them to clear the area. Richard and Klaus were already fleeing as carefully as they could, so Chase followed Remi's lead. Once they arrived at their frightened horses, they comforted the animals and watched the scene unfold from afar.

The furious beast that had attacked them shook its head, grunted, and stomped a hoof on the ground before striding towards its new foe with a furious roar. Unphased by the display, the gryphon spread its great, golden-brown wings outward in a slow, deliberate motion. At the last possible moment, the gryphon leapt upward with a single strong flap of its wings.

A gust of air battered the earth, nearly toppling the charging beast. A slight loss of balance was all the gryphon needed, and in a flash, it was upon its prey. The horned beast roared in pain as talons and claws dug into its back. The gryphon ripped and tore with wicked speed. For a moment, Chase thought the gryphon would get bucked from its prey, but to his relief, no such thing happened.

Using its great, outstretched wings to keep its balance, the gryphon grabbed the beast's horns before driving it to the ground with a final snap of its beak around the monster's neck. A silence fell on the clearing while the predator held its prey. After ensuring its foe was finished, the gryphon raised its eagle's head high and stretched its wings outward. It let out a long, piercing screech that rattled the travelers to their bones before tearing into its kill, feasting in the aftermath of the successful hunt.

"Don't get too close," Remi spoke softly while she silently returned her spear to her saddle. "The gryphon didn't help us out of kindness. My best guess is that it had been stalking that thing for quite some time. We were just a distraction that created an opening. We need to leave—now."

Klaus nodded in agreement and readied his horse. Richard followed his lead, and Chase quickly did the same.

His legs and ribs aching with every movement, Chase gingerly climbed into his saddle. The group carefully and slowly fled the scene before the gryphon decided they had overstayed their welcome.

CHAPTER 20
A MATTER OF TRUST

Once they were far enough not to be bothered by the gryphon, Chase looked over to his friend. "Richard, are you alright? I saw that thing hit you hard." He tried to keep the question casual for his friend's sake but concern unmistakenly laced his words.

Richard grunted and smiled. "That thing grazed me. I reckon I'll get off with a nice bruise on my thigh where his damned horn got me but that's all. You're the one we should be asking, mate. That bastard threw you near twenty paces! You sure nothing's broken?"

The muscles in Chase's back tensed while he rode, but there weren't any signs of injury that he could tell. His thick, black cloak and leathers must have padded his fall enough. After a brief inspection of his limbs, Chase finally responded. "I'll be fine."

Richard snapped his gaze to the foreigners that led the group forward. "By the way, what the bloody hell was that thing? I've never seen anything like it. I've never even *heard* of a beast like that."

Klaus smiled and replied coolly. "Rannock. Or, if you prefer the Gallander name for it, a charger. The Azaleans call them bruuts, and the Magi name for it is the tzalgor. I'm sure they have as many names as the places where they've appeared over the years."

Clearly seeing the mixed looks of concern and confusion painted across Richard and Chase's features, Remi chimed in to elaborate. "They are demon spawn, lads. There is not much known about why they came about or why they appear in some areas over others, but they almost always arise from some sort of nest. Think of it as a portal, usually in caves or abandoned buildings. Although, I know of more than one occasion where a nest formed between the branches of a particularly large tree. I must admit, the beast just now was quite the specimen."

"Should we do something about it?" Chase's stomach twisted, and an acrid, sour taste festered in the back of his throat. "I mean, if there's a nest or portal or whatever you call it, won't there be more of those things? That seems... problematic at best."

Remi paused thoughtfully before answering the question with a clear tone of sympathy. "That's true, most likely, but no. I don't think we should worry ourselves over such things. There are great deal of demon hunters and poachers here in Galland that make it their livelihood taking care of such things. Some are native born Gallanders, hearing all sorts of stories about wild adventure and the thrill of the hunt from the time they were babes.

"Others are exiles or sell swords and mercenaries from distant lands that depend on the extra coin." Remi looked off in the distance, suddenly lost in thought. "I came across a young Magi demon hunter a few years ago. It was quite impressive what the lass had managed to do with our sorcery. I believe her name was Thelise, though perhaps she went by Thel or Fel… These hunters are much more appropriately equipped and experienced than you or me in the practices of killing demons." She returned her gaze to her questioner. "I assure you, lad, the issue is in good hands."

"Maybe not *good*," Klaus chuckled more to himself than to the others. "But well-practiced. That is certain."

"We can't just do nothing," Richard barked in rebellion refusing to acknowledge Klaus' joke. "If one of those damned charger things wanders into a town or into someone's camp, it'll kill them!"

"What do you propose we do, young one? Even if we rode in and drove the beasts back through the portal from which they came, what then? Do you know how to close a demonic portal? I'm not ashamed to say that I do not." Klaus' voice was even and flat. He held no resentment for the notion of helping, but his statement was undeniably realistic.

Chase intervened before Richard could respond. "We should send word to the people in Redwood. That monster wasn't very far from them and if there are any of these hunters staying at one of the inns there, they should jump at the opportunity to make some coin."

Remi smiled warmly while her stallion strode forward, bouncing her gently back and forth. "Very well," she said. "The next opportunity we have I'll purchase a pigeon, or perhaps a raven, if we're fortunate enough to come across one. We'll send word to Redwood so they can properly prepare. That's all we can do, I'm afraid, and it's more than most would. For two men who call themselves assassins, you are both rather charitable." She winked as she finished, a dazzling smile splitting her face.

Chase nodded in agreement, suppressing a laugh. "It's the fresh air and clear skies, I think." Logically, he knew there was nothing more they could do, but that did nothing to remedy the guilt growing in the back of his mind. Trouble seemed to be following the unfortunate pair of Bergman ever since they were exiled. Not to mention the smell that flooded the air when the demon arrived was so close to that of his nightmares. *It's too much of a coincidence. Will didn't mention demons or the like, but still…*

Chase tried to force his thoughts elsewhere by practicing his sorcery from his saddle. He managed to condense the air above his hand into a small round icicle three times before his curiosity broke the silence hanging in the air among the travelers. "Remi. If you don't mind, could I see that spear of yours for a moment? I wasn't aware you had such a weapon. It seems much shorter than any spear I've seen any soldiers in the Berg use."

Remi brought her hand to her braid in

contemplation. "Short spears are much less cumbersome when traveling, and with the right training, it can still manage to reach farther than any conventional blade. Although, I have seen poleaxes, pikes, and long spears handled as delicately as daggers in the hands of the appropriate combatant, of course." After a short pause, her hand dropped to the spear in her saddle. She handed the weapon to Chase and smiled. "It was a gift, lad. Try not to break it, if you would be so kind."

Chase laid the spear across his lap. What appeared to be a simple oaken spear from afar was much more ornate. Intricate carvings of various animals were spread throughout runes of some sort, embedded in gold leaf. Various inlets of bronze and copper held the occasional sapphire or ruby, and the carved wood had been dyed with dark oil. The odd blade at the spear's end was long with a single curved edge narrowing to a slanted point. Chase had never seen such craftsmanship for something as simple as a spear.

He drew the weapon up in his hand and raised it to chest level. It was much lighter than he expected, and superbly balanced. The dark leather handle that split the haft near its center was worn from years of use, yet still supple and well kept. Chase studied the spear, rotating it slowly to admire how the light played on the weapon before handing it back to its owner. Remi sheathed the spear and covered it in a length of purple silk, concealing it from unfriendly eyes.

Without speaking to Remi, Chase turned to Klaus. "If you don't mind, I'd like to have a look at that handheld crossbow of yours, as well. The crossbows I'm familiar with are much larger and take longer to load. I'm curious about how yours works." Chase made sure not to allow his tone to betray his skepticism, but Klaus glanced at Remi and raised his eyebrow. Remi returned Klaus' suspicion with a short nod before Klaus handed the crossbow over.

Made from a black wood Chase had never seen before, the crossbow was a magnificent contraption. There was a smooth, silver end cap on the bottom of the handle that shimmered in the sunlight, engraved with intricate flowers and thorn-covered vines. Matching silver-plated rods were used as stiffeners in the short arms of the crossbow and Chase suspected there was a matching rod in the weapon's core, judging by its surprising heft.

Chase turned the weapon over in his hand slowly. The string was a deep brown color that he guessed was due to an oil treatment. The joints and pivots that held the crossbow together were reinforced with steel rivets adorned with polished silver caps, each one engraved to mimic a blooming flower. A strange, gear-like mechanism was fixed to the body that he guessed allowed Klaus to load and fire the weapon so quickly and effortlessly.

He handed the crossbow back to his companion and paused for a moment to contemplate his exact words. *Regular people don't carry weapons like these. I don't care where we are, they just don't.*

Richard twisted his face in frustration. "What the hell are you on about, Chase?"

Chase turned his gaze to the strangers. "Just who

are you two, and I mean who are you *really*? You knew about my dragonmark the moment you saw me, and you seem a boundless source of knowledge no matter the subject. You both seem to be experts of your own crafts, and as it turns out, you're both carrying weapons that appear to be worth more than all our supplies and valuables combined.

"I don't believe two simple traveling friends, no matter how long they have been out in the world, could be quite as exceptional as the two of you. I want the truth. We've been traveling together long enough, and we've told you more than enough to earn the same privilege in return." Despite his best efforts to remain calm and collected, heat rose in his voice betraying more hostility than he intended.

Klaus remained silent, deep in thought. But after a long pause, Remi sighed. "It's true, lad. We've not been completely open to you and your friend. For that, I apologize most deeply. You must understand, and I'm quite sure that you and your assassin colleague do, that due to our particular situations, it's important that Klaus and I stay as anonymous as we can. There are those that would see us in a dungeon or in chains or worse, although I can assure you, they are few and far between. Many others may recognize us, that is surely an inevitability, but we mustn't go out of our way to make that inevitability come any easier than it already will."

"Why, *exactly*, do the two of you need to keep such low profiles?" Richard snarled more unpleasantly than his question warranted.

Klaus was the first to reply, his cool tone level

and even. "Just like you, young ones, Remi and I have had our fair share of unpleasantries. Most of which have ended in certain parties wanting to run us through with a good cut of steel."

"While Richard and I understand, we have to know what kind of people we're dealing with." Chase shifted in his saddle slightly. "You've been nice enough to us, and we're grateful for that. But to expect that we should just trust you on your word alone goes against the very reason you've been keeping things from us. Not to mention, it would be fortunate for *all* of us to know that our trust in you is not misplaced." His face was cold and hard as a stone.

Remi nervously twisted the end of her braid. After a moment of silent reflection, she looked Chase in the eye with a soft expression. "Very well, lad. You and Richard have earned our trust as well as any I've had the pleasure of accompanying for such a time as we have. I may be inclined to say you have earned more than just our trust." The woman's smile faded. "My full name is Remylara Drakolar. I was a commander in the Royal Soulesian Army, and a leader of a battalion of Magi sorcerers. My official rank was Master Fire Spinner. My sister, Salyn, was murdered in the ongoing conflict with the Beast-men of Black Rock, but not in battle as one would expect."

A pained sadness washed over Remi's round features while she continued. "No, she was murdered by a Beast-man spell breaker—aided by a traitor Frost Weaver—in her sleep the night before she was ordered to leave the warfront. I was... boisterous concerning my dismay for the leniency afforded the parties involved. I insisted the traitor should have been exiled along with the guards stationed at her tent that night. Although, many claimed I was too invested in her well-being." Straightening in her saddle, she composed himself, sticking her chin forward in defiance. "As such, I was stripped of all rank before I voluntarily left Soule in favor of a more peaceful life. Aye, I've made my fair share of enemies—although, I like to think that I've made a few friends along the way as well."

"I would say so." Klaus continued with his dazzling, crooked smile before the others had a chance to speak. "I just so happen to be Klaus Svoct of the Death Valley Svoct's. No doubt that title means very little to you, young ones. I'm the son of a very powerful and equally disliked politician by the name of Volnar Svoct. While I've done a fine job of ripping myself from the family infamy and disappointing my father—and his father—all at once, most people who know the name look coldly upon me.

"As for my skills in wielding blood magic? I'd like to think it's simply a gift, and while I insist that I'm blessed in our ways, it may also be due in part to my training with Talvenna's First Legion. It's a national service that people of affluent backgrounds are required to serve a decade in as an act of service to those less fortunate, while commoners can voluntarily join the Second Legion. It may not have been as exciting as fighting in a war, but I learned a few things here and there about working with my hands."

"What the bloody hell are you two on about?" Richard snorted with a hearty laugh. "A damned commander in the Magi army and a crooked politician's rebellious son? And how is it that those two people from countries on opposite sides of a bloody continent meet and become best of friends?"

"Well, that's an easy one, little cub," Klaus smirked and tipped his brimmed hat slightly. "Remi saved my life."

"That's true, lad," Remi affirmed. "Shortly after I arrived in Galland, I found myself in a spot of trouble with a few former colleagues from a campaign we conducted in Black Rock. I must admit, I didn't blame them, but Klaus intervened before they could manage to strike. We thought our troubles were at an end, so we parted ways. Come to think of it, I believe we were staying at the same inn without realizing it. It's quite humorous how things like that can happen. Later that night, the three Magi took Klaus by surprise and stripped him of his dagger before he could defend himself."

"I maintain that they took advantage of a drunken man in a dark alley. Sober in the daylight I would have given them a real fight." The smile widened on the pale man's face, emphasizing his somewhat oversized incisors.

"I'm sure you would have, old friend. Anyway, I made short work of the old washouts and since then, my colleague and I have been as close as kin."

Chase mulled over the answers for a moment. "Fair enough. I just have one last question. Considering everything you've shared, how are we to believe that our chance encounter with people of such status and skill was a mere coincidence? How *exactly* can we know that it was simple happenstance that brought us together?"

Remi smiled and responded kindly. "Lad, we could ask you the same question from our own perspective. How exactly can it be that two assassins from a land shut out from the rest of the world *happened* upon the tavern where Klaus and I *happened* to be enjoying a few drinks? There are those who believe in a greater power or predetermined destiny. Yes, in fact, some of the world's religions preach and praise such doctrines, though I cannot say whether this qualifies as such. We cannot trouble ourselves with such matters. Whether you believe in cosmic coincidence or a higher power with a guiding force, the result will not change. You walked into a tavern. I recognized your dragonmark. The rest is neither here nor there."

Chase eyed Remi intently, trying to discern any ill intentions. Klaus saw the unease in his expression. "We cannot explain it in any clearer terms than we have, young ones. You know who we are, where we came from, and why we are together. The rest will come in time. You must trust us just as we trust you."

"Aye," Richard grunted. "Suppose that's that, then."

Chase somberly nodded. "I apologize for our suspicions."

"We understand, young one. Know that I speak for us both when I say that you've grown to more than just traveling acquaintances. You have gained some friends in us." Klaus smiled and patted Chase's shoulder kindly. He kicked the sides of his horse urging it forward, and with that, the group rode in silence for some time, enjoying the peaceful sounds of the Gallander landscape.

CHAPTER 21
A ROSE AND A SHADOW

The four companions rode north until the sun began to set just to be sure they were clear of the gryphon's territory. After a pleasant dinner of salted pork stew with field onions, tomatoes, and hot spices, they shared a drink around the fire from one of their wine skins.

It was all the group could do to forget about the uglier parts of travelling the countryside on their own, but Chase's mind wandered, nonetheless. He couldn't help it. People like Sasha seemed fit to take care of themselves, but who else could hope to survive against something as terrible as a charger? Four trained fighters—two of which were accomplished magicians—could hardly scratch the thing before yet another monstrous beast swooped into their unintentional rescue. What hope was there for a traveling merchant without anything but the clothes on their back? What hope was there for all the people like Sasha?

It was a feeling of helplessness that haunted Chase, reminding him of how life in the Berg had been for so long.

Allowing the heat of the fire to cradle him pleasantly, he thought back to before he had been exiled. He had felt bad for the people of the Berg for a long time, but it was a defeated feeling that betrayed a grim acceptance of the way things were. The High Council's rule over Rakksberg carried with it an implacable finality. In a way, it made life easier knowing there was nothing that could be done. The Council would rule, the people would suffer, and the assassins in the Burrow would continue their misgivings under the guise of survival.

But after leaving the Burrow, things were different. If magic and dragons were real, why couldn't something be done? Chase didn't need to accept the lot in life given to him. He could do *something* for a change. He knew, deep in his heart, that not everything could be changed. The High Council would remain the dominating force that hung over Rakksberg until long after Chase was gone from the world.

That didn't mean he couldn't do what he could with the gifts he had been given to help people along the way. Did it?

What a strange thought.

***

Chase woke the next morning covered in sweat

with a sharp, stabbing pain in his chest. His eyes struggled to adjust to the dim light of the morning. Heaving with each stabbing breath, Chase blinked furiously. One moment he was on his cot, and the next he was in an empty field, a fiery sky bathing a massive charger in ominous red light.

He coughed in his hand. His vision blurred. With each heartbeat, the spittle that wet his palm flashed to a spot of deep, dark blood before flashing back to nothing more than sweat and spit.

A blinding pain shot through Chase's ribs when he tried to move. He heaved yet again, desperate to regain his senses. He was back in the clearing—his stomach wet with blood. The charger stood over him, huffing with that same blood dripping from its massive, twisted horn.

The beast drew closer. Its breath steamed in the damp, cool air. Its fanged maw widened. Chase closed his eyes.

After a deep, ragged breath, Chase opened his eyes. He was back in their camp, lying in his cot, drenched in sweat. The pain in his stomach was gone, and he was back with his friends.

Slowly, Chase stood and looked out to the horizon toward the sunrise. Just when he had hoped the horrors of the night before were behind him, his breath caught in his throat. Nearly thirty paces away, the Man in Red stood under a small maple tree in the dim light of the morning with a wicked smile slashed across his face. Chase blinked and rubbed his eyes, but when he looked again the man was gone. Only the tree stood, its red-kissed leaves shining in the light of the sunrise.

"Are you okay?" The question made Chase jump slightly. It was Richard from his own sleeping mat, his blonde hair matted in a tangled mess.

Chase smiled. "Yes, Richard. You don't need to ask it every morning. Another night, another nightmare. I *do* think I'm getting better, though." It was a lie, but there was no need for Richard to worry himself over it. The previous night's dream of the charger ravaging their entire group while Chase was powerless to help them was one of the most visceral ones yet. "I'm just stretching."

"If you are *just* stretching, make yourself busy and cook up some breakfast. It feels like I haven't eaten in days."

I should tell him.

It's my fault he's here right now and not in some warm bed somewhere.

"Don't you always feel that way?" Chase laughed nervously before digging through one of Remi's saddlebags for something to eat. Richard rubbed the sleepiness from his eyes and yawned, but the expression of concern that had been there for weeks now was unmistakable.

He didn't *have a choice because I* made it *for* him. *I should tell him.*

Chase found some eggs and a few potatoes that would suffice. He chopped the potato with a small dagger—all the while Richard watched him closely. It was as if his friend was inspecting him, expecting something strange to happen.

I can tell him while the food cooks. Yes. That will give me some time to think it through.

He grabbed a cooking pot from one of Remi's saddlebags and winced at the metallic clanking that rang out in the silent morning air. Chase nearly groaned aloud when the clattering of pots caused their guides to stir within their tents. They would soon be joined for a hearty breakfast and casual conversation to start their day.

I'll tell Richard later, then. Now's not the right time.

I just need to wait for the right time.

By the time the aroma of fried eggs and potatoes filled the air, the camp was alive with the chorus of morning pleasantries.

After several days of casual riding and friendly banter, the group arrived at the bank of a massive river. The immense span of water shined brightly in the light of the autumn sun. The river spanned the width of many roads with no discernible end in either direction. Its banks lacked the brilliant swaths of flowers that the Amaranth had, but there was no shortage of wildlife. A small group of mallards swam in a bed of reeds nearby while songbirds flew overhead in vibrant flocks. The fragrance of fresh water and wild grass filled the air, accompanied by the sound of steadily stirring water.

They made steady progress, following the river west. To keep himself busy, Chase continued practicing the things Remi taught him. After days of effort, Chase could now produce simple spells while holding a conversation. On occasion, he would condense large amounts of vapor too quickly, but that led to little more than a damp lap. As they rode, Chase enjoyed watching the changing landscape pass them by, even if it was overwhelming at times.

In Galland, the wildlife was more numerous than Chase had thought possible. He saw various fish and reptiles, birds of all shapes, sizes, and colors, and even the occasional deer or rabbit before they fled from the travelers' horses. Remi assured them that the river they had been travelling along, the Harp, was the central lifeblood of the country and the rest of the land was not quite as exciting at this time of the year. Even so, Chase took in the sights with a smile.

After some rather uneventful days of riding, a small town at the base of a hill settled on the southern bank of the Harp came into view. "That is Glarrus," Klaus explained. "Completely unremarkable in just about every way you can imagine."

"So, what's the way that it's remarkable?" Chase teased with a sarcastic tone. "You said just about every way. That must mean there is at least one thing that's special about the place."

Remi laughed. "If I may be so bold, I can surely think of one thing. There is a delightful tavern called The Fiddler's Rest that serves a delightful ale made with berries that positively dances on the tongue. I'd rather not return to The Dancing Mare, if I can help it. After my particularly long stay during the storm I mentioned, the folk there seem to think that my pockets are endless. Every time I go, they charge me triple the prices of the local folk." She paused for a moment, smiling as if she was recalling a nice memory. "At any rate, I seem to recall a wonderfully pleasant man who worked at The Fiddler's Rest that liked the way my hair shined in the candlelight. Was his name Brendan or Brandon? What was his name, Klaus?"

"I don't ever seem to recall half the men you conjure up in that head of yours," Klaus teased. "I don't recall half the women you conjure up either. Quite the imagination, old friend."

They quickly found a stable for their horses attached to a small hostel where they could store their belongings and book lodging for the night. Chase soon found himself standing on the steps of a small wood and stone building with a thatched roof. A sign swung above the door with a picture of a violin laid in front of a goblet of wine with the name "The Fiddler's Rest" painted across the top in fanciful script. Music and candlelight leaked from every crack in the walls like water from a broken cup.

Richard smiled and pat Chase on the back. "This seems like my kind of place, mate."

The smell of ale and wine filled Chase's nostrils, accompanied by the sweet aroma of baked lamb and wild berries as the sound of fiddles and drums rang through his ears. A few men played their various instruments joyfully while a woman in a low-cut, green dress that was almost too thin twirled and sang, her golden hair swaying to the tune of the music. The dim light bathed the room in a warm, orange glow that felt oddly welcoming. It was as if everything about the place was asking people to venture through its doors and stay for good food, fine drinks, and great company.

Remi claimed a small table for their group while Richard rushed to the bar for some flagons of ale. Klaus began to wax poetic about a previous visit to Glarrus that he insisted had ended with the pair of old friends bargaining with a farmer to lend his pig to the town guard, but Chase only partially listened. Instead, he scanned the bar for anyone or anything that looked out of place or suspicious; something he had done by habit since he was an initiate.

Chase had always felt more comfortable in crowded and busy places than during quiet times. When things grew quiet, it was often the case that danger was lurking in some unseen corner. In larger crowds, however, he found it easy to blend into the chaotic masses and enjoy a sense of anonymity. Even so, old habits die hard.

Cole burned into the assassins' minds that their survival depended on unwavering vigilance in these situations. They needed to ensure they were the most dangerous people in the room to guarantee their safety. If they didn't, there was no telling who might be waiting for just the right time to strike them down. At that moment, however, all that way from the Berg in such a warm and welcoming place, Chase only felt paranoid.

As he scanned the crowd, his breath caught in his throat. The Man in Red stood beside the modest band of gleemen. His presence oozed around him, tainting the innocent charm of the ambience until Chase was certain he would vomit. For far too long, the Man in Red watched the festivities of the place with a sneer, his eyes shining sickeningly in the warm light of the tavern.

Chase rubbed his eye with the back of his hand, and the Man in Red was gone. He tried to ignore the bead of sweat running down his temple. *It's warm in here. That's it. Nothing else to worry about tonight. Not here.*

Swallowing the lump in his throat, Chase returned his attention to the lively crowd of guests.

A pale Drakthul man with midnight blue hair—wearing flowing shirts even more elaborately stitched and ruffled than Klaus'—sat chatting with a chestnut haired Gallander woman in an embroidered, blue dress that she clearly reserved for nights out such as this. Further down the bar, a bald Magi in a flowing linen outfit wrapped in colorful silk spoke behind a flagon of ale to a woman with shimmering black hair that fell almost to her waist in an elaborate set of braids.

After passing over a few patrons that were laughing at something one of them had said, Chase's eyes finally landed on a woman alone at the bar. She was standing with her back to him, resting her elbows on the nearby counter. Dark mahogany hair fell upon her shoulders, shining beautifully in the flickering candlelight. She wore a lightly embroidered riding jacket, oddly cut at the waist, with a matching pair of leather riding pants that flattered her feminine figure. Her red-brown boots had a short heel appropriate for notching the boot loops of a saddle, and she wore a belt around her waist that held various pouches, fit for a long journey.

Chase's eyes lingered longer than he had intended.

Even from this distance, something about the woman was enthralling. He couldn't peel his eyes her.

"Chase!"

He jolted back to his table. Richard had returned with the ale, barking his friend's name until he realized that Chase was apparently preoccupied. Chase took a flagon of the auburn liquid and shivered in his seat. "Sorry, I saw someone…"

"Someone you thought you recognized?" Richard snorted and smacked the table with a smile. "We are on the wrong side of the bloody mountains for that nonsense. Who could you possibly know?"

"I'll say he recognized someone," Klaus jested after taking a healthy drink from his flagon. "He recognized a possible dancing partner in the crowd. I've seen that glint in many eyes before, young one."

"You have quite the way with subtlety when it comes to the finer things in life, old friend." Remi remarked with a massive grin. She returned her gaze to the flustered Bergman before continuing. "Although, you weren't exactly hiding it, lad—if I may be so bold to say. I was beginning to wonder what ill fate would fall upon you if we left you for much longer. Surely, your jaw might have fallen off completely if left to hang for another moment!"

Richard twisted around toward the bar, craning his neck around the crowd of bustling patrons. "Who? That one over there at the bar with the red hair? She is quite the looker." He swiveled back to his friends. "I prefer blondes, myself. Never seen you to be much with women, though, Chase."

"I see you and Klaus share your way with words." Chase's cheeks flushed, so he tried to hide it behind a large mouthful of ale. It was sweet enough, if a little too bitter for his liking, but it was strong all the same. *Wish I could say Richard was drunk, but he hasn't even touched his flagon yet.*

Remi grinned, holding her drink in the air above the table. "Life is short, lad. Go and talk to her. You never know the day the Sisters will come for you, welcoming you to great expanse beyond the veil. You might as well enjoy your youth while it lasts, and with any luck, you'll stay youthful for as long as it takes to grow old and pass on to the next life in peace."

Chase resentfully clanked his flagon against Remi's and lifted it to his mouth. He drank slowly, trying to think of anything else, but his efforts were futile. Veronika was the last woman he had shared any amount of time with, and that felt like a lifetime ago. Perhaps it was. *Has it been weeks? Months? It feels like years.*

Finally, after much consternation, Chase stood from the table and straightened his cloak before approaching the bar. The woman with the mahogany hair shifted her weight from side to side absentmindedly while she enjoyed her drink. Chase blinked abruptly before leaning against the bar next to her.

He ordered a drink for himself before glancing her way. She turned to him and smiled. "Hello, stranger."

Chase tried with all his might not to stare, but he couldn't help it. Her smile was dazzling, and her features were as perfect as they possibly could be. The woman's olive skin was flushed from the heat of the room and the ale in her hand, but her expression held an undeniable wit that Chase found transfixing. Yet, there was a kindness to her that Chase had never seen, and the way her nose wrinkled while she smiled made his heart flutter.

The woman was remarkable, but all her beauty paled in comparison to her eyes. Chase's chest grew warm, and his stomach turned as he stared into her bright, round, golden eyes. They were the color of the sun in the moments before a sunset, like the most precious golden amulet. Chase struggled to find the right words, but after a painfully long pause, he managed to stammer, "H-hi."

The woman shifted from one side to the other, inspecting Chase to see if he was injured. "Are you okay? You seem out of sorts. Did you hit your head? I can wave over the barkeep to fetch you a bandage or some cool water if you'd like."

"N-n-no," Chase replied, desperately trying to regain his composure. "No, I'm okay. My apologies… my name is Chase."

The woman smiled, her lips pursing pleasantly, eyes aglow with excited enthusiasm. "Well, then, Chase. My name is Rose. Rose Delain." She held out her hand expectantly. Chase grasped it softly and gave it a single shake before clumsily letting go. When he failed to respond after a moment, she continued. "So, are you from around here? I can't help but notice you seem a bit lost. I do hope you know your way home."

"Uh, no. No, I'm not… From around here, that

is. I'm not lost either, mind you, I'm just not from around here." *Carpenter's Hammer, what the hell is wrong with me? I feel like my tongue is too thick to speak.*

"Well," Rose jabbed Chase's ribs lightly with her elbow and gave him a playful wink. "Don't hide it. Where are you from? You certainly look like a Gallander, even if your hair is a bit dark."

"Rakksberg," Chase blurted without thinking. He closed his eyes after the word left him. *First, bloody nightmares, monsters, magic, and now I can't even speak to a woman without making a damned fool of myself. I am going mad.*

Rose frowned slightly causing her lips to fold in a way that made Chase's heart pound even harder for a moment. "Hm," she finally responded. "I can't say I'm familiar with the place. Is that to the south? I must admit my Gallander geography isn't what it should be. You must be from the south with hair that dark."

"Y-yeah, sure. It's in the south, not far from Redwood. I don't get north often." The lie felt awkward. He was sure the woman with her keen golden eyes would know he was hiding the truth.

Rose's eyebrow raised. "Redwood, you say? I haven't been. Though, wherever you're from, I suspect I know why you are headed north." Chase's eyes widened slightly. "You certainly seem to have a mark that's not been seen in quite some time. You're not really trying to hide it either." Rose smirked, causing her nose to wrinkle once again, and Chase's stomach whirled so much he felt he might become ill.

She can't know what it means. Three people is too many. The woman winked again and sipped her own flagon of dark ale before continuing. "My father, Arnaud Delain, is rather... influential in Azalea. I'm not exactly dim-witted, nor am I without a proper education. Gallanders tell tall tales that almost everyone agrees are false, but I know a dragonmark when I see one."

Carpenter's Bloody Hammer, one day I'll learn not to go to taverns. "What makes you think that's what it is? Maybe I just have strange tastes." Chase felt hot. It couldn't simply be the heat of the room. *How much ale have I drank? It* must *be the ale, right?*

Rose chuckled. "You *do* have strange tastes, that's for certain. All black leathers? You would do well to contrast, maybe with some white linen or silver silk. Silver and black are quite the dashing pair." Her eyes gleamed in the light. Her smile made Chase's chest tighten. "The Azaleans were, and are to this day, the Heralds of the Dragons.

"Many of our people still teach our children about them in hopes they will return some day. Most people doubt it will ever happen, but we're still taught how to recognize a rider when we see one. That mark on your face is done in ink that is much too dark, and when you become flush, I can almost see it shimmer." She lifted a hand to Chase's cheek and stared at the mark. Then she stared into his eyes.

Chase's tongue felt thick, and his mind went blank before the barkeep set another drink on the counter demanding payment. He fumbled with the coin purse Remi had given him, so Rose placed three gold coins on the counter between them. The gruff tavern owner inspected the coins suspiciously before grunting and returning his attention to the other patrons of his establishment.

Before Chase could properly thank Rose for the drink, a tall, long-haired man with broad shoulders leaned against the bar, causing her to turn away from him. He sighed to himself in defeat and grabbed his flagon of ale before abandoning his endeavor, face still hot and flushed. When he turned to leave, Rose touched his forearm gently. Chase looked back at her glistening golden eyes. "It was nice to meet you, Chase."

"It was nice to meet you too, Rose."

Chase returned to his table, defeated, staring at the grains of wood near his fingertips. Before he said anything, he turned his new flagon of ale end over end, emptying its contents in his mouth as quickly as he could. He wiped his mouth and remained silent while he stared forward.

"Well, how did it go, already? You going to shack up with her? She's bloody well worth it, I'd say." Richard's blunt demeanor was always worse when he was drunk.

"It went…poorly."

Remi and Klaus laughed outwardly before Remi finally spoke, still struggling to contain herself. "At least you got a good look at the lass! Was she as pretty as the rest of the people here would lead us to believe from the number of men that stare in her direction? I haven't seen so many sidelong glances at a woman for quite some time."

"More so." Chase shook his head, running a hand through his hair dejectedly. "She's... gorgeous. Her eyes are golden like the sun. I've never seen anyone like that."

Klaus stopped laughing and eyed the boy suspiciously. "Did you just say that she had golden eyes? Are you sure about that, young one? They aren't orange or amber?"

"I could hardly look away. She said she was from Azalea. Great Carpenter, I've never felt so dull." Chase looked at Richard, who had moved on to yet another flagon of bitter ale. "This must be how you feel on a good day, mate."

Richard snorted and raised the drink to his mouth to stifle a laugh. Remi simply smiled and continued. "Of course she is, but she's not just any lass from the land of the flower folk. Golden eyes are a sign of great reverence. Most of the Azaleans north of these parts will have lavender, magenta, or even teal eyes. I once saw a lad with silver eyes, but it's truly a rare sight to see gold. Those born with golden eyes are said to be descended from an ancient bloodline of very powerful crystal-singers. You have just stumbled upon a very special lass, indeed."

"Yes," Chase answered curtly with a large gulp of ale from a newly filled flagon. "Yes, she is." *Shame that I won't get to speak with her again.*

After a long pause, Richard blurted out, "I don't get it. You kill people for a living—bloody dangerous people. You've seen things that would make most men soil themselves, and you can make ice with nothing more than your bloody mind. How the hell is it that you can't rope yourself a woman at a tavern?"

"We can't all have such a way with words as you, little cub," Klaus retorted with a dazzling, almost hungry smile. "You clearly would have no trouble at all, now wouldn't you?" The sarcasm was evident, but even still, Chase noticed Richard blush slightly before stammering out a rebuttal.

The group continued to tease one another for quite some time. Flagons of ale came and went while they enjoyed each other's company in the lively tavern atmosphere. Chase glanced back to the bar every now and then only to see that Rose was still speaking with the broad-shouldered man that had interrupted their earlier conversation.

Richard seemed much more interested in the dancing woman with the revealing dress, swaying to the sound of music. Eventually, he mustered the courage to ask the entertainer for a dance while Klaus enjoyed a dance of his own with a dark haired and pale Drakthul man to the busy sounds of fiddles and raucous laughter.

Remi caught Chase glancing at the bar later in the night. She snorted and with a final gulp of ale, smiled brightly in the dim light. "Young lad!" She yelled the words much louder than was needed. "You've been peeking at that Rose lass for far too long! Does her company upset you?"

Chase's head was clouded, and his inhibitions were gone. He felt heat rise in his cheeks. "Maybe," he spat. "He's not so special! I think he's a sort of ugly bloke, anyway!" *I bet I could take him. He's big but I still bet I could take him. Stupid big head with his stupid broad shoulders. I could kill him.*

No.

That wouldn't work out right.

Remi roared with laughter. "That man just so happens to be a knight. Sir Calloway has won the annual tournament held just south of Glarrus for three consecutive years now. He's *quite* the man. I once watched him knock a man from his mount with a single swing of his great sword. Reminds me of a lad I knew in Soule, though I believe *he* would not know me now."

I could take him. "And I kill people for a living. Killed my fair share bigger than that sod. What's your point, Remi?" *Can't imagine that knight has much real experience anyway, ugly bugger.*

Remi lifted her hands defensively, her smile growing wider by the second. "Fair enough, lad. Fair enough. This all reminds me of a time I saw a lad I was quite taken with in my youth. The sweet boy—I recall Melodas was his name—was Azalean as well and just as I did then, I believe you may require a small nudge."

"Wait, what? What nudge? I don't need a nudge. There is no need to nudge anyone to do anything! I am sure things will be just fine without any nudges anywhere."

No nudges.

Remi stood up, swaying slightly on the spot before clumsily walking over to the bar where Rose conversed with the knight. She threw her arms in the air shouting incomprehensively at the broad-shouldered man. Sir Calloway looked startled at first but quickly recognized who approached him. He yelled as well, returning Remi's smile with one of his own. The pair embraced before parting from the bar, leaving Rose by herself.

Chase froze, watching the mahogany haired woman look around at the remainder of the tavern's patrons. Rose's eyes met Chase's and she smiled. She grabbed her flagon of ale from the bar and approached him. Chase's stomach tied in a knot when she sat on the stool next to him and scooted it slightly closer.

"Hi, stranger," Rose said, throwing Chase a playful wink. "I'm glad to see you're still here. You're the most interesting person I've met here tonight."

Ha! Take that *Mr. Knight. I am interesting and you still have a big head.* Chase's voice caught in his throat again, but this time it loosened quickly. He had more than his fair share of ale, but he still managed to hold on to his calm demeanor. "I… I'm glad to see you as well. My friends told me that the man you were speaking with was a knight. Won some sort of tournament or something?"

Rose laughed as she reached out and touched Chase's forearm. It made his chest warm, his heart flutter, and his stomach tumble. "Yes. That was Cairon, son of Mairon, or *Sir Calloway* as he is all too quick to remind everyone. He was rather enthusiastic in telling me all about his conquests and his glorious showings at the annual tournament. However, to be completely honest, Chase, the man was a bit of a creep."

Chase chuckled, feeling more relaxed than he had been earlier even if his stomach was still tied in a knot. "I can't imagine a woman such as yourself would go for someone like that, anyway." His mouth was dry despite the ale, but his words were finally coming to him more easily, so he pressed on. "You're far too observant to fall for tricks and posturing. You'd be better off finding someone with a wit to match your own."

"Oh?" Rose raised her eyebrows and smiled. "And where exactly would I find such a witty man, Chase?"

"Certainly not here, I can tell you that right now." Chase grinned. His nerves melted away like ice by a fire. "You should probably leave now to better your chances of finding somebody like that by the end of the night."

Rose's hand moved from Chase's arm to his hand. She smiled, moving the hair from her face gracefully before meeting his eye.

His heart was pounding like a drum, and his face felt hot. *Uh oh. Is my face shimmering? Can she see my face shimmer? Dammit, what if it's glowing? It feels like it's glowing.*

Rose simply continued to smile and finally replied. "I like my chances right here."

They talked for hours.

Chase divulged things he never thought he would to a stranger. He told her about the Berg, although he felt it best if she thought it was in the south of Galland rather than across the Blackridge Mountains. Chase spoke lightly of his work as an assassin, and about his journey so far against his better judgement. She didn't seem to mind any of it. In fact, her smile never faded for a moment, even if her eyes betrayed that she knew he was no Gallander.

Rose told him much about herself, as well. She spoke of growing up in a prominent and influential family in Azalea. Chase had asked what exactly her parents did to make them so important, but she largely avoided the subject, and Chase didn't bother to press it further. It didn't matter. Nothing mattered beyond the beautiful woman who shared his table in that moment.

The Azalean spoke more about her home, her mother, and her travels. She offhandedly shared that she had some sort of duty to her people that she would eventually need to honor, but she wanted nothing more than to travel and see the world beyond Azalea. Wanderlust was not something Chase had ever felt before, but after speaking with Rose and hearing her enthusiasm for a life of travel and mystery, Chase had half a mind to abandon his entire endeavor altogether and join her in seeing as much of this strange world as he could.

Before either of them knew it, the night had passed, their flagons were empty, and the barkeep was asking them to leave.

Chase walked with Rose arm-in-arm back to his hostel to retire for the night. Reluctantly, the pair stopped. Chase took her hands in his and met her beautiful, golden eyes. "You are a truly magnificent woman, Rose. It makes my heart heavy that I may not see you again."

Before saying a word, Rose threw her arms around Chase's neck, stood on her toes, and pressed her lips to his. Chase's face grew warm, and his cheeks flushed. His chest tightened, and his stomach turned over until the world around them melted away.

He took Rose in his arms and kissed her.

She was the only thing that mattered. There were no quests or prophecies. There were no dragons or monsters. There was only Chase and Rose, and nothing could take that moment away from them.

They enjoyed a tender embrace for what seemed like hours and yet, when their kiss ended, it was too soon. Rose's brilliant golden eyes pierced through the night to meet Chase's gaze. She reached up once more and kissed his cheek gingerly. "Don't forget me, little shadow."

"I won't as long as you don't forget me."

"How can I forget a shadow? All I have to do is look down." The pair laughed in each other's arms for a moment before kissing again. The world melted away and flooded back in a whirlwind. With a pang of apprehension, Chase let go and made his way up the nearby stairs to the inn. He only made it halfway up the steps before hearing Rose call out to him. "Oh, and if you ever find yourself around Crystal Lake or Parth, find me."

Chase nodded before Rose turned and walked away. She glanced back and smiled before rounding a corner and venturing into the cool night completely out of sight.

Heart pounding in his ears, Chase proceeded into the inn, continued to his room, undressed, and slipped under the sheets of the modest straw mattress. He smiled and closed his eyes, the room slightly spinning around him. Inevitably, Chase knew that in moments he would open his eyes and find himself in yet another nightmare, filled with death and dismay. However, he had to admit to himself that after a night like that, he did not care.

CHAPTER 22
DOWN THE HARP

Chase woke the next morning to the sound of chickens clucking and dogs barking through the window of his room. Sweat soaked the cotton sheets of his meager bed, and his clothes clung to his skin unpleasantly. His eyes adjusted slowly to the dim morning light, but it wasn't the plain oaken ceiling that he saw above him. The roof of the inn had been ripped open, giving way to a deep red sky. Screams rang out all around him, the grating sound splitting Chase's head nearly in two.

Pain searing through his every muscle, Chase tried as hard as he could to move. No matter how hard he tried he was stuck there in his bed. Not even his fingers would obey his command, paralyzed by some unseen force. He tried to open his mouth, but his efforts were futile. He couldn't call out to his friends. He couldn't scream for help. He couldn't do anything beyond lying in his bed, gazing up at the fiery sky above him.

The room's nearby door slammed open. A monstrous huffing that sounded like gravel scraping against stone in the wind was soon followed by the massive thuds of hooves on hard wood.

Chase panicked. It was hard to breathe. His heart raced, threatening to leap from his chest at any moment, and it felt like an unseen band squeezed his chest so hard he thought it might crack his ribs. Chase wanted nothing more than to jump from his spot and run as fast as he could, but he could do nothing to stop what was coming next.

A massive, fanged maw came into view from above. Beady, enraged eyes stared down at him. A twisted ram's horn scrapped against the bed. The jowls of the beast opened, and Chase closed his eyes to accept his fate.

When he opened his eyes again, he was alone. The inn was whole again, and the air was filled with little more than the sounds of chickens clucking and dogs barking through the window of his room.

Chase gingerly looked to his side, and to his great relief he could finally move his neck freely. The rest of his body soon followed, although the aches and pains that coursed through him nearly constantly now seemed worse than normal. He reached into a nearby satchel and procured a jar of pleasantly smelling cream before applying it to much of his arms and shoulders.

Begrudgingly, Chase hobbled to his feet before

dressing for the day. He elected not to wear his heavy leathers and instead settled for a simple linen shirt and brown cotton pants. Remi and Klaus were waiting for him to join them in the hostel's common area by the time Chase forced himself out of his room.

Chase's head screamed at even the slightest of movements, but his body was at least his own again. He joined his guides at their nearby table before croaking, "Where's Richard?"

"The little cub seems to have drunk a little too much after your Azalean princess joined you," Klaus replied wryly, clearly enjoying the state of things that morning. "Come, young one. Remi saw our drunken friend earlier this morning."

Trying to hide his pain as much as he could, Chase followed them out of the inn. Two blocks away, lying on a pile of potato sacks under the awning of a deli, was Richard. He was lying face up snoring loudly while holding a particularly large sack of the tubers in his arms.

With the distinct sound of muffled laughter, Remi waved her arm over the sleeping man with her palm to the ground. In the trail of her arm, ice cold water was conjured from thin air before falling on the drunkard.

Richard howled, scrambling to his feet and swinging his arms violently, grasping for his battle axe. When he finally realized who had woken him, he spit a mouthful of water onto the ground and nodded.

Chase rubbed his eyes, trying to get some sort of

relief from his headache. "Where are we headed now?" he asked. "I'd rather we leave sooner than later. Anything to take my mind off this headache."

"There is a small dock here in Glarrus." Remi suppressed more laughter. "After we replenish our supplies, we should buy passage on a ferry to Haven. It'll be quicker than riding and our horses should finally get some much needed and well-earned rest. Although, if you do not mind me saying, and I mean this with the utmost sympathy, I assure you. It seems to me you lads need the rest more than the horses do."

"Can you please stop your bloody yelling," Richard complained despite their quiet tone. "My head is about to burst. I need eggs."

There were no protests to seeking an easier route to Haven. After procuring some food at the various delis, bakeries, and butchers of Glarrus, they readied their horses. The town was small, but the streets were narrow and uneven in most places, so it took a painfully long time to make their way through the market all the way to the docks.

The rickety wooden docks weren't much to behold. A simple deckhouse sat at the base of a long row of aged wooden planks.

Only one ship remained in the port this morning. It was a small vessel, but wide and sturdy with a large white sail and two massive water wheels that Klaus explained helped with traversing the river's currents. A meager crew was tending to the boat, checking lines, and moving around cargo this way and that.

Without delaying any more than was needed, they approached a thin old man with a scraggly, grey beard that was sitting in the deck house. The man spat on the ground before scratching his cheek. "Oy. Name's Welland. Captain Welland of the *Water Thrush*. What can I do ya' for? Long time since I seen a Magi and Drakthul in close company with Gallanders. Lookin' for passage down the Harp?"

"Aye." Remi dipped her head in a respectful manner before standing upright once more, though the short woman was only a forearm's length taller than the counter of the deckhouse. "My name is Remi, and these fine gentlemen that I have the pleasure of accompanying are my companions— Klaus, Richard, and Chase. We seek passage to Haven for us, our supplies, and our horses. I can certainly assure you, we have plenty coin to pay your services and require little in the way of commodities or conveniences."

The captain spat again. "Ack. *Water Thrush* got more than enough space, but I'll not be takin' ya' as far as Haven. I got no ill will for the city folk, but my route only goes as far as our tradin' post upriver from the city walls before I got to turn back and head upstream. Even if it wasn't, river's got a mighty current this time o' fall and it only gets worse nearin' the sea. Only 'bout a day's ride from the city at any rate, if ya' manage a good pace."

"That is more than adequate, captain," Klaus raised his brimmed leather hat to the man who shrugged and spat yet again. "I suspect your vessel will provide an enjoyable voyage." His voice was smooth like running water as he placed the purse of gold coins suitable for the ship's fare on the counter.

The captain took a single gold coin embedded with a curved-necked heron and bit down on the metal. Tossing the purse in one hand, he seemed satisfied enough. "Pack yer things and climb aboard. We leave within the hour. Just keep that Drakthul smooth talk 'way from the lasses on my crew. Don't want ya' gettin' any ideas."

As the group boarded the ship, avoiding the bustling crew of shirtless men and cloth wrapped women alike, Chase looked back at the town of Glarrus. Smoke poured from numerous chimneys while the sound of children playing and dogs barking quickly faded under the growing sounds of hard footsteps on wood and the water beneath the docks. The horses were uneasy to board a ship at first, but they soon relaxed and were secured in animal pens hidden below deck.

His gaze soon returned to the nearby deckhouse and his stomach twisted on itself. The Man in Red stood behind the counter with a wicked smile and a crazed look in his eye. For a moment, Chase could not shake the dreadful feeling that the figure was about to speak to him, but Captain Welland's waving arm directing the nearby dock workers broke the illusion and the Man in Red vanished as quickly as he had appeared.

Rubbing his eyes and forehead, Chase rolled his shoulders with an unpleasant cracking sensation. His headache was fading, but it was taking much longer than he would have preferred.

After a few hours of sitting on the ship's deck

practicing some simple spell crafting, his head had thankfully returned to normal. Even though the Man in Red hadn't shown himself again, Chase couldn't shake his unease. The nightmarish apparition was appearing more often, and the dull, persistent ache behind his eyes was a bitter reminder of his constant struggles each night.

Thankfully, the following days of traveling on the *Water Thrush* were long but uneventful. The gentle sway of the ship's hull bouncing in the river's current was comforting while the sounds of bank swallows, blackbirds, and mallards created a soothing ambience behind the bustle of the ship's crew. Chase enjoyed the smell of river water and mud that filled his nostrils while the landscape shifted before their eyes. Hills flattened to plains, and maples and birches gave way to elms and poplars, their leaves embracing a dazzling range of oranges, golds, and reds as they approached the heart of fall.

The ship's crew grew suspicious of Chase's ragged appearance, but he could dismiss the cold sweats and aching joints as sea sickness easily enough. To distract himself, he focused on practicing his sorcery. He enjoyed the routine it provided him, and he was excited when Remi shared that he was progressing quite quickly compared to most students. Chase was now capable of weaving the toams mid-conversation with relative ease, faltering only with more complex tasks unless he gave them his full attention.

They spent most of their spare time playing simple card and dice games below deck. Remi often conversed with the crew, although Klaus politely heeded Captain Welland's warning and stayed mostly to himself to avoid giving anyone the wrong impression. Richard and Chase prodded their guides for casual information while they ate slowly from their rations and drank steadily from their water skins. No crew member seemed to take much note of their passengers, but judging from Welland's harsh demeanor, Chase suspected that was on the order of their captain.

On the fourth morning of sailing down the river, a meager outpost came into view from the deck of the *Water Thrush*. By midmorning the riverboat had docked next to a watchtower on the northern bank of the Harp. The outpost was comprised of little more than the tower and a few stock houses that accompanied some simple cottages. The buildings were made of more stone than wood, from a strange beige rock that made the structures look dirty.

Chase watched the shirtless crew members unload the group's possessions as well as several small wooden crates that had been stored in the ship's cargo hold. They carried many more crates back aboard the *Water Thrush* before Captain Welland bid the travelers farewell. Even though it was nearly midday, the captain insisted the party could make it to Haven by nightfall if they hurried.

After a few hours of brisk riding, Chase was trying to remain in high spirits despite his diminishing mental state. He was eager to reach the nation's capital, but he feared his attempts at some semblance of optimism were in vain.

He'd been having the horrific dream of the woman being beaten in the cellar repeatedly the last few nights, and each time it became harder to clear his mind in the morning. The Man in Red would stand over him in his cot or in the corner of his room laughing at him, or he would think he was back in the cellar for long, hard minutes after opening his eyes. One night, the woman had even been replaced by Rose, which forced Chase into a fit of screaming the following morning, shaking in fear of what he had witnessed.

I can't be losing it. Not now. These dreams have got to go away some time.

Please, they have to stop.

Once we get to Haven, they'll surely stop. They just have to.

Please, not like this.

Klaus noticed Chase was struggling with something while they rode. "Trying to remember the face of your Azalean princess, young one?" he teased. "You weren't that drunk, I hope. I seem to remember she was quite pretty."

"I've been meaning to ask," growled Richard with a growing smile. "Do we have to call you a *little* shadow now, or will shadow suffice?" They had overheard Chase murmur that in his sleep and were not going to let him forget it any time soon.

The other three travelers laughed haughtily from their horses while Chase snickered. "If you call me little shadow, Richard, I reserve the right to refer to you as my little bear cub like that one woman from Haverson did. I remember she was quite taken with you even after you sobered up and realized she was married. Her husband nearly ran you through with a pitchfork when he found out. You almost swore off grain liquor after that entire debacle—almost."

Remi snorted a puff of smoke from her pipe, choking on her own breath. "It would appear that our Drakthul friend was not entirely wrong after all."

Richard's cheeks grew flush with embarrassment. "Aye, Chase, fair enough." He turned to Klaus and Remi. "Just how far away is this damned city, anyway? My rear is as raw as that jerky we've been gnawing on, even after our ferry down the river. My stomach still doesn't sit right, mind you. Bloody boats. Man was never meant to ride the water like that. I'm ready for a decent meal and a great big tankard of ale." Richard licked his lips as he finished.

Remi chuckled. "Not far now, lad. We keep our pace up, and we should arrive by sundown just like Captain Welland said we would. Say what you will, but I've always known ship captains to be honest enough men. Surely their tales can be something to behold, and I've had my fair share of run-ins with unruly men in the Royal Navy, but they were honest enough, all things considered."

"Bloody sundown?" Richard shifted uncomfortably in his saddle. "I don't know if I can take another full day of bloody riding. This horse is fine enough, but a man can only spend so much time in the saddle. We've been on horseback more than not since this damned journey of ours started."

"Indeed, young one," Klaus sneered with a glimmer in his eye. "I can understand your concern, but it looks to me like your rear will be just fine."

Chase chuckled while he rubbed his fingers together causing sparks to fizzle above his hand. The group continued onward, stopping very briefly for another meal upon Richard's request. As the day approached evening, Chase could see the city of Haven peeking up from the horizon. True to the captain's word, the river's current had grown much stronger by then, and it stretched out to almost double the width it had been when the group left Glarrus.

Richard had grown weary from the continued riding, insisting stubbornly that the group stop briefly again to stretch their legs. Chase didn't mind. His own limbs had begun to ache despite Madelyn's creams, and his leathers had grown uncomfortably warm from the sun beating down on the group all day.

He hopped down from his mount and raised his stiff arms upward as he stepped down the river's embankment. The cushion of the sand under his boots was a welcome relief from his rigid saddle. Against his better judgement, his mind wandered while he looked down at the flowing river.

Chase could faintly make out large fish swimming just beneath the water's glistening surface. He blinked and the fish were dead, rotting with exposed skeletons and missing pieces of flesh that floated just below the surface. He blinked again and the fish returned to normal. Insects buzzed around the reeds along the shore among packs of hunting herons and egrets that screeched the awful, pained screams of children between innocent squawks and chirps. Ducks waded through the shallows around charred, dead bodies that were there one moment and gone the next. Gusts of wind occasionally flowed across the water that filled Chase's nostrils with the smell of smoke and brimstone, but it was quickly replaced by the pleasant aromas of sweetgrass and cedar.

Hoping his senses would return to him soon, Chase bent to his knee and reached his hand into the cold flowing water. He splashed a handful onto his face before cupping his hands to take a small drink. The cool liquid was crisp, putting his mind and heart at ease for a quiet moment. It ran down his cheeks into his ragged beard. The breeze across the river's surface crawled up his spine, sending a shiver across his skin that seemed to echo the wind.

As he shook his hands dry, the sand beneath him began to shift. His stomach lurched uncomfortably, and he stood only to be nearly thrown off his feet. The very ground beneath him lifted upward with a violent jerk.

A massive creature burst from the riverbank with an agitated groan.

The beast stood on two legs, towering well over the height of three men. Its thick gray hide was covered in mud, sand, and rocks from the riverbank, and it reeked of rotten fish and stale water. Its legs were short and massively thick, supporting a hulking hunchbacked behemoth with arms as large as the tree trunks. On a bulging neck sat a large, misshapen head with a flat brow. Its massive, under-biting jaw held three immense rectangular teeth that appeared to be carved from river rocks. Alongside a lumpy and battered nose, two beady, bloodshot eyes glared at the intruder. Sand, mud, reeds, and stones fell from its back and limbs.

It let out a hulking roar.

Nearly stunned by the odor of the thing, Chase staggered up the riverbank. He stumbled to his hands and knees, kicking furiously while trying to ascend the hill. He finally caught the heel of his boot in soft earth and sprang to his feet only to hear Remi yell from behind him. "River troll! Hurry, lads. Get to your horses, now!"

Chase didn't hesitate. Even so, he had to leap quickly to his left when the monster slammed its arm downward, narrowly missing its mark. He cursed and ducked under another brutal swing, a gust of wind rushing past him. His heart sank when he realized his horse was running away, but the sand and mud was making it nearly impossible to get away from the monster quickly.

With a frustrated roar, the troll wildly pounded the ground with both arms. Chase whistled repeatedly in a desperate attempt to get his horse's attention, but it failed. He swore again at his carelessness in missing the troll's resting spot, frantically dodging its onslaught of attacks.

A blast of heat flew past Chase followed by a roar of pain from the troll. Remi's distraction was just enough to knock the beast off balance, causing it to stumble clumsily over its thick limbs. After what felt like ages, Chase's frightened mare finally heeded his call and halted just long enough for him to leap into the saddle. He gave his horse a brisk strike on its flanks with his heels, and it cantered into a fierce gallop.

By then, the troll had diverted its attention to its new attacker, who had been throwing blasts of fire at the monster from horseback. A sudden realization dawned on Chase that he could help the group escape as well.

His mind racing, he desperately tried to think of a spell he could cast to slow the troll's pursuit. *I could trip it. How the bloody hell would I do that? Maybe I can make Remi's fire bigger or hotter somehow. No, that won't do much either. That thing seems hardly bothered by it.* His gaze fixated on the water still dripping from the troll's legs. His mind went back to his bowl of water by the fire.

That's it.

While his horse galloped to catch the rest of the group, Chase reached out and grasped at the air in front of him as though he were holding an invisible goblet. He clenched his fist and the air around the troll crackled. A cold mist hung in the air for just a second before a boom rang out and the water streaming down the troll's legs violently froze.

Legs locked in place, the troll grunted and fell forward, slamming its jaw on the hard packed road beside the river. The group took the opportunity to gain as much ground as they could, but they only managed to retreat a few cart lengths away before the monster broke free from its icy shackles and resume its pursuit.

The troll was immensely quick for its size with shocking endurance. They fled at a brisk gallop, looking back on occasion between frustrated roars to see that the troll was chasing them with a wild vigor that Chase never would have imagined from such a creature. An entire hour later, and the troll was still rampaging behind them, slobbering as it scrambled to catch its prey.

Finally, the gates to Haven stood before them. The troll roared again in anger, but this time it was answered by the distant bellow of a guardsman's horn. Chase strained his eyes, his horse recklessly charging forward. Just as the group was almost within shouting distance of the ramparts, he saw a rank of archers rise from behind the garrison and let loose a slew of arrows. Chase gasped and ducked, but to his relief, the quarrels flew behind them and battered the ground in front of the rampaging troll.

A final scream erupted from the monster, and it stumbled to a halt. The troll pounded the ground in anger while arrows peppered its back. Shielding its face with massive arms it turned away from the city and retreated into the distance in defeat.

Chase relaxed in his saddle and allowed his horse to slow. By now his joints and muscles screamed in silent protest at even the slightest of movements. He longed for the comfort of a soft mattress. *Hell, even a hard mattress would be welcome after that ride.*

Breathless and exhausted, the group slowly approached Haven's gate. The tall stone wall that barred their entry, constructed from the same beige stone as the trading post that had long since fallen behind the horizon, loomed over them. It was marginally better than the monolithic gray walls of Corina or Edenhall, but this close to the base of the wall it still exerted a crushing presence that was hard to ignore.

The great wooden gate swung open with a worn, tired groan to allow their entry. Several armed guards, standing with their hands resting on their sword hilts and crossbow handles to remind the visitors of their presence, met the strange group that had just led a troll to their doorstep.

Carpenter's bloody Hammer, I'm tired.

CHAPTER 23
THE DEMON OF SOULE

"You, there," a chainmail-clad guard holding a crossbow spoke, his crude accent betraying his humble upbringing. He wore a light blue tabard stitched with a great white heron holding a silver fish in its mouth. "What business you got 'ere in Haven? It ain't every day we see armed men running through these parts carryin' a troll behind 'em. You some kind of soldiers or somethin'?" He spoke through gapped teeth and had a lightly faded scar across his cheek.

Klaus was the first to respond, his voice still shaken from the ride, but still more composed than the rest of his friends. "We are travelers, friend. One of ours managed an unfortunate moment of bad luck which placed him on the back of that river troll. We had been running for quite some time when your archers were kind enough to lend us a hand."

A second guard, wearing the same heron on a

field of blue and holding a long bow with a sword at his side spoke up this time. "That still don't explain why y'all are armed to the teeth. Just who do ya think y'are?" He spoke in a nasally voice, his crooked nose making the nose piece of his steel cap look awkward and unnecessary.

Still raggedly panting, Remi slowed her breathing with a concerted effort and spoke levelly. "My name… is Remi… and these are my companions. We are here to visit the Grand Market and buy passage on a fishing vessel from the Golden Harbor. We've been on the road the past few weeks, traveling all the way from Redwood and we are very tired. I would appreciate if you and your fine guardsmen would allow us to continue so that we may rest."

The first guard with the crossbow wiped his nose with the back of his leather glove. "Just how do we know you're tellin' the truth? You folk come bearin' weapons and that troll. I don't know 'bout that."

Richard grew tired of negotiating and growled in response. "You know our business and given we haven't skewered the lot of you, I'd say we're safe to let through."

Chase couldn't hide the smile that crept across his face, reminded of his days carrying out assassination contracts with his friend. *Cole never appreciated how blunt Richard could be.*

He looked down at the guards from atop his saddle. "If we were trying to bring some kind of danger to the city, don't you think that crashing straight through the main gate would be less than ideal for us? Surely, your strapping young archers would have stuck us like pin cushions if we had brandished our weapons. We just want to rest before we're on our way. Nothing more."

Silence dragged on for an uncomfortable moment while the guards digested what the would-be visitors had said. The guard with the crossbow spit on the ground before nodding. "Aye. Seems fair enough to me and mine." He turned to the second, inner gate behind him. "Let 'em in, boys. Don't think they'll bring us trouble." The guards stepped to the side and allowed the party to enter the city of Haven.

The city was organized into tight rows of cobblestone roads between wooden and beige stone houses that crawled upward multiple floors, built in a fashion that allowed for little extra space. Streetlamps were being lit for the evening outside each of the buildings, giving the entire city an orange warmth that almost made the strange stone glow.

Remi was the most familiar with the city—and as such—led the way to an inn for the night. They passed more taverns and various storefronts than Chase had ever seen in any of the cities of the Berg. Even as the establishments were closing for the evening, people of all sorts walked the narrow streets. He recognized several dark-skinned Magi dressed in a mix of beige tones and colorful silks, along with a few pale Drakthul clad in flowing linen and cotton under thick, darkly dyed leather. He assumed that the olive-toned people dressed in leather overcoats with gem-colored eyes were Azaleans, but there were still many people that were completely foreign to him, each looking stranger than the last.

Eventually, they arrived at The Drunken Demon, adorned with a painted board depicting a strange red man with horns holding a tankard of ale—which Klaus insisted was the most comfortable inn in the entire city. They purchased their beds for the night, requesting their horses be fed generously before they were brought to the nearby stable after such a hard ride. After moving their belongings into each of their rooms, they met in the tavern beneath the inn for a drink to relax after a tiring day.

The tavern was dark, lit only by numerous candles that lined the walls and filled the tables. The dark, stained furniture was draped with white tablecloths spotted by melting wax. It was a strange décor but seemingly suited the inn's namesake. A ragged old man with a greying mustache sang a harmonious tale while he strummed an ornate harp from his seat in the center of the room. The sound filled the air with a sense of life that would not have left, even if all the patrons had.

Klaus had insisted they try a dish from his homeland that the locals had started to refer to as black bean stew. The inn keeper's reluctant son placed a bowl in front of Chase that was overflowing with beef, black beans, various mushrooms and cabbage stewed in beef broth with garlic, onions, and black coffee. Shortly after eating the strange but delicious meal, Chase relished a goblet of sweet mead and retired for the night long before the rest of the travelers had eaten their fill.

Lying on his bed, Chase stared at the ceiling of his room. The place was simple, with a surprisingly soft mattress on a sturdy oak frame. It was cramped yet comfortable with only enough space for the dresser, end table, and coat rack all made from the same stained wood.

His body ached from the day's excitement, and without much thought, he allowed himself to sink into the mattress, closing his eyes and breathing in the cool air as deeply as he could.

*****

When he opened his eyes, Chase was lying in the same bed in the same inn, but the smell of fire flooded his nostrils, and the room was bathed in an eerie red glow.

He sighed and rose to his feet. *Here we go again.* He cracked his neck before walking through the door to the rest of the inn and eventually out the inn's front door. The city was most certainly Haven, but the buildings around him were set ablaze. Screaming filled the air, accompanied by the crackling of fire and the occasional boom of a collapsing building somewhere far off in the distance.

"Where are you going so quickly, old friend?"

Chase closed his eyes in despair and turned to the owner of the familiar voice. He saw the mirror image of himself, clothed in blood red trimmed with splashes of grey, standing just outside The Drunken Demon. Chase nearly spat at the wicked man. "What do you want?"

"Now, now, Chase. Where are your manners?" the Man in Red smiled. "I'm simply opening your eyes to your future. Our future. Is it not the most wonderful, beautiful sight you have ever had the pleasure to behold?"

"You're lying," Chase grunted, his teeth involuntarily grinding as he spoke. "Is this some kind of sick joke to you? You force your way into my head and parade around these scenes like some kind of theater, and now you expect me to believe they're visions?" Chase resisted the urge to rub his aching eyes. "Whoever you are, you must be slow. Only a fool would believe you. And even if I did, what's to stop me from doing everything in my power to avoid all of this?" Chase gestured to the ruined world around him as he finished his defiant statement.

The Man in Red laughed. "*That* is where you're mistaken. These aren't images I am creating, nor are they visions I am conjuring. They are simply a glimpse into your future. This world is not a choice that can be decided against. It is an inevitability. You *will* see this fate come to pass, because it already has. This is a set course, and you are sailing right for it. Have I spoken plainly enough for you, or shall I continue? I know you cannot be as dense as your friend. After all, I never was."

Chase looked at the Man in Red and his deranged smile. Simply standing in the man's presence made him feel unclean somehow. "Don't take me for a fool. None of this started until I set out from the Burrow. I have no doubt that these little fantasies of yours are only meant to scare me. How else would you explain the dream with Sasha or the charger? And what about the dreams with Rose? They're twisted perversions, all of them, and none were revealed to me until after I already knew their context. It's nothing but a trick."

The Man in Red cackled at the remark. "So, I can't have a little fun on the side? Curse me for being a man who enjoys his work. As for the timing of it all, your friend in the Blackridge Mountains may be able to shed light on the subject. Then again, he may not. Who am I to say?" The wicked man looked down at his feet as if to see if he had stepped in something, then back up at Chase. "You've seen what I have to show when you needed to, and you will continue to do so from now on. There are such glorious things you can and *will* do in time. It will all come in time. Don't worry. You are going to do great and terrible things. It's going to be so much fun."

***

Chase fell from his bed with a heavy thud, panting and sweating profusely. He desperately rubbed his eyes. *I won't go mad. I don't care what that man said. That won't be me.*

He opened his eyes and through his blurred vision, he saw the Man in Red watching him. One moment, he was sitting on the nearby chair with a scowl on his face. The next, he was lying in the bed laughing maniacally. His voice rang out in Chase's mind, saying a hundred things at once.

He was sitting next to Chase. He was standing over him. He laughed. He screamed.

The world rushed around Chase as he curled his arms around himself.

"See you soon."

With that single, solemn statement, the Man in Red vanished and the room fell silent. Chase's ragged breathing and racing heartbeat slowly steadied. His hair clung to his brow uncomfortably, but eventually, the cool morning breeze through the window was enough to put him at ease.

Please. I can't go mad. Not now. Please.

Slowly, with shaking hands and wobbling knees, Chase gathered his belongings and left his room to join his companions. He was the first one to wake up that morning, so he found a quiet table in the inn's tavern and ordered a mug of coffee to occupy his hands while he waited. The steaming black drink filled his chest with a warm sensation that was always sapped from him in the night.

Chase finished his drink and was halfway through his second mug when he was finally joined by his companions. He welcomed their slower pace now that they had reached the city. Ever since he had left the Burrow, there was hardly time to sit, let alone relax and share a casual conversation over morning coffee or tea. Even still, he couldn't help but feel his stomach twist in knots again while he contemplated his next steps. He was eager to keep moving forward, desperate to rid himself of the Man in Red once and for all.

Haven's Grand Market was nestled in the center of the city, so it took the group quite a long time to reach it. Along the way, the city seemed even livelier than it had the night before. Men and women of all ages bustled through the streets on their way to and from their homes, jobs, and the myriad of vendors that lined the walkways.

When they finally arrived, Chase couldn't help

feeling overwhelmed by the scope of the marketplace. Stands selling various goods were packed in as tightly as the space would allow, crammed in until the place was overflowing with carts, wagons, stalls, and storefronts each with their own small crowd of passersby.

Merchants selling various exotic spices, produce, baking goods, and meats were scattered randomly among fine silk and cloth vendors, smithy supply stands, and tanning suppliers. With such a vast number of vendors, each individual seller could afford to specialize beyond any store Chase had ever seen. Smiths that only worked with specific metals, butchers that slaughtered only one breed of animal, and even bakers that worked with a single type of grain were only a few of the stands they passed as they eagerly searched for goods to carry on the next leg of their journey together.

Chase departed from the others and wandered through the immense market looking for anything that caught his eye. He felt himself getting distracted by the faces within the crowd as much as by the goods in the stalls. Gallanders with all sorts of hair and fair skin, dressed in simple cotton and linen that seemed suited for a farm as well as a marketplace crowded next to exotically garbed Magi, wrapped in silks with shining dark skin and glimmering black hair. The occasional Drakthul made their way through the crowd dressed in dark leather, though man and woman alike wore hats that shielded their ghostly pale skin from the sun.

Most unsettling among those in the crowd were the olive-toned Azaleans in their fine dresses and shirts, partially covered by odd overcoats that didn't extend beyond their waists. Many of the foreigners with gem-colored eyes shot Chase sideways glances and suspicious looks when they saw his tattoo, making the hair on the back of his neck stand on end. *Perhaps Rose was right. They suspect they know what the mark is, although the question now is what will they do about it?* Shaking away his unease, Chase tried to distract himself with the rest of the crowd.

Several people with sharp features and pointed ears hidden beneath ragged, tangled hair passed over him showing little or no interest. Their builds varied as wildly as their features did, but they all wore the same hand-stitched garb of natural greens, browns, and yellows that were decorated with various beads and claws and trinkets. Chase could have sworn a few of them had fangs even larger than Klaus', while others looked like they were covered in a fine coat of fur that shimmered in the sun. Realizing that none of the onlookers in the market seemed to think twice about the strange folk, Chase tried not to draw attention to himself by prying too closely with his gaze.

While most of the strangers in the market seemed little more than simple foreigners, there were those of a more monstrous nature that nearly made Chase reach for his blade before he caught himself. The Beast-men that Remi had spoken so poorly of were nothing like Chase imagined they would be. Broad chests held abnormally thick arms that extended well passed their hips. Their fingers were long with dagger-like claws, and their bodies were covered in coarse fur that varied in shades of brown, gray, and black. Most striking and terrifying of all their features were the bear-like heads that rest upon their shoulders, always raised high with the utmost sense of pride.

Through the madness of the crowd, Chase managed to find a few stands that caught his eye. He bought several finely balanced throwing knives made in Soule and paid a smith to sharpen his cleaving dagger. He also filled a large leather satchel with bread, jerked beef and pork, a few spices from a Drakthul merchant, a length of fine corded rope, some segments of cloth, and a small collection of sharpening stones.

It felt strange to be browsing goods at his leisure, buying and bartering like any other commoner. It was not a luxury he could ever afford in Rakksberg as a child, and he was never welcome to as an adult. *I suppose I could get used to this. Although, I don't suppose I'll be able to do such things if we make our way back home somehow.*

Sometime later, Chase found himself chuckling when he bought a length of silver silk that could be wrapped around his leathers in a similar fashion to his Magi friend. *Rose did say it would look nice.* After spending hours among the stalls in the Grand Market, Chase only failed to find an adequate sword. He longed for a replacement to the blade that had snapped in the charger attack, but the swords he found were either poorly crafted, much too expensive for his humble budget, or simply felt wrong in his hand.

Finally, Chase made his way out of the swarming hive that was the market. It took him a long time to figure out exactly where he had wandered to, but he eventually found his friends resting in a nearby park, sharing what they had bought with one another while they waited. With full sacks and lightened hearts from the day's endeavors, they continued toward the Golden Harbor.

The streets were much less crowded than the marketplace. Peddlers that clearly could not afford a better selling space, or vendors that simply did not want to move their products still yelled eagerly at passersby, but they could at least speak to one another normally this far from the Grand Market.

Shortly after the group had departed from the market, Chase saw a woman with dreadfully pale skin, but her features were soft and rounded and she lacked the pointed ears and slender frame of the Drakthul. When she glanced at him, Chase was startled to see that her almond-shaped eyes were a light, cloudy gray color. She wore a strange, dark silk dress—cut in a way he had never seen and embroidered in golden thread—under a thick fur cloak. Her leather boots were fur lined as well, along with the cuffs of her sleeves

They soon passed a peculiar man selling beads that struck Chase's eye. He was a handsome man, clearly from somewhere in Soule. Beyond that, there was nothing of note about him beyond the abnormally large crowd of women huddled around his wares.

Remi looked at the man in disgust. "If I am not mistaken, and I can assure you I am quite confident in the matter, I suspect that man is burning heart-thorn.

It's a rare weed found only in Talvenna on the banks of certain river. When it is mixed with spices found in Soule and Shi, it can entice people into becoming more agreeable and compliant. That scent is quite unique, and the effect is plain to see, but I sadly only have my suspicions. If I had some proof of the matter, I would report him to the guard."

"What kind of proof would you need?" Richard seemed oddly bothered by the spectacle, though Chase suspected a certain amount of jealousy may be the reason why.

Klaus raised an eyebrow, clearly suspecting the same thing Chase did. "The incense burner used would have a strange residue left behind from the spices mixing while they are burned."

"Richard, I know it seems wrong, but even if we had time to stop to look into it, how would you expect us to—" Chase was so distracted that he didn't see the hulking form before it slammed into him square in the chest. The force of the blow as the Beast-man walked by was almost enough to throw him completely off his feet. He wheeled around in anger. "Hey! Why don't you watch where you're going next time?"

The man turned his head and grinned, bearing a row of sharp ivory teeth that shined against his black fur. He wore nothing but tattered linen pants, allowing his rippling muscles to be displayed even beneath his thick fur. "Mind your words, pale hide. You stink of frost weaver Magi filth. I should rip out your tongue with my own teeth and rake your bare back just for showing me such disrespect. You would be eaten as a morsel in Black Rock, not fit for a meal."

"Now, black fur, we mean you no disrespect, to you, your clan, or your ancestors," Klaus smoothly interjected before Chase could respond. "My friend is not from these lands and is... unfamiliar with Tor customs. I will personally see that he is reprimanded by my own customs and laws before the sun sleeps and the moon wakes. We apologize for any inconvenience we've caused. May your teeth be sharp, and your claws never dull." He bowed his head and lifted his brimmed hat slightly as he finished.

"Spare me, *blood elf*." The bear-like man snarled and bared his fangs again. "Your ways are weak, and your blood is thin. I would sooner be put to the pike than accept such patronage." The man turned his head slowly to look at the travelers one by one. His eyes finally rested on Remi.

An uncontrollable rage filled his expression while his muscles twitched and clenched. "Remylara Drakolar! Slayer of Children—the Demon of Soule! How dare you stand before a Child of Tor with such pride? You should be on your knees begging for me to rake your oily hide. I should rip out your throat and tear your limbs from your trunk, you spineless butcher!" The words sounded thick and clumsy coming from the man's fanged mouth, but the threat was not lost on them.

Remi sighed, her chin falling slowly to her chest. Chase stared at her in bewilderment before noticing sadness and regret flowing through the woman's expression.

He glared back at the Beast-man and felt his hand clench the handle of his dagger under his cloak. Eyes scanning his surroundings, Chase saw three of the man's kin that would most likely join if their conversation came to blows. Richard's stance widened very slightly. The air buzzed in anticipation and silence fell around them.

Before anything else could happen, Remi stepped forward. "What is your name, lad?"

"Coal-Brynn-Skor," the Beast-man snarled. Chase watched his muscles continue to flex and strain. "You killed my moon brother, Coal-Koran-Skor, and your men killed my cousin by blood, Iron-Gnag-Troga. You murdered countless of my people to force your filthy Magi ways on my kin. My home is gone because of you, Demon of Soule."

Remi's face became sunken and solemn. She lifted her gaze to look the Beast-man in the eye. "Nothing I can say will change the things I've done, and nothing I can do short of offering you my life will ease your suffering. You disdain my people as I do yours, although I would suspect you personally are more justified in such matters. That much won't change. That doesn't justify what I've done, and I am pained to accept that nothing will.

"I long for a day when the Magi of Soule and the Children of Tor can put down their weapons and allow peace to prosper between us. I've grown tired of our conflict. You, Coal-Brynn-Skor, black-fur spell breaker of the Children of Tor, deserve my most sorrowful apologies." Tears were streaming down the Magi's cheeks, even though her voice stayed composed. "What happened in Coal was despicable. I have no other words for it."

Coal-Brynn-Skor scowled. "Your words are shallow, butcher. Your actions and the actions of your people say otherwise. All this talk of sorrow taints your meat. Cowards always taste of pity and shame. You treat us like savages who don't know our right from our left and yet you burn your meat to tasteless bark and wrap your wounds in dry sheep's fur. Our people will never have peace, not as long as the pale hides and oil hides decide what is and is not *proper* for those they have no claim over."

With that, the Beast-man left the travelers to stand alone in the road. Remi sighed in relief, her muscles visibly relaxing as she did. Chase felt himself ease as well, and his hand fell to his side. The spiteful remarks had cut through the air like a dagger, but it was Remi's apology that lingered far into the silence.

CHAPTER 24
CASHING IN A FAVOR

"What the hell was that, Remi?" Chase asked in a hushed tone so his other companions would not hear him while the continued toward the harbor.

"I don't wish to speak of it, Chase. I have done things I wish to forget."

"I don't think that's an option at this point, Remi." He stepped around a cart someone had left in the middle of the walkway before returning to the Magi's side. "We've been down this road before and when we spoke about it then, you told me to trust you. You know I'm an assassin—that I've killed people for most of my life. Enough to make a living from it. I don't see what can be worse than that, and frankly, I don't care if it is. If you can't be honest with me, then how am I supposed to trust you?"

"I would hope that I've done enough for you that my trust would not *still* be in question," Remi snapped in a heated tone. This was clearly a sore subject, but Chase had to be certain whatever this was wouldn't come back to harm them later.

When Remi realized Chase wasn't about to let the subject go, she sighed. "Alas, you aren't wrong, lad. For all my faults, I still like to think I can be open with those closest to me." She pulled her pipe from her satchel with quivering hands and packed it with dried tobacco. After lighting it with a snap of her fingers, she drew in a long puff of smoke. "When I was a younger woman, the commander of an entire battalion in the Royal Army of Soule, I had a company of Spellswords under my command—unlike anything in the rest of the army. They were brigands and mercenaries. Some were assigned to my battalion to keep them in line while they served out prison sentences, while others were simply in it for the coin.

"I quickly established myself as a particularly efficient leader. Although, I must admit, I am no longer proud of such recognition. After a few of my more successful endeavors, I was charged with leading a campaign on Black Rock soil. It was the first time the Magi had set foot in Tor territory in nearly fifteen years. My company of lawbreakers led the assault and quickly established forward outposts, dispelling the Tor presence from large portions of Black Rock. It was not a glamorous operation, nor was it the thing of stories, but it worked in the eyes of my superiors. After all, as you might expect, what was the cost of losing a few criminals if it meant we were to take Black Rock once and for all?

"It looked like the Royal Army was on track to achieve swift and decisive victory over the Children of Tor until we arrived at the settlement of Coal." Remi shook her head as smoke shot from her mouth in a sorrowful sigh. "You see, all Children of Tor are named first after the settlement from which they were birthed, and last after the name of their mother or father. That man was a survivor of what we had done, and his brother was one of the victims."

Chase stepped around another bump in the road and returned his attention to Remi. "Survivor of what, exactly?"

Remi drew deeply from her pipe before solemnly recalling the tale. "After seventeen days of fighting with no signs of victory over the spell breakers in Coal, my men began to feel doomed to retreat and admit failure. They felt that there was no hope for victory, or even survival over the savages, and I cannot say that I didn't feel the same. So, on the seventeenth night, I called my officers into my command tent, and we devised a plan to ensure our victory in Coal and later in Black Rock. I see now that the wiser solution would have been to accept our failures and retreat." She allowed tears to fall from her eyes once more. "We were to send most of our remaining forces, all the remaining criminals, in a frontal assault on the settlement before retreating on the eighteenth evening to feign defeat. The war party was mobilized and on the move away from the settlement to complete the illusion.

"Then on the eighteenth night, I led a small group of my best sorcerers under the cover of exceedingly complex illusions conjured by my second in command to the heart of the settlement. It was there that I gave the order to drop the illusion and commence the final phase of the plan. We set fire to the settlement from the inside..." She stopped for a moment, struggling to continue. "I... I gave the order to kill anything in sight that did not wear the colors of the Royal Army. We spent the next *three hours* slaughtering every man, woman, and child we could reach. And I gave the order. It was done by my voice and by my hand."

Remi nearly choked on the words, her voice shaking with each breath. The blood left Chase's face and his stomach twisted in his gut. *I've done many things, but to lead a massacre?*

He wanted to let the whole thing go. He wanted to forget Remi had ever shared her grim tale, but something urged him forward. He remembered his numerous dreams, and the vile acts carried out by the Man in Red.

You are going to do great and terrible things.

"So, what happened after it was done?"

Chase felt the sting of regret as soon as he asked the question, but Remi cleared her throat and continued while she smoothed her silks with trembling hands. "After victory was won over Coal, three of my most talented sorcerers were so beset with grief and guilt, they took their own lives. I continued to lead the campaign for a short time, but my heart wasn't in the fight. No one's heart was. The full might of Black Rock fell upon our forces and drove us out of Coal and off the shores of their homeland. All that bloodshed, all those broken hearts, and all those lost souls were for nothing. We didn't accomplish victory over the Children of Tor. We didn't accomplish anything...

"In a matter of days, I left the army. Deserted. I traveled to Dren Talar, or rather Muqadasan, my nation's capital. The blasted *city with two names*..." Remi paused for a moment and shook her head. "I was there only long enough to hand them my officer's blade before stowing away on a cargo vessel headed to Azalea. There were those eager to see me leave after I had raised such a stir around my sister's death.

"I made my way through the country of flowers to Galland. I eventually met Klaus and tried to forget my past. Rellun Ajhara, my second in command and a powerful illusionist, took my place as leader of my battalion and to my knowledge still wages war on the Children of Tor to this day, for all the good it will do."

Chase walked in silence for a few paces. He struggled to find something to say. *Bloody hell. I'd want to forget that, too. I have my own fair share of sins I'd rather everyone forget...*

He finally looked at his travelling companion to see the tears had been wiped away. "Thank you, Remi. You've shared more than you needed to. I won't ask about it again."

Remi wiped her eyes again. "Know that I hold no love for the Beast-men. They're monsters that feast on the flesh of my people. They copulate under the moonlight under the guise of spirituality and condemn all that fail to conform to their blood-crazed ideals.

"I hold no love for the Children of Tor. But what

I did… I have no words for what I did to those souls at Coal. I burned them in their beds as they licked their wounds and slaughtered more in that night than I had killed in the entire campaign. I hold no love for the Children of Tor, but I do hold my sorrow for them close to my heart."

"I can see that now, Remi." Chase placed a hand on the woman's shoulder. "We all have memories we wish to remain hidden, and I won't uncover those again. I would never think to do that to a friend."

After waiting for some time, the pair walked briskly to rejoin the conversation with Klaus and Richard, who had at this point decided that Gallanders, while modest and charming, did not hold a candle to the Azaleans where beauty was concerned. Chase awkwardly joined the conversation, glad to have a distraction from more serious matters, but Remi took considerably longer to compose herself.

They soon arrived at the gates of the Golden Harbor. Upon reaching the clerk at the gate, Klaus handed over a shipping pass he had purchased at the market, allowing them to enter the docks. Chase's nose filled with the scent of salt water while his eyes adjusted to the sunlight that glared off the vast blue sea before him.

The harbor was massive, stretching up and down the coast as far as he could see through the crowd of busy workers. The calls of sailors to one another on nearby ships filled the air over a backdrop of clanking boots on wood while people loaded and unloaded goods from various vessels.

Remi abruptly called out to Chase and Richard,

"This way, lads. The fisherman we seek owns a small yet sturdy vessel, and he usually pulls into port north of the main gate. He is a fine enough man, though not quite as fine as others, if I may be so bold to say. I believe him to be an honest man, and after all, he does owe me a favor. This will certainly be a hefty favor to ask, but I have noticed in my days that I can be quite persuasive when I need to be." She winked at her friends as she finished her statement with a devilish smile.

The harbor was filled to the brim with all sorts of magnificent ships. A giant galley made of a bright yellow wood adorned with black and gold plating carried the largest crew Chase could see. The name *Goldfinch* was inscribed in gold letters on the hull. Next to that, a smaller vessel made from stained oak with blue sails labeled *Blue Jay* was securing itself to the docks in a mess of shouts and flinging lines. These were followed by the *River Swallow*, a schooner with a modest crew adorned with dark blue sails, and the *Night Raven*, a frigate made from pitch black wooden planks.

Chase noted that nearly every ship that they passed, large or small, was packed with cargo with only a few ships holding passengers. None carried weapons or armaments of any kind as far as Chase could tell.

Richard, never a particularly avid fan of subtlety, remarked, "Why is every ship we pass named after some damned bird? I was always told it was good luck to name a boat after a woman."

Klaus smirked. "Most cultures have their own

superstitions. For some it's women. The Drakthul prefer to name a ship after their family's patron star while the sailors of Galland put their faith in birds. If I recall correctly, a ship here is normally named for the last bird to land on the site of construction before wood has been lain. Though sometimes, it's named simply for a bird that the captain prefers."

"And in Soule we name them after flowers," Remi added. "While in Shi, they name their small number ships in honor of their gods of death. If I am not mistaken, the Elvari name their own vessels for various nature spirits. Although, I must confess that I do not know for certain. The Elvari certainly are a guarded folk at best." She gave a friendly chuckle with a warm smile.

"I suppose whatever works to keep the crew from jumping ship at the first sign of rough seas." Richard shrugged while he withdrew a piece of jerky from his belongings before tearing off a large mouthful with considerable effort. "Though, a bird's name doesn't quite roll from the tongue like a woman's."

Klaus laughed. "If you always have women on the mind, mighty bear, your den will be empty of mates. I am sure there are others who would share you company just as eagerly."

"It's not always," Richard retorted with a broad smile, ignoring the latter half of Klaus' comment. "Just *most* of the time."

They continued down the docks for a while, making their way slowly across the wooden walkways. Chase tried to take note of all the ships as they walked past, but there were far too many to keep straight without stopping to watch them for longer than they cared to.

After they passed what felt like hundreds of ships of all shapes and sizes, Remi saw a man she recognized and trotted over to greet him with her arms stretched to either side.

Chase looked at the nearby ships, guessing which he would have the chance to board. To his left, there was a galley made from spruce with deep green sails—*Country Chickadee* set in large bronze letter work across the bow. The *Tree Sparrow* was docked next. It was a schooner made from oak with modest trim of silver accents and red sails. Finally, there was a frigate made from redwood with orange and black sails labeled in blue paint as the *River Wren*.

"Chase!"

His observations were abruptly interrupted by Remi when she approached with the man she had recognized. "Chase, this is Parrus, captain of the *Tree Sparrow*. He's the fisherman I told you about that owes me a few favors."

"Now, now, Remi," the ship captain interjected with a smile. "If we're keeping track, I'm sure you'd owe me quite the debt for all the rides you've enjoyed on the *Sparrow*."

The captain was a gaunt man although he was strong in stature, and his posture was that of a man that had been to sea for many years. The whiskers on his chin, as well as the hair at his temples, were peppered with silver while the creases in the man's skin embellished his hardened features. His piercing blue eyes betrayed no ill will, but Chase saw the years of experience and hardship behind the man's gaze.

Parrus waved an arm dismissively, allowing his loose white shirt to sway in the gentle breeze. "And besides, I'm much more than a fisherman. I'm shocked an old friend would think so little of me!"

"Hardly," Remi held a hand in the air in dismissal. "However, regaling the tales of all the adventures we've shared would require many more days, and of course, many more tankards of fine Gallander ale than we've had in the last few weeks. Perhaps one day I'll tell the lad about the expedition north around the tip of Shi and into the heart of Cendralli. What was the sharp, young lad under your command, then? I seem to recall his name was Drellas. Although, it may have been Pellas. That lad could throw dice with the quickest."

The captain's expression cracked with a toothy grin. "Kellas is still my first mate, even with that young lass pulling him ashore whenever she can. Seas bellow, Remi, you're still lost with your names, I see." He folded his loosely covered arms across his trunk and frowned. "Fair enough. Now what is this so-called *favor* that I owe you?"

Remi waved an arm lazily in Chase's direction. "As you can plainly see, my traveling companion has a peculiar tattoo." The captain nodded in response. "I can assure you—the stories are true—and I do not say that lightly in the least! I wouldn't have come to you with such a task as this if I suspected the tales were false, and though I've been known to be incorrect on occasion, I suspect *this* is not mere suspicion. This is no simple tattoo. It's a mark."

Parrus raised an eyebrow. "Oh? What sort of mark?"

"A dragonmark." Remi smiled wryly, but the smile faded quickly when her friend began to scowl.

"Shit," the captain shook his head. "That means you need me to sail my bloody ship to Dragonstone."

"Precisely."

"Well, that isn't going to happen any bloody time soon, is it? If I pretend for a moment that this fool didn't just draw on his face with some funny ink, and that this Dragonstone is more than a story told to cabin boys to keep them good to their mothers, that island is in the middle of forbidden waters—and for good reason. No ship has gone into the mists and come back to tell the tale. None. There's a reason trade ships ride the Azalean coast, Remi. The whole damn thing is surrounded by enough rocks to beach a naval fleet, and that's if the storms don't put you at the bottom of the sea first! *And* that's all only true if the bloody thing exists in the first place. I know my ship isn't the biggest of vessels, but even I can't hope to get close to the damn thing."

"Relax, Parrus. I'm almost hurt that you have so little trust to think I've not considered our situation as thoroughly as I could. If what I've heard and read is true, that mark makes Chase immune to any magical protection that hangs over the island. And I'm sure he may be able to remedy the mist, so long as it is not hiding anything too unexpected. As to the validity of my claims, I can assure you we are not mistaken."

Remi placed a consoling hand on the captain's shoulder. "Please, Parrus. I don't believe we can find another captain who would dare to sail that far west."

The captain objected with an increasingly annoyed tone. "Promises and assurances don't get me close to the damn thing without breaching the *Tree Sparrow's* hull. And even if I can sail close enough, what then? There's hardly a reason to think Dragonstone is more than just a rock. A damned rock in the middle of the damned sea. Nothing more. It's a bloody fool's errand."

Remi's expression darkened while she spoke in a hushed tone. "Need I remind you what happened the last time I was in Nareem? I seem to remember a particularly perturbed merchant that claimed you were stealing cargo from him until a certain Magi convinced him otherwise." She was clearly growing impatient with the captain's stubborn demeanor.

"As if that even comes close to this," Parrus shouted before pausing to calm down. After a long moment the captain finally relented. "Dammit, Remi. I hope you know what you're doing. I'd rather not die this month. I quite like living."

This man is as stubborn as Richard. Maybe more. Chase found this as good a time as ever to chime in. "We won't be a bother. We can keep to ourselves in whatever quarters you provide us."

"We?" Parrus raised his voice again and looked back at the Magi. "Remi, do you plan on sinking the *Sparrow*? Who else is coming beside the boy?"

"No one." Remi turned her attention to Chase.

"You'll have to go on without us. Don't worry, lad, you are in the best of hands. When you get back, I'll have to tell you some of those stories Parrus and I share. We'll meet you in Parth, on the shores of Crystal Lake to the northeast. We should be waiting there for you by the time you get there. It's an easy enough ride, or I should hope it's easy after that troll business of ours. Parrus will make sure that you get through this ordeal in one piece."

Chase reluctantly accepted the Magi's directions in silence, although he regretted having to leave his companions behind. He felt especially wrong for leaving Richard after all they had been through.

I should tell him now. There may not be another time, and he needs to know... It's my fault we're here. I made this choice for both of us, and now I'm leaving him.

But when he glanced over at his friend, Richard nodded in agreement.

Dammit. I can't tell him now. Not here, with all these people around.

Chase finally returned his gaze to the captain. "I stand by what I said. I won't be a burden to you or your crew."

"You're damn right you won't, boy." Parrus looked like he wanted to spit, but he suppressed the urge, oddly twisting his mouth. "I won't have any nonsense on my ship. We eat three meals a day in the crew's quarters. If you aren't there, you won't eat. You'll rise at sunup and bed at sunset. Keep out of trouble and I won't have any more reason to resent a certain Magi friend of mine for taking you on."

Remi patted the captain on the shoulder. "I'm sure Chase will prove an easier passenger than I was during my days on the *Sparrow*."

The captain finally spat on the wooden walkway before allowing himself to smile slightly. "Nobody could be as bad a passenger as you, old friend."

Chase shared a lengthy farewell with his friends. Knots twisted in his stomach when he watched them walk toward the harbor gate. He felt a lump in his throat and his mouth had grown dry.

Richard nearly bumped into a passerby, clumsily apologizing for getting in the way.

I need to tell him.

"Richard!"

The man stopped in his tracks and turned to his friend. "What is it?"

Chase froze.

Every ounce of him wanted to call out to his friend. He wanted to tell Richard that it was all his fault they were stuck so far from home—that *he* was the reason their entire life was uprooted following some *quest* from a mysterious man in the middle of a mountain. Richard had given up his life the moment Chase was exiled, but Chase had been the one to ultimately seal their fates. To make matters worse, he had been keeping this from Richard because he was afraid the man would get upset and leave, but he was the one leaving Richard behind now. All he could think about was the crushing regret hanging over him.

I might never see him again. For all I know, the journey to

Dragonstone will be as perilous as Captain Parrus fears. This might be my only chance to tell him...

"Take care of yourself, mate. Be safe."

Richard saw the uncertainty painted across Chase's face. For a moment, it looked like he was about to ask what was wrong, but he simply nodded. "You, too, mate."

He turned and walked away through the crowd.

Chase wiped away the beginnings of tears at the corners of his eyes, and his heart nearly stopped. The Man in Red stood near a pile of crates, laughing as he watched Chase's friends leave. He turned back to Chase and flicked his nose with his finger before disappearing as quickly as he had appeared.

Chase jumped at the sound of Parrus' voice. "You coming, boy? We're better off leaving while the seas are calm. Got a long voyage ahead, and Kellas heard whispers from some of the other crews of a storm brewing to the south. Wouldn't doubt it either. Fall is storm season on the open waters. May be in for a rough voyage if we don't get a move on."

CHAPTER 25
CURSED WATERS

Without any further delay, Chase grabbed his pack and boarded the *Tree Sparrow*. The sturdy wood flexed very slightly under his feet while the crew rushed aboard, busy gathering the lines and preparing the ship to leave the port. Trying to stay out of the way as best as he could, Chase followed Parrus below deck to a cabin reserved for the occasional guest.

The room was small, but more than he had expected. A straw mattress sat atop a wooden frame that had been permanently secured to the floor. Next to the bed sat a small end table that had also been fastened so it wouldn't slide during rough waters. A small mirror hung on the wall farthest from the door, but there were no other decorations besides that simple adornment.

Chase dropped his pack near the end table and looked back at the captain. "Thank you, Parrus. I'm not sure what I'll find on that island, but I thank you for getting me there in one piece."

"You can thank me when we get there, boy," the captain growled. "And one last thing. I'm not doing this for you. Follow my rules and stay out of the way or we'll have a problem. My crew is a friendly enough lot, and I have no plans to keep you to yourself, but I best not see you keeping my crew from their work. I run with just enough to keep the *Sparrow* afloat—no more, no less. That understood, boy?" Chase nodded in agreement before the captain left, returning to the cargo hold before climbing the steep steps to the upper deck.

Chase sat on the bed and took a deep breath. It had been a long day, and he was tired. Thanks to Madelyn's salves and the renewed supply of creams he bought from a peddler in Haven, his joints and muscles didn't scream as much as they had recently.

He rubbed his eyes and felt the flicker of the Man in Red across his eyelids for the slightest moment. He opened his eyes and his stomach dropped. The Man in Red stood next to the mirror, leaning against the wall of the cabin with a wicked grin painted across his features. Chase quickly shut his eyes and opened them again to see an empty cabin once again.

Carpenter's Hammer, I am *losing it.* He leaned against the wall of his cabin and allowed his heavy, strained eyelids to fall shut.

***

The stink of sulfur and smoke assaulted Chase's senses.

He opened his eyes, and he was sitting on a stool in the middle of a deserted storefront. The all too familiar backdrop of screaming and crying was thankfully muffled behind the shop's closed door. He took a deep breath, allowing his nostrils to fill with the foul stench of burning bodies before rising to his feet and proceeding to the door. To his surprise, the door was locked.

What Chase thought was a storefront was a tavern. The bar in the back corner of the room was covered in an assortment of broken glass and haphazardly strewn flagons. Any scrap of food had been ransacked long ago, and many of the chairs and tables in the room had been knocked out of place or broken. There was a set of stairs to Chase's left, but they were blocked by a massive pile of rubble where the second floor had collapsed.

He returned to the stool and waited. While he was glad the sounds outside were muffled, they weren't muted. Chase sat, listening to terrified screams beyond the distinct crackle of fire for several long minutes. Finally, the disturbing ambience was broken by a crash through the wall behind the bar.

An explosion of fire and black smoke erupted through the wall in a wave of intense heat. With ringing ears, Chase scrambled to his feet just in time to see four men entering the tavern dragging a fifth behind them.

Two of the men were adorned in black armor with wolf-head helmets and red tabards depicting a man surrounded by sharp, black teeth. The third wore the same armor and tabard, but his head was bare revealing a long face crowned by a gnarled mess of grey hair. A long scar ran from the corner of his mouth to the base of his skull, severely disfiguring the side of his face. The fourth man—trailing behind the ragged prisoner his soldiers were dragging into the tavern—was the Man in Red wearing a sneer across his wicked face.

The men threw their captive in the center of the tavern, who crumpled with a weak groan. He began to cough and choke, writhing in pain while he struggled to breathe. The Man in Red turned to his men. "Ensure we have no unwelcomed guests." The armor-clad men nodded and obeyed their master promptly. The Man in Red focused his attention back to the prisoner on the floor. "Do you see?" The cold, heartless man's smile twisted in a manner that made bile rise in Chase's throat. "Do you see what happens when you dare to defy my order?"

"Order?" the old man on the floor croaked. "What kind of order is this, Chase? What have you become? Bloody order. It's bullshit, and you know it is just as well as I do."

The Man in Red waved his hand and the prisoner on the floor twisted in pain. His dirt-covered face shined in the dim, red light that flooded the inn. The years had not been kind to him, his mop of dirty gray hair hanging from his head and a large scar running from his eye to his chin, but there was no mistaking it. He looked a stone's throw away from death's door, but Chase would recognize that face no matter what.

It was Richard.

No. It can't be. Please, not this.

The Man in Red smiled in twisted pleasure while he spoke with a cool and level harshness that made Chase's skin crawl. "You dare say my name? Maybe this old bear *does* still have his teeth."

"And why shouldn't I?" the old and battered image of Richard yelled. His captor's spell had left him breathing heavily with blood dripping from the corner of his mouth. "You were my friend once, Chase. You were my brother. You betrayed me just like you betrayed the rest of us. What would Remi say if she was still here, if you hadn't killed her along with her new apprentice?"

The Man in Red paused at the mention of the woman's name. He stood thoughtfully before his smile returned. "Betrayed?" The entire world shimmered and flickered as the deranged man cackled. "As I remember it, *you* were the ones that rebelled against me. Were you not comfortable? Did I not provide for you as long as you stayed in my kingdom? Remi and that filthy Gallander girl got what they deserved. Klaus was the only one smart enough to see exactly what we could do together. What was I to do? Let you take my throne and cast me aside?"

"You know exactly why we did it."

"Ah, yes," the Man in Red quieted his tone. His cold voice pierced Chase's mind like a dagger, ringing in his thoughts and drowning out all other sounds. "Her."

Richard grunted, mustering every bit of strength that he could. He stood before the Man in Red with a scowl painted across his features and spoke through gritted teeth. "Nothing you can do will make me kneel to you again, not after what you did to Rose. If you're going to torture me, you might as well get on with it. I'll not give you the bloody satisfaction of hearing me scream, you dirty bastard. You might as well just kill me."

"Oh, I won't kill you, old friend," the Man in Red smiled and turned his gaze across the room to Chase. "He will."

Chase felt a black-bladed dagger appear in his hand. His stomach twisted into a knot and his breath caught in his chest. The room was suddenly so small. It was so warm. His hands shook, his mouth as dry as a bone.

No.

When he lifted his head, Richard was there, gazing deep into his eyes. Chase's heart pounded in his ears. It was hard to think. He just wanted to close his eyes and be gone from this place. He wanted never to return—to be rid of the Man in Red for good.

But he knew that wouldn't be the case.

Chase knew that no matter what he did or how long he prolonged the inevitable, he would not be allowed to wake from his dream until the deed was done. Defeated, with tears streaming down his cheeks, he met the gaze of the time worn image of his friend.

"I am so sorry, Richard."

Tears streamed down the old man's face, as well. He placed a hand on Chase's shoulder. "I wish we never left the Burrow."

Anguish nearly overcame him. This was his fault. Chase lifted his shaking hand and swallowed the lump in his throat.

This was it.

He sunk the dagger into his friend's chest. Everything faded to black around him and before long, the tavern, the Man in Red, and his oldest friend in the world were all gone.

***

Chase was back on the *Tree Sparrow*.

Tears wetting his cheeks, he scrambled to a seated position, wildly looking around his tiny living quarters. His heart pounded like a herd of thundering hoofbeats. It was hard to breathe. Sweat drenched his clothes, waves of hot and cold rushing over him.

He's coming. I know he is. He'll be here soon.

Don't come. Leave me alone.

I can't stop it. He's coming.

No. He's not here.

He's going to be here soon.

Stop! The bloody Man in bloody Red isn't even real! I need to get ahold of myself.

Over and over, Chase mumbled himself. "You're on a ship to Dragonstone. You're on a ship to Dragonstone. You're on a ship to Dragonstone…"

One moment he was in the meager cabin on the *Tree Sparrow* and the next he was in the horrible tavern looking down at his friend's lifeless body. His world flickered back and forth until he wanted to scream. He clenched his hair in balled fists and rocked in his seat.

"You're on a ship to Dragonstone. You're on a ship to Dragonstone. You're on a ship to Dragonstone…"

Chase looked down at his shaking hands. They were covered in blood. Richard's vacant eyes stared up at him.

"You're on a ship to Dragonstone. You're on a ship to Dragonstone. You're on a ship to Dragonstone…"

The world closed in around him. There was nothing he could do. He was trapped, helpless to suffer in his own personal hell of fire and death.

And then the world went quiet, and the noxious smells that assaulted his nose faded. His shaking hands were clean, and clean air filled his lungs until finally, he could breathe easier. Chase was back in his bed in his tiny living quarters below deck on the *Tree Sparrow*.

The Man in Red was seated on the floor in the opposite corner of the room—smiling—leaning back against the wall. Chase tried not to react, but his hands still shook, and his ragged breaths were still shallow and labored. Without thinking, he hissed, "*Are you real?*"

The man laughed. "As real as you."

Chase blinked and the Man in Red was gone.

It took a long time and a considerable amount of

effort, but he peeled himself from his bed all the same. Barefoot and clothed in a fresh linen shirt with clean cotton breeches, he walked out of his room and onto the deck. The sun hadn't risen yet, but Chase suspected it would soon. For a long moment, he focused on nothing more than the smell of salt water and sounds of the calm sea lapping against the ship's hull. The shaking in his hands eventually relented and his breath returned to normal.

Finally, the sun painted the sky with a wide array of reds and oranges that shined beautifully off the calm surface of the sea. Captain Parrus appeared shortly thereafter wearing his flowing white shirt, untied at the collar to show dark chest hair speckled with gray. "Breakfast is below deck, boy. Get it or lose it, but don't come crying to me if you choose the latter."

Chase nodded silently, staring at the horizon.

The captain shifted slightly, awkwardly noticing his guests' pale skin and the dark bags under his eyes. Parrus cleared his throat and nodded. "Fish and fruit... it's uh... good for the teeth." He gave a strange, toothy grin that resembled a grimace before frowning. "Well... don't just stand there."

Chase smiled weakly. His eyes were heavy, and a dull throbbing lingered in his temples, but he was happy to be awake all the same. "Thanks, Captain."

Parrus looked like he was unsure if he should say more, but he relented and swiveled on the spot before returning to his crew below deck.

The dining quarters were cramped with a table

and chairs secured to the floor, just as they had been in the guest cabin. Despite the early hour, the crew was in high spirits, laughing and sharing stories over the morning meal. Although his portion was small, the food was better than Chase thought it would be.

All the *Tree Sparrow's* crew were Gallanders with messy mops of tangled brown, red, or blonde hair. Each member wore a lightweight, loose-fitting shirt that hung from their well-muscled bodies to expose sun-kissed skin with sack cloth pants and oddly small deck shoes. At the sound of a sharp order from Captain Parrus, the crew sprang to their feet and spilled from the dining quarters to attend to their duties for the day.

The midday and evening meals were more of the same with slight differences in the fruit and fish served. The evening meal was accompanied by a sweet, spiced rum that burned horribly. One of the sailors, a red-haired young man named Gaerin, clapped Chase on the back as he choked the liquor down. "Not a strong stomach there, laddy?" the man jested. "I remember when Teresa first joined the crew. Took the lass nearly a month before she could stomach the stuff."

A woman sitting across from Gaerin cracked her mouth in a large smile. Her blonde hair contrasted her sun-darkened skin wildly, even in the dim light of the cabin. She slapped her hands on the table before standing and grabbing the drink out of Gaerin's hand. "I could drink your skinny arse under the table any day of the week, you little gobshite." The woman upended the mug of rum, allowing a trickle to slip passed her mouth before slamming the empty mug on the table upside down.

The table roared with laughter. To Chase's surprise, even Parrus smiled behind his cup of rum. Chase gladly joined in the ruckus while several sailors continued to challenge their peers' drinking prowess, thankful for the distraction from his worries.

Eventually, the conversations slowed, and the cabin calmed to a dull murmur. Peaking up from his conversation with the sailor named Teresa, a young brown-haired sailor with a scraggly mustache raised his voice from across the table. "What business do we have at this rock, anyway? I heard its cursed or some such nonsense, Capt'n."

"Damn right, it's cursed," a red-haired woman with thick arms and a heavy brow shouted from the other side of the table as she finished another mug of rum. "Last I heard a ship sailed into the mists—the crew went mad. One little shite slit the helmsman's throat in 'is sleep before he threw 'imself from the crow's nest. Rest of the crew started seeing things in the mist—terrible things. Whole damn ship disappeared, too. Place is cursed, all right."

Captain Parrus stood leaning over the table in a commanding gesture before raising his voice to the crew. "Dalby, Moira—that's enough. I'm the captain and you blimey lot will do as I say! And you'll like it, else you won't eat for a week. I'll not have my crew questioning me on my own ship. Unless you mean to mutiny, I suggest you shut your gobs and buck up before I throw you both to meet the Smithy himself." The crew fell silent, the two young naysayers wordlessly looking down at their empty plates. "I'll not abide superstition on my ship. I don't care whatever bloody prayers to whatever bloody sea spirits you lot do on your own time, but you'll not bring talk of curses and crews long lost to my table on my ship. That rock is about as cursed as my arse, and if I say we sail to Dragonstone, then we sail to Dragonstone."

"I-I'm sorry, Captain." Chase felt lightheaded from the rum, but speaking up seemed the right thing to do. "I don't mean to cause problems with your crew. I'm not sure how much you've told them, and that's your decision to make." Chase pushed himself up from his chair awkwardly, still not used to chairs that didn't move beneath him. "I should head back to my cabin for the night."

The captain's hand shot up in defiance. "Nonsense, boy. Sit your arse down. Dalby and Moira are as bloody thick as tree trunks." The two crew members still looked down at their plates in silence, their faces reddening. The captain raised his voice, addressing the crew. "Now, I'll have no more of this talk. You're all going to drink your share or find your bunk and shut your bloody gobs for the night. Am I understood?"

The crew responded with a chorus of, "Aye, aye, captain." A few of the sailors dismissed themselves from the table, including Dalby, Gaerin, and Moira—although Teresa poured her and Chase another mug of rum with a seductive wink.

Chase raised the mug to her with an awkward smile and drank. After he finished, he excused himself from the table and thanked Parrus for the meal. The captain may have waved his hand dismissively, but Chase swore he saw the corner of the man's mouth turn upward slightly when he left the table for the night.

The next day, Chase spent much of his time on deck, watching ocean birds twirl above with the occasional pack of dolphins or school of fish swimming below. He practiced his sorcery, allowing the sound of sea water on the *Tree Sparrow's* hull and the smell of salt in the air to ease his mind while he worked. He condensed the thick vapor above his hand and began to thoughtlessly spin the shimmering icicle on the spot. A gruff voice startled him from behind. "So, you're like that old fool, Remi."

Captain Parrus stood in a loose red shirt not unlike the white one he had been wearing the previous day. The old man's skin seemed more wrinkled in the midmorning sunlight, and his features somehow seemed harder. He wore an expression that looked like a bitter mix of happiness and contempt. Chase accidentally dropped the misshapen lump of ice on the ship's deck. "Excuse me. If you mean the sorcery, I can stop if you'd like me to."

"Bah." Parrus waved an arm in the air before approaching the deck's railing. He rested his hands on the gray-dyed wood and sighed. "I don't bloody well give a shite what you do, as long as you're keeping out of my crew's business. I know you've been nothing but agreeable, boy. And I see you've been trying—don't think I haven't. I'm thankful for that. But Kellas don't trust you and I can't say the rest of my crew takes kindly to you. Sure, Teresa is having trouble keeping her bloody legs shut, and most of the folk don't harbor any ill will…" The old man rubbed his forehead with a callused hand before shaking his head. "They're scared. You scare them."

Against his better judgement, Chase laughed. When the captain shot him a sour look in response, he quickly composed himself. *Sleep must be getting to me. Need to get my act together.* Chase went silent for a while, but before the captain could leave he saw the first mate scowling at him from beyond the helm. "Do you believe in the curse?"

"Do I look like a cabin boy barely off his mother's milk?" Parrus spat off the side of the deck. "I believe that no ship's gone into the mists and lived. That's enough for me."

"Fair enough." Chase leaned against the railing next to the old man. They stood in silence for a moment before Parrus nodded at nothing and dismissed himself. Chase saw Kellas say something to the captain only to be dismissed with a tired wave of an arm.

The first mate was a gaunt man with dark hair and abnormally dark skin, even compared to the sun-darkened crew members. He wore the same flowing shirt, cloth pants, and oddly small shoes as the rest of the crew, but a red cloth that matched the *Tree Sparrow's* sails was wrapped around his left bicep. Kellas scowled at Chase before turning his attention back to the crew.

Chase spent a great deal of his time in his meager quarters, sharpening his blades or reading a small collection of books that Remi had given him to pass the time. Thankfully, Gallander written language was very close to what they used in Rakksberg, a trend that Klaus assured could not be coincidental. Apart from a few words and phrases, the books held his attention nicely, but he eventually grew bored enough to return to the deck.

They sailed at a steady pace and the seas remained calm, so most of the journey was anything but exciting. To fill time, Chase stood at the stern, looking out behind the small vessel where he could practice his sorcery away from the prying eyes of the crew. He held out his hand, concentrating deeply, and closed his fingers slowly to make a fist. Larger and larger portions of the seawater froze, forming floating masses that he melted before repeating the process over and over.

Occasionally, Parrus would join him to share weather conditions or tales of his travels on the open seas. He was a pleasant enough man, contrary to his rough manner of managing his crew, and he seemed to take a liking to Chase even if the man wouldn't openly admit such a thing. Teresa also tried to keep Chase company on many occasions, although he adamantly declined any advances the woman made, much to her growing frustration.

Switching between various activities helped pass the time. Days passed without any sign of an island or mist until Chase was half-convinced there was no island at all. Parrus insisted the wind was just too weak to sail much faster, but Chase had his doubts.

That was until the eighth day at sea. A dense fog descended on the ship over the course of the day until Captain Parrus had no choice but to drop the anchor.

Chase joined the captain at the ship's bow and waited. The crew looked uneasy, some of which started to mutter what sounded like prayers under their breath.

Parrus stood with his hands resting on the grey wooden railing of the *Tree Sparrow*, dressed in a flowing, pale blue shirt. He was accompanied by a scowling Kellas, who still bore the red cloth around his bicep.

Chase sighed. *Here goes nothing.* He focused on the droplets of moisture in the air. For a long time, he stood in silence, breathing as evenly as he could while he pictured his spell. He heard a few of the crew start to whisper and murmur to one another, but he tried his best to ignore the noise and concentrate.

Finally, Chase threw his arms outward. To his surprise, the way was cleared before them for hundreds of yards. A bed of rocks shot up from the surface of the sea like a hundred sharpened spears for as long as the eye could see. The closest of which were no more than fifty paces from the *Tree Sparrow's* hull. Chase didn't have to look to know that it was far too close for comfort for the weathered old captain beside him.

Parrus looked at Chase as the fog crept back around the ship. "I think this is as far as I take you, boy. There's a raft on the port side that you can take the rest of the way. I'll not be risking the *Sparrow* in waters like that."

"You sure we shouldn't make him swim?" Kellas interjected with a grimace. "Or fly? Or whatever the hell the damned sorcerer can manage on his own? Not sure the *Sparrow* can spare a raft, sir."

"Shut your damned gob, Kellas." The Captain looked as if he were about to strike the gaunt first mate, but the man didn't react. "The boy was trained by a Magi we know and trust, not some evil sorcerer from one of your mother's bedside stories. The *Sparrow* has an extra raft, and you damn well know that. The next time I hear you question my command, you'll be emptying the chamber pots for a week—first mate or not."

Chase was amazed to see the first mate submit, turning his gaze back to the crew as a distraction from the conversation. Pretending the interruption had not occurred, Chase leveled his gaze at his host. "I understand, Parrus. Thanks… for everything you've done for me. No matter what you owed Remi, you didn't need to do this for me, and you certainly didn't need to house me so generously."

"Aye." Parrus paused, trying to find the right words. "I must admit, the crew and I *did* want to see if the rumors were true. You've heard enough of the… bad luck that falls on those who venture to the mists. Even so, I suspect you just might make it out the other side of all this."

"That certainly is the idea."

The captain chuckled. "You're alright by me, boy. Stayed out of trouble fine enough and gave the crew something to talk about with all that Magi business. If you do get out of this alive, come see me in Nareem. Dragon or not, I'd like to hear what's on the other side of them rocks."

Chase nodded before following the captain to the ship's spare raft. Gaerin was sent to Chase's quarters to gather his things while Teresa and Moira helped prepare the raft for release. After everything was ready, Chase thanked the captain again and stepped onto the boat. The crew lowered the vessel carefully into the water and once it was released, Chase grabbed the boat's oars.

He began rowing deeper into the fog.

CHAPTER 26
THE ROCK IN THE MIST

Chase sat for over an hour gazing into the thick fog around him, pulling his rowboat along stroke by stroke. Within the eerie silence, the smell of salt and shale hung in the air, and an uncomfortable chill ran down Chase's spine. Slowly, he rowed past the large rocks rising from the water's surface, trying his best not to get lost in the ominous maze.

Occasionally, the fog thickened so much that it became hard to breathe. With a flick of his wrist, Chase could disperse the fog momentarily, but it always crept back in. He rowed for what felt like days until finally his grip weakened, and his arms screamed in silent protest. Chase rubbed his eyes with his shaking palms and shook his head.

When he opened his eyes, he was joined in the rowboat by another. Sitting on the bench across from Chase, looking at him intently, was the Man in Red.

Chase tried not to react, but his heart raced and hands trembled. His mouth went dry and a lump formed in his throat while sweat beaded on his brow. He desperately hoped he had simply fallen asleep in the raft after days at sea without a decent night's rest. But it was quickly apparent that he was still wide awake. Resigned to his fate, Chase sighed. "What do you want?"

The mysterious man in blood red leathers splashed with touches of grey laughed. "You wound me with your suspicion. I merely wanted to talk. I get lonely, and your company is always quite entertaining."

The man's voice was cold and piercing. It made Chase's skin crawl. He wanted to throw down his oars and leap into the sea. Resisting the urge, he clenched his hands around the oars tightly.

He's not really here.

It was hard to breathe. His chest was tight.

Carpenter's Bloody Hammer, if he is, I really have gone mad.

He shifted uncomfortably in his seat, trying to maintain eye contact with the mad man. "Talk about what? What could you possibly have to say to me?"

The man smiled. "Well, Chase—I hope I can call you Chase. I am sure you have many questions for me: some villain that haunts your every night's dreams. Flesh and bone, sitting in this very boat when, just a moment ago, your only company was your knapsack. I'd surely hope that your curiosity would conjure a question or two. I'd be disappointed

393

with myself if you didn't. I don't ever remember being that content."

"Fine." Chase admitted to himself that he was curious, even if it was mostly born from desperation. *Maybe now I may finally get some answers.* "Are you real or an illusion?"

The stranger's smile became a frown, and his voice grew cold. "You already asked me that, and I gave you my answer. I am as real as you—as real as the water we float on or the boat we sit in."

"Are you lying?"

"I'm appalled that you would think so lowly of me," the Man in Red recoiled, but he couldn't hold back a smile. "I suppose that's a fair question, given the circumstances. However, I'm not so mundane that I'd forgo the opportunity to stir up some doubt here and there. Your question is one that I have decided *not* to answer. You can find out for yourself whether my words are true or false."

Chase grinded his teeth in frustration. He continued to speak while he rowed the boat further into the fog. "Alright then. Why am I having these dreams? Why do you *insist* on making me witness such terrible things?"

"The answer to that isn't that simple, dear Chase. Although, I promise to try my very best to answer clearly." The wry grin on the man's face, accompanied by his sarcastic tone, made Chase roll his eyes. "You have these dreams because someone wants you to. Someone wants you to see all the wonderful things you'll do, and that man gets what he wants—one way or another."

"No," Chase interrupted. "I refuse to believe that these visions are prophetical. I'm not that person, and I swear I will never *be* that person."

The Man in Red shrugged, grinning widely. "Oh? An assassin with a body count higher than most of the monsters in children's stories? I hate to break it to you—and please don't take this the wrong way, because I love this about you—but you are that person. You *are* that monster."

"No, I'm not. I did what I did because I had to."

"So, what? Do you really expect me to believe that you'll put down your blades for the good of the people in the Berg? *Rakksberg*? The country that threw you aside for dead when you were cast away as an orphan by a mother who didn't care for you and a father who deserted you?

"Please, Chase. Don't make me laugh. You're an *assassin*. A killer. A member of the Black Blades: a ruthless, glorified mercenary band that manipulates the land from the shadows. You haven't changed and you won't change. You'll always be that killer, even when you think you've turned over a new leaf and cast your black blade aside. Have you forgotten so quickly that part of you that's buried deep inside? Does it revel in what you do *because you have to*? You'll never change the darkness that taints your soul. Believe me, Chase. I know. I've lived it."

Chase flushed and his grip tightened on the oars. "You can say whatever you want about my soul, but you don't know who I am or *what* I am. You don't know what I've done or why I've done it."

"On the contrary, I do know. I know because I can feel it, smell it—even taste it. I am your lament and your terror. I am your wrath and your despair. I *am* your soul."

Chase felt a wave of cold wash over him. An eerie shiver ran down his spine. Disbelief flooded him for a moment before he felt something else entirely: recognition. That sick part of him that he had been trying so hard to forget had been quiet since he left the mountains, but it had still been there before. It had always been there, waiting for the moment when he would end someone's life.

It can't be true… can it?

It was almost enough for him to lean over the side of his rowboat and empty the contents of his stomach into the sea.

No. It's not true. He's just trying to get under my skin and into my head. It can't *be true.*

"Do you know what I'm going to find in this fog?" asked Chase, trying to think about anything else.

The wicked intruder smiled and folded his hands behind his head. "Yes, I do. But I'd rather not tell you. I wouldn't want to ruin the surprise, now, would I? It's going to be quite a shock—I'm sure of it."

"Did you know you're a real prick?"

"I've heard worse."

"Fine." Chase was growing irritable. It was like his skin was trying to crawl from his body. "How much longer am I going to have to deal with your…appearances. I'd rather enjoy a good night's rest for once. I haven't had the pleasure in a *very* long time."

The stranger's face grew solemn for a moment, but his expression was soon replaced with twisted glee. "Oh, I won't accompany you for much longer, but that doesn't matter. I'm here the way you see me today because you will it. You are a frightened little boy, because you know deep down I speak the truth. You have those nightmares, but you don't fear the things I've shown you. You're afraid because deep in your heart, you enjoy them. You know there's nothing you can do to avoid your inevitable fate. But rest assured, you'll forget your fears, for a time.

"Your life is about to change, and in the whirlwind of that change, you'll forget about me. About us. I imagine it will be quite a long time. But eventually, when your knightly deeds are done and you find yourself alone in the dark with nothing to drive you forward, the fears will return. I will return to you, but not as a dream or as an apparition of a man sitting in a boat. I will return as your actions. You'll succumb to the darkness in your soul, and you'll feel the power within yourself just like I have shown you."

Chase averted his eyes from the man. *I refuse to believe any of that nonsense. But still… what if he is telling the truth? What if I really am doomed to carry out all those terrible things. Should I just end things here and now? Save Richard from—*

Richard.

397

Chase sat in silent contemplation. His heart sank and he felt the threat of tears behind his eyes. *No. I can't do that. I won't.*

"I don't care what you say, I'm not going to—" By the time Chase lifted his gaze again, the Man in Red was gone. He took a deep breath and slowly exhaled.

With arms growing weary and a burning sensation growing across his chest as he rowed, Chase continued through the mist, not knowing how far he had gone or how much further it was to Dragonstone.

Chase shook his head in frustration and stood on the rowboat, surrounded by dense fog and jagged rocks. He inhaled deeply, concentrating on the water vapor hanging in the air. After a moment collecting his thoughts, Chase threw his arms out and as he did, the fog around him retreated once more.

The sight that revealed itself nearly took Chase's breath away. A craggy, rocky island stood with a massive stone building stretching far down the nearby shore. The building's modular, rectangular shape was unlike anything Chase had ever seen, built into the side of the island as though it were carved from the cliff itself. The dark grey stone was engulfed in shadows, but Chase could make out thick, rectangular stone accents along the building's edges and bordering a series of thin window slits that dotted the structure's walls.

A small stone dock protruded into the sea, but the fog quickly crept back around Chase's meager boat, obscuring his vision. Soon, he was standing in an endless gray void, unable to see anything beyond the dagger-like rock that rose from the sea a few paces away.

Chase carefully guessed where the simple stone dock stood and rowed. After fumbling around a few jagged rocks and missing the platform entirely at first, he secured his tiny rowboat as best as he could. The breath caught in his throat while he gathered his things and clambered onto the aged stone platform.

Awestruck, Chase slowly stepped forward. The strange, rectangular building towered high above him and extended down the coast until it was swallowed by the dense fog. Odd, angular stone with no sign of tooling or joint work made the structure look unnatural somehow, and its immense size made Chase feel small and insignificant. A simple, rectangular stone door stood at the end of the dock and with no clear signs of any other entrance, he made his way to the portal.

Chase grabbed hold of the simple, flat door handle and heaved with his shoulder until he could step through the opening, revealing a strange chamber that resembled a massive reception hall. It was lit by a series of torches that made the grey stone glow with a flickering orange hue. The room was nearly barren, aside from a few small tables and empty weapon racks. A stale, damp scent hung in the air that reminded Chase of a closet that had been kept shut for a very long time. Dim, blue light descended in a column from a hidden skylight high above to illuminate an imposing stone slab that stood in the center of the chamber.

It was an intimidating sight to behold, but it was the figure behind the stone slab that made Chase involuntarily shiver.

A massive, humanoid creature sat cross-legged behind the slab, bathed in blue light. Its limbs were as thick as tree trunks and Chase imagined that if it stood, it would be as tall as one, too. Its face was human, though it was heavy set, wide, and flat with a thick brow and a stub nose. Its long black hair fell upon its bare like cords of rope, and it was staring at its new guest with unblinking eyes.

At first it spoke in a language completely unfamiliar to Chase. After waiting for the guest's response and hearing none, it tried another. The second language still made no sense, although the words somehow sounded less clumsy. Finally, the giant smiled and spoke slowly and surprisingly gently. "It's nice to have a visitor for a change. Please come and sit. I'm sure you've been traveling for quite some time." The creature motioned to a small stool near the immense stone slab.

Chase moved toward the giant, joints shaking as he slowly made his way across the massive chamber. He reluctantly sat in the stool and fidgeted uncomfortably. *What the bloody hell is that thing, and what am I supposed to say? It could probably crush me with its little finger.* Chase rubbed the back of his neck, failing to conjure words until he finally blurted awkwardly, "H-Hello."

The giant laughed, nearly shaking the room while his shoulders and chest heaved with every sound. His voice was slow, deep, and boisterous. "My boy, I doubt you made it all this way just to say 'hello.' Now, I can clearly see your mark which means you must be here for a dragon. I'd be happy to point you toward the Dragon's Mouth, but I suspect you may be quite confused. Longing for the company of another after all these years, I don't see a need to rush quite yet. So, young man, how may I help you?"

"Uh…" Chase clambered to string together coherent thoughts. "Right. Well… Thank you for being so polite. I don't really know what to say. To be honest, I don't really know what any of this is, so I guess we can start there."

"Ah, yes. Where are my manners? My name is Gron, and you have arrived at the sanctuary on Dragonstone. You can clearly see that I'm a giant—pure bred—from the Chi Sin Lo Mountains in Shi. My parents were asked to bring me here about… oh… five or six hundred years ago, when I was merely a whelp not yet even as tall as a horse. Since then, I've been here, looking after the grounds and escorting any new riders to their partners. Although, I have not needed to perform that duty since shortly after I arrived. What is your name, little one?"

"Chase," he replied almost too quickly. His nerves eased slightly, but he was overwhelmed. "My name is Chase. I am from Rakksberg—the Berg—beyond the Blackridge Mountains. I was sent here by… by a stranger who marked my face. A Magi named Remylara Drakolar directed me here, so here I am… I don't really know what happens next. I didn't exactly expect to see anyone, let alone a giant."

"I don't blame you, little one. The secrets of

Dragonstone are well kept, and for good reason. There are many things about this place that even I don't know after all these years. Did I hear right? You said you are from Rakksberg?"

"Yes, I did," Chase eyed the giant suspiciously. "Why do you ask?"

The giant paused, rubbing his face with a massive, thick fingered hand that was covered in coarse, dark hair. "Bah, nothing. There's only ever been one other rider from the land behind those mountains that I know of, and I am not terribly fond of that one. He snuck past me and stole a fire drake right out from under my nose. I didn't know he was here until it was too late, and by then they had already fled."

Chase suddenly recalled the man who stole Terror. He looked up at the giant to see his large grey pupils shining blue in the dim light. "I'm sorry that happened. I don't intend to do anything as sinister as that while I'm on your island."

"I can see that clearly, little one. I can see it in your *kahnra*. You have a fair amount of darkness about you, but there is light in there. Now, I suppose you are eager to meet your own drake. We can continue our conversation as we proceed, I think. Come, now."

The word *kahnra* meant nothing to Chase, but he dismissed the strange comment before following the giant through a large archway in the back of the chamber. Struggling at first to keep sure footing as the ground shook with each of the giant's steps, Chase scrambled to stay alongside the monster of a man.

Beams of blue light burst through small window slits down the entire length of the hall, bathing them in a strangely calming ambience. With eyes straining against the dim light, Chase couldn't see where they were walking and instead he turned his attention to Gron. "What can you tell me about the island?"

"You mean to tell me the mystery of an island full of dragons isn't enough?" The giant winked and shrugged his massive shoulders. "A long time ago—long before I was born—the great, green dragon known as Wisdom commanded the dragons to retreat to this very island. I'm not sure what the reason was for this retreat, but according to legend, Wisdom knew something of the fate of the dragons that compelled him to do so.

"There was a great schism between the dragons that caused a revolt somewhere around that time. Although, details about the events so long ago are few and far between. Wisdom made a treaty with the giants of all the nations, back when we were still a united and proud people. My ancestors built this place as a sort of...groundskeeping complex. We were to ensure that the dragons upheld their side of the treaty while providing them with protection and whatever services we could offer." The giant's excited expression grew somber. "Once there were a great many giants that looked over the island, but now I am the only one. It has been this way for far too long, I am sad to say."

Chase staggered when the giant stubbed his toe on a stone bench, nearly pulling it from the floor. It didn't seem to bother the giant, so Chase didn't bother to ask. "What sorts of services do you provide them, exactly? I mean, they're dragons, aren't they? What exactly do they need from anybody that they can't do themselves?"

Gron snorted happily. "Not much if I am honest. The shrouding mists that were conjured long ago seem to repel most unwanted visitors well enough. Beyond that, we make sure future riders are equipped to meet their bonded partners, which is much simpler than you would think. The hardest part was making all the saddles, but since that was completed long before I was born, I simply keep them oiled and make sure the rats stay away from their straps from time to time.

"Otherwise, the dragons don't ask for much. It makes for a dull life, but I find peace in the silence. I do miss my people from time to time." The giant turned his gaze down to his tiny follower. "I must ask, how are things going in Shi? Have you heard much from their people? Maybe a word on how the giants are handling things in the mountains?"

"Sorry, but I'm afraid not," Chase replied, stepping through the blue light of one of the windows. "The Berg is cut off from the rest of the world. I only just learned about life beyond our own borders recently. My traveling companions taught me as much as they could in our short time together, but they are from Soule and Talvenna. They don't really talk about Shi all that much." Chase paused for a moment, unsure of what else to say. "Forgive me for changing subjects, but what exactly am I supposed to be looking for?"

Gron waved a massive arm slowly. "No need to

apologize, little one. I understand that this all must be quite the sight to behold. I once met a Magi, not long after I began my service here. I thought he was quite rude, until he found his partner and his demeanor changed entirely. It must have been the nerves, I suppose.

"Yes, when it concerns your dragon, there really isn't much that I can tell you. Drakes come in all shapes and sizes. My people have some rough categories for them, but I am no expert on the matter. My mother was quite the scholar on the dragons and their kind, but she has been gone for a long, long time."

Chase nodded and noticed they had almost made it to a second archway that clearly designated the next room. A few more of Gron's paces and they were standing before a massive storeroom stretching endlessly into the distance. On either side of the chamber, there stood a massive wooden rack with rows of leather harnesses stacked all the way to the incredibly tall ceiling. The air was still damp, but the smell of wood and oil replaced all other odors and the room almost glowed with an orange light that flickered from the nearby torches.

Chase looked up at his guide. "Are those all what I think they are?"

"Yes." Gron nodded with a satisfied smile. "Saddles. One made for each and every dragon that would ever come to be, or so the legends are told. Judging by your mark, your saddle shouldn't be too far. You can wait here while I fetch it if you'd like."

Chase agreed to stay, and the giant walked down

the storeroom hall, shaking the ground with each step. He took a deep breath in anticipation and searched through his pack. He found some pork jerky and stale bread that he hoped would ease the butterflies that ravaged his stomach before sitting on a nearby stone bench. Chase chewed the tough food and watched Gron rifle through various racks, looking for the saddle for his dragon. It all felt surreal.

The bloody dragons are real! Richard won't believe this. I'm still not sure I do.

It was not that long ago that Chase would never have believed such a creature could exist, and now he was getting a saddle as casually as a noble would be fitted for his evening attire. He had no way of knowing what waited for him on this strange rock, or if it would be happy when it saw him.

What if I'm not what the dragon *expects? Bloody hell, I never considered that. To think, I could come all this way, and the dragon could see me and just… walk away. Or worse, what if this is all still some kind of dream? What if this is all still some sick game orchestrated by the Man in Red? What if I died in the mists and this is all just my imagination?*

What if I'm actually mad?

I can't be mad. Can I? Not after all this. Please. Not now.

Gron stopped abruptly in the distance, causing Chase to jump slightly as his thoughts returned to the chamber full of saddles. The light was dim, but he saw the giant pull an entire row of saddles out from the rack, halfway from the ground to the ceiling. The saddle rack slid out into the hall to reveal even more harnesses draped over wooden frames. After a moment's deliberation, Gron procured a mass of leather straps and metal buckles before sliding the rack back to its place.

The giant returned with a smile on his face and the mass of leather draped over his shoulder. "Your saddle was right where I suspected... almost. That mark you wear is embroidered into the seat just as all saddles are marked in such a way."

"That makes about as much sense as everything else has today," Chase chuckled nervously. "So, what now?"

"There is a door, not too far back that we passed. You may not have noticed it, but it leads outside to a staircase that will take you to a cliff looking over a large canyon. That canyon is known as the Dragon's Mouth. *That* is where you will meet your dragon."

My dragon. My *bloody dragon.*

Chase's heart fluttered and his stomach twisted uncomfortably. Sweat beaded on his forehead, despite the cool dampness of the sanctuary. "Alright, then. No time to lose, I suppose. Lead the way, Gron."

CHAPTER 27
DESTINY REVEALED

Chase followed Gron along the path the giant had described. Before long, he was outside again, breathing in the fresh, salt-ridden air from the sea below. Fog cloaked most of the island, but after climbing the long, winding stairs that crawled up the rocky cliffside, the air cleared. Soon, the blazing sun above shined down on Dragonstone like a precious jewel sitting in an endless blue-green sea.

It took the odd pair a few hours to climb stony cliff, but they eventually stood on a small plateau overlooking a vast gully. Nothing stood on the plateau, save for a small hut made from the same grey stone as the rest of the island's structures. The platform was bordered by large rock formations, as if the island itself was dissuading adventurers from continuing any further.

Unsure of what he should say, Chase looked at his

guide. "Thanks for your help, Gron. Excuse my candor, but... now what do I do?"

The giant laughed and patted Chase on the back, nearly knocking him to the ground. "Your *kahnra* is wild, little one. Unfortunately, all you can do now is wait. That hut was made for just that reason. There is a small well behind it for fresh water, and there is even a proper bed. Your dragon sensed your presence as soon as you stepped foot on Dragonstone. Now, you must wait."

"For how long?" Chase tried to hide his concern, but he could feel it bleeding through his statement. "It looks like I could be here for a while."

"I don't know, to tell you the truth. I wish I could say more, but it's quite different for every rider. It's hard to say how far the dragon must travel or if it's ready to join its rider. I've even heard that a dragon may not come at all if it feels its match is unworthy, but that is rarely the case. It could be a day, or it could be a month. You must only be patient, and surely, your partner will join you when they are ready."

Chase sighed. He wasn't looking forward to being constrained to the small platform, but he had no other choice. Thankfully, his pack was filled to the brim with provisions that could last a few months if he was careful. Richard saw to that before they had parted ways. Chase looked back at the giant. "Are you going to stay with me?"

"No," Gron replied, his face falling into a frown. "I do have *some* duties to attend to. But more importantly, my presence masks your own. Your *kahnra* is strong, but you are no giant. If I stay, I'm afraid that your partner may not realize you are ready for them. I'm sorry, but we must say our goodbye's for now."

After a long pause, lost for words, Chase nodded to himself before clearing his throat. "Fair well, Gron. And thank you again—for everything."

"It is my duty and pleasure." The giant tucked an arm under his bare stomach and lowered into a hulking bow, still much taller than Chase. "Good luck, little one." Gron heaved the mass of leather straps and buckles he carried to the ground and returned to the cliffside steps, leaving Chase alone on the Dragon's Mouth.

Chase walked to the edge of the platform and took a deep breath.

The sunset over the horizon bathed the gorge in red, orange, and gold light that made the gully glow. The odd gray stone from the shore below was now joined by red clay and pale limestone to form stunning segmented rock formations. Towers of jagged stone rose like daggers from the basin below. Cliffs, mountains, and countless rocky hills dotted the rugged landscape as far as the eye could see.

To Chase's surprise, he could make out the dim outlines and blurred shapes of several animals. What looked like oddly shaped deer and thick-shouldered goats dotted the landscape while the occasional bird soared overhead. He wasn't sure why, but he had assumed when he got to the island he would find a barren landscape, void of all life. That was, of course, a foolish notion. If there really was an island full of dragons, they must eat something, after all.

After gazing out at the landscape for much longer than he had intended, Chase yawned and made his way to his humble abode. The hut may have been modest, but it still had more amenities than he would have expected. A small bed with a stone slab foundation lay with a matching stone end table and stool. There was even a separate room for a latrine.

With arms and legs that screamed in protest at every move, Chase placed his weapons on the table, draped his cloak over the stool, and stored his leathers in the end table's drawers. By the time he was finally ready to sleep, his eyes were heavy, and his thoughts were clouded. It had been a long day after what felt like an endless string of long days. His stomach ached unpleasantly, acrid from nerves and anticipation.

Months. I hope it doesn't take bloody months. I don't think I can stand the Man in Red's company for that much longer. Chase swore he heard something from outside the stone hut, but he quickly dismissed it as nothing. Soon, his eyes were hazy, and the room seemed to shift and swirl on its own.

Please. I need this to be over.

I'm not mad yet. Am I?

No. I can't be. Please.

Let the Man in Red leave. Let him leave me for good once this whole blasted quest is over. Please.

Chase had no choice in the matter. He finally relented and let sleep take him once again.

***

He woke in a daze, drenched in sweat after yet another nightmare. Unfortunately, it seemed he was stuck with the Man in Red for the time being.

Time crawled by in monotony. Fortunately, Chase had grown accustomed to filling his time to distract himself from the nightmares that continued to ravage his thoughts. He hadn't finished the books that Remi had given him, and there were a few novels that he enjoyed a great deal. When he needed to get up and move, he ran through his sword stances or found ways to burn off energy with exercise on the strange, rocky platform.

Above all, however, Chase practiced his sorcery. With little else to do on the Dragon's Mouth, Chase found that it was the best way to stay preoccupied. There was a certain comfort in the calm meditation that was required to channel the toams in the arid, dry air. It was as if the magic in the air on Dragonstone was somehow more elusive. On more than one occasion, Chase lost his hold on the toams altogether, which had not happened since he started practicing the Magi sorcery.

It felt like it was so long ago to him now.

Has it been weeks? Days?

No. Not days. Longer. I just need to think.

How long has it been? Carpenter's Hammer, it feels like a lifetime ago we set out from the Berg.

For six days, Chase meandered around the Dragon's Mouth, desperately trying to pass the time without thinking about the Man in Red. It was harder now that he was alone. Chase had thought that he had missed being alone after being gone from the Burrow for so long, but any time he stopped to think about his solitude, the man from his nightmares would appear to taunt him. He was never there for more than a moment, but it was always a moment too long for Chase's liking.

Chase drank deeply from the well behind the hut, allowing the cold liquid to fill his stomach before walking to the center of the plateau. When he closed his eyes, a great flaming ruin came into view, burned into his mind like an image after staring into a bright light. He shook his head.

Damned nightmares.

They are just nightmares.

They aren't anything more. They can't be more.

Please. Not more.

Chase slowly shuffled back to the center of the plateau.

He's not here. He can't be here.

He's not here. He can't be here.

With a rasping sigh, Chase leveled his gaze at the dusty ground at his feet. For the better part of three days, he had been trying to draw different pictures in the rocky earth using only his sorcery. It was a difficult and unwieldy practice, but he had managed a few crude images. A passable iteration of the cliff outside the Burrow sat next to an almost unrecognizable sketch of his old quarters. Chase took a deep breath and closed his eyes, reaching out with his mind to the toams in the dry mountain air one more time.

Just a moment before Chase was about to swirl his hand in a distinct circular motion, he heard a grating, scratching sound.

He's not here. He can't be here.

Chase frantically searched for the source of the sound and realized it was coming from the edge of the plateau that overlooked the valley beyond.

He's not here. He can't be here.

Step by step, Chase made his way to the cliff.

He's not here. He can't be here.

Almost too late, Chase scrambled back to the center of the platform. Panic overwhelmed him when he realized whoever or whatever was making that odd scratching sound was almost upon him.

He's not here.

He can't be here.

He's not here.

He can't be here.

Scratching, clawing, and clicking erupted over the edge of the cliff until a massive, clawed foot grasped at the dusty earth. A scaled beast of immeasurable bulk pulled itself onto the platform with a series of heavy grunts and wicked snapping sounds. Once the monster had planted all four feet on the platform, it shook slowly before gazing at the man that dared to stand before it.

The beast was massive—larger even than the

charger in Galland. It almost resembled a cat, skulking its way across the plateau, but it had a long, reptilian tail and massive, powerful limbs. Covered in mottled, leathery scales in a sickly shade of green with dark stripes down its spine, the creature stepped forward with careful, calculated steps that made its skin shimmer in the sunlight. Step by step, it drew closer to its prey.

Fixed on a thick and muscular neck that was wrapped in folds of leathery, scaly skin was a massive, reptilian head. Chase shuddered at the unnatural appearance of the thing. Rather than a set of jaws one would expect to find on such a creature, its head bore a hulking black beak that was faded from the sun and chipped from a long life of constant use. Its eyes were small, red, and feral, and they blazed with hatred as they fixed on Chase.

The reptilian beast took another step forward, shaking its massive head to click its beak.

Chase's skin crawled at the sound, like a hammer slamming against a broken rattle. Without thinking, he took a step back. Moment after moment, step after step, the beast drew nearer, snapping its head and whipping its tail with each monstrous stride.

A moment of silence fell over the plateau when the beast suddenly stopped. Chase didn't know what to expect, but what followed nearly made him wretch in disgust.

The monster lurched with a horrible gagging sound, thrashing its head from side to side. Terrible gargling sounds erupted from the thing's throat until it finally opened its beak and a putrid, sickly green gas poured onto the ground at its feet. Rot and decay assaulted Chase's nostrils, nearly forcing him to his knees. With a concerted effort, he covered his mouth and stood his ground.

Anticipation hung in the air. The strange beast eyed its prey with an eager hunger that made Chase's heart thump uncomfortably in his chest. Slowly, warily, he prepared for an onslaught. The silence that followed was deafening.

A soft breeze blew across the platform. The putrid green gas that flooded the area shifted.

Without warning, the beast threw its head back and roared. A piercing screech assaulted Chase's mind finally bringing him to his knees and forcing his hands to his ears. Without thinking, he breathed in the terrible fumes that surrounded him and nearly emptied his stomach on the ground. His throat burned, and his eyes watered, his chest screaming in agony. It was as if someone had lit the air aflame in his lungs, and he could do nothing but sit with his hands over his ears, desperately hoping the beast would cease its terrible roar.

Before Chase could clamber to his feet, the monster pounced.

A bone-shattering crack rang out when the beast's terrible beak snapped shut nearly hard enough to split Chase in two. Without a moment to spare, he had leapt out of the way, scrambling to get to his feet as fast as he could. Unfortunately, he was still too slow. With a dull thud, the monster's club tail slammed against his shoulder.

He felt a distinct crunch in his arm, but Chase had no time to dwell on the injury. He had to move.

The beast let out a wild, frustrated screech. This time, Chase was ready for the noise and dove behind a small rock at the edge of the platform. With immense frustration, the monster snapped its beak violently with a series of clicks and hisses that made Chase's blood run cold.

He took a deep breath and tried to calm himself. His hut was on the other side of the platform, but for just a moment, the path was clear. Chase knew he would only have one chance to reach his belongings, but he needed to get there if he had any hope of surviving the next few minutes.

Amid the monster's wicked snapping, snarling, and hissing, Chase sprang to his feet and bolted for the small stone hut no more than thirty paces away. His heart thudded in his chest, and the world went quiet. He breathed heavily, charging forward step by step—hoping the beast would be too slow to react.

Soon, he was halfway to the hut. Chase's mind went blank. The only thing that mattered was reaching his pack to retrieve a blade.

Chase turned his head and saw—to his horror— the massive beak of the beast about to snap shut around him, sickly green smoke pouring from the corners of its mouth. The sight of the horrible beak, lined with rotted, pocked gums with a putrid smelling gray tongue that reached out to Chase like a desperate child's hand, nearly made him vomit. But there was no time.

The beast was upon him, and he had to act.

In the moment before the beak snapped down on him, Chase felt the world slow down to a halt. Instincts taking over, he ducked his shoulder and dove as hard and as fast as he could.

A dull pain throbbed in Chase's hip as the bottom jaw of the monster slammed into him. The massive beak clamped shut with a wicked snap, but to Chase's relief he ducked clear of the attack. He nearly rolled into the hut through the small doorway, but he made it all the same just in time for his foe to crash into the stone structure with a loud boom and a pained grunt.

The hut stood strong, just as Chase had hoped it would. He felt the ground shake and heard the monster scream in frustration, beating its head against the walls trying to bring the entire thing down. There was no time to dawdle. Chase rifled through his things until he found his black-bladed cleaving dagger. Without a working sword, the dagger was the next best thing. It would have to make do.

After a deep breath to steady his nerves, Chase sprang from the hut and rolled. A harsh slam rang out, and the world shook as the beast's tail hit the ground hard, missing Chase by a mere hand's width. The monster roared in anger and threw itself upon him with massive foreclaws raised. Rather than rolling further out of the way, Chase scrambled beneath the creature's immense form.

Holding his breath, surrounded by toxic smoke, Chase thrust his cleaving dagger upward and dragged the blade across the monster's leathery underbelly. It screeched, louder than ever before, and thrashed violently, almost crushing him beneath its hulking hind legs.

Chase darted away and clambered to his feet. He eyed the monster warily, waiting for its next move while it regained its composure with a harsh clacking of its beak.

The monster screeched yet again, and the world echoed with its terrible sound. It wretched and gagged until a stream of putrid gas poured from its wicked maw. More and more of the toxic gas erupted from the beast until Chase was in an endless void of fowl smelling, sickly, green fog.

The taste and smell of rotten flesh assaulted his mind and his throat seared with white-hot pain.

He couldn't move. He couldn't think. There were only pain and the sick stench of death.

Chase dropped his dagger and clasped his hands to his throat. He screamed in pain, only for more of the miasma to force its way into his lungs. It was too much to bear. He fell to his knees and began to wretch.

This is it. I'm sorry, Richard. I've failed.

A deafening sound filled the air: a terrifying, bone shattering, prehistoric roar. Through the toxic fog, Chase could just barely make out a strange shape darting through the sky. In a flash, the shape descended on the plateau and collided with his foe.

The pair slammed into the rock wall behind the hut with a deafening boom. Stones and dirt and dust erupted from the impact. The beaked monster screeched in terror while the new combatant ripped at its side with massive claws and sharp teeth.

With the toxic gas dissipating, Chase scrambled to be clear of the fog, gasping desperately for any shred of clean air. His vision blurred and his head throbbed, but he could still make out the terrible form of a huge, silver beast thrashing and snapping at its victim's bloody flank. After struggling with its assailant to no avail, the wingless beaked monster shrieked and fled from its foe. With a series of snaps and hisses, the defeated beast scrambled off the edge of the Dragon's Mouth and retreated to the gorge below.

Another deafening roar filled the air in triumph. A single gust of wind emanated from the silver beast, and with it the gas was swept away from the platform. Chase's vision slowly returned to him, and he was left to stare in awe.

It was as if a dragon had stepped right out of a children's story, standing in all its magnificent glory before Chase—head held high, and silver scales gleaming in the sunlight like polished steel.

The drake stood nearly twice as tall and three times a wide as the largest warhorse Chase had ever seen. It had a slender yet powerful body with four thick legs and a long, whipping tail. Upon each of its muscular limbs sat ridged paws that ended in wicked claws as black as night. Pride seemed to exude from the beast, standing with its head held high to expose its black-scaled underbelly, as if to challenge any who opposed it to strike at its vulnerable underside if they dared.

Atop its lean neck sat an angular head with a long,

horned snout that held a terrible set of jaws, lined with massive fangs that made Chase feel weak at the knees. Two gleaming black horns protruded from the back of its skull along with a crest of smaller, more jagged ones that resembled a nightmarish cowl. The beast huffed and eyed Chase with narrow, black, slitted eyes for a moment. It was as if the creature was trying to weigh and measure the man that stood alone on the plateau.

The air caught in Chase's throat and his mouth went dry. Before he could do or say anything, the dragon stretched out two massive, leathery black wings to their full length. In that moment, Chase could do nothing but sit in awe of the beauty and terror of such a magnificent beast.

Silence, save for the sound of a gentle breeze flowing over the plateau, hung in the air for far too long. Chase was about to speak, his lips parched and his throat still burning from inhaling toxic fumes, when the dragon shifted. It folded its wings to its sides and took a single step forward with black claws digging into the hard packed earth below.

The dragon's throat vibrated, and Chase expected to hear a guttural, rasping growl that would match the beast's mighty roar. However, the sound that fell upon his ears was quite unexpected. The voice of a young man, no different than any other man Chase had ever heard before, spoke to him. "Hello. My name is Diligence."

Chase faltered. His head swirled and his mind grew clouded. He half expected the Man in Red to show his wicked face, but the man never came. Chase was truly alone apart from the wonderous silver dragon that stood with him on the plateau.

Stunned, Chase looked up at the approaching dragon, its scales shining magnificently in the sunlight. "What did you say?" he croaked. "I... I don't quite understand. What *was* that?"

With an odd snort that sounded like laughter, the dragon replied, "Oh, that? Remorse, being the flightless bastard that he is, has grown jealous of the surface world. Even more than usual for one of the dragons bound to the Catacombs. I would venture to guess that he caught your scent and crawled to this plateau before I could arrive." The dragon paused for a moment. When he continued, his tone had leveled, and his voice sounded more serious than before. "I know you have many questions. I may not be able to answer them all, but I'll try my best. Bring a chair from that hut out here. It'll be more comfortable than the ground."

It's a bloody dragon, like from all those story books, and the damned thing is talking to me?

Chase wasn't sure what to say, so he simply did as the dragon asked. When he reemerged from the hut dragging the stone slab that passed for a stool behind him, the dragon had taken it upon himself to lie on the ground. The shimmering silver mass of muscle stretched slowly and lazily, allowing his scales to dance with dazzling light from the sun above.

The dragon yawned, exposing countless daggerlike fangs. Chase shifted on his stool and cleared his throat before speaking. "I don't quite know what to say. This is all so... unbelievable. Not that long ago, I thought dragons were a myth told to children before they were put to bed and now—I'm looking at one. I was never really convinced you would come at all, even until this morning. But here you are."

Diligence flicked his tongue to one side before his throat vibrated again. His mouth moved in a strange manner while he spoke, as though he was speaking in a way that didn't match the words Chase heard. "I suppose I could say the same about you. The man-races of the world haven't come to this rock since before my parents were hatchlings. I heard unbelievable tales of your kind, but here you are, as well."

Chase took a deep breath. "I have been looking for answers since I left the Burrow, and it feels like each question answered leads to three more that need to be asked. I'm not sure where to start."

The dragon seemed to smile. "I'll start slowly. You must be curious about me and my kind, are you not?"

Chase nodded.

"Try to keep up." The dragon winked wryly. It was odd to see the reptilian form smile, but Chase found it strangely comforting. "You know my name, which is a start, but you should probably know a small amount about the dragons here on Dragonstone." Chase nodded in agreement before the dragon continued. "Legends say that long ago, dragons roamed the entire world. The early dragons were among the oldest creatures to grace this land with their presence. However, when the man-races emerged, they began to hunt our kind until a fierce battle raged between them. The dragons were quickly outnumbered and eventually they were forced to retreat completely or be faced with utter extinction.

"When the dragons knew they were defeated, they called for a truce. They agreed to live out their days on Dragonstone as long as the man-races left them to relative peace. To ensure both sides of the agreement upheld their promises, they agreed that ambassadors to either side were needed. Dragonmarks were meant to link the soul of a dragon and a member of the man-races. The dragon riders oversaw many of the goings on of the world in those days, and the peace that followed lasted generations.

"Wisdom, a great green dragon, felt that the deal was fair and would allow dragons to flourish alongside your kind, while Wrath, a terrible dragon with scales like the night, insisted that the man-races were weak and that dragons should rule over them. The riders bonded to dragons loyal to Wisdom maintained that peace was the best way forward for everyone while those loyal to Wrath desired the great power that their dragons promised them.

"After many years of peace and order, a civil war nearly tore the world asunder. It's said those were the darkest days the world has ever seen, but after much turmoil, Wrath and his followers were pushed back into the Catacombs beneath this island where they remain imprisoned to this very day."

Chase frowned in concentration, trying to take in every word the silver dragon spoke.

Diligence clearly saw it as well and smiled.

"Wisdom taught the early dragons on the surface to respect the man-races, among many other things. Much of what we dragons do and how we act today is thanks to Wisdom's original teachings."

Slow and clumsy words finally fell from Chase's mouth. "This is all quite interesting, but how do you fit in all of this? Were you a fighter in this civil war?"

Diligence snorted and his immense, black-scaled underbelly shook while he laughed. "No, of course not. I can't look that old, can I? I only hatched three and a half decades ago in your kind's time. Wisdom has been dead and gone for nearly a thousand years if the stories they tell are true. I learned all of this from my mother, who learned it from her father, who learned it from his mother, and so on. I just want you to understand what it means when I tell you that I was hatched and raised on the surface while you most recent admirer, Remorse, lives in the Catacombs."

Chase nodded, but the words in his throat stuck uncomfortably. Finally, he found his voice. "S-so, why am *I* here? Surely there's someone who deserves it more." *More than a murderer. It can't be true, can it? Will had to have been lying or exaggerating...*

The silver dragon cocked his head to the side in thought. "I can't tell for certain. Some others of my kind who fancy themselves as scholars may know more, but I'm far from that. Would you mind if I take a guess?" Chase shook his head. "I think you've been summoned to answer for an intrusion here. It happened long before I hatched, but those that were alive at the time made sure every dragon knew the tale. A wicked man from beyond the Great Scar found a way to forge a dragonmark. None of the dragons here have the slightest idea how that could be possible, but it happened, nevertheless. Soon, the man arrived right where you sit now and met his red-scaled fire drake, Terror."

I guess Will wasn't lying after all. "I know the story," Chase replied. "But how do I fit in?"

"I don't think that your arrival here is a coincidence. I think you've been marked to answer for the other person's crimes."

Nothing more than a glorified weapon meant to carry out someone else's judgement. "So, I'm being punished?" Chase frowned deeply. "Am I to serve as payment?"

Diligence shook his head. "No. You're to serve as his executioner."

Chase's heart sank. *I'm an assassin. Will's gift is nothing more than another contract. I never should have thought otherwise.* A sense of dread and disappointment filled him. *Traveling so far from the Burrow has clouded my judgement.* He sighed. "If the shoe fits, I suppose."

The Man in Red was right.

The silver scaled dragon cocked his head to the side once again. "I don't think you understand the bond between a drake and their rider. Our souls have been woven together by a very ancient magic that finds the two souls that are best matched for one another. The very fact that I am here to answer the call rather than a drake from the Catacombs should be enough to put away any doubts from your mind."

Chase thought for a moment. *The magic could be mistaken. Or this could be more of Will's handiwork. Maybe he had some ulterior motive for granting me a mark…* All the events that had led up to this moment gave him hope that he may be able to put his past behind him, and in a single, terrible moment, that hope was shattered. The realization nearly brought him to tears.

However, if what the dragon said was true, there may still be some hope for Chase. The overwhelming sense of dread outweighed anything else in his mind, but he desperately latched on to the glimmer of hope that was buried deep beneath the waves of uncertainty.

It can't be right. I won't let it end like that. The Man in Red can choke on his words, and Will can eat his with ashen food and spoiled wine for all I care.

Chase leveled his gaze at the heaping pile of shining silver scales. "…Very well. So, what happens next?"

"I'm not sure, but I'd suspect Terror and his rider still have their eyes on the man's homeland. Do you know exactly who may have been behind their exile?"

"The man supposedly came from Rakksberg, like me." Chase noticed the dragon eye him over at that, but he tried his best to ignore it. "The High Council resides over the Berg as they have for generations. I suppose their predecessors must have been the ones responsible for the banishment."

"Hmm…" Diligence lifted a claw on his foreleg to the base of his neck and scratched in thought. "I suppose we have our answer. If we can somehow remove your High Council from power, Terror and his rider may try to seize their opportunity to return.

It's said that the man who came for Terror thirsted for control above all else. Why he would is beyond me, but if that's true, he may be lying in wait for the right moment to reclaim your land for himself."

Chase closed his eyes in quiet contemplation. He had seen how the people of Galland thrived and how the people of the Berg struggled or starved at the mercy of a careless and callous governing council. He had seen what good people were forced to do when they had no other choice, and he knew that as long as the High Council remained in power, those people would remain hopeless.

Chase steeled his nerves and pushed any lingering apprehension away. *If Will sent me here just to fulfill another damned contract, so be it. That doesn't change that this is* my *gift, now. It's mine to do with as I see fit, and with Diligence by my side I'm sure we'll put our bond to good use.* "We have a long road ahead of us, Diligence. I'm not sure I'm ready, but Carpenter's Hammer am I tired!"

The dragon nodded his massive head in agreement. "Aye. We'll have plenty of time to speak more later. Go get some rest. I'll stay nearby in case Remorse decides to show his ugly face again."

Chase chuckled and trundled back to his bed in the hut. He didn't even bother to drag the stool back inside. He was so tired he just left the thing where it was.

Slowly, he lowered himself into the surprisingly soft bed on its strange stone frame.

Bloody hell. He's here. He's actually here. It's all true.

I can't wait until Richard finds out.

He smiled. His throat still ached from the toxic gas, and his muscles screamed in silent agony, but at that moment he didn't care.

Chase slowly closed his eyes, and the world around him faded away once again.

***

Chase opened his eyes to... nothing. Nothing happened. There was no fire, no eerie orange glow, and no stench of death hanging in the air. The world was silent, and he lay in the bed that sat in his meager hut at the top of the Dragon's Mouth.

Carpenter's bloody damned Hammer. Thank the stars it's over.

With a tired smile, Chase closed his eyes again and listened to the gentle sounds of the morning, tears streaming down his face.

GLOSSARY

Azalea (ah-ZAY-leya): The northernmost nation of the Moon Isle, named for its vast fields of azalea flowers.

Azalean (ah-ZAY-lee-an): Natives of Azalea known for their olive-toned skinned and gemstone eyes. The "flower folk" practice a form of magic that involves singing the crystal from the earth.

Black Blades, The: A mercenary band in Rakksberg known for using black-dyed steel while adorned in black leather.

Benjyn: A hermit from Rakksberg.

Cendralli (sen-DRAH-lee): Heavily forested nation on the Northern Sun Isle, home to the Elvari.

Chase: A Bergman assassin from the province of Haverson. He favors a bastard sword and cleaving dagger. He has become to be known as "the Shadow."

Children of Tor: Bear-like Beast Men, natives of Black Rock on the Southern Sun Isle. Followers of a shamanistic religion, and the most violent opponents to the Magi of Soule.

Drakthul (DRAHK-thool): Natives of Talvenna on the Northern Sun Isle, characterized by pale skin, sharp features, and pointed ears. Practitioners of Blood Magic.

Elvari (el-VAR-ee): Native people of Cendralli characterized by pointed ears, sharp fangs, and a fine fur covering their skin. Druidism is intrinsically linked to every aspect of their culture.

Galland (GAL-and): A country on the Moon Isle, home to the Gallanders. This once-lonely nation of fair-skinned folk has grown into a welcome destination for travelers of all cultures. The marketplace in Haven, the nation's capital, rivals in in all the world.

High Council: The ruling government of Rakksberg. A single representative from each province composes the council that dictates laws and sees them carried out in the Berg. These men and women tend to live on vast estates that rival most castles.

Klaus Svoct (KLAUS SVOTE): A Drakthul Blood Mage and son of a harsh politician.

Madelyn Taph: A strange woman from southern Rakksberg with mysterious origins. Self-proclaimed alchemist, herbalist, and botanist.

Magi (MA-jie): Dark-skinned natives of Soule. Magic is extraordinarily common amongst Magi which has caused conflict with nations that oppose their practices.

Rakksberg (RAKS-berg): A country on the Moon Isle, home to the Bergman, otherwise known as "the Berg." Devoid of magic and outside influence, the country has been ruled by the High Council ever since a catastrophic event occurred nearly a century and a half ago.

Remylara Drakolar (REM-i-lar-ah DRAH-koe-lar): Otherwise known as Remi, a Magi Fire Spinner from Soule and former officer in their military

Richard: A Bergman assassin and best friend to Chase. "The Bear" prefers a double hefted great axe.

Shishussan (shee-shoo-SAHN): The natives of Shi on the Northern Sun Isle, spending most of their time secluded in the mountains. Pale-skinned and round featured with almond shaped eyes. Known for open practice of necromancy.

Soule (SOLE): The native land of the Magi, characterized by harsh deserts and an arid climate. The nation has been at been at war with Black Rock over magical doctrines amongst the people of the Sun Isles.

Talvenna (TAL-ven-uh): Home of the Drakthul on the Northern Sun Isle. Little is known about these lands apart from the legends the Drakthul allow top spread. The land is said to be black and twisted.

Toam (TOME): The center of Magi traditions of magic. The smallest known unit of energy.

ABOUT THE AUTHOR

Zach Otto was born in 1992 in Grand Rapids, Michigan. After moving frequently as a child, he was raised in Marinette, Wisconsin. He received his Bachelors of Science in Biology in Minneapolis, Minnesota before attending the Minnesota College of Pharmacy in Duluth, Minnesota where he received a Doctorate of Pharmacy. It was there that he met his partner, Kait, and where they still live together today. Writing has always been a loving hobby, ever since he played "pass the notebook" with his family as a child. Zach also enjoys hiking, birding, painting, movies, and board games with friends.

www.ingramcontent.com/pod-product-compliance
Lightning Source LLC
Chambersburg PA
CBHW030617250626
47154CB00006B/1823